NOAH'S ARK

McAnally Flats Press
4809 Riversedge Road
Louisville, TN 37777
www.McAnallyFlatsPress.com

Library of Congress Control Number: 2013921341
ISBN: 978-0-9819209-4-8
Copyright information available upon request
v. 1.02

Cover Design: MSDesigns / iStockphoto: Zurijeta, weible1980
Interior Design: J. L. Saloff
Images ©Larry Henry except page 3, © iStockphoto/atikinka2; and
page 139, Huey ©army.mil
Typography: Minion Pro, Bordeaux Roman Bold

First Edition, 2014
Printed on acid free paper in the United States of America.

For Mildred and Jay

"I can give you nothing that has not already
its origins within yourself,
I can throw open no picture gallery
but your own,
I can help make your own world visible
— that is all."
~ Herman Hesse

Also by Larry Henry:

Garden of Eden

Plato's Cave

NOAH'S ARK
DRUGS, MURDER, & TREASON

Larry Henry

MCANALLY FLATS PRESS

Chapter One

Roger & Shannon

Sha Doobie

"How do you do that?"

"You're just a girl. You can't learn nothin.'"

"That's not fair. I'm gonna tell my mom."

"You do and I'll put a frog down your britches."

"You keep your stinky old frogs away or I'll tell my daddy."

"I'm getting' that frog right now!"

"Mommm!"

"Oh, shut up! I don't even have a frog."

"I'll show you if you'll teach me."

"You will?"

"Yes, but you have to teach me first."

"You said that last time, an' you never did nothin.'"

"You teach me and I'll show it to you, I promise."

"No."

"Oh, all right then. Come on. We'll do it in the garage."

Shannon lifted her dress, pulling her panties down, then bent over so Roger could see her bottom. Shannon and her parents had moved in next door to Roger and his family eleven months earlier after Hurricane Donna laid waste to the Eastern Seaboard. The two had become playmates, but they argued over just about everything. Their parents joked that they behaved like two young married people, fighting over who wore the pants in the family. Shannon had a crush on Roger, but Roger was still at that awkward age where he thought girls were dumb. Nevertheless, Roger was beginning to notice little Shannon.

"Can you see it?"

"Yeah. It looks like a biscuit or something."

"Mama says that's where babies come from."

"I don't believe it. How do they get in there?"

"Mama says daddy puts them there."

"That's crazy. It ain't big enough."

"Mama calls it my 'Virginia.' She says they grow in there."

"How do you reckon he gets 'em inside?"

"Maybe they have the doctor do it. Doctors take babies out, you know."

"Does it hurt?"

"Mama said I came out easy as pie."

"My mother never tells me anything."

"Now you have to show me yours."

Roger undid his shorts and pulled down his Jockey underwear. He had never shown Shannon his penis before, but the two children where uninhibited and it didn't embarrass Roger like it would most little boys, age eleven.

"It looks like my finger."

"Yeah, I write with it sometimes."

"You do not. That's where you pee."

"Daddy says when I get big I'll have one like his."

"What's his look like?"

"It's bigger than mine."

"Much bigger?"

"It's as big around as the rake handle."

"I see Mom's all the time. She has hair on hers."

"So does my daddy."

"You think we'll get hair?'

"Probably."

"You said you would teach me."

"All right, come on."

The children ran back outside onto the sidewalk in front of Shannon's home. It was a perfect spring day. School was out for the summer. Traffic along the two lane street was light for the Turnberry neighborhood. Several kids were riding their bicycles or playing on skates. Mary Leibowitz waved from down the sidewalk. Mary was in the same grade with Shannon and Roger.

"It's like walking backwards. You just lift your knees and your heels while you slide your feet backwards."

"Do it again so I can see how."

Roger turned his back and started down the sidewalk doing his backwards maneuver. Shannon turned her back and started in the same direction. Shannon hadn't gone but a few steps when her heel caught in a crack and she fell over backwards, banging her head on the concrete. Roger rushed over, sliding his ball cap under the back of Shannon's head.

Roger was experiencing strange emotions that confused him. He felt a compulsion to comfort his little neighbor with the pretty red hair and big brown eyes.

"Are you okay?"

Shannon sat up with tears streaming down her cheeks.

"Do you want me to get your mother?

"I hurt my neck. Will you rub it for me, please?"

"Sure."

Roger massaged Shannon's neck tenderly where a piece of gravel had bruised her, causing a purple spot to appear. Shannon had on her mother's perfume. Roger had never noticed before. She closed her eyes, leaning her head back against Roger's shoulder.

"Feel better?"

"Yes, Roger. Thank you. Let me try again, please."

"Okay, watch now … raise your knees and slide those feet. Backwards, like this."

Roger Overstreet was in the same musical groove as a Cuban kid he had seen at school who called his strolling maneuver the Sha Doobie. Roger was quite the athlete. It was as though he could hear the music inside his head. He was a good Pop Warner player too. At four feet nine inches tall and seventy eight pounds, Roger excelled at the halfback position with his football team.

Mary had abandoned her bicycle to come and watch. So did Fred Roberts from across the street. They asked Roger to teach them the Sha Doobie like he was doing with Shannon. Roger led them over to his driveway where there were no cracks to trip over.

"Watch now, it goes like this … raise your heels, and slide your feet."

Mary was getting the gist of it, but Shannon and Fred kept having difficulty. This went on for five minutes with Fred and Shannon losing their balance every few steps.

Shannon was frustrated. "Why can't I do it?" she exclaimed.

Roger thought for a minute. "I forgot something." he said. "You have to say 'Sha Doobie' first."

"Sha Doobie?" Fred was the neighborhood skeptic. "That's silly."

"Sha Doobie!" said Shannon. She went scooting backwards down the driveway like a little professional.

"Sha Doobie!"

Fred began his backwards stroll. He tripped twice. Then he got the hang of it.

"I love it!" Shannon squealed, clapping her hands. "Sha Doobie! Sha Doobie!"

Roger's mother came out on the front porch to see what all the excitement was about. Joyce Overstreet took a seat on the porch swing, marveling at the four children strolling backwards all over her driveway. *What fun*, she thought.

Joyce walked down the front steps to where the children were showing off their skills. "May I try?" she asked.

Fred Roberts grinned. "Sure, but you gotta say 'Sha Doobie' first."

"What does it mean?" she asked.

Roger answered his mother. "It's magic, Mom."

Mrs. Overstreet responded. "If I say the magic words can I Sha Doobie too?"

Roger replied. "Sha Doobie is when the Great Spirit grants you a wish."

"Sha Doobie!" Joyce Overstreet went gliding across the driveway pretty as a picture. "This is fun, Roger. This really is fun."

Shannon and Roger stood side by side smiling at his mother. All the kids were impressed with Missus Overstreet and her first Sha Doobie experience. Half an hour later she had them all in her kitchen for milk and fudge brownies.

When Shannon's father got word about the kids and their Sha Doobie activities, he decided to do something special for the neighborhood children. Being a trial attorney over in Hallandale, he took one of the firm's letterheads and drew up a legal document using their finest parchment paper.

SHA DOOBIE

This august document represents a Platinum Membership in the Sha Doobie Tribe of Moon Walk Boulevard, Turnberry, Florida. We of the Sha Doobie Tribe do hereby pledge allegiance to our brothers and sisters, the Great Spirit, and his beautiful daughter Moon Walker. All who sign this document become members for life, promising loyalty and good fellowship to all Tribal Warriors until Happy Hunting Ground.

Tribal Council shall consist of Chief Moon Dog, Luna Treasurer, and First Warrior. Tribal Council shall be elected by secret ballot and majority vote. All remaining members shall hold the honorary title of Tribal Warrior.

Monthly fees of one dollar per Warrior shall be collected and held in escrow by Luna Treasurer for Tribal events. All who join the Sha Doobie Tribe shall sign the secret pledge, swearing Honor Bright on their Ancestor's Bones. So stated before God and Country this Age of Aquarius, 1962.

Eleven children lived on the street and all eleven signed as Tribal Warriors. Barrister Parker made each child an original copy on the same parchment paper. He then had each document framed in tulip wood.

It was as though a miracle had taken place in the neighborhood. The children seldom fought or argued anymore. They had become the Sha Doobie Tribe. They played together, attended picture shows together, outings at the beach, and shared weenie roasts in their own backyards.

For his twelfth birthday all the members were gathered at Roger's home for cherry ice cream and chocolate birthday cake. Roger asked Shannon if she would consent to becoming his Tribal Princess.

Shannon gave Roger a big smile. "Yes!" She answered.

Shannon hugged Roger and kissed him on the cheek. All the children hollered and clapped their hands.

The Parkers and the Overstreets were proud of their children. Shannon and Roger made a darling couple. They were the light of their parent's eyes. The Sha Doobie Tribe had just acquired their first pair of Lovie Dovies.

Chapter Two

Young and Beautiful

Pastor McFarland was speaking.

"Adam was an irresponsible husband. Noah was a drunk. Jacob deceived his father and tricked his brother out of his birthright. Moses was a murderer. King David was a murderer and an adulterer. Yet God called on each one of these men to serve as an inspiration for those who followed His teachings. God calls on unlikely people for the purposes of His Kingdom."

Shannon punched Roger with her elbow, whispering. "There may be hope for you yet."

Roger whispered back, smiling. "You'd love me if I was Blackbeard the Pirate."

"I certainly would not. I'd turn you in to the Shore Patrol, and watch them hang you from the yardarm."

"Yeah! And probably swing from my feet, you blimey wench."

"Oh, but they're such adorable feet. And pink little toes."

"Pipe down, you two. Have a little respect in the Lord's House."

"Yes, ma'am."

Twenty minutes later the service let out and Roger walked Shannon home. The birds were singing and the butterflies were fluttering about the pretty flowers on the manicured lawns. Their parents were proud and thankful for the way their children were growing up. Roger and Shannon were in love. The two were going on fourteen and shared classes together in the eighth grade. Roger made good grades and excelled at Pop Warner football. Shannon was a straight "A" student, having made the cheerleading squad with the football team.

Roger had changed over the past twenty-four months, maturing into a fine young gentleman. Shannon had changed too, evolving into a beauty, a bit of a coquette but she worshiped her Roger. Shannon often changed clothing in front of Roger, proud of her shapely bottom and budding breasts.

She invited him to touch them, telling him, "Someday we'll be married and these will be for you."

Nothing Shannon did embarrassed Roger for he did love kissing her and fondling her pretty breasts. His erections were another matter. He wanted to wait until they were older. Shannon did too, but sometimes she unzipped Roger's pants, taking him out and stroking his penis until he ejaculated. Roger, in turn, pushed Shannon's panties down, gently using his fingers to arouse her to shuddering climaxes. This was becoming more and more of a ritual which concerned them both.

The big game between Roger's Blue Emus of Turnberry, and their archrival the Blue Dolphins from Hallandale was scheduled for Friday evening at the Eleanor Roosevelt High School. This was for the Miami-Dade County championship. The winner would go on to the state finals. Excitement was in the night air. Many of the townsfolk were sports enthusiasts, and the prospect of one of their Pop Warner teams capturing the state title had the sports community all abuzz. The stadium was packed when the referee blew his whistle. Sixteen thousand cheering fans rose to their feet as the football tumbled through the air.

Shorty Dog with the Dolphins received the ball on his twelve and ran it back to the twenty-nine yard line. Next play, their fullback, Eric Taylor, ran the ball off right tackle for eight more yards. Then Goose Gunzburg, the Dolphin quarterback, lobbed one downfield to his left end, Too Tall McBride, for twenty-one additional yards. The Blue Emus had been thrown off balance by a coordinated running and aerial attack. By the end of the first quarter, the Dolphins were leading Roger's Blue Emus by seven points against a big fat hen egg.

First play of the second quarter, the kickoff came to Roger on his own ten. Away he ran, cutting upfield with his Emus forming a blocking wedge which carried Roger to the twenty-three before Badass McCoy knocked him to the turf, stepping on his right hand. Badass had a reputation for dirty tricks seldom detected by the referees. Next play, Little Willie John faked right, going up the middle for five more yards before Badass tackled him, bloodying his nose with an elbow. The refs saw that one, which cost the Dolphins fifteen yards for unsportsmanlike conduct. The ball was on the forty-three with the Emus threatening downfield in Dolphin territory.

Three Sha Doobie Warriors played on the Emu team. Roger at left halfback, Little Willie John at right halfback, and Moose Jordan at right tackle. Four plays later, they were on the Dolphin thirty-one yard line. Quarterback Pretty Boy passed the ball to their right end, Snake Wilson, on the twenty-four with nine minutes left to play in the second quarter. Try as they may, they could not get the ball into the end zone. With no time-outs remaining, fourth down and four on the nine, Coach Caputo elected to go for three points. Pretty Boy kicked the field goal, and the score was seven to three.

A near riot erupted when Badass McCoy kicked an Emu player in the groin after he was down at the end of the Dolphin runback. Again, the referees failed to see the infraction. One of the Emu players punched Badass in the face, and was promptly ejected from the game. Badass just grinned. The Emu players objected vigorously, but to no avail. Linebacker Kyle Fulmer was helped from the field into the locker room where an ice pack was placed on his "bruised ego." The half ended three plays later with neither team able to score. The rivalry remained seven to three.

In the locker room, Coach Caputo was informed about the cheating Badass was getting away with on the playing field.

Phillip Caputo was a Korean War veteran, and a member of the Old City Kiwanis who attended Miami Shores Presbyterian Church. He always tried to set a good example for his boys. But today they were about to learn something different. Coach Caputo bragged on his Emus, telling them they were the best team he had ever coached. He praised them for their heart and determination in the face of unsportsmanlike behavior. He spoke of their history, about how they had prepared all year for their physical and mental challenges on the gridiron. He explained that life was not always fair. Sometimes one had to improvise to overcome adversity. Then he outlined something they had learned running the fifteen-yard obstacle course through a parallel row of old automobile tires.

Franklin "Badass" McCoy was the only child of a middle-class family living in Hallandale. His father was a decorated police detective with the Miami Police Department. Daisy McCoy was a sweet lady who attended church every Wednesday evening and Sunday mornings, praying for their immortal souls and her husband's safety on the Force. Badass had gotten his nickname in the sixth grade after whipping a school bully on the playground after class. Following his pugilistic success, it wasn't long before Franklin himself began bullying his classmates.

His father was known for bending the rules, sometimes beating confessions out of felony suspects before taking them downtown for booking. It didn't bother him that his son was acquiring a reputation similar to his own. He was proud of young Franklin, coddling and spoiling the boy.

Detective McCoy's partner was a fearsome-looking character from the lowlands of the Okefenokee Swamp in southern Georgia. He was a former bootlegger, six feet six with muscular arms and broad, powerful shoulders. A knife scar down the side of his face just below his left eye gave him the appearance of something grotesque and sinister. Everyone called him Cottonmouth because of a white birthmark on his mouth and chin. Black people were afraid of him, saying he had the Mojo sign. People steered clear of Cottonmouth because he exhibited a persona of someone prone to violence. But he and Detective McCoy got along like brothers. They shared a camaraderie which accounted for more arrests than any other detective team with the Miami Police Department.

Third quarter was two-thirds in the record book with the players battling back and forth, but neither team could gain the advantage. Then disaster struck. With four minutes left in the third quarter, the Emu center snapped the football over the quarterback's head on the twelve-yard line. Little Willie John went running back to save the football, but was tackled in the Emu end zone for a touchback. The quarter ended with the score nine to three. Coach Caputo addressed his players in front of the bench, praising their courage, and telling them there was still time for a victory. Roger Overstreet had his doubts.

Fourth quarter began with the kickoff coming to Roger on his fourteen. He ran the ball back eight yards before a wave of Dolphin tacklers plowed him under at the twenty-two. Next play, Little Willie John faked right, running a reverse for seven yards before Badass tackled him, jamming a finger in his eye. Little Willie John had to be led off the field with an ice pack over his injury. Something had to be done.

Coach Caputo called Time-Out.

"Men, remember what I told you about those tires. Now is the time. Pretty Boy, you take the snap on two, fake a pass then give the ball to Roger. Moose, you and Catfish take down the guard and tackle in front of Badass. Tommy, you block the linebacker. The rest of you boys, block anybody you can downfield. Roger, you know what to do. What's that magic word you boys use with your social club?"

"Sha Doobie, Mister Caputo."

"Right on! Now get out there and Sha Doobie some Dolphin ass!"

Wampus Kat centered the ball to Pretty Boy who faded back to pass, handing the ball off to Roger. Moose and Catfish leveled the two defensive players in front of McCoy. Wampus Kat slammed into the defensive center, driving him sideways to the left. Tommy knocked the linebacker flat on his back. The die was cast. Roger charged up the middle for five yards. From the right he saw Badass coming. Roger pivoted right pumping his knees high in the air just like Coach Caputo had trained them running through the automobile tires. With McCoy bent down low for the tackle Roger's knee connected with Badass's chin, and blood flew everywhere. McCoy fell to the ground. Roger ran over the top of him, and into the open field.

Downfield blocking was picture-perfect. Only one remaining Dolphin had a shot at the ball carrier. It looked like he was going to be tackled on the twenty-five, but Tommy caught up to Roger and cut the legs out from under the last defensive player between Roger and the end zone. Roger trotted in those last few yards, spiking the ball and throwing his arms to the heavens. The crowd went ballistic! Badass was carried off the gridiron, minus a front tooth. The Emus gathered around Roger, yelling and cheering as they returned to their side of the field. Out came the cheerleaders. Shannon was there, proud as a peacock, laughing and prancing and holding Roger's hand. The extra point was good. Coach Caputo just grinned and winked at his boys. Then he set about getting his defensive unit ready for the kickoff.

The game lasted another twelve minutes, but with their star player out with a concussion, the fire dwindled and went out in the Dolphin players. McCoy had been the glue that held them all together. He was a fine athlete. Had he been a fair-minded individual, the Dolphins might have won, but like his father he broke the rules. The game ended with the Emus on top ten to nine.

Next day, Roger's touchdown run was featured on the front page of *The Miami Herald*. A celebration got underway. His mother and father threw a barbecue out on the sidewalk for the whole neighborhood. All the neighbors came, and once again the news media was there. More pictures appeared in the paper with Shannon and Roger mugging for the camera. Coach Caputo and the Emu team were featured, and all the lovely cheerleaders.

Turnberry was extremely proud of their Pop Warner team. That autumn held special memories for the Sha Doobie Tribe, their families and friends, and the residents of Dade County, Florida.

But all was not well in the land of the Flower Children, with their bell-bottom jeans, their psychedelic music, and their multi-colored beads. Dark forces were afoot both in America, and in a distant land called Indochina. John Fitzgerald Kennedy had just defeated Richard Milhous Nixon in the closest presidential election in American history. No sooner had President Kennedy and wife Jackie settled in at the White House than John was confronted with the Bay of Pigs decision. President Eisenhower, in league with the Pentagon and the CIA, had orchestrated an invasion plan to overthrow Fidel Castro. JFK was intrigued with the thought of thwarting the communist regime in Cuba and gave the go-ahead. But Kennedy lost his nerve at the last minute, personally bungling the invasion. The Castro forces carried the day. A corrupt President Batista fled the island nation. Premier Khrushchev sensed weakness in the young American president and began shipping missiles to Cuba, tipped with nuclear warheads. An American U-2 spy plane discovered the threat, and the Kennedy Administration locked horns with the Soviet Premier.

For thirteen days in October 1962, the world held its breath as the two superpowers faced off at the brink of thermonuclear Armageddon. America was poised and ready at DEFCON 2. DEFCON 1 would mean war. Khrushchev had badly misjudged the resolve of the American president, who had matured and learned from his mistakes in the Solomon Islands, and his Bay of Pigs fiasco. Khrushchev finally realized his mistake before the mushroom clouds began rising over the Soviet Union. B-47 bombers, B-52s, missile silos, and nuclear submarines around the globe were waiting for the signal to strike the Soviet Empire. The Russian Premier ordered his nuclear missiles shipped home. The world was saved. Dallas, Texas, and Lee Harvey Oswald awaited the president's arrival thirteen months down the crimson trail of history.

Mister Overstreet and Mister Parker were second lieutenants with the United States Army Reserves in Miami. Believing it their patriotic duty and a good opportunity for serving their country, the two had volunteered for military service soon after the Overstreets moved in next door to the Parkers. John's law practice and Steve's managerial experience with the Burdine Department Stores afforded them excellent leadership qualifications for the Army Reserves. Joyce Overstreet and Katherine Parker were proud of their husbands. They were successful businessmen, and they cut dashing figures in their military uniforms. Every other weekend, their husbands met at the Reserve Center for classes and close order drill. Two weeks each year, they flew away to various Army installations around the United States. There they went through simulated combat training, the rifle range, familiarizing themselves with tactics and weaponry, and more close order drill. It kept them sharp mentally, and afforded them good physical conditioning.

Rumors about a conflict in a place called Vietnam began filtering back to the United States, but nobody paid it much attention. Asia was on the other side of the world. Florida was the vacation capital for North America. Life was good for the majority of US citizens in the 1960s.

The assassination of John F Kennedy, November 22, 1963, broke Miss Liberty's heart. The nation grieved as though struck a mortal blow, while allies and foes alike looked on in disbelief. Hearings were held to get to the bottom of the evil deed, but the Warren Commission withheld part of their findings, believing it more prudent to calm fears rather than stir up additional conspiracy theories. A poplar American president lay dead at Parkland Memorial Hospital in the blue bonnet State of Texas. President Kennedy wanted to end the Vietnam War if elected for a second term, and bring the boys home. That was a fading memory now. Vice President Johnson was administered the oath of office onboard Air Force One. Then the pilot took off from Dallas, Texas, for Washington, DC, with Jackie and the president's body onboard. Nobody was thinking about Indochina. It was a time for mourning and saying goodbye.

The Beatles landed at the Miami International Airport, February 13, 1964, aboard a DC-8, and nothing was ever the same again in Dade County, Florida. The music spoke of love and peace and charting one's destiny among the stars. Beatlemania blitzkrieged the fruited plain, sea to shining sea, and the Sha Doobie Tribe became some of their most ardent admirers. It wasn't long before the disc jockeys began playing, "I'm Into Something Good." Herman's Hermits quickly became a household name. The British Invasion had established a beachhead.

More English groups followed in their musical footsteps: Dusty Springfield, The Animals, Petula Clark, The Rolling Stones, Peter and Gordon, Manfred Mann, The Who, Donovan, Cream, Joe Cocker, The Moody Blues, and Procol Harum. *A Hard Day's Night* and British fashions from Carnaby Street set the tone for Hollywood and the American media to proclaim England as the center for the music and fashion industry. The British Invasion spelled the end of beach music, most of the female groups, and for a time it hampered the careers of such teen idols as Chuck Berry, Jerry Lee Lewis, and Elvis Presley.

August 2, 1964: The destroyer USS Maddox reported being under attack by communist torpedo boats in the South China Sea. Two days later a second attack was reported against the Maddox and the USS Turner Joy. Citing the attacks as justification for military action, President Johnson and Defense Secretary McNamara convinced Congress into approving troop deployment for South Vietnam.

It has never been established if the second attack actually took place. Some believe it was the nervous reaction of sailors misinterpreting their sonar equipment.

The Marines landed on the Da Nang beaches in South Vietnam, March 8, 1965. That initiated the beginning of a nondeclared war. General William Westmoreland, Commander of American Forces, found himself under the micromanaging thumb of his Commander-in-Chief, President Lyndon Baines Johnson. Military victory was never the intended goal of President Johnson, only Communist containment of North Vietnam. This was more a wish-dream than a political reality. The nation soon found itself torn apart by political ideology, historical ignorance, media bias, and military blunders. Country Joe and the Fish released their 1967 protest ballad, "I Feel Like I'm Fixin' To Die." Two years later Creedence Clearwater Revival sang "Fortunate Son." The Flower Children dug it!

"Oh, Mom, thank you for my pretty birthday cake and all the decorations. Everything is just perfect."

"Have a nice time, dear. Your father and I will be next door if you need anything."

It had been decided the week before that Mister and Missus Parker would allow Shannon her privacy for her sixteenth birthday party. Shannon had begged them to stay, but after a little coaxing she relented to their wishes that she perform as party hostess. To her parents, that was the symbol of a young lady coming of age. The house on Judith Drive would be filled with Shannon's and Roger's friends, and the Parkers didn't want to inhibit them in any way. Shannon had been voted Sophomore Beauty. Roger was a proud member of the varsity football team. The Parkers and the Overstreets viewed their children as young adults.

Roger was the first to arrive. He kissed Shannon sweetly, mussing her lipstick. She set about repairing her mouth in the hall mirror while Roger answered the front door. Soon the Sha Doobie Tribe was all present, plus the cheerleaders and the Pop Warner team Roger played on in grammar school. They had lost the state championship to a team up north, but what a grand experience. It bonded them together as brothers, especially beating Hallandale. Shannon and the cheerleaders had become close friends.

Jane Kendrick was a buxom Southern belle from Savannah, Georgia. Miss Jane spoke with a magnolia accent often imitating Scarlett O'Hara to the delight and amusement of her friends.

"I do declah! Looks like a wagon load uh barnyard mysterians … an' hay market queens! But I do love it so. What's on the menu, sugar plum, hog jowls an' chitlins?"

"Not a bit of it you sweet thang, you. Y'all done been voted Miss Georgia Puddin'. These Confederate gentlemen heah been a cogitatin' over competin' for yo' little hand on tha dance flo.'"

Shannon loved the camaraderie she shared with Miss Jane. The two of them often put on a show, talking like King Cotton plantation belles.

"Shoot! Them ole horny toads couldn't boogie-woogie my ole granny. They'd kick over dead, like June bugs in a lightnin' storm."

"Oh, fiddle-dee-dee. They're strong as plow mules, an' neigh on half as smart."

"Well, I reckon I could give 'em a try. Say, who's that short drink uh water over yonder on the faintin' couch? He looks plum bodacious."

"Why that's Little Willie John, our football hero. He's a good ole boy."

Little Willie John flushed as crimson as his cherry red motor scooter. Willie was a fine student and a star athlete, but he was extremely shy around females. Miss Jane had him licked in height by two inches.

Kevin was a handsome individual from Goose Creek, South Carolina, with ice blue eyes, a muscular physique, and a mop of curly black hair. His mother and Jane's mom had been sorority sisters back in Athens at the University of Georgia. Miss Jane had developed a crush on Kevin after asking him to jitterbug at a sock hop in the high school gymnasium. Over she went and plopped down on the fainting couch. Little Willie John blushed an even brighter red, but his smile spoke volumes for the lovely Miss Jane.

The house was full to overflowing, thirty-eight teenagers all teasing and flirting with one another. The French doors were opened and part of the menagerie spilled out back onto a screened-in marble porch. Happy Birthday was sung while the cheerleaders served up ice cream and chocolate cake. Shannon Parker glowed as both party hostess and birthday girl. Roger turned out the porch lights, and piled a stack of 45s on the record player.

The sun was setting beyond the tops of the trees, purple and lavender and gold, accompanied by a salt breeze blowing in from the Atlantic Ocean. It was a time of innocence and romance for tender young hearts in the ancestral lands of the Tequesta Indians. No one imagined the sun was setting on Lady Liberty's innocence.

A dozen couples were dancing. Others were standing around the dance floor enjoying their fruit punch, chatting about Thursday's sock hop in the school gym and the pending game Friday night against Orlando. The Beatles were compared with Bob Dylan and The Moody Blues. The Beatles won handily. There was a new picture show in town, *Doctor Zhivago*, but getting a learner's permit was the most serious topic under discussion. Having one's license to drive was cool beans. It meant getting away from the physical confines of Mama and Daddy, and hanging out at the drive-in restaurants.

Pretty Boy was dancing with Mary Leibowitz. The sophomore class had voted her "Most Likely to Succeed." Shannon's birthday party was their first date unescorted by Mary's mother. Johnny Mathis began filling the room with "The Twelfth of Never. Miss Mary melted into the arms of her adoring quarterback.

"You gettin' yours soon, Moose?

"My father said I could have one soon as he gets a Jeep from that surplus store up in Cape Coral."

"A Jeep, huh? That'll be cool, man.

"Dad said it wouldn't hurt none if it gets banged up some. It's old Army stuff, anyway."

"What about you, Carl? When you takin' your test?"

"Mama said I gotta wait 'til I'm older, eighteen she said."

"That sucks."

"That's what I said. Mama grounded me the rest uh the day."

The telephone rang. Shannon answered it.

"Your father and I have decided to go see *Doctor Zhivago* with the Overstreets. We'll be back around 10:15. You and Roger clean up after your guests leave. Don't let them stay past eight o'clock. Their parents will be worried and start calling."

"Okay, Mom. My birthday party was great. Thank you and Daddy for everything you did."

"We're happy for you, dear. Goodbye, now."

"'Bye, Mom."

Kevin and Miss Jane were the last to leave. Shannon and Roger set about gathering up the plates and party paraphernalia. The dishwasher was loaded, and the remainder of the birthday cake placed in the refrigerator. Then Shannon ran the vacuum cleaner over the carpet in the living room. Finally the two of them sat down to rest. Shannon laid her head over on Roger's shoulder.

"I wish we could stay like this forever. You and me and our friends here in Turnberry. I don't want to get old and have disappointments. I want us to stay just the way we are, young and beautiful and always in love."

Roger placed his arms around Shannon and held her. "I don't know what I'd do if something happened to you. I'd go jump in the bay and float off with the Vikings."

"You'd probably meet some ole mermaid and forget all about me."

"Yeah, and have lots of little mermaid children that bark like seals."

"I'm prettier than that ole mermaid."

You're prettier than all the mermaids that ever were."

Shannon smiled and kissed him. Roger kissed her back. "I have a surprise for you," she said

"Is it a good surprise?"

"It's very good, something we've waited for a long time."

"What is it?"

"I'm on the pill."

"No kidding!"

"Mom got them for me last month. She knows we'll be married someday so she told me it's okay."

"You mean tonight?"

"Yes! They won't be home 'til after ten. I want us to do it on my birthday. We have two whole hours to ourselves."

Shannon went around the back of the house turning out the lights. Then she lit a candle on the porch table. The two of them stripped naked and stood gazing at one another as the shadows danced about the walls from the flickering teardrop of fire. The freedom, so new and delicious, of knowing they didn't have to wait any longer was intoxicating. Shannon shuddered with each kiss as Roger caressed her tender breasts and silken thighs. Their labored breathing ushered them down that yellow brick road traveled only once in a lifetime.

"Honey, do it to me now."

She lay back on the sofa, drawing her knees apart, guiding Roger's penis with both hands. It hurt Shannon at first, but after a few careful movements her discomfort gave way to the most exotic sensations she had ever imagined. Having Roger inside her was an exquisite awakening. The sex was so grand she felt faint. Almost immediately she experienced a climax. In seconds, she climaxed again. Shannon clung to Roger with all her feminine being. She willed herself into him, wrapping her legs around his hips, thrusting her pelvis with loving abandon. Shannon climaxed a third time just as Roger released his seed into Shannon's body.

"God, I love you. I love you so much."

"Roger, honey, let's get married as soon as we can."

"Gosh, Shan, imagine us in a little house someplace. We'd make love every day."

"Twice a day. Once is not enough."

Shannon reached down, taking hold of him again. In no time Roger was ready.

Their second union lasted several minutes. Shannon climaxed again and again, trembling with passion and desire. Roger was euphoric. Their love for one another washed over them in waves, carrying them aloft to those celestial heights of Xanadu. For the handsome Roger Overstreet and the lovely Shannon Parker, sweet sixteen could not have been any more adorable.

Chapter Three

The Payoff

In 1943 eighteen motor torpedo boats were designed and built for the Navy by the Huckins Yacht Corporation in Jacksonville, Florida. Those were considered the best of the torpedo boat series. The Huckins was a 78-foot craft with a top speed of 43 knots, featuring a deep V Quadraconic hull which allowed for smooth sailing at any speed in reasonable weather. Full load displacement exceeded 40 tons with a crew of 11 to 12 men. PT boats were designed to plane off in operation the same as motorized pleasure craft. Their hulls consisted of two one inch thick layers of double diagonal mahogany planking, utilizing a glue-impregnated canvas sheet between the inner and outer hulls, held together with bronze screws and copper rivets. Three Packard 1,350 HP V-12 engines powered the Huckins boats driven by three separate propellers. Her fuel tanks held 3,000 gallons of gasoline.

Dutch Henry purchased a Huckins boat from a shipyard in New Orleans with money he saved selling marijuana to pot dealers at various Southern universities. Wayne "Boogie" Compton, his first cousin, put up half the purchase price. The music, the ganja, and millions of women no longer in fear of getting pregnant because of the "pill," created a carnival atmosphere unrivaled by anything since the Roaring Twenties. Marijuana was in great demand.

Dutch used Wayne's marina at Daytona Beach for making repairs. He employed his engineering skills acquired at the University of Florida, plus a year's tour of duty in Vietnam with the Army Corps of Engineers. He labored on the engine assembly for weeks, replacing the superchargers, fuel lines, intercoolers, and dual magnetos while adding new fuel pumps, spark plugs, seals, and generators. The torpedo tubes and weapons platforms had been removed by the Navy. Dutch gutted the interior of his craft, turning it into a cargo hold. He kept the two officers' quarters plus a small space for cooking. Lead ballast was secured forward to counterbalance for weight loss. He installed 1 x 12 poplar planking every six feet, soaked in water, to conform to the inside curvature of the hull. The old canvas machine gun emplacements on either side of the armored cockpit were refitted with stainless steel gun tubs. Then he steamed and waxed the hull. On her trial run the *Sea Queen* clocked in at 51 miles an hour.

"What'd you come up with?"

Dutch opened his notebook. "Storage can hold 900 of those compressed bags, 925 if we stuff the mothers in there. That's 18,500 pounds. $40 a bag comes to $37,000. We can carry another 440 bags strapped down on the fantail. That's 8,800 pounds and another 17,600 bucks. Wholesale the load for $25 a pound comes to $682,500. Gas and oil should run around $2,000. That'll net us about $625,000, but we still need another $7,000 Where we gonna get that?"

"I'm working on it. 18,500 pounds is over nine tons. Can she handle that much weight below decks?"

"Those torpedoes she carried weighed 2,600 pounds each. That was 5,200 pounds. Torpedo tubes, guns, engines, gasoline, and all the rest ran up around 42 tons. My guesstimate, loaded and fueled, is probably 16 tons less than what she weighed on patrol. The engines are like new, and her reinforced hull can handle the weight in heavy seas."

"Okay. Give me a couple a days to get with my old college buddy. He told me to call him if anything special ever turned up."

"I'll be at the apartment if you need me."

Boogie Compton's contact in Panama had called the week before saying she had located fourteen tons of high-quality merchandise. "Panama Red" was good stuff. A load that size didn't come along very often. Wayne and Dutch had pooled all their cash, but were $7,000 short. Part of their savings was tied up in the boat. Dutch set out for the bank to empty out his lockbox. Boogie went back in the office and pulled out a Miami telephone directory.

"How's the family?"

"Everybody's fine. And you?"

"I lost a hundred and twenty-two pounds."

"What?"

"I got divorced."

John laughed. "I remember she was awfully pretty."

"She was that, all right. And a spoiled pain in my ass every day of the week."

"So what's the occasion?"

"You said to call if something special turned up."

"Is it safe?"

"I think so. Dutch Henry and I are betting the farm on this one."

"I'm free Wednesday if you can get loose."

"How 'bout that British restaurant in Vero Beach, say three o'clock?"

"I'll see ya there, Boogie Man."

Chapter Four

Mad Dogs and Englishmen

"We have dark beer, cider, apricot brandy … "

"I'll have a pint of cider and the plowman's lunch."

"I'll have a toad in the hole and the cider."

The waitress turned and left for the kitchen.

"I wonder if the owner knows Joe Cocker?"

"Probably where he got the name for his marquee."

"How was the drive up?"

"The usual traffic out of Miami. Pretty light on the highway. What've you got, Wayne?"

"Dutch and I are going after a load of grass. A big one. We fixed up a boat to run down to Panama, and haul the stuff back up here. Fourteen tons, but we're short $7,000. The trip will take about two weeks. Your share would be $45,000. I'll round that off to $55,000, counting your investment. Dutch and I keep the lion's share. We're taking all the risk."

"What kind of boat is it?"

"It's an old PT boat. Dutch renovated the whole thing. She's a beauty now."

"What about the Coast Guard?"

"That's not a problem. Their ships average about 20 knots at flank speed. The *Sea Witch* can turn 50 knots. But get this, Sarah tells me the Coast Guard isn't wise yet to all the smuggling going on. That's a big advantage in our favor for pulling this thing off without a hitch. "

"What do you know about this Sarah person?"

"Sarah is an airline stewardess. We dated some before I got married. I should have married her, but that's a long story. Anyway, we got back together after my divorce. Sarah told me about all the smuggling going on up and down the Florida Coast. She's been involved once before. I knew about some of it, but nothing like she told me. People are getting rich every day in this business."

"If something goes wrong and you guys get caught, what then?"

"Marco Robles is the president of Panama. His administration is full of the usual bullshit and corruption, but Sarah told me if there's trouble she would ask her stewardess friend to go see Omar Torrijos for help. Her girlfriend dates one of his officers. Sarah met Colonel Torrijos at a wedding reception. She says he's the main man in Panama, besides President Robles."

"What might that cost?"

"Too damn much! I want you to take power of attorney over my marina. If Dutch and I get in trouble, use the title to bail us out."

"How do you plan on getting rid of the stuff?"

"I got buyers out the ass. One dealer in Miami wants $250,000 worth as soon as we get back. I can sell the whole load in five or six days."

"What about fuel and navigation?"

"We'll top off in Key Largo then make our run for Cancun. I have all the ports mapped out, tides, ocean currents. We got a radio, a compass, an old radar set. Dutch knows the stars. It'll be cool, man.

"Looks like you've covered your bases. What's your gut feeling about all this?"

"You always ask that question, don't you?"

"It helps me decide how to handle a case, especially one like yours. I don't want you two getting your tails in a crack. And I don't want to lose my money, either. That's nearly all my savings."

"My gut feeling is this. With Sarah's connections in Panama and you up here as backup, I don't foresee a problem other than the weather. That, Dutch and I can handle. Once you get your money back, consider letting some of it ride. Dutch and I will cut you in as a full partner our next trip south."

"Sure beats our Kentucky Gentleman days bootlegging whiskey at the college. I bet we never made more than six hundred dollars selling booze.

"How's that daughter of yours?"

"Shannon is a delightful young lady. She's grown up into a real beauty. Got herself a boyfriend, a real nice fella. They'll be getting married one of these days."

"So what do you think?"

"I have to talk it over with Katherine first. I always bounce ideas off her."

"I like Katherine. She's a cool lady."

"Katherine has street smarts. I'll let you know something by tomorrow afternoon."

Katherine Mosley was a thirty-eight–year-old beauty who spent her youth in an orphanage in Milledgeville, Georgia. The day she turned eighteen she left the children's home with twenty-four dollars in her jeans and a cardboard suitcase, and hitchhiked her way to Jacksonville, Florida. Three days later she was working at a truck stop on the outskirts of town. Seven months of serving tables and fending off male customers proved to be a dead end so she hitched another ride to Saint Augustine. The men there were just as enthusiastic as Jacksonville. She dated a few of the Army Air Force pilots, but all they wanted from Katherine was to get in her pants.

It was in the spring of '47 when a stranger walked in and sat down at the lunch counter where Katherine was waitressing for the F.W. Woolworth Company. The stranger was a student at Florida State University. Katherine found herself intrigued by the young man. John Parker was handsome and intelligent, a real Southern gentleman. One look at the redhead taking his order and John stopped in midsentence.

"Ma'am, would you give me the honor of joining me for a picnic on the beach? I'm a senior at the college, over here on spring break."

Seven months later they were married.

"Your friend is completely crazy."

"So you don't like the idea?"

"It's not that. He reminds me of Errol Flynn in those old pirate movies."

"You should meet Dutch Henry."

"What's he like?"

"He's big and tall. He's a tough-looking character."

"Is he cute?"

"I guess so. He's a six-foot-four version of William Holden."

"Big hands and big feet?"

"You're a naughty girl."

"Sweetheart, you know I'm teasing you. I could never sleep with anyone but you."

"Then stop distracting me or we'll spend the rest of the afternoon in your favorite position."

"Promise, sweetie?"

"Yes, Katherine. You're my baby doll."

"Sarah's connection in Panama intrigues me. Who would suspect such a thing from an airline stewardess? Or a boat dock guy and his engineer? Their cover is perfect. Being his lawyer makes sense since the two of you went to school together. Nobody would believe we have money in this thing. I'm for it if you feel comfortable about our savings."

"There's something else, Kat. If they pull this off, and I'm confident they will, I would like for us to invest in some of their future ventures. As long as it's safe and the boys don't get in trouble, we could make a fortune doing this."

"I knew on our first date I should marry you."

"Why's that?"

"'Cause you make me so damn horny!"

John laughcd. "You are a naughty little girl!"

Katherine smiled and turned out the light.

Chapter Five

The Dual 90s Caper

A special meeting had been called for the Sha Doobie Tribe. Mischief was afoot. All eleven tribal members were in attendance. Mary Leibowitz's mother and father had arranged their playroom with card tables and folding chairs to accommodate Mary's teenage guests. Bowls of potato chips and pitchers of lemonade were set out. Mary, their newly elected Chief Moon Dog, called the meeting to order.

The topic under discussion was Badass McCoy, and his three football buddies who had beaten Roger up when he stopped for gasoline over in Hallandale. They roughed up Shannon too, dragging her out of the car and pulling her panties off for a trophy. Roger told his mom and dad he got the black eye at football practice. Shannon managed to slip in without being seen by her mother, and put on a summer dress to cover the bruises on her arms and legs.

"Those guys hang out together. They call themselves 'The Four Horsemen.'"

"More like The Four Assholes, if you ask me."

"What are we gonna do about this? The way they treated Shannon an' all?"

Moose was in whupass mode. "I say bust some heads!"

"I'll second that." Little Willie John was still pissed over the football game where Badass poked him in the eye with a finger.

"Hold on, Warriors."

Mary turned to Roger. "I think we should hear what Roger has to say regarding the matter. Then we can hear Shannon's side of the story."

Roger addressed the group from his place at the table beside Shannon. "Well, it happened this way. They beat me up some. Then they insulted Shannon by pulling her panties off. They rattled our cages pretty good. Badass is bad news, I won't argue that. But they did show some sense of fair play. They didn't hit me when I was down. It was mostly pushing and shoving."

"That's crazy. They gave you a black eye and busted your mouth. They need their asses kicked."

"Maybe so, but not by me."

"Why not?"

"I got in a few good licks. They knocked me down a couple a times."

"So what?"

"Each time I was on the ground they waited 'til I got back up. Does that sound like they really wanted to hurt me? McCoy was just showing off."

Shannon spoke up. "It's true. As bad as it sounds they didn't kick Roger or anything like that. When they grabbed me they weren't really rough. I got my bruises fighting them, but nothing real bad."

"Then what the hell are we doing here?"

Roger continued. "I didn't say we couldn't have some fun with this. I just don't want anybody getting hurt, that's all."

"Yes, we don't want anyone getting hurt," Shannon said. "That's not the Sha Doobie way."

Pretty Boy rose to the occasion. "Shannon and Roger are right. That's not the Sha Doobie way."

Moose argued for a minute then finally gave in. Calico and the others nodded their heads in agreement.

Little Willie John was slowly brailing his way around to their way of thinking. "Okay, what's this fun stuff you talk about? We can't just forget what they did to you guys."

"I don't know. Play a joke, maybe?"

Mary was smiling. "I'm very proud of the Tribe. This is what they teach in synagogue, about kindness and doing the right thing. What McCoy and his friends did was wrong. We don't want to compound that wrong by doing something equally mean or ugly."

"Whatever we decide, the Warriors should vote on it," Pretty Boy said.

Mary had a serious crush on Pretty Boy. Pretty Boy felt the same way about his "Miss Mary."

"Yes, we'll put it to a vote. In the meantime the Tribal Council will entertain suggestions from the Warriors. Think of something funny, but legal. We don't want Moose and Little Willie getting thrown in the pokey … again."

Everybody laughed.

The Sha Doobie Tribe had chosen wisely when they elected Mary Leibowitz their Chief Moon Dog. Mary had an amusing sense of humor, an IQ in the stratosphere, and was planning on becoming a member of the Cape Canaveral Space Program after she earned her PhD in Physics. Pretty Boy's immediate ambition, besides marrying his Jewish Princess, was a football scholarship with The University of Florida.

"First Warrior, you may bring in the hotdogs now. Girls, you'll find potato salad and Cokes in the refrigerator."

A week passed with various suggestions entertained before Council regarding what action to take against McCoy and his teammates. Calico suggested pouring oil in his gas tank. Not good. That would smoke like the dickens, and could damage his engine. Charlie thought it would be funny to spray paint the shrubbery in his parent's front yard. Bad idea. That might kill the plants. Little Nelle wanted to egg the house. Not good, either. That might involve Detective McCoy. Moose and Little Willie John came up with the notion of jacking up Badass's convertible, taking the wheels off, then dropping them down the flagpole at McCoy's school.

The two had scoped out the scene. There was a twenty-foot extension ladder behind the gymnasium they could use. Splendid! Everyone would know The Four Horsemen had been made to look less than cool. Better still, no one would know who did it. Chief Moon Dog called the Tribe into session the following Saturday. The vote was unanimous.

A full moon shown down on a nocturnal wonderland awash with an atmosphere of intrigue and mystery, it's quicksilver brilliance a white mantle across the subtropical landscape. An owl hooted. In the distance a dog barked. Trucks shifting gears out on the freeway gave rise to a sense of impending peril. Beneath the trees lurked a pair of Warriors.

"What time is it?"

"You just asked me that question five minutes ago."

"Well, tell me again."

"It's 10:45! Five minutes ago it was 10:40! Five minutes from now it'll be 10:50. You're the biggest worrywart I ever saw."

"Well, I'm nervous. This place is full of snakes and spiders."

"Great ole big ones ... hungry too, I bet!"

"Now cut that out!"

"Stop thinking about it! You're driving me crazy."

"You were crazy when you were born, Moose."

"You got a point there ... hey look, the lights went out."

"Thank goodness."

"We'll wait a few more minutes. They should be in bed by then."

Moose and Little Willie John were a quarter block south on the opposite side the street in a vacant lot thick with crape myrtle, sand oak, and banyan trees. They had hidden four concrete cinder blocks there the week before. Moose had a car jack with him he'd borrowed from his father's automotive repair shop downtown. The pickup truck they came in sat parked behind the bushes and banyan trees. The stage was set. They took off running in the shadows toward the McCoy home.

"These things are heavy."

"I'll trade you my jack an' lug wrench."

"No thanks. You get busy. I'll go back for the other two."

Moose set about jacking up McCoy's convertible in front of the McCoy residence while Little Willie John ran back for the two remaining cinder blocks. Moose had one wheel off by the time Little Willie John returned.

"These things weigh a ton!"

Little Willie crawled up under the back of the automobile. Moose scooted a cinder block on either side of him. Willie pushed them under the steel frame opposite the rear wheel hubs then crawled back out. Moose began unscrewing the lug nuts on the second tire.

"Roll these back to our hiding place. I'll have the others off in a jiffy."

By the time Willie returned, Moose had both front wheels on the ground. Willie slid under the Mustang again, placing the last two cinder blocks underneath the steel frame opposite the front wheel hubs. Moose let the car down on the blocks then the two of them lit out for the truck, Moose carrying the lug wrench and jack, and Little Willie John rolling the two front wheels as fast as he could go.

A porch light came on across the street. Willie and Moose fled into the bushes with their cargo. An elderly woman came out on her front stoop.

"Is someone there?" she called out.

Another porch light came on next door. A young man appeared in the doorway. "Is something wrong, Missus Weinstein?"

"Little Pooh was barking. I think he heard something."

"You stay here. I'll go take a look."

The young man's wife standing behind him in the foyer called out to her husband, "You be careful, dear."

Missus Weinstein responded, "Yes, Brian, please be careful."

Little Willie John found himself in a dire predicament. Right beside him beneath the bush he had chosen to hide under was a multicolored snake as big around as his wrist. Its colorful markings resembled those of the deadly coral snake. Willie was too scared to move. So was the snake. Moose saw the reptile in the moonlight, reached over and flipped it away with his hand. The snake coiled up.

"It's a rat snake. They're called tiger rats. It can't hurt you."

"Looks like a coral snake to me!" His serpent phobia fully engaged, Willie began wedging himself through the sand oak branches to distance himself from the black and yellow viper.

Brian was standing in the middle of his driveway listening to what he thought were marsh rats in the underbrush.

Moose got tickled. "Coral snakes are little suckers. You got a King Kong rat daddy over there." He bit his tongue to keep from laughing out loud.

Little Willie John's wiggling and squirming reminded Moose of a raccoon after a saltwater crab. After much straining and grunting, Willie landed on top of Moose.

"I hate snakes!" Willie whispered.

Moose placed both hands over his mouth to stifle himself.

"Stop laughing at me, you asshole."

"Be quiet, damn it. He's gonna hear us."

Curiosity finally satisfied, Brian went back inside his townhouse and closed the door.

Roger, Shannon, and Pretty Boy were waiting beside the Hallandale High School flagpole when Moose and Willie John came running out of the trees rolling four automobile tires with the rims still attached. Roger and Pretty Boy had just brought up the extension ladder from behind the school. Shannon had a fifty-foot roll of clothesline she'd purchased at a hardware store in town.

"You bring the gloves?"

"Two pairs ... got 'em right here."

Roger climbed the ladder holding the clothesline, which he draped over the top rung of the ladder, letting both ends drop to the ground. Little Willie John tied off one end to a General Dual 90 with a slipknot. Wearing the work gloves, Moose and Pretty Boy took hold of the other end, hoisting the tire up. Roger positioned the rim around the top of the flagpole, pushed his ladder out a ways with Pretty Boy, Moose, Little Willie John, and Shannon supporting the ladder from below, and down it fell. Three more hoists, and they had all four wheels around the twenty-foot steel pole. Roger and Pretty Boy carried the ladder back to the exact location they found it.

"Remember now, not a word to anybody except the Tribe."

Shannon, Roger, and the quarterback hustled back to their Oldsmobile across the street in the school parking lot. Moose and Willie retraced their steps through the trees to the pickup truck. All five would be home in bed by half past midnight.

"You gonna tell about the snake?"

"Yeah! I'm gonna run me uh ad in the school newspaper."

"We ain't got no school newspaper!"

"Then I'll be the editor of our first edition."

"The Klan would burn a cross on the front lawn!"

"Hey, that would be some killer news."

"This ain't funny, okay?"

"I can see it now, 'Night of the Tiger Rat.'"

"Now listen, you!"

"Ten cents a copy!"

"Damn it, Moose!"

"I won't rat you out, Snake Man. But it was pretty funny. You climbing around in that bush like a dang monkey."

"I guess it was pretty funny at that." Little Willie John chuckled at himself.

They both laughed.

"You're a pal, Moose."

"You're a good sport, Willie. Tonight was great, wasn't it?"

"We pulled a good one, didn't we? Badass is gonna have a cow."

It had been a memorable adventure for the young Warriors, five high school friends who would share the moment with laughter and fond memories for the rest of their lives.

Chapter Six

The Voyage

Dutch and Wayne left from the marina with several fishing vessels a little before sunup. The eastern horizon turned bright yellow as the sun rose above a green ocean into a pale blue sky. Its golden reflection across the waters boded well for the mariners going to sea.

"'Red skies at morning Sailors take warning.'"

There was no breeze, only a three-knot current flowing north with the Gulf Stream.

Bubba-J, a weathered old salt with a handlebar mustache, was left in charge of running the marina. Bubba-J came with the package when Boogie's father retired, giving Wayne ownership to the three acres of land that went with his commercial boat dock. Two years after retirement Mister Compton died in his sleep. That was a sad moment in the lives of Wayne and Bubba-J. Bubba-J and Lyle had served as seamen during the First World War.

Conrad Adalmann was fished out of the North Sea following

the Battle of Jutland. His German cruiser had been sunk by a pair of British battleships. That's when he and Lyle met and a friendship developed. After the war ended in 1918, they came to live in the United States where they settled at Daytona Beach. Seaman Compton opened a small fishing marina, and Seaman Adalmann helped him manage the business. Over the years it grew into a docking facility with a hundred and thirty-four boat slips.

Lyle hung the title of Bubba-J on Conrad during the Second World War when Americans became suspicious of Germans. Conrad still had the accent so Lyle passed him off as a Russian. They laughed about that one. The two were a pair of characters, finding humor in everything they did together. A lover of Great Britain passed from the scene when Lyle Compton died. His German comrade grieved the loss of his British friend.

"Tell me again about our trip."

"Once we top off at Key Largo we got about 480 miles from there to Cancun. It's another 950 miles to Panama as the crow flies, but we'll add 130 miles by refueling in Trujillo. I want our tanks full in case we run into trouble. From here to Miami is 560 miles then about 55 more to Key Largo. All told, I estimate 2,200 nautical miles.

"Divide your mileage by 20 knots and you get 110 hours. We'll have to average 23 knots to compensate for the current. A hundred and ten divided by 24 comes to four and a half days. Nothing ever goes according to plan so figure six days. No big deal. We'll get a nice tan and get to see the whales."

"I've never seen a whale before."

"They got twenty or thirty varieties down there, mostly humpbacks and sperm whales. Dolphins are all over the place."

"You read much?"

"Some, why?

"I read *Moby Dick* in Vietnam."

"I read that book and saw the movie. Gregory Peck was great as Captain Ahab. Remember when he caught St Elmo's fire in his hand?"

"That was pretty cool. Another book I liked was *The Scarlet Pimpernel*. It reminded me a little of Vietnam. The North and South killing each other just like France and England. I hated what I saw over there."

"You mind talking about it?"

"I guess not. It still gives me bad dreams. I saw a lot of dead people. Some with their heads chopped off. I never knew people could be that mean to one another. We had an Army chaplain who cracked up. They sent him back to the States."

"I thought you were building bridges and bunkers."

"We were, but sometimes the fighting came in right on top of us. Twice we had to defend our positions."

"That must be scary as hell getting shot at."

"It was scary, all right. And the heat and mosquitoes were fucking awful."

"Sounds like the usual military stuff."

"We had this one lieutenant who worked with the ARVN helping with our construction and whatnot. ARVN was the South Vietnamese Army troops. Anyway, this particular day he was talking with one of their officers when the man's head exploded right in his face. A sniper got him. Our lieutenant wasn't right for a week after that."

"Hell, who would be? I saw this little girl brought in who drowned a few years back. I can still see her little face. It was awful. It doesn't go away, does it?"

"No, you just learn to live with it. That's why so many soldiers become alcoholics."

"Speaking of which, it's five o'clock someplace. How 'bout a beer?"

"Sure thing! All this talk about 'Nam gave me a headache."

The men toasted one another with frosty bottles of Pabst Blue Ribbon.

They were steering south against the Gulf Stream. It would take until morning to reach Miami. The ocean was calm with three-foot swells running thirty yards apart. They were traveling at twenty-five knots on one engine to conserve fuel. Two hours later the first dolphins appeared.

"Hey, look over there."

"I see 'em."

"See the way his nose sticks out? Those are bottle-nose dolphins."

"We had those in Vietnam. The men used to feed them off a pier at Cam Ranh Bay. There was a village there called the 'Meat Market.' For a few bucks a GI could rent a girlfriend for the day. Beer and beach parties, man. All the comforts of war."

"You've done it all, Dutch. A degree in engineering, Vietnam, now this."

"You're the lucky one, Boogie Man. That marina must bring in a lot of dough."

"It does pretty well. But we got taxes and maintenance, and every once in a while some dickhead from city hall shows up with another regulation to gum up the works. I'm grandfathered or I'd have to replace the whole deck area."

"I like ole Bubba-J."

"That ole Kraut bastard! I love that old man. He and my dad were like brothers. I wish you could have met my father. He was something of a visionary. He could see what was coming before it got here. I couldn't see past the end of my nose 'til I took over the marina. Bubba-J helped a lot. He's like my father now."

"I read *The Battle of Jutland*. I can't imagine what it was like with those big shells landing around."

"Dad never talked about it much. He did say when his battleship fired a broadside the ship went sideways about a foot."

"Did he talk much about England?"

"He was from a place called Bath. They have lots of flowers and architecture there. Stonehenge is between there and London. He was proud to be a Brit. Talked about Winston Churchill all the time. Said Churchill saved England, and probably saved the whole world."

"I read *Their Finest Hour*. The Battle of Britain was unbelievable. So was Dunkirk. Churchill and Hitler were great speakers. So was Roosevelt. I don't think much of President Johnson. A colonel I know said Johnson could lose the war."

"How so?"

"Political meddling."

"Why don't we just blow the place away and come home?"

"China and Russia are involved. Our own politicians are running the thing into the ground."

"I never heard that before."

"You won't hear it on the six o'clock news. Walter Cronkite and the other networks are covering for the White House."

"The colonel told you that?"

"No, one of the reporters with *The New York Times* told me. She said everybody is covering for Johnson.

"What do you think?"

"The colonel said the White House is afraid China might get in the war. That would mean trouble."

Wayne fell silent. His sense of pride in the American political system had just been deflated. He had a cousin in Vietnam. And one of his buddies from high school had left three weeks ago. Wayne wondered if it was going to turn out like the Korean War.

They journeyed on beneath the afternoon sun, passing one freighter after another. Hours later the sun began spreading its magnificent colors when it sank in a western sea. The stars came out.

Dutch pointed behind the boat. "See the little dipper?"

"Yeah."

"The end of the handle is the North Star. We're running south so it's behind us. When we leave Key Largo and head out in the Gulf, it will be on our right. Actually it'll be a little behind us to the northeast. We'll be going southwest toward Cancun, about 230 degrees on your compass."

"Where'd you learn that stuff?"

"Building firebases. We moved around sometimes at night. We always had a compass, but it helped to be able to read the stars. When it wasn't cloudy or raining our gunny sergeant went by the stars. Gunny served in the Pacific. He taught us how to do it."

"How 'bout teaching me?"

"See the big dipper up there? It's upside down now which means it's spring. If it were right-side up it would be fall. When the handle is pointed straight down, it's February. Straight up is July. The top front of the big dipper is always pointing toward the North Star, the little dipper. The big dipper rotates around the little dipper. Same way the earth rotates around the sun. The stars don't move. We do. The sun doesn't move either. We rotate around the sun."

"I'll never remember that."

"Sure you will. It just takes practice. By the time this trip is over you won't need your charts and radar. Just locate the North Star. Then use a nautical map to plot your heading. "

"If the sun doesn't move, how far away are we when winter comes?"

"That's a misconception a lot of people make. The earth always stays the same distance from the sun. It's tilted on an axis of 23 degrees. If you were out to the west in space looking back at the earth and North America, winter comes when the Northern Hemisphere is on your left, tilted away from the sun. Summer comes when the Northern Hemisphere is on your right, tilted toward the sun. The equator stays the same the year-round. It's always pointed toward the sun."

"That gunny sergeant must have been something else."

"He didn't talk much about his past. He stayed busy looking after us, telling us what to look for, booby traps and such. Don't build cook fires or wear aftershave in enemy territory. Bury everything, cans and toilet paper. Stick together. Don't' make no noise. All our guys got back safely."

"I'm worried about what you said about Johnson. I got friends over there."

"Say a prayer for them, Wayne. I prayed when the bullets were flying."

They journeyed on through a platinum ocean. Overhead a million stars blanketed the *Sea Queen*, resembling tiny diamonds in a black void.

By 10 a.m. they were well past Biscayne Bay following the island chain down to Key Largo. Boogie knew one of the marina captains who worked the piers at Rock Harbor. A twenty dollar bill was passed. No mention would be made about the *Sea Queen* passing through. Boogie stayed onboard with the money while Dutch went ashore to rustle up some breakfast.

Three miles out they dug into their bacon, lettuce, and tomato sandwiches.

"Something funny happened in the restaurant."

"What?"

"There were these three guys sitting at a back table, a Mexican and two white men. The Mexican came over and asked me something in Spanish. I told him '*No comprende*.' Then he went back and sat down."

"Maybe he wanted a date."

"Get outta here!"

"You are kinda cute."

"That'll be the day!"

"Probably looking for a job or something."

"I don't think so. His hands were soft. The men with him were soft-looking too."

"You noticed his hands?"

"You notice everything about a person after Vietnam."

"That's good thinking, Dutch. We'll gas up at Stock Island or Pirate's Cove on the way back."

"I think we better get ourselves some weapons in Panama."

"I brought Dad's old .45 with me."

"We need something with some range to it in case we run into trouble."

"I'll ask Sarah. She knows those military guys."

"We have a probe in the medical kit, don't we?"

"A probe, a scalpel, and sutures."

"That's cool. I'm gonna take me a nap. Wake me up when you get tired."

The day passed quickly as the men maneuvered through the blue fathoms of the Florida Straits. Ninety miles to the south lay Havana and Castro's Cuba. Four hundred miles southwest, the city of Cancun perched above the Caribbean on the eastern tip of the Yucatan Peninsula. Hundreds of miles north, oil rigs and natural gas platforms dotted the coastline around the Gulf of Mexico. Night fell as the sun disappeared into a sparkling marmalade sea.

"Hear that?"

"What is it?"

"Whales."

"Sounds like a squeaky door."

"Listen, it's really beautiful."

"Must be a lot of 'em."

"We better slow down or we might hit one. The moon will be up in a few minutes."

"Let's drift awhile. I want to see one."

Wayne turned off the engine. Low in the east the moon was rising. The moon cast enough light for Dutch and Boogie to distinguish the dark shapes in the water. The whales were moving north with the Gulf current on their way to the Grand Banks to feed on the tiny plankton and octopus squid out in the North Atlantic. One of the whales was passing nearby off the port bow. The others were farther out, singing back and forth to stay together.

"That's a sperm whale. See the head, blunt and squared off? That's your Moby Dick. It's damn near as long as the boat so that's a big male. He'll go forty tons or better."

"That's the biggest thing I ever saw."

"Watch when he rolls again. He's looking over here to see what we're doing."

"Would they attack if we disturbed them?"

"Not likely unless we hurt one of their young."

"It's a beautiful creature, all right."

"They're wonderful animals. I couldn't kill one. The Japanese do it all the time."

"I read where the Canadians club baby seals for their fur. That's shitty."

"The world is full of shitty people, Dutch. I wonder if what we're doing is wrong."

"I've asked myself that question a dozen times. If someone wants to smoke herb and get high, I don't see any difference between that and drinking whiskey or smoking cigarettes. Nicotine is more addictive than the chemicals in marijuana. Of course if they smoke weed all the time, that's not good."

"I'm glad you said that. I'd hate to think we're supplying addicts."

"Think about it this way, Boogie Man. Besides good health men want two things in life, money and pussy. Money gets 'em the pussy. Mary Jane is gonna get us the money."

"There's a certain mad logic there, but I like it!"

"Right on!"

"You think we'll see more whales?"

"Once we start down the Nicaraguan coast we should see lots of them."

"Looks like they've gone their merry way. Ready to crank up again?"

"Sure. You steer awhile. I need some sleep."

At two in the morning Dutch saw his first meteor shower. It lasted the better part of thirty minutes. Tiny streaks of fire burning across the heavens. Life was like that, a flash in the pan then night. He mused about growing up in South Carolina, his education in Florida, and his experiences in Vietnam. Now he had a new life as a smuggler. Wayne was right to question their morality.

Wayne was wise in ways he wasn't. Wayne knew about the sea, about boats, and he understood business. He was a gentle soul. The two of them made a good team. He could have done a lot worse in life, like those crippled GIs coming home from 'Nam. Or the girl he almost married in college who was off her rocker. Vietnam had taught him that life was a roll of the dice. Sometimes you pick up the cash. Sometimes you roll snake eyes.

Smuggling was going to make them rich. They could have anything they wanted. Wayne wanted Sarah. Dutch wondered what she was like. And the girl she was fixing him up with in Panama? If they got in good with the Panamanian authorities, that would be the real jackpot.

Dutch wondered what they would do if the law got on their tails. Live in South America probably, maybe even Panama. He hoped he would like Sarah for Wayne's sake. Bummer if he didn't. He hoped she would like him. Being twenty-five with the potential that lay before them was a little bit frightening. He didn't want to screw it up over some dumb mistake.

Another meteor flashed across the sky. People believed those things were good luck. Dutch thought for several minutes. Were they destined for good fortune? Or were they sailing into trouble? He vowed that night before God and his deceased father that he would engage all of his military knowledge and all of his educational ability for the successful completion of their mission.

Dutch was aware of the evil in men. He had seen it at Dak To, Kontum, and Hoi An. He saw it again in that little restaurant in Key Largo. He knew men were out there who might try and take it away from them. It reminded him of Vietnam and how fragile life really was. Beneath a starry sky, in the middle of a dark and mysterious ocean, Dutch thought again about the bloody ambush upriver from An Khe.

The hand of Fate was about to roll the cosmic dice for two Americans.

Chapter Seven

Detective McCoy

The Fallen Idol

Detective McCoy was on top of the building looking down on an alleyway three floors below. Cottonmouth was across the street behind a trash dumpster with his .12 gauge riot gun. Enrico Basilio, a capo with the Cosa Nostra, had informed them of a drug shipment en route to the Colombian headquarters in Opa Locka. The Mob didn't like competition. Nor did they relish a turf war with the smugglers from Bogotá. The South Americans had already killed two of his crew and wounded five others. Basilio was letting his cop connection settle the score.

McCoy spoke to his partner using a two-way radio. "Cotton, you see anything?"

"Naw, they ain't come yet."

"Radio back the minute you see something."

"I got 'er covered, Bill."

A tractor-trailer loaded with thirty-nine hundred kilos of cocaine and eighty eight-five pound bags of pure heroin was in transit from the Miami waterfront to the Opa Locka warehouse. Dock workers had been paid five hundred bucks a head for offloading the drugs from a rusting Colombian freighter whose manifest read bananas, coffee beans, and tobacco. Three cartel members were waiting inside the 1940s freight office for the shipment to arrive. Two more Colombians were shepherding the truck through the rain-swept streets of Miami.

It was midnight when Cottonmouth radioed McCoy. There was no traffic, only the ghostly image of a silvery moon overhead. Streetlights cast eerie illuminations amidst a continuing drizzle as the eighteen-wheeler came rolling down the rain-blackened street. The driver stopped just past the alley then began backing his rig into the narrow brick corridor.

McCoy positioned himself above the office door. Cottonmouth scuttled from behind his dumpster, crouching down behind a '58 Chevrolet several feet east of the big diesel. The driver stepped down from his cab, and went around to unlock the trailer doors.

"*Ay Caramba*! What a beautiful sight we have here."

"More *loco* dust for the stupid *gringos*, eh?"

"Julio, you are the happy-face comedian."

"We make the big money, Miguel. Four and a half tons of shit for Uncle Sam and his French whore, Lady Liberty."

"That was a good one, Julio. You get the job on Ed Sullivan."

"Get to work, you pranksters. We got five hours before daylight."

Four of the Colombians went to work loading handcarts while a fifth man stood guard near the entranceway to the alley. They labored for an hour neatly stacking kilos inside the warehouse on sheets of marine plywood with 4 x 4s underneath to keep the cocaine from ab-sorbing moisture through the concrete floor.

"Give 'em another few minutes, Cotton. We promised Rico part of the load."

"I want a bag or two, myself. My old lady uses the stuff."

"That coonass is gonna cut your balls off one a these nights."

"Yeah, but she's a hot little mama. Says my face turns 'er on."

Gunfire shattered the stillness of the evening. The lookout had spotted Cotton across the street talking to McCoy. Bullets rang off the pavement, slamming into the Chevrolet, ripping bark off a bitterwood tree. Then a Russian AK-47 opened fire. Ricochets whined into the drifting fog. Cottonmouth was trapped behind the automobile.

Bill McCoy stood up on the perimeter of the flat roof and pulled the trigger. The roar of a Thompson submachine gun filled the night. Sparks shot from the pavement, debris flew in the air. Men screamed and fell, clutching their bodies. McCoy continued to fire until the fifty round drum was empty.

Cotton walked across the street with his shotgun in his hand. Flying shards of glass had cut a gash in his forehead. With blood running down onto his raincoat he looked like something out of *Inner Sanctum*. The lookout was still alive. The other four men lay dead, crumpled like bloody rags on the wet pavement.

Struggling to raise his weapon, the Colombian whispered up at John Franklin, "Fuck you, *gringo*!"

Cottonmouth pulled the trigger. A load of double-ought buckshot ended the conversation.

"Come on, man. We got work to do."

The detectives entered the delivery office searching for money. There was usually cash around where drugs were concerned. It took just minutes to locate the suitcase.

"Holy shit! Over here!"

"Damn, man! We hit the mother lode."

"Get this shit out to the car while I call Basilio. No, wait!"

Detective McCoy grabbed two handfuls of cash, stuffing them in the top drawer of an office desk. Cotton was out the door and headed for the car when McCoy made his call.

"We heard the chopper. You guys okay?"

"You bring a truck?"

"Sure thing, we're right around the corner."

"Get over here before the whole neighborhood wakes up."

"We're on the way."

A heavy van came to an abrupt halt in front of the bullet-riddled truck cab. Twelve men piled out, forming an assembly line passing kilos of cocaine into the van. Enrico stepped down from the front of the unmarked vehicle.

"Get yourself a good taste, Rico. Then beat it. You got ten minutes."

"You're a dirty cop, McCoy, and I love you for it."

"And you're a lousy dago, but we sure make the cash registers ring."

"Know what I like about you, McCoy? You'd make a great hit man."

"Cottonmouth's your hit man. He'd shoot his own grandmother for a cold Blue Ribbon."

"Cottonmouth scares the shit outta ever body."

"He has his moments."

"You find any money?"

"That's my business. Nose candy is yours."

"I'll wager there was fifty, sixty grand at least."

"Wager all you like, Basilio. You got a load of free dope, and we took all the risk."

"You got me there, McCoy. I owe you for getting these wetbacks off my neck."

"They'll be more."

"I know. They're a resilient bunch uh pricks."

"Tell your boys to keep their mouths shut. We don't want those bastards finding out about us."

"Boss, we got a thousand bags just like you said."

"Make your call, McCoy."

The van was a mile away when the first squad car arrived. In hot pursuit came a reporter with *The Miami Herald*. An ambulance had been summoned. A pretty female paramedic cleaned the blood off

Cottonmouth's face, placing a bandage across his forehead. The reporter, a young man fresh out of Miami University turned white at the sight of the bloody bodies strewn about the crime scene.

"Good God! Does this happen very often?"

"Shit happens, son. Take a look inside."

The young reporter went inside the warehouse where he inspected the mounds of cocaine. Satisfied, he came out and climbed up inside the tractor-trailer. This was a big story. Detective McCoy and Detective Franklin had busted a shipment of more than three tons of cocaine. Five Colombians had been killed in the gun battle, and Detective Franklin wounded. In addition, $34,600 in cash had been found in a desk drawer inside the warehouse office.

No one suspected that 2,200 pounds of coke had been taken by the Miami Mafia plus eighty-eight bags of heroin. Or that $242,400 was locked in the trunk of William McCoy's squad car. To everyone present, Bill McCoy and John Franklin were heroes. The young reporter wrote it up as if crime had been expunged from the precinct of the Dade County Police Department.

Badass was so proud of his father he could bust. Everywhere he went people patted him on the back, telling him how glad they were his dad was on the Force. They told him he was a lucky young man and he was going places someday. Businessmen asked him to come see them after he finished school. A job would be waiting. Frank McCoy had never had a steady girlfriend. Now he found one on every street corner. He had become a celebrity just like his father.

In a matter of five days it went straight to his head.

"I think I know who took my wheels."

"Who's that?"

"Remember that kid we pushed around in the gas station?"

"Yeah. It was that football player that knocked you on your ass!"

"Fuck you!"

"And knocked out your front tooth!"

"Cut it out, Eric."

"And scored a touchdown that cost us the game!"

"I told you he did something illegal."

"Like you didn't?"

"Well, whatever, I think he did it!"

"You're just pissed 'cause it was the talk uh the school for two weeks."

"You turnin' chicken?"

"No, I just know trouble when I see it. And you're headed straight for it."

"I think that car wreck addled your brain."

"Uh-uh ... It knocked some sense in me. We're always in trouble because of some shit you've cooked up. Your dad gets you out. The rest of us get screwed. That last trip downtown cost my father thirty-four dollars and sixty-two cents to bail me out. He works hard for his money. And that's the second time in seven damn weeks!"

"Want me to buy you a crying towel?"

"I want you to pull over in that parking lot up ahead."

Frank looked over at Eric sideways then wheeled into the parking lot in a cloud of dust. Both young men jumped out, slamming the car doors behind them. Before Frank could utter another word, Eric knocked him flat on his ass on the pavement.

"What the hell did you do that for?"

"Ever since your dad got in the newspapers you've been so full of shit none of the Horsemen can stand your ass. Your dad is famous. Great! But you ain't done shit to go strutting around like a damned peacock. You're still a Horseman, just like the rest of us. So get over it! Or the Four Horsemen are washed up, done, finished. Even Shorty Dog said it, your buddy."

"Shorty does drugs."

"Maybe so, but he's got your number."

Frank McCoy got back in his Mustang and peeled off, burning rubber. He had always been the leader of the Four Horsemen. He was so angry he felt sick to his stomach. How dare Eric talk to him that way, and knock him down! Even Shorty Dog was against him. He tasted blood in his mouth.

Back at the house he pulled around in the backyard to wash his automobile. Frank needed time to think. He loved his beautiful convertible. His father had bought it for him the year before. He pulled out the hose and started soaping when he noticed a small nick on the right rear fender. That could be fixed with his mother's nail polish.

Upstairs in his parent's bedroom he was rummaging through his mother's vanity searching for a proper shade of red when he noticed the carpet had come loose in the corner behind her mahogany desk. Frank got down on his hands and knees to see what the trouble was. The floor wiggled. He pulled the carpet back to see what was causing it. There was a cut in the subfloor made by a skil saw. It needed repair so he went out to the garage for some eight-penny nails and a hammer.

Back upstairs he inspected the loose plywood again. It had been taken up and put back down wrong. He pulled it loose to place it back the right way. A long metal box was resting between the 2 x 10 floor joists.

Frank pulled the box out and opened it. Inside he found packets of $100 bills, fifty bills to a bundle. He stacked them out neatly on the bedroom floor. He counted thirty-three packets, $165,000. Frank placed them back in the metal box the same way he found them, secured the plywood back in place so it fit correctly, tucked the carpet down neatly, and left the house. He got in his car and drove for the beach.

His beloved father whom he idolized as his hero was a crooked cop. Two emotional shocks in one afternoon had thrown Frankie off balance. He didn't see the red light at the intersection. He didn't see the white Cadillac, either.

A four-door Eldorado T-boned the red Mustang, knocking it

seventy-nine feet across the intersection onto the sidewalk. A million stars exploded in Frankie's head on impact. His life flashed before his eyes like the lighted windows of a passenger train racing through the night. The last thing he remembered was his father's concerned face staring down at him at the football game.

Chapter Eight

To Every Thing There Is a Season

The death of Frank McCoy was a shock to the Hallandale Community. His father and Detective Franklin had just received their third commendations for bravery. Frank's mother was a well-known and respected member of the Catholic Church. Hallandale High School revered young Franklin as their football hero. He was team captain and a good student. Frankie was Mister and Missus McCoy's only child. Some remembered him as a showoff and a troublemaker. Nevertheless he possessed the potential for a bright future someday. Numerous young men of the 1950s and '60s were rebels without a cause. James Dean had been Franklin's matinee idol.

The three survivors of the Four Horsemen felt both shame and guilt over their rejection of Frank McCoy as their leader just hours before his death in a mangled automobile accident. Shorty Dog idolized young Franklin. Shorty and his girlfriend had gotten themselves involved with a Mexican drug smuggling ring. Frank's accident sent Shorty Dog into a tailspin. Tampico heroin became their drug of choice.

The woman who smashed into Franklin, a snowbird from New York City, thought little about the man in the red Mustang. She was more concerned over the damage to her white Cadillac. The Sha Doobie Tribe was of a different mindset.

Mary Leibowitz called a tribal meeting the day after the news broke.

"We had our differences with Badass, but that's all behind us now. From now on I suggest we refer to Frank McCoy as Franklin or Frankie or just plain McCoy. He was a young person just like the rest of us. We all make mistakes. That's part of life. Franklin made his share, but I suggest from now on we refer to him in a friendly and respectful manner. That's the Sha Doobie way."

"Good point, Mary!"

"I agree."

"Shouldn't we do something nice like send flowers or a sympathy card or something?"

"Good idea, Shannon. Luna Treasurer, how much money do we have in the kitty?"

Calico dug in her purse to find her notebook. Then she dropped it on the floor. Moose picked it up, handing it to Calico with a silly grin on his face. Everyone laughed and joshed the little lady with the long blonde hair and sparkling green eyes. Calico was overly conscious about her bosoms. Her breasts were referred to by the young men at school as "The Twins." Calico was a popular majorette.

"Y'all just stop it now! Let me see … okay, here it is … uh … sixteen dollars and forty-four cents."

"Any suggestions how much we should spend?"

Little Willie John raised his hand. "I never liked Frank McCoy, but this is different. The way I see it he's gone on to that big football stadium in the sky. I vote we spend whatever it takes, and get him something nice."

Fred spoke up. "My dad's company does business with a flower shop downtown. I'll ask Daddy if he can get us a discount."

"Find out by tomorrow afternoon. The family's receiving guests this Friday."

"I'll ask him as soon as he gets home tonight."

The meeting adjourned, and they all loaded up in three automobiles for the beach. It was a beautiful spring day. A crisp breeze was blowing in off the Atlantic causing the waves to crest at four feet. Tourists lay about sunbathing on the golden sand. The Sha Doobie Tribe found their favorite spot on a dune overlooking the ocean. Moose set down the heavy picnic basket and the girls spread out the blankets.

"Wonder if he saw it comin'?"

"I hope he never knew what hit him."

"He wasn't that bad, was he?"

"He had some issues. I guess having a father like that is a hard thing to live up to."

"I guess so. His old man's a tough cookie, all right."

"I'd be proud if he was my father."

"You don't know. He might be like Biggie Rat or Itchy Brother."

Little Willie John admired Detective McCoy. "He don't look like no rat to me."

"He's a tough one, all right. That's the third or fourth gunfight him and Snake Eyes been in."

"It's Cottonmouth. He has that birthmark on his face."

"You reckon he's got a tongue like a snake?"

"Yeah! Probably goes around bitin' people."

"Maybe his pecker has rattles on it like a rattlesnake."

"You boys hush up right now!"

"Okay. We was just funnin'."

"Well, cool it. Ladies don't want to hear about men with rattles on their thing."

Calico snickered. Moose cackled. They all laughed.

Mary just shook her head. "What am I going to do with this bunch?"

"They're hopeless, Mary. I'll cut a switch and we'll tan their bottoms good."

"Don't bother, Calico. They'd probably like it."

More laughter!

The procession into the church stretched outside the building and down a concrete sidewalk. Students from Hallandale were present, the Miami Police Department, a reporter with *The Miami Herald*, and several people from Detective McCoy's neighborhood. Four hundred mourners had shown up. Roger and Shannon stood in line waiting to pay their respects.

"At least it's a good turnout."

"Yes, I'm glad we came."

"I am too. It feels funny, though."

"Why do you say that?"

"I guess because of the fight and them pulling your panties off and all."

"Frank was just showing off. They didn't hurt us."

"It's like football, I guess. You get knocked down and just get back up."

"I wish Franklin could get back up."

"I do too, Shannon. I really do."

"Let's not talk about it anymore. I'll start crying."

"Okay. Look at the pretty flowers. Let's try and find ours."

There were standing wreaths, urns with flowers, hanging wreaths, flowers in baskets. The scent from all the colorful bouquets filled the church with a pleasant aroma. It reminded Roger of his grandmother's funeral when he was a little boy. He remembered afterwards they ate fried chicken and potato salad. He was too young then to understand that grandmother wasn't coming home anymore.

It took forty minutes before they got down the aisle toward the front of the church where the family was receiving friends. A tall policeman standing beside Detective McCoy reminded Shannon of Mary Shelley's Frankenstein. He was muscular and raw boned, rough-looking with a terrible scar down his face. His had eyes with the blue intensity of someone who could see inside a person's soul, short-cropped brown hair, and gray sideburns which stuck out on both sides of his bullet-shaped head like the spines on a blowfish. The nose was broken and flat from numerous fistfights when he worked in the white lightning trade up in Georgia. His most prominent feature was his mouth and chin. His skin was dark like an Indian, but the birthmark and his chin gave him the resemblance of a cottonmouth water moccasin.

"That's him, isn't it?"

"God, he's scary looking."

"That's Cottonmouth, isn't it?"

"Yes, that's him."

When they came before Missus McCoy she nodded her head, smiling at Shannon through her tears. Shannon reached out to touch her hand, a big lump in her throat. Then it was Roger's turn. He said how sorry he was, that Franklin had been a friend. Daisy McCoy thanked Roger, wiping away her tears with a little yellow handkerchief.

When they stepped in front of Detective McCoy, he turned and looked at the name tag on a burst of white lilies and little blue forget-me-nots directly behind him. It bore the names of the Sha Doobie Tribe.

"You're that football player that ran over my Frankie."

Roger swallowed hard, fearful of a scene. "Yes, sir."

"You knocked his front tooth out, and scored a touchdown."

"Yes, sir. That was me."

"Franklin told me you were the one that put his tires down that flagpole."

"I won't lie to you, Mister McCoy. I did it."

McCoy's grim expression faded to a reluctant smile. "You know something, son. Frankie admired you for your grit. He told me about the fight. He said you never reported it."

"No, sir. I didn't want to get him in trouble."

"Frankie was always in trouble. That was my fault. His mother warned me not to spoil him."

"I'm sure you did your best, sir."

"I can see why he respected you. You're smart like a diplomat. Meet the other side of that equation. This is my partner, John Franklin."

Cottonmouth had been staring at them the whole conversation. He reached out a hand to Roger. The hand was scarred, some of the knuckles broken. Shannon noticed his thumbnail was black. When Roger took the gnarled fingers in his hand it felt like an alligator had gotten hold of him. The skin was rough and calloused, the fingers leathery. Cottonmouth looked down at Shannon and Roger.

"You're uh sweet girl, an' you're uh nice boy. You need help, you call my partner."

"Thank you, Mister Franklin. We appreciate that."

They moved on before the open casket where Franklin lay at rest wearing a blue summer suit and his favorite pink silk tie. He looked almost natural. There was a slight depression on his forehead which had been filled in and powdered over where the steering column had smashed his skull. The impact had broken his neck. Death was almost instantaneous.

Shannon reached out and touched the back of Franklin's hand. It was cold and hard. She pulled away, shocked by how it felt. A pair of tears rolled down her cheeks. "He feels like stone." she whispered.

"That's how they embalm people."

"Let's get out of here. This is terrible."

Outside, Shannon squeezed Roger's hand. She was trembling. "My parents are gone for the afternoon. Take me home, Roger. Take me home and make love to me."

Back at the house Shannon pulled down the shades on the back porch, and stripped naked. Roger followed her lead. She took him by the hand, pulling him down beside her on the couch. There she did something she had never done before. She prayed, asking God to protect Roger. Then she straddled his hips, taking him inside her warm, moist body, thrusting her pelvis until he cried out in ecstasy. Shannon had tears streaming down her nose and cheeks.

"Honey, what's wrong?"

"I could not stand losing you. I love you too much."

"Shan, baby, I'm not going anywhere. I'm right here, always."

"Don't ever leave me. I would die without you."

"Are you upset because of Franklin? Is that what's wrong?"

"Yes!"

Shannon burst into tears. Roger held her against his chest while she sat naked on his thighs, her knees resting on either side of his hips. He rocked her gently until she cried it all out. After the tears had stopped, Roger scooted her over on her back and lay down beside her on the couch.

"Feel better?"

"Yes, Roger."

"You know how much I love you. I'll never go away."

"What if you get killed?"

"In that case, I'd wait for you in Heaven."

"You silly, you'd fly off with those pretty girl angels."

"You're my angel. I won't fly anyplace without you."

"I read an article in one of the magazines at the beauty parlor last week."

"What did it say?"

"It said some women please their men by doing it doggie style. It said it gives the man 'authority' and makes him feel like 'the captain of his ship.'"

"You're the captain of my ship."

"I'm serious, Roger."

"Is that what you want to do?"

"I want us to do it every way there is. Then start all over again."

"Then I suggest we hoist anchor and get under sail."

"Oh, you masterful sailor, you!"

Before he could say another word, Shannon was off to the bedroom to get a little sailor's hat she wore for Halloween. Back she came, placing it squarely on Roger's head. Shannon got down on the sofa on her knees and elbows.

"Is First Wench ready?"

"Yes, my Captain."

Roger assumed his position of authority.

"Ohhhh, Captain!"

Roger used both hands to steady the shapely vessel. First Wench was ready and waiting. Their love for one another made it all the more romantic. Roger began their rhythmic voyage with Shannon holding tight to the armrest on the sofa.

Shannon regaled Roger with a poem they memorized in the eighth grade. "'O Captain! my Captain! our fearful trip is done.'"

He responded merrily. "'The ship has weather'd every rack, the prize we sought is won.'"

She giggled. "'The port is near, the bells I hear, the people all exulting.'"

Roger concluded the famous stanza. "'While follow eyes the steady keel, the vessel grim and daring.'"

Shannon loved to improvise. "O Captain! my Captain! a storm inside, I feel to be a brewing."

Roger thought for several moments. "'Tis … the goal we sought … First Wench of love … a treasure worth renewing."

Shannon sailed on. "Hurry, my Captain! Oh hurry, please! … I long to be with you."

Roger held fast to his tumultuous craft. "Light the cannons of love, … O Heart … for now … our voyage is through."

They climaxed together as one glorious seafaring mariner, Captain Overstreet and Wench Parker collapsing facedown on their imaginary pallet of seaweed and flamingo feathers. Walt Whitman would have been speechless.

"Besides our first time" … catching her breath … "I think that was the best ever!"

"It certainly was" … he kissed her sweetly … "You sure have gotten to be a spunky wench lately."

"I'm your spunky wench" … she kissed her Captain … "Any time you want me."

"We'll be eighteen next year. Want to get married then?"

"Yes, honey, if our parents will let us."

"We could room together in college and everything."

"If 'everything' means doing it every day, I'm all for that."

"Do you know what you're going to study?"

"No, do you?"

"I'm going to study Shannon Parker."

Shannon reached over and tickled Roger. He was ticklish, squirming about on the couch, laughing. She got on top of him, tickling his ribs and stomach. Roger begged for mercy. Shannon leaned over Roger, her sensuous nipples brushing his face and lips. Roger felt himself getting excited. Shannon felt it too.

"Don't you ever feed that thing? It's hungry again."

"I love you, Shannon Parker."

Shannon took Roger's penis in her hand then slid under him wrapping her legs around his waist.

"Do it to me real slow this time, honey."

The loving was grand and delicious, a youthful exuberance of love, sex, and emotional embrace. Afterwards they fell asleep, fulfilled, in each other's arms. Shannon awoke when her parents pulled up the driveway. A comedy ensued, rushing around getting dressed. The Parkers came bustling in loaded down with groceries. Roger was invited for dinner. Missus Parker got busy with the tossed salad and baked potatoes while her husband went out back to grill the steaks.

It had been a marvelous evening for Shannon and Roger, and a totally miserable experience for William and Daisy McCoy. Cottonmouth returned home that afternoon to his Cajun princess with a fifth of bourbon whiskey under one arm. Frankie McCoy had been like a son to John Franklin.

Chapter Nine

Captain E'Manuel

Rendezvous

Swells were running at eight feet with a brisk wind blowing from the southwest. Boogie had cut their speed to fifteen knots so as not to plow into one of the waves and swamp the boat. The craft would sluice through a valley, climb a mountain of water then sled down the other side into another trough between the rolling seas.

Sunup found them refueling in the port city of Trujillo, Honduras. They ate breakfast on the pier, tacos with scrambled eggs and green fried tomatoes. Back out on the Spanish Main the ocean was deep blue, almost purple where they passed along the Mosquito Coast.

That evening the sun cast a magnificent array of colors where it sank into the Caribbean. A waterspout appeared briefly on the horizon where the moon rose up into a star-spangled night. Phosphorus sparkled in the wake of the boat. Flying fish leapt and soared, cavorting amongst a trio of porpoise shepherding the *Sea Queen* on her journey south.

"This wind will die down soon. Then we'll get back up to speed," Wayne said.

"How big do these waves get in a real storm?"

"Thirty, sometimes forty feet."

"Good God! How would we manage that?"

"Just keep your nose to the wind and maneuver up one side then down the other. We'd head for shore. A boat this size might not last long in seas that rough."

"I bet a lot of boats are on the bottom out here in the shipping lanes."

"Davy Jones put in some overtime, that's for sure. Centuries ago pirates sailed these waters. They raided the Spanish treasure fleets. Then the Spaniards would chase after the pirates. Later on the French and the British got in the act. There was always a war going on in Europe or a plague or something so people came to the Americas to get away from all the taxes and bullshit."

"How much longer, you reckon?" Dutch asked

"Day and a half, two maybe."

"I'd like to see some more whales. That was something."

"Whales are marvelous animals. Smarter than some people I know. They keep their young inside the pods. That's so the predators can't get at them. Some do of course, but it's not like letting your kids run loose in the streets."

"Elephants are like that. We saw herds of them in Vietnam."

"Elephants and bears, all kinds of critters care for their young better than some parents."

"It wasn't like that in Vietnam. As poor as they were the mama-sans looked after their kids. But God were they poor. Whole families lived on a few dollars a month. Everybody worked. The government was crooked as hell. I felt sorry for those people."

"The world is a fucking mad house. China, North Korea, Russia, all run by assholes."

"I wonder what Panama will be like?"

"Assholes! But Sarah says we're in like Flynn so we'll roll with the punches. Someday we'll look back on this from our penthouses in Daytona or Jacksonville and say … 'Assholes!'"

"That's what I like about you, Wayne … a man of few words."

"That lady Sarah has you fixed up with is supposed to be a real looker. Think you can handle that?"

"We'll see. I ain't had a date in a coon's age."

"Well, just be your deboner, gormat self. She's from an old Atlanta family that has money."

"Money is good. I'll try not to wave my Johnson around in public."

"That would be a novel introduction. I wonder how the Panamanians would take it."

The whales appeared a little before ten o'clock. Dutch heard them singing while Wayne was down below preparing supper. Dutch slowed the boat to five knots, motoring alongside the creatures for a better look. It was a pod of humpbacks, twenty or more traveling north with the current. The sea had calmed to a flat silver surface. Wayne came up from the galley with shrimp cocktails and a thermos of hot coffee.

"They sound different," Dutch observed.

"Those are humpbacks. See how their backs are humplike with a dorsal fin set back toward the tail?"

"They sound like cows."

"They do a little, don't they?"

"They're not as big as those other whales."

"You mean sperm whales. Humps are ten to twenty tons lighter. The blues were hunted almost to extinction. They're the monsters of the deep, a hundred tons or better. I saw a blue whale just once about five years ago."

"You know a lot about the ocean, don't you?"

"I was going to be an oceanographer before dad gave me the marina. My studies helped a lot with running the place. Bubba-J was a big help too. He taught me the lore of the seven seas, pirate tales, sea battles, ocean currents. There's tons of gold and silver off the Florida coast and out in the Gulf. You just have to go out there and find it."

"Didn't Blackbeard sail in these waters?

"Blackbeard operated off the Southern Colonies, and around the West Indies, Cuba, the Bahamas, and Andros Island. He lasted about two years as a buccaneer. Edward Teach had a fearsome reputation, but he was a gentleman pirate. There's no record of him ever killing a hostage.

"Blackbeard would lay in wait for merchant ships in the Florida Straits. He sacked Charleston in 1718. That same year the British Navy cornered him in an inlet on the coast of North Carolina. That was the end of our Captain Teach.

"Henry Morgan was my favorite. Now there was a real swashbuck-ling son of a bitch!"

"You mean that Captain Morgan on rum bottles?"

"That's the one. He was British like my father. Errol Flynn played Henry Morgan in his 1935 classic, *Captain Blood*. Morgan pillaged the Spanish colonies and sank their shipping. I believe it was 1674 when he was awarded the governorship of Jamaica by the British Crown.

"He sacked Panama City in 1670 with a fleet of thirty-six ships, and burned it to the ground. That led to the eventual downfall of the Spanish monopoly over the Caribbean. He was a brilliant tactician like Lord Nelson, and ruthless to the bone. Morgan and his buccaneers plundered the Spanish Main for eleven bloody years."

Boogie radioed ahead to let Sarah know they were three hours north of Kusapin on the Valienta Peninsula. Sarah instructed them to proceed down the coast to Old Bess Point, where a patrol boat would be waiting two miles offshore. Rendezvous went well. The Panamanian captain led the *Sea Queen* to a small shore installation just south of Old Bess. The facility consisted of two large corrugated metal warehouses, an assortment of military trucks and Jeeps, plus a brand new Caterpillar crane. A long, dilapidated wharf led inland along the banks of a waterway once used by commercial fisherman. Wayne spotted Sarah standing on the end of the pier, waving to them.

"Ahoy there, *gringo* devils!"

"Sarah, you sweet thang, you!"

"Come get me, Bilge Rat"

Wayne nudged the *Sea Queen* up against the docking bumpers, and Sarah hopped onboard.

"You must be Dutch Henry." Sarah touched his cheek, taking hold of his hand.

"You must be Sarah Ferguson."

"I like him, Boogie. He's a keeper."

"That's cool. Where's Trudy?

"Flying. She'll be in tonight."

Sarah flung her arms around Boogie's neck and kissed him. He kissed her back, allowing the boat to drift alongside the creosote pilings.

"I missed you, Stud Muffin."

"You probably flirted with every man between here and New York City."

"Of course I did. That's what they pay me for."

Dutch Henry could see why Boogie was enchanted with his fly girl. Sarah was intelligent, amusingly sarcastic, and bubbling over with personality. She was a dead ringer for Jennifer Jones, but about two inches taller, light brown hair, brown eyes, great legs, and a pair of lungs that caused TWA pilots to perform double takes.

"Where can I park this tub?"

"Up ahead. You'll be safe there from the breakers."

A Jeep sat waiting on a concrete apron above the wharf while Dutch and Wayne secured the *Sea Queen*. A gravel road leading to a grassy airfield took only a few minutes. They disembarked in the parking lot of an aging Quonset hut. It was the only other building besides the two warehouses within a thirteen mile radius. Four friendly soldiers came out to greet them. Sarah spoke to them in Spanish. They began laughing. The soldiers loaded their gear onboard a Cessna AT-17, dubbed "The Bamboo Bomber" by American airmen who used the craft for training purposes during the Second World War. The pilot powered up, and they were airborne.

"What was that all about?"

"I told them you were sweethearts."

"Good grief, Sarah! You'll get us kicked out of the country."

"They knew you were coming. That's our protection."

"Oh!" Boogie and Dutch looked at one another. "Is something wrong?"

"The airfield isn't on the map. The soldiers keep the bandits away."

They flew in over the mountains, landing at the city of David situated on the David River a few miles inland from the Pacific Ocean. Taxiing down the runway they could see the bell tower of San Jose rising above the town. Sarah ushered them through the military section of the terminal, and once again the armed soldiers nodded and waved to her. A black Mercedes was waiting outside.

"The hotel I've chosen is a nice one. Lots of Army personnel stay there. You can leave your money in the hotel safe. The front desk is secure, but you never know about the chambermaids. Captain E'Manuel is our host. Tony is one of Colonel Torrijos' fair-haired boys. Tony's the gentleman my girlfriend Amanda dates."

"When does Trudy get in?

She's with another flight crew this month. She'll be here around seven. In the meantime I suggest we freshen up a bit. Boogie and I have our own room. You and Trudy have rooms beside each other. We're on the fifth floor overlooking the David River."

Dutch Henry sat down on a luxurious chair inside his suite overlooking a beautiful river scene. Sarah amazed him. Sarah Ferguson was the most efficient women he'd ever met. His apprehensions about any difficulties in Panama had evaporated onboard the aircraft. He liked Sarah and trusted her. The long sea voyage had taken its toll. Sleep came easily.

A knock on the door awakened Dutch. He rubbed the sleep from his eyes and got up to answer it.

"Dutch?"

Standing before him wearing a black evening gown was a gorgeous blonde, six inches shorter than himself, blue eyes, hourglass figure, in high heels and carrying a Gucci handbag.

"Trudy?"

"I've awakened you. I'm sorry. I can come back later."

"No, wait … please … come in. May I offer you a drink?"

"Yes, I would like that. Vodka rocks with a slice of lemon, please."

Dutch busied himself at the well-stocked bar.

"I'm afraid I fell asleep when I should have been getting ready. I can shower and be dressed in a few minutes. Are the others ready yet?"

"I just looked in on them. Wayne and Sarah were busy dressing. Your trip must have been tiring."

Dutch Henry took a quick shower, brushed his teeth, splashed on aftershave, combed his hair, put on his suit, and rejoined Trudy before her cocktail glass was empty.

"So tell me, Dutch. What possessed you to get involved in the smuggling business?"

"You know about that, do you?"

"Sarah and I are confidantes. She told me all about you, your service in the military, your schooling, that boat you and Wayne fixed up. You're an impressive young man, Mister Henry."

"I'm at a disadvantage, Trudy. I know nothing about you."

"Don't be. I'm a little old country girl from Georgia whose grandfather made a fortune in the stock market. We're what Atlanta society calls, 'The Magnolia Peters.' I've always found that a bit distasteful, referring to one's social status like it has a price tag on it. Most of them inherited theirs, anyway."

Dutch laughed. "And down to earth, to boot!"

Trudy smiled. "I am, aren't I?"

"You're a breath of fresh air. Too many people take themselves too seriously."

"I'll let you in on a little secret about flying. You see lots of good stuff out there, but you see the other side too which breaks your heart sometimes. Americans have no idea how lucky they are."

"I saw that in Vietnam. They're as poor over there as these people down here."

"Tell you what, Dutch. Amanda, Sarah, and I built a little infirmary south of the Canal Zone near San Miguel. When this is all over, chip in a few dollars with us. We plan on building another one up here in the mountains as soon as we get enough money together. You'd be surprised what $10,000 can buy in one of these Third World countries."

Dutch Henry sat quietly contemplating the blonde beauty from Georgia. Trudy watched him, saying nothing. A feeling of warmth crept over Dutch Henry. He felt excited, happy, and oddly vulnerable. She reminded him of women he'd always admired, but never expected to socialize with. Her magnetism was drawing him into deep uncharted waters.

"Makes you think, doesn't it?"

"Actually I was wondering why you aren't married. Any man would be proud to call you his wife."

"You interested?"

Her direct question startled him. He hesitated, eyeing her, then took hold of his pride with both hands. "Yes, Trudy. I am."

"Excellent!"

"A woman like you? Surely there was someone in the past."

"There was. He died five years ago."

"Why me?"

"Sarah has psychic abilities. Some call it 'second sight.' Her mother had it. Her grandmother was written up in one of the Boston medical journals. Whatever it is, Amanda and I confide in her about everything. She touched you, didn't she?"

"I think so. Yes, when she got on the boat."

"She told me you were one of a kind. I didn't want to get my hopes up until you opened the door, and I saw you standing there with your hair down in your eyes and your shirttail hanging out."

"Not one of my better impressions."

"Good impression. Sarah was right. You're a keeper, Mister Henry."

"I can't believe this is happening. I'm about to make a fortune, and up pops a woman I'd fight for in the parking lot with bare knuckles and tire tools. I like you too, Miss Magnolia."

"A wise old bomber pilot told me something when I first started flying. He said relationships and marriages are hard things to manage. But he said there is a special way that works."

"What's that?"

"He said, 'Hold on loosely but don't let go.' It gives a couple their space. At the same time it keeps the flame alive between them."

"You just made the sale, lady. I'll give you $10,000 from my share. I know Wayne will. He's in love with your witch friend."

Trudy giggled. "I'll tell Sarah what you said. She'll put the bad juju on you and turn you into something for us girls to play with. A kitty or a puppy, maybe."

"Remember *Casablanca*?"

"Yes. I cried at the end."

"This could be the beginning of a beautiful friendship, Trudy."

Dinner was scrumptious, Sancocho soup, empanadas, savory slaw, and seasoned prime rib of beef, medium rare. For dessert, *pastel tres leches*. Beverages were white wine sangria and ice coffee. After dinner cocktails were cognac with orange peel and slices.

"To a successful business venture!"

"Hear! Hear!"

Trudy raised her snifter, smiling at Dutch. "To my new companion, Dutch Henry."

Tony E'Manuel rose from his chair at the head of the table, addressing the two couples in the private dining chamber with him and Amanda. Captain E'Manuel was a handsome man, tall and slender, dark complected, 31 years of age, with black curly hair and pale green eyes which seldom left Amanda's smiling face. His ancestry was Spanish and Portuguese. The uniform he wore was handcrafted by a master tailor in Panama City. He'd graduated third in his class from Harvard University.

"Welcome to our new colleagues, Dutch Henry and Wayne Compton. What you have undertaken is very rewarding, but there are risks involved. One obvious risk is the authorities. Getting caught can mean going to jail. We have some control over that through our connections with the various judges and politicians in America. Don't be too surprised. They like money just as we do. At any rate, if we can't get someone set free we can usually minimize their prison sentence.

"A more serious risk is pirates. These are ruthless men and women, criminals who intercept boats, stealing money and any cargo onboard. Some murder their victims. That is why you must never allow yourselves to be stopped on the high seas. To protect yourselves I suggest allowing my men to arm your *Sea Queen*. You have gun emplacements we can arm with .50 caliber weapons. Those can easily be disassembled before entering port.

"A third factor is the weather. Always check the weather reports. If a storm is brewing stay in port or head for shore. The winds and the seas can become extreme here in the Southern Equatorial Zone. Trudy and Sarah would be quite unhappy if their men ended up sleeping with our aquatic life forms.

"If you have a breakdown at sea I have a number for you to call. One of our patrol boats will come as quickly as possible. If you encounter sea pirates and need help, radio this number and fighter aircraft will be dispatched to deal with the situation. A spool of white tape will be placed onboard your boat. Make a white cross on top of your cabin so the pilots can identify you.

"I think that covers everything. There are many people in this business, but only a few enjoy our protection. Sarah Ferguson and her TWA angels have done a great service for my country. This is my small way and that of my colleagues of saying, Thank You.

"Do you want those machine guns installed?"

Dutch answered the handsome captain. "Wayne and I appreciate your advice. I assume they'll reinforce the decking inside the gun tubs?"

"A metal plate goes down which the gun mounts attach to. Your field of fire is 180 degrees."

"That's cool."

"It's been a pleasure doing business with you, Captain. Dutch and I will be back as soon as I get my buyers organized."

They were strolling in the moonlight, laughing, talking, and holding hands. It was a balmy evening with the moon overhead and the stars twinkling in a velvet night sky. All around, the trees and bushes reflected the moon's silver radiance. It was as though a tropical paradise had been arranged just for them. Sarah was right. Trudy found herself wishing the night would never end. She couldn't recall ever feeling that way before, about anyone. What was it about Dutch Henry that made her feel safe, and giddy, all at the same time?

He was an exceptional individual, tall and attractive, but in a masculine way she wasn't familiar with. For one thing he had an Alpha personality with the soul of a Beta, compounded by a sharp intellect. That confused her. Hard men aren't tender, are they? At any rate, this one was holding her hand and telling her things she wanted to hear, all of which she found intoxicating.

She felt the sum of her universe balanced that moment in time and space at the apex of her cosmic identity. It stole her breath away, making her fearful and adventurous all at the same moment. She felt drawn to Dutch, emotionally, physically, and intellectually. It was exhilarating, something she had dreamed about all her life.

Was it the alcohol, the lonely nights, her yearning for love? Maybe it was the salt breeze in her hair, the serenade of the night creatures, those sappy love novels she read during layovers? Or was it the nearness of someone intriguing and tender, a man she knew she could adore. It was all of those things, and so much more. Trudy Peters was losing her heart to a man she had known less than twenty-four hours.

"I'm worried, Dutch."

"What about, Trudy?"

"I feel like I've known you all my life. I don't want it to end."

"I plan on sticking around."

"I would be very unhappy if something happened to you."

"That makes two of us."

She laughed.

He took her in his arms and kissed her, holding her close and tenderly. She snuggled against him, eyes closed, breathing his masculine scent. Dutch recalled a novel he once read about a British soldier standing on the white cliffs of Dover gazing out across the English Channel. A storm was raging, the seas crashing against the rocks below. On the other side of the Channel lay the Nazi juggernaut, a terrible war, and man's destiny.

Looking into the blue eyes of Trudy Peters, Dutch imagined his own destiny smiling back at him in the silvery moonlight.

Standing before the door to her hotel suite, Trudy asked Dutch a question. "You do understand, don't you?"

"Of course I understand. First dates are very important for ladies."

"You won't be sorry."

"I know."

"You know a lot of things, don't you, Mister Henry."

"I know you're the best thing that ever crossed my welcome mat."

"We're moving pretty fast, aren't we?"

"I'll go whatever speed you like, Miss Magnolia."

"You already know that one … Hold on loosely, but don't let go."

"I'm missing you already."

"I'll fly up to Daytona if I get a decent layover."

"Boogie and I will be there two maybe three weeks. He has to get his buyers organized."

"Do be careful out there on the ocean. I'll worry about you guys."

"Worry about getting that next hospital built, not about me and the Boogie Man."

"You sweet thing, get your butt to bed. I'll come wake you for breakfast."

They kissed goodnight.

Dutch lay awake unable to sleep, thinking about dinner, his and Trudy's walk in the moonlight, and the journey that lay ahead tomorrow morning. Trudy was unbelievable: brains and beauty plus she was funny. And the lady was sexy as hell. Her passion for helping the poor was amazing. He envisioned her beside him in bed, naked, making love.

As soon as she knocked, Dutch opened the door. He was dressed and ready for his lady in waiting. Downstairs they joined Sarah and Wayne. The sun was up and the birds were singing. Unable to sleep half the night thinking about each other, Trudy and Dutch were both sleepy. Coffee and orange juice was served. Two cups later Dutch and Trudy were holding hands.

Sarah was animated, enjoying her breakfast. The others could tell by her gay demeanor. She was happy to be back with her man again. The problem started when Wayne met Sarah on a flight to Atlanta. He'd already made plans to stop seeing Jane before he encountered Sarah. Janie got wind of his intentions, and his interest in Sarah Ferguson. So Janie told him she was pregnant. Wayne married Jane to give the baby a name. Later on, she faked a miscarriage. Boogie found out, and filed for divorce. Jane got the house and a small financial settlement. Wayne kept his boat marina.

"The Boog and I been talking, Trudy Girl. How would you like for us ladies to accompany the boys up to their first layover? It takes about two days. We can get off there and fly back to work."

"Oh, Sarah! I'd love to!"

Dutch pushed back from the table, grinning at Trudy. "Great! When do we leave?"

"Tony called this morning. We'll be loaded by noon."

They caught the Bamboo Bomber back to the airfield, motoring down the gravel road to their weather-beaten pier. The *Sea Queen* was riding two feet lower in the water. Her aft deck was piled with tarpaulins, secured by ropes and cables holding down four and a half tons of compressed Panama Red. In the hold they found hundreds more of the bundles, stacked floor to ceiling.

"My word! That's what I call a load!"

"You boys are gonna have soooo much money."

"All of us are going to share in this, you ladies and us Florida rednecks."

Sarah asked, "Are you saying I'm in love with a redneck?

"Damn right! Y'all both are!" Wayne replied.

Trudy laughed merrily, squeezing Dutch's hand. "Oh golly, Sarah. I guess I am."

Sarah squealed happily, throwing her arms around Dutch and Trudy.

"Cast off, Dutch … let's show these womenfolk the Caribbean."

Chapter Ten

For God and Country

The letter was lying on the coffee table in the living room when John Parker arrived home from his law practice over in Hallandale. Katherine had wanted to open the letter, concerned about what might be inside, but she waited, respecting her husband's privacy. The brown manila envelope bearing his name and address was from the Department of Defense in Washington, DC.

John left it lying on the table.

"I know what it says. We were told last weekend at the Reserve Center. I didn't tell you because I wanted to spare you as long as I could. Our unit has been activated. We're being deployed to Vietnam. Steve is going with me. All the Reservists are going. We're scheduled to fly out the first of the month."

Katherine sat down on the couch, dumbfounded. Her worst fears had come to pass. The man she loved, her husband, her life, the father of her daughter was going away to war. She felt sick to her stomach.

Finally the tears came. John held her in his arms until she stopped crying.

"You're my husband and I love you. But I'm very angry with you. You're leaving me! What about Shannon? What about me? What if something happens to you? I don't want to be alone again. I love you, John. I had my fill of loneliness in that orphanage."

"I understand, sweetheart. I don't want to leave you. There was no Vietnam when Roger and I joined the Reserves. We signed the papers and took the pledge. It was fun. Now the Army tells us they need us."

"Damn the Army! I need you. Shannon needs you."

"Kat, I wish we could turn back the clock, but I have no choice. Steve and I are bound by law. Please try and understand. I'm not leaving you. You and Shannon are my life, my every reason for living. I'm just going away for a little while."

Katherine burst into tears again, clutching John in her arms. "Oh, God!" she wept. "Please, please protect my baby."

They sat on the couch talking, crying, holding hands, reminiscing about the good times they shared over the years. The front door opened and Shannon walked in from school. When told about Mister Parker's leaving for Vietnam, Shannon rushed into her father's arms, burying her face in his chest.

"I don't want my daddy going away." she said, weeping.

The doorbell rang. Katherine got up to answer the front door. It was Joyce and Steve with Roger. Her eyes were swollen and red from crying. Joyce was still shaky so Steve led her over to the couch and they sat down together. Roger stood off to one side in front of the fireplace, fidgeting with the buttons on his shirt, not knowing what to do with himself.

Mister Parker spoke. "Roger, come sit with Shannon. I think it's time we all had a drink. I'll do the honors."

Katherine Parker placed her arm around Roger Overstreet's shoulders. For the first time in his life the boy was afraid. He loved his father and was frightened for him. He didn't understand, but a great chasm of dread and uncertainty had opened up before him and his mother.

Joyce laid her head on her husband's shoulder, tears streaking her mascara, clutching Steve's arm with both hands. Shannon took Roger's hand in hers, smiling through the tears for her young sweetheart. The group sat quietly, waiting for Mister Parker to return from the kitchen.

John came out balancing six cocktail glasses on a Coca Cola tray.

"We have eleven more days before we leave. That gives Steve and me time to get our affairs in order. In the meantime, let's do things together. We can go to the beach, cook dinner together. Take in a movie. Maybe go dancing. Let's celebrate like a family. Steve and I will be gone for twelve months. That's not the end of the world. Let's be happy, and share what we have as neighbors."

Mister Overstreet spoke. "Twelve months is a long time without a kiss."

Joyce poked Steve in the ribs with her elbow, smiling for the first time. "It is for me too, you silly thing."

Shannon spoke up. "Roger and I will be eighteen next year. We want to get married then."

Katherine thought for a moment before addressing the adults. "These two were made for each other, but I'm not sure about eighteen. What do you think, Joyce?"

"Steve was twenty-two when we got married. I was twenty. I'm not sure either, Kat."

Steve voiced his concern. "They have their college to think about. What do you think, John?"

"I suggest the two of you wait until Steve and I get back from overseas. If you can schedule your classes and find a reasonable place to live, I see no reason why we can't have a big wedding right here at the house. We'll invite your old Sha Doobie gang, and the whole neighborhood."

Shannon jumped up and hugged her father. "Oh, Daddy, I love you so much."

Roger spoke up with a big smile on his face. "Don't I get a say-so here?"

Shannon turned, answering Roger with an impish grin. "No! You be quiet!"

Everybody laughed.

The days and nights passed quickly. The wives prepared the men's favorite meals, pampering their husbands in loving ways, surprising them with little gifts. They made love every night. It was a second honeymoon for the Parkers and the Overstreets. Shannon and Roger never left their side, asking what they could do to be of help.

At night after their parents had gone to bed, Shannon and Roger would slip off to their screened porch on the back of the Parker home. They awoke just before sunrise, hurrying back to their own bedrooms. Both families were aware of the children's charade. It didn't matter. The kids loved each other and would be married someday.

Everyone cried at the airport. The Army was everywhere, wearing their brown uniforms. The press was there too, the city mayor, a congressman from Tallahassee, plus a number of bosses who came out to see their employees off. A great mystery beckoned from the East as though some phantom lurked among the clouds just beyond the horizon. Would they see action? Might some of them get hurt? Questions and rumors swirled through the crowd like confetti.

A television reporter caught sight of a pretty young redhead, asking her what she thought about the men going off to war.

"I don't know anything about that. I just know my daddy's leaving and I love him." Tears pooled in her eyes.

Roger pulled Shannon away from the reporter. "Come on. They're getting ahead of us."

They huddled together before the entrance to a secured passageway leading into the aircraft, embracing one another, kissing, whispering tender secrets, saying their goodbyes. Final call sounded over a loudspeaker.

"I love you, darling. Please take care."

"I love you too, sweetheart."

And they were gone.

The wives and children stood before a crazy quilt of glass windows watching as the airplane flew away into a blue Florida sky until it was just a speck, then winked out of sight. A terrible loneliness descended upon the room. Then the sadness took hold.

Driving home, Joyce summed up her opinion of the operation. "This has been the worst day of my life."

Roger slid his arms around his mother as much to comfort himself as to comfort Joyce. The fear came again, a cold malignant force sweeping him along a dark underground passageway where one's imagination runs wild, where monsters trod basalt corridors, and no songbirds sing.

Chapter Eleven

Master Sergeant Cody

Delta Dawn

Gunnery Sergeant William Cody, "Wild Bill" to his men, was standing in the middle of the aisle addressing his soldiers. Wild Bill had seen action in the Pacific, and again in Korea. He was decorated with two purple hearts and a Silver Star. More important, the men respected him.

"We ain't goin' to Japan an' we ain't goin' to Korea, so listen up an' listen up good. We're headed for Da Nang up near the Demilitarized Zone. Our job will be patrollin' the DMZ. You weren't told before 'cause the enemy's got big ears. So's our dumbass press."

A stir went through the aircraft. They had just flown out of San Diego and were a hundred miles out over the Pacific Ocean. Two of the men cursed. Somebody laughed nervously, whether from relief over knowing their final destination or just being scared shitless. Da Nang was a hot zone, and everybody knew it.

"Don't get het up on me, now. You've had your trainin', damn good trainin'. You're all good men an' a force to be reckoned with. We're United States Army, an' we kick ass!"

"Right on, Gunny!"

"You tell 'em, Wild Bill!"

They flew southwest the rest of the afternoon, landing at Midway for refueling. The men were allowed to get out and stretch their legs. An hour later they were flying through a thunderstorm. The men slept fitfully, not accustomed to airplane seats for beds, the drone of the engines ever reminding them of their rendezvous with destiny. Breakfast was served by four Delta stewardesses pushing metal carts up and down the aisles. Gunny lit the smoking lamp. Then the scuttlebutt started again.

Lieutenant Overstreet turned to Gunny Cody, presenting him with a hypothetical situation. "Gunny, if we get in a firefight and I freeze up, will you kick my ass, please?"

"The first few minutes are the worst, Steve. It scares the shit outta ever body. It does me too so don't feel like the Lone Ranger. You and Lieutenant Parker know the basics. I've taught you ever thing I know 'cept the shootin' part. Vietnam won't be like Bougainville or Iwo Jima. They ain't no front lines. Keep your eyes open and your heads down. I'll be with you ever step uh the way."

"You think they'll be firefights?"

"I spec so. DMZ is Charlie Country."

Lieutenant Parker spoke up. "Gunny, you have permission to kick my butt up between my shoulder blades if I panic. Punch me, slap me, but don't let the men see me afraid."

"Hell, lieutenant, you'll have your hands full looking after the men. You won't have time to get scared. When the bullets start poppin' an' crackin' they's always a few that needs help. That's where we come in. Don't let 'em bunch up. Keep the men spread out so's a grenade don't get 'em. An' keep 'em busy shootin'. Gives 'em less time to think about the shit they've stepped in."

"Did you ever freeze up, Gunny?"

"About fifty times, but I don't tell nobody about it."

Lieutenant Overstreet and Lieutenant Parker laughed out loud. Gunny Cody just grinned, and winked. There was an ongoing camaraderie between the three men. The master sergeant looked upon his young charges as fine Army personnel. They were mature, professional, and intelligent second lieutenants. He knew he could count on them if they encountered the Elephant.

They passed over the northern tip of Luzon flying out over the South China Sea. Sixty minutes later they were looking down on the tropical jungles of South Vietnam with its rice paddies, and creeks and rivers crisscrossing a beautiful, exotic landscape. Circling above Da Nang they could see the Central Highlands off to the west. Down below were the military runways built by the French during the Colonial Occupation.

After the men offloaded and got their duffle bags out of the cargo hold, they were loaded on three transport trucks and driven through a sprawling military complex. Mile after mile of Quonset huts, tanks, wooden buildings, artillery pieces, trucks, ammunition depots, warehouses. It appeared every conceivable caution had been taken to defeat the unseen enemy.

The drivers delivered them to a two-story barracks on a cul-de-sac where they observed four additional buildings of the same vintage olive drab. Two-thirds of the company had arrived earlier, squared away their gear, and gone to chow. Captain Bloom ordered Gunny Cody to fall the men out, and march them down the street to the mess hall. They could deal with their duffel bags and footlockers when they got back. Captain Bloom asked Lieutenant Parker and Lieutenant Overstreet to remain behind.

"I wanted to give you a head's up so it'll appear we know what the hell we're doing. We'll be here five days. Then we're going out in the field. I want you and Gunny to school the men on what we're dealing with before we go. The military is notorious for sending men into combat situations they know damn little about. I brought eleven pages of notes I copied before we left. This is everything I could find at the newspaper and the library. Thank God for Wild Bill. He's been through all this before. I'm as green as you fellows. Now let's go get ourselves some breakfast!"

Wild Bill was ending his afternoon lecture.

"The Pentagon thinks this is gonna be a cakewalk, be home by Christmas and all that happy horse pucky. They don't know shit from Shinola! Said the same thing about them Jap fliers in World War Two. Zeros shot our guys down like clay pigeons 'til we got better airplanes. Told ever body how great the Sherman tank was. Kraut panzers blew 'em to hell the whole damn war.

"Charlie is not some peckerhead running around in pajamas like you've all heard. He's tough, he's damn smart, and he knows the jungle. He uses mines an' booby traps so watch out for tripwires and metal prongs stickin' outta the ground. You hear something strange, take cover! Me or one uh the lieutenants will be there mucho quicko. You see Charlie up ahead, wait for one of us. If he's already in your face, blow the bastard away.

"Two years ago communist troops damn near wiped out two Army battalions in the Ia Drang Valley just south uh here. Intelligence fucked up. Westmoreland fucked up. The only thing that saved their asses was the Air Force. The Vietcong use hit-and-run tactics so keep your eyes peeled and your ears open on search and destroy operations. Take nothin' for granted. If something can go wrong it usually does. An' stay off the trails! You're liable to step in a punji trap or blow your ass away with a mine.

"If somethin' don't seem kosher, it sure as hell ain't kosher. Tell your sergeant, tell Lieutenant Parker, tell Lieutenant Overstreet, or come tell me. When the shootin' starts we'll get you through it. After a few weeks you'll be old hands at this stuff. It ain't half as bad as it sounds. Just keep your heads down an' use some common sense. In twelve months you'll be home tellin' Sweet Thang how you won the damn war.

"Treat the villagers with respect. The French treated 'em like red-headed stepkids. They had this big-ass battle back in '54 called 'Dien Bien Phu.' The Frogs lost to the Viet Minh communists. They coulda won, but the politicians were too damn chicken-shit to send in a relief column. Then the French politicians did what French politicians do best. They quit and went home with their tails between their legs."

The helicopter ride over the coastline was exhilarating. In one clearing they spotted a herd of elephants. Farther on they flew over a village beside a muddy river inlet. Twenty miles north of Quang Tri the pilots turned west, parallel with the Demilitarized Zone. Tuttle Company was on deployment for fourteen days. First Platoon, Second Platoon, and Third Platoon boasted a roster of one hundred and thirty-five men. The choppers set down in a long grassy meadow. Thick jungle surrounded the landing zone.

"Head for them trees yonder, boys. Don't be lollygaggin' out here in the open."

They assembled on a dimly lit jungle floor beneath a canopy of tualang trees, kapok, ta prohm, and strangler figs. Colorful birds and monkeys chattered nonstop, calling back and forth to one another high above them in the branches. The temperature was ninety degrees, the air fetid and humid. Mosquitoes began arriving to welcome the new dinner guests.

"Toto, I don't think we're in Kansas anymore."

"Damn bugs!"

"Are we having fun yet?"

"Listen up, men." Captain Bloom was addressing his troops. "We're going to be out here two weeks. Drink plenty of water so you don't get dehydrated. Use your mosquito repellant, and take your salt tablets.

We'll be moving west parallel to the North Vietnamese border. Our assignment is to make certain the Vietcong aren't infiltrating down across the Demilitarized Zone. They're more than 400,000 Americans in country now so we have excellent tactical support. The flyboys at Da Nang can be here in fifteen minutes. Stay alert and keep your eyes open.

"Move 'em out, Gunny."

An hour later the column had covered approximately two miles. They were strung out between the tall trees, the undergrowth, and the low hanging vines which reminded Captain Bloom of his studies in college about the Mesozoic period. Blue-bearded bee-eaters, parrots, ruby-cheeked sunbirds, chestnut-eared laughingthrush, and dozens more of the feathery choir serenaded them with gleeful exuberance. Carroll and Hollis got the scare of their lives stepping over a leaf-covered log, when the log suddenly moved. A fourteen-foot python went slithering off into the underbrush. Overhead, curious monkeys monitored their progress, swapping stories back and forth about the strange intruders.

They arrived at a clear stream where Captain Bloom signaled a break.

Gunny spoke to them. "Fill up your canteens an' put them iodine pills in so you don't get the crud. Give 'em a few minutes to dissolve."

The men did as they were told.

"Damn! This stuff tastes like medicine."

"Recommended by snakes and skeeters ever where."

"Hey, what's the crud?"

"That's when you get the jungle rot, and your dick falls off."

"Get outta here!"

"Wonder if they's any dead people around here?"

"Somebody at chow called this place 'The Widow Maker.'"

"Well I ain't married so that makes me copacetic."

"Reed, you're too ugly to get married."

The men were still laughing when Gunny Cody come running back through the trees from the forward column. Lieutenant Overstreet was with him, speaking softly to the men.

"Lock and load ... lock and load ... there's an enemy force up ahead. We're pulling back. The Air Force is on the way. Stay alert and be quiet. That means no talking."

"Follow me!" Gunny led them south, away from the advancing column of Vietcong. He found a low-lying hill he liked, and began forming a skirmish line. "Dig in, boys."

Captain Bloom and Lieutenant Parker remained behind, hidden in a pine thicket observing the enemy movement. PFC Smith, one of the radio operators, was with them.

"Gator Two to Gator One ... Kilroy here, bearing gifts for One Hung Low ... What is your position?"

"Gator One to Gator Two ... We're about seventy meters east of the enemy column ... Can you see them yet?"

"That's affirmative, Gator One ... Bookoo papa sans! ... Better get your asses outta there ... We're starting our run now."

Lieutenant Parker noticed the radioman's hands were shaking. John finally understood what Gunny meant when he told him he wouldn't have time to be afraid. He reached over, touching the sleeve of the young soldier.

"You did a good job, William. Take it easy. We'll be leaving soon."

Captain Bloom spoke. "When the bombing starts, run like hell!"

Two F-105s came down in single file at 350 miles an hour. The air vibrated when they thundered past. The thick greenery of the dark jungle appeared surreal for the next few seconds. A Technicolor dream in slow motion as four silver canisters tumbled end over end through the early morning dawn.

WHOOOM! WHOOOM! WHOOOM! WHOOOM!

Exploding napalm hurled thirty-four-hundred-degree jellied gasoline into the ranks of the terrified Vietcong. There was horrific screaming and men on fire, clawing at their flaming uniforms! The stench of burning flesh filled the jungle atmosphere. The Angel of Death had just deployed.

Another Thunderchief exploded past overhead. A thousand-pound fragmentation bomb convulsed the jungle floor. Earth, weapons, trees, and men blasted skyward delivering sons of Buddha to the iron gates of Valhalla.

PFC Smith sprawled to the deck when two additional bombs detonated right behind them. Running was difficult with the radio on his back, a carbine and ammunition, and the earth heaving beneath his feet.

Gunfire! Bullets cracked and whined. Leaves fluttered to the ground. Rocks and sticks flew.

"I'm hit!" Bloom had taken a round through the calf.

"Can you walk?"

"I think so. Help me up."

With Parker on one side and Smith on the other, the three went hobbling through the jungle with Captain Bloom between them. A bullet ricocheted off Lieutenant Parker's helmet. The enemy was only yards behind.

Gunny Cody, Corporal Higgins, and PFC Cassidy appeared out of the trees with an M-60 machine gun. Higgins was lugging the weapon. Gunny was carrying a canister of ammunition in each hand with his rifle slung across his back. Higgins opened fire. Tracers went slicing through the trees.

Billy Cassidy fired his M79 grenade launcher.

BLAM!

He fired another projectile point-blank into the advancing Vietcong.

BLAM!

Half a mile away columns of black smoke were boiling up into an aquamarine sky from the flaming napalm.

"Incomiiing … Hit Tha Deck!"

Chapter Twelve

Jimmy Four Eyes

The station house had been slow most of the morning when a call came through dispatch asking for Detective McCoy. Jimmy Four Eyes was on the other end, rattling on about something he had seen Saturday night down on the docks. Jimmy was an ex-pug who fought his way up for a shot at the middleweight championship only to have his brains punched out for ten rounds in his last fight before the big match. Jimmy never recovered. His doctors had a special name for it, but what it boiled down to was his motor functions had been K.O.'d. That affected his speech and vision.

"I seen 'em … I seen 'em … you told me … them men … to look for."

"Which ones, Jimmy?"

"Them dark ma-men."

"South Americans?"

"Them's the ones. They … they was unloadin' a ba-boat."

"Where at, Jimmy?"

"You gonna pay me?"

"Don't I always?

"I want … uh… let's see … I want fifty dollars."

"I'll give you ten for the tip. And two twenties if it's something good."

"Okay … Gimme it!"

"Where are they now?"

"I want … umm … I want … give me my money."

"Goddamn it, Four Eyes! What's the fucking address?"

"It's right here."

"Where the hell is right here?"

"Pa-Pier 5 … it's uh … it's the uh … "

"Meet me at the Three Feathers. We'll be there in twenty minutes."

Detective McCoy hung up the receiver, pulled out a .45 from his desk drawer, and went downstairs looking for Cottonmouth. He found him at the water cooler mixing bourbon whiskey in a paper cup.

"Four Eyes called in … I think he's spotted something."

"Nose candy?"

"Pier 5 down by Three Feathers."

"I gotta get my shotgun. I just cleaned Mister Whupass."

The Three Feathers was a strip club where mariners, whores, and downtown businessmen hung out. It was also a favorite spot for the college crowd, and the occasional faggot hoping to get his lollypop treat. Truman Capote had visited there once while on a book-signing tour. The blue-haired madam who ran the place, Mama Maybell, had a signed photograph of Truman hanging above her teakwood counter-top. Cottonmouth and McCoy found Jimmy sitting at the bar talking with Babe, one of Mama's twenty-dollar specials.

"Hey, Jimmy. Buy me a beer?"

"Nawww … you ba-buy me one."

"Set 'em up, Mama. Whatever Jimmy wants. Pabst Blue Ribbons for me an' Cotton."

"Cotton, you're such a handsome devil. You give a girl a wide-on."

"One uh these days, Mama. I'm gonna ring your bells like the Salvation Army."

"Promises! Promises!" Mama Maybell went to get the beers.

McCoy handed Jimmy a ten dollar bill. "They'll be more if something good turns up. What were they unloading, Jimmy?"

"You swear?"

"I swear on Frankie's grave."

Cottonmouth turned and looked at McCoy. So did Jimmy. That was the first time he'd referred to his son since the funeral.

John placed a size thirteen on his partner's shoulder. "Frankie was like my son too, Bill."

"I … I liked him. He always treated me … sq-square."

"Where is it, Jimmy? That place you told me about?"

"It's … uh … round tha corner. That old … pl-place … they ma-made stuff."

"The glove factory! You stay here, partner. We'll be back."

McCoy dealt a five on the countertop, downed his beer, and out the door they went. Both men were dressed in civilian attire so no one besides a few of the locals recognized them as cops. As they neared the two-story brick factory building, a dark-complected man with multiple tattoos sitting on a wooden crate stood up. The two loading-dock doors were pulled down shut.

"Hey, mister. Y'all got work here?" Cottonmouth stood a foot taller than the Colombian.

"We got no work."

"They told us down at that Feathers joint you got work. Me an' my buddy here will work for minimum wage. We need work, mister."

"We ain't got no stinkin' jobs. You go away now."

"Tell you what, Chico. You hire us an' we'll give you ten bucks outta our first paycheck."

"You crazy *gringos*! They ain't no jobs here!"

"How 'bout we go inside an' ask tha boss?"

"NO!" YOU GO AWAY!" The tattooed man flashed a gun butt sticking out of his pants.

"Come on, William. This asshole ain't gonna give us no job."

Half a block down the sidewalk, McCoy spoke to Franklin. "They got something in there, all right. We'll come back tonight. One o'clock?"

"I reckon maybe two. They should be asleep by then."

The skeleton key they brought with them worked on the 1920s door lock. Cottonmouth crept up on a sleeping guard, knocking him unconscious with a lead-lined slapjack. McCoy was right behind him with Mister Whupass. Cottonmouth had modified the shotgun, sawing four inches off the barrel which gave the .12 gauge riot gun a wider shot pattern.

Moonlight filtering through dozens of square-cut windowpanes revealed four men sleeping on army cots. The place was run down, dilapidated, smelling of dust and machine oil from a bygone era. On a long workbench between the sleeping Colombians lay an assortment of rifles and handguns. Food wrappers and paper cups littered the concrete floor.

Detective McCoy nudged Cottonmouth, pointing at a man sitting on the floor with his back against one of the 14 x 14 wooden pillars. Closer inspection revealed the man was bound to the post, and appeared to be asleep.

"See if the lights work," whispered McCoy.

Cotton was feeling his way along a wall in the shadows when he tripped over a bucket, sending it clanging across the concrete floor. He flipped a light switch the same instant the trespassers went scrambling for their guns. Automatic weapons fire shattered the stillness of the night. Sparks and pieces of brick flew. Cottonmouth felt three slugs impact the back of his bulletproof jacket.

BOOM!

Nine double-ought lead shot blew the gunner through the plate glass window of the front office.

BOOM!

A second man was blown backwards across the floor, a .44 magnum in his hand.

"Up against the wall, you sons a bitches! Cotton, get that asshole over here so we can watch him."

The tattooed man from their encounter on the sidewalk was cursing a blue streak, tugging at a pistol hung in his leather belt. Cottonmouth struck him with the slapjack just as he fired, knocking the man sideways into the army cots. His Smith & Wesson went flying across the concrete floor. Tattoo jumped back up, grabbing for a handgun on the table. Cottonmouth knocked him into the cots again.

The man began screaming, demanding his civil rights. Cottonmouth grabbed Tattoo by his belt and shirt collar, swung him high in the air, slamming him against the office wall, knocking down the rest of the plate glass window.

"That's for not givin' me a job, you sumbitch!"

McCoy summoned the paddy wagon and an ambulance. Cottonmouth went through their pockets. The captive, beaten black and blue, was untied and placed on one of the cots. The young man appeared to have no serious injuries, but he was incoherent. A small wooden box sitting on the table invited inspection.

Cotton found five Spanish dollars plus $2,700 in one hundred dollar bills. He stuffed the pieces of eight in his pockets and eighteen of the bills. There was a glass vial in the box. Cottonmouth unscrewed the lid and sniffed.

"Aww, Jesus!"

He grabbed a rag off the table, blowing his nose repeatedly. McCoy rushed over, asking what the hell was the matter with him?

"Devil's Breath! That crazy kid that hanged his ass snorted this shit. It's what voodoo priests use to turn people into zombies. Stuff will fuck you up!"

"Let me see that. It says here on the label, Scopolamine."

"I bet they used it on our friend over there. He looks out to lunch."

"Keep the bottle. We might need that someday."

It took fifteen minutes for John to shake off the mind-numbing effects of the drug.

The same reporter from the cocaine bust arrived with the ambulance crew and the paddy wagon. He couldn't believe his good fortune. Two scoops in a row with the same two detectives. That secured young Randolph a star position with *The Miami Herald*. Taking their statements for the newspaper, Randolph noticed blood on Cottonmouth's trousers.

"You've been hurt, sir."

"Yeah, that tattooed sumbitch shot me in the ass."

"Why didn't you say something?" Detective McCoy was concerned.

"I was too busy keepin' alive."

The reporter walked over to view the hostage. Moments later he whistled. "You guys know what you got here?"

"Naww! Who is 'e?"

"His picture is all over the wire service. There's a big reward."

"I was too busy keepin' alive" ran in *The Miami Herald*. The headlines read, "Miami's Finest Do It Again." John Franklin and William McCoy had become hometown heroes. The young man they rescued was a kidnap victim from a wealthy family in Brazil. The Colombians had smuggled him into Miami to escape the manhunt taking place all over South America. Detective McCoy brought Jimmy Four Eyes with him to the presentation ceremony where a $100,000 reward was divided into three separate checks.

A .32 caliber slug was fished out of Cotton's rear end. He was told by his surgeon to take it easy a few days. Forty-eight hours later he and McCoy were down at the Three Feathers celebrating their reward money with Jimmy Four Eyes. Jimmy was so excited he couldn't sit down.

"I ba-been in thirty-one fights … an' … an' … I never got a pa-purse no mor'n … forty-four hundred. You guys … you guys … I love ya'll!"

"You're Number One, Jimmy. Don't spend all your dough on broads and booze."

Mama Maybell had Jimmy fixed up with her best $50 call girl, no charge. Jimmy was good for business. Randolph had been invited, so he took pictures of Jimmy standing beside Betty Lou for the newspaper. McCoy, Jimmy, and Cottonmouth took turns setting up the house with rounds of free drinks. It was the best party Mama had thrown since the Enola Gay and Bockscar dropped atomic bombs on Hiroshima and Nagasaki.

Six days had elapsed when McCoy and Cottonmouth received a call from Mama Maybell. "You better get down here. They got Jimmy."

The alley had blood splatters on the brick walls and pools of blood on the asphalt. Jimmy's wire rim glasses lay crushed at his feet. Detective McCoy noticed something white on the pavement. He picked it up, wiping off the grime and blood with his fingertips. It was a human front tooth with a gold crown. Half a cripple, Jimmy had put up a respectable fight before they murdered him. McCoy wrapped the tooth in a handkerchief and stuck it in his hip pocket. There was a paper sticking out of Jimmy's shirt.

"McCoy & Snake Face—You're Dead Meat!!"

Cottonmouth stuffed the note inside his sports coat. "No sense tha paper gettin' holt uh that. You think it was them Bogotá shit asses?"

"If they're in town, Rico will know where they're holed up. Let's get back to the station house and make that call. You still got that voodoo dust?"

Chapter Thirteen

Dutch and Trudy

Blue Whales

The *Sea Queen* was two hours north of Old Bess when Sarah spotted the whales. She and Trudy were sunbathing on top of the cabin sporting their new two-piece bathing suits. Boogie was driving while Dutch was below in the galley preparing lunch.

"Swabby! What kind of whales are those?" she shouted.

Wayne was preoccupied, thinking about his crew. Trudy and Dutch had taken to one another like a couple of love-struck teenagers. He was pleased about that. Dutch seemed at peace for the first time since returning home from Vietnam. Wayne was happy about that too.

Wayne loved Sarah. She was intelligent and beautiful, and a priceless asset to their business ventures. He planned on willing his estate to Sarah once he reached home port. No sense taking a chance if something happened to him. He'd cut Bubba-J in for thirty percent, and designate him as manager for the marina.

"Swabby!"

"What?"

"Whales, Blind Tom, over there!"

"Oh, wow! Blue whales! Blues are the biggest things in the ocean."

"Take us closer so we can see."

Wayne maneuvered the boat to within thirty yards of the massive creatures. Trudy called down to Dutch to come topside and see the whales. There were six of them swimming north with the Equatorial Current.

"Whoa! I thought sperm whales were big. Those things are longer than the boat!"

"Over a hundred tons. A hundred and thirty or forty tons is my guess."

"That is the most amazing thing I have ever seen."

"They were hunted almost to extinction back in the thirties. There aren't but a few thousand left. This is really something seeing six of them like this. They're going north to feed. They'll come back down here for the winter."

"Get the camera!"

They took turns snapping pictures of each other with the whales in the background. It was a sunny day with clear skies and gentle seas. Life had never been so good. Each time Dutch looked at Trudy his heart skipped a beat. Trudy viewed Dutch as the grand finale in her search for the righteous man. She could hardly believe it was happening so quickly. For Dutch it felt like a dream. A woman like her! He silently thanked God for his amazing good fortune.

Trudy only nibbled at her baked grouper and macaroni salad. Love had stolen her appetite. Dutch was starving. He wolfed his food when he was in the midst of big doings. She enjoyed watching him eat. There was a hairline scar above his left eye she hadn't noticed before.

"What caused your scar?"

Dutch stopped eating, touching a hand to his brow. She could see his demeanor changing.

"I'm sorry. Did I say something wrong?"

"No, honey … it happened in the war."

"Can you tell me about it?"

She had seen it before in men coming home from Vietnam. They would be talking one minute. Then they were back in the jungle reliving events from the past.

"You darling man. I didn't mean to upset you."

"I thought maybe it would go away."

"We won't talk about it anymore."

"I want to talk about it … it's … in my dreams."

They were alone in the galley. Dwayne and Sarah were up on the bridge operating the boat. Trudy came around the table and sat down beside Dutch, placing an arm around his waist.

"Tell me, darling."

"I never told anybody before. We … uh … we were repairing a railroad trestle so we'd bivouacked underneath the tracks on this riverbank. It was a wide river and pretty deep. Some of the men were fishermen so they kept us in fresh fish. There was this little village upstream about a mile or so. The kids would come every day and visit. We gave them candy or whatever we had lying around. We had a medic in the outfit so he checked the kids over, and gave them vaccinations.

"One morning the children didn't show up. That was unusual so Gunny took the Indian to go check it out. Two hours later they were back. Gunny told us to saddle up.

"When we got to the village we saw this pile of little arms beside a bloody tree stump. The Vietcong had come during the night, and used that stump as a chopping block to hack off the children's arms with vaccinations. They killed the adults. Their throats were cut. Three little girls and three little boys bled to death.

"The medics managed to save one child. He was about four. Gunny asked for a volunteer. I stepped forward. I went with Gunny and the Indian. His name was Moses Blue Pony.

"Blue Pony tracked, while Gunny and I walked behind him watching for the enemy. It got dark so we bedded down for the night. Next morning we were moving at first light. We'd gone about a mile when the Indian signaled a halt. There they were in a clearing eating breakfast, seven of them. We could tell who the leader was. He talked all the time.

"We spread out, and on Gunny's signal we opened fire. It was over in a few seconds. We went out then to examine the bodies. I was bending over Big Mouth when he came up with a knife and just missed slitting my throat. I rolled away, but he was on me like a duck on a June bug. Blue Pony knocked him out with his rifle butt. I had blood all over, but it wasn't too bad.

"The Indian made a suggestion and we said okay. We pulled his clothes off, tied Big Mouth to a tree, and waited for him to wake up.

"Blue Pony scalped him. The bastard kicked and screamed just like those kids he butchered. We left him there tied to that tree. The Indian understood some of the language. He told us the man begged us to shoot him. I asked why? Blue Pony said, 'He knows the tigers will come.'

"I don't regret what we did. I'd do it again. But I dream about those children, and those seven little arms beside that bloody tree stump."

Trudy had tears in her eyes. "Sweetheart, I want you to meet the bomber pilot. He's my father."

Trudy Peters was on Cloud Nine. All her life men had thrown themselves at her feet. Few saw her as an intellectual, educated and bright. They were too busy staring at her boobies or her caboose, as she called her shapely bottom. Other men were intimidated by her intelligence or the way she looked. Insecurity was the hallmark of the Bullshit Boys, men who never grew up. Some of the pilots were like that. But she knew flight attendants who were just as silly and immature. Poor self-esteem wasn't a male characteristic. The whole species had its share of dysfunctional personalities.

She recalled what her father told her four years earlier when she joined the airlines. "You're a beautiful woman, Trudy. Don't let that distract you from your purpose in life. Look for a man who appreciates you for who you are, and not just another roll in the hay."

The bomber pilot had a way with words. Over the span of four years she had become just as direct as her father. Speaking one's mind often shocked people. They were accustomed to the social platitudes. Flight Commander Peters had taught his daughter well.

She thought about her sick mother. Mother had slipped away from Father with Alzheimer's. The war years had been their day in the sun. How grand she looked in her uniform with the Women's Auxiliary Air Force. Father had told the story a dozen times how he met her mother in a Piccadilly air-raid shelter. Trudy wished she could give Father some of her happiness. The WAAF seldom recognized her Army Air Force pilot anymore.

Standing beside Dutch with the wind in her hair and the stars overhead filled her mind with questions. Where would they live if the authorities became involved? What would she look like after childbirth? Trudy didn't want to be all fat and stretchy for Dutch. She wanted him always to be her champion, her six-foot-four Casanova, her White Knight whom she adored. Gosh, he sure knew how to please a girl. She loved the way he held her afterwards. It made her feel special and appreciated.

"Daydreaming, Miss Magnolia?"

"I was thinking about you, dear."

"A penny for your thoughts?"

"I was wondering where we might live if you and Wayne get in trouble."

"Good question. I don't know about extradition. Australia, Thailand, Panama? Boogie has a lawyer friend. We could ask him."

"Father knows lots of lawyers."

"Wouldn't he object if he knew what Wayne and I do?"

"I'm not sure. Grandfather made a lot of money in the stock market, but he lost most of it when the market crashed in '29. None of his friends ever knew. He let on like he was still rich. There wasn't much left after Grandfather died. When Father came home from the war he still had his pilot friends all over the world. That's how he made his fortune."

"Is he still in business?"

"He retired after he crashed a cargo plane in Ethiopia. One of his best friends was killed in the accident. Father gave his share to the widow."

"Your daddy sounds like quite a man."

"He's like you."

"Your father's a war hero. I was just an Army grunt building roads and bridges."

"You're my hero, and what you did for those children …"

"Gunny took it harder than any of us. He cried when we got back to the village and saw those little graves. I guess I did too."

"It takes a strong man to admit crying."

"I never knew they made women like you, Trudy."

"There's a few of us around: my mother, Sarah, and Amanda."

"I'm sorry your mama has that illness."

"Alzheimer's is a terrible disease. We keep her comfortable. That's about all we can do."

"I like the way you confront things. I think I'll try the 'Trudy' approach."

"How you gonna manage that, wise guy?"

"Well, it goes something like this … will you marry me?"

"Wow! That really does take the cake!"

"Will you marry me, Trudy Peters?"

"Of course I will, my darling."

He held her in his arms and kissed her. She snuggled against him, smiling up into his suntanned face.

"You said a mouthful this morning when you made love to me."

"I meant every word." he kissed her again.

"I can't wait until your watch is over." Trudy squeezed his butt with both hands.

"You're a shameless woman!"

"I'm your shameless woman, Sugar Britches."

"Being out here with you and the whales, it's like a dream."

"Pretty groovy, isn't it?

"The grooviest, dream girl."

"I want us to have a proper wedding in Atlanta so my father and his friends can be there."

"Mom will be thrilled. She hasn't had much to smile about since Daddy died."

"It's wonderful the way couples bonded together during the thirties, and the war years."

"I think you're pretty wonderful."

"Grew on ya, did I?"

"Like Cupid's arrow, straight through my heart."

"Oh, look! A shooting star! That's good luck!"

Chapter Fourteen

Lieutenant Parker

Sacrifice

A mortar shell landed twenty feet from PFC Smith, jarring him an inch off the ground. Captain Bloom absorbed the blast, his body between Smith and the explosion. Bullets were clipping tree limbs, clods of earth were flying in the air. Another mortar round exploded, showering the men with dirt and leaves. Gunny's skirmish line lay 80 meters straight ahead.

Crack! Bullets impacting the trees and soil were unnerving. *Crack! … Crack!*

A squad of Vietcong had flanked the six infantrymen, firing into their position from a low lying ridge 100 meters to their right. More Vietcong were behind them. Billy Cassidy got off an M-79 round. Corporal Higgins opened fire with his M-60 machine gun. Gunny found himself and his men in a precarious predicament. If they got up and ran for it they would be shot down and killed. If they stayed where they were they were going to die anyway.

"Smith, get over here! Gimme that radio!"

William Smith did the Olympic Belly Crawl. Death howling above their heads was prime incentive.

Billy Cassidy was firing his M-79 grenade launcher as rapidly as he could load, aim, and fire.

BLAM! BLAM!

Higgins was nearing the end of his last ammunition belt.

"Gator Two! Gator Two! Come in Gator Two!"

Crack! … Crack! Crack! … Crack!

"I read you loud and clear, Gator One."

"It's Shit City down here. I want you guys to bomb a smoke round. Repeat. Bomb a smoke round!"

"Can do! Light one up!"

"Cassidy! Put some smoke on them assholes."

Thuung!

A 40 mm smoke projectile arched up into the sky falling down into the trees directly behind the Vietcong position. Moments later a Thunderchief roared by overhead, strafing the ridge with 20 mm cannon fire. Another 105 screamed past at 400 feet, releasing two 500-pound canisters of napalm. The ridge lit up bright orange, boiling flames, and agonized screaming.

"Come on, lads!"

Halfway to their lines Corporal Higgins cried out, and fell.

"Lieutenant!" shouted Gunny.

Lieutenant Parker snatched up the M-60 then grabbed Higgins by the arm. He and Wild Bill ran the corporal to the foxholes. Billy Cassidy and William Smith stumbled along close behind dragging Captain Bloom between them.

"Medic! Medic! Over here! Parker! Go check on Overstreet. He's down yonder a ways. Cassidy! Go with Lieutenant Parker!"

Running behind the foxholes, John Parker was thinking about Katherine and his daughter. How would they manage if he went home in a box? Ten thousand dollars was a lousy dividend for getting killed.

"Billy, scoot in behind that dead tree. It's good cover. Make your rounds count, son."

A mortar round exploded in a treetop. Enemy fire was escalating.

Up ahead he spotted Lieutenant Overstreet directing his men. Tuttle Company had held their fire, waiting for Parker and the others to reach the safety of their position.

"John! God, I'm glad to see you! Olson got shot, but he'll be okay. I was worried when we heard all the shooting and those planes overhead. You look like shit!"

"Welcome to Green Acres! Bloom is hurt bad. Higgins got shot in the stomach. What about here?"

"We're taking fire from the left and some out front. Nothing we can't handle."

"Our planes chewed up their main force. But there's more of them, lots more. We heard 'em coming through the trees."

"The mortar crew is ready to go. I placed an M-60 behind those rocks over there. Is Wild Bill okay?"

"Wild Bill is A-OK!"

A mortar shell impacted twenty meters behind them. Moments later another round burst ten meters closer.

"Take Coveeer!"

An 81 mm landed in the foxhole between PFC Johnson's legs. Blood and tissue splattered the soldiers on both sides of Johnson's hole. His helmet landed at Lieutenant Overstreet's feet, his head still inside.

"Goddamn It! Watch the skyline! You'll see it!

"I see it, sir! I see one!"

"Take Coveeer!"

The mortar shell exploded three meters forward of the lines.

"Where is it, Kirby?"

"About three hundred feet that way, sir. I saw it go up."

Mortar Crew! You heard the man. Give us two rounds at one hundred meters, thirty degrees left. Space your secondary rounds ten meters apart, left, right, forward, and back. Gun Crew! I want two- and three-second bursts. All Guns! Commence firing! Commence firing!"

The perimeter lit up with muzzle flashes.

Another mortar came whistling in. Two more shells exploded down the line.

Gunny landed in the trench beside Lieutenant Parker. He had Smith and Cassidy with him. "Crank up that radio! Hand it here! ... Hey, sky monkeys! You got anything left up there?"

"We got one ... two ... six 500-pound frags. And a shitload uh 20 mike-mike."

"They's a pesky varmint down here needs a good ass whuppin."

Crack!

"Smoke the bastard!"

A mortar round exploded to their right wounding two soldiers.

Crack! ... Crack!

"Cassidy!"

Cassidy aimed at a tall cypress tree three hundred feet to his left. The smoke round hit the tree, falling down into the underbrush. A 105 swept down, scything the rising smoke with his electronically fired minigun. Whole trees fell before the onslaught. A second Thunderchief loosed another torrent of 20 mm shells. A third and fourth 105 thundered past, dropping 500-pound fragmentation bombs. The jungle rocked with explosions.

The six aircraft formed up single file, plowing the jungle floor with their 20 mm cannons. Then they flew away for home. The jungle fell silent except for the cries of the wounded. The mortar bombardment had stopped. The fighting was over.

"You done good, Billy ... Hey, Billy."

Billy Cassidy was kneeling on the ground hunched over his M-79 grenade launcher as though he were praying. Lieutenant Parker touched Billy's shoulder. His helmet fell off. There was a round hole in the center of Billy's forehead. There wasn't much blood. An armor-piercing bullet had passed through the front of Billy's headpiece.

"Jesus God! Johnson is blown to hell, now Billy. Fuck This Shit!" Lieutenant Overstreet flung his M-14 down in the dirt.

Gunny Cody was by Overstreet's side in seconds. Gunny took hold of the Lieutenant's bicep with an iron grip. "Lieutenant! Remember what you said? Don't let the men see you like this. Cassidy was a good soldier. He's with God now. Your job is looking after the men still here. Pull yourself together, Steve."

"I'm sorry. I'm sorry, Gunny."

"I know, son. Just deal with it. You okay now?"

"Yes, sir! Thank you, sir. If I pull another stunt, kick my ass again, please."

"You'd do the same thing for me, Steve." Wild Bill winked, smiling at his young lieutenant.

Lieutenant Parker and Lieutenant Overstreet gathered up what they could find of PFC Johnson. Billy Cassidy was the hardest casualty. A freckle-faced kid from Boca Raton, Billy wanted to be a veterinarian when he returned home from Vietnam. Billy loved animals. Oftentimes he would spend the day feeding and petting the stray cats in the alley-ways and parking lots along the Florida beaches.

Captain Bloom died on the floor of the Huey helicopter on the flight back to Da Nang.

Corporal Higgins was sent back to the States for reconstructive surgery. Five soldiers were killed that day and eleven wounded. Tuttle Company grieved their losses, but took solace in the fact a hundred and thirty-one enemy bodies were discovered following the firefight.

A driver sat outside the barracks waiting for Lieutenant Parker to finish dressing. Colonel Brown had sent word he wanted to see Lieutenant Parker. It was 6:25 a.m. Five minutes later Parker was on his way through the compound, riding shotgun in an open Jeep. When he walked into the colonel's office, an Army major was sitting in the corner. Lieutenant Parker saluted and was told to take a seat.

"I understand you had some trouble up along the DMZ."

"Yes, sir. We engaged a large enemy force."

"This is Major Stone. He's with Army Intelligence. Tell us what you saw up there."

"Captain Bloom and I and the radio operator were hidden in a stand of pine trees. We radioed Da Nang for the airstrike. We couldn't see the enemy very well, but we could hear them coming through the jungle. Sergeant Cody had pulled the company back to a defensive position about two hundred meters behind us. The planes came and really clobbered them, sir."

"Go on."

"When the bombing started, Captain Bloom told us to run for it so we did."

"What happened then?"

"Captain Bloom got shot in the leg. The radio operator, PFC Smith, and I got Bloom between us and headed for our lines."

"Tell Major Stone about Sergeant Cody."

"We were in deep shit, sir. The VC was right behind us. I didn't think we were going to make it. Next thing I knew Gunny and Higgins came out of the trees with an M-60. They had Billy Cassidy with them. Corporal Higgins cut loose with his machine gun. That stopped them for a little while.

"Then we got pinned down out in the open. Gunny got on the radio and called for an airstrike against the ridge. Billy marked it with an M 79 smoke round. The planes came, and we made another run for it."

"Would you say Sergeant Cody exhibited sound judgment?"

"Yes sir. He saved all our lives."

"What then?"

"Higgins got hit so we got him and Captain Bloom back to the foxholes. We were taking mortar fire the whole time. A mortar shell killed PFC Johnson right after we got there. PFC Kirby spotted where the mortars were coming from so Sergeant Cody called for another air strike. Billy marked it with another smoke round."

"Where were you when this was taking place?"

"Sir, I was on the left flank assisting the men. Billy Cassidy was there and Lieutenant Overstreet. Gunny ran over to help out when the mortar shell killed Johnson. That's when Billy got shot."

"Do you know why I called you here this morning, Lieutenant?"

"No, sir."

"I'm recommending you, Sergeant Cody, Corporal Higgins, PFC Cassidy, and Captain Bloom for the Bronze Star. I'm also appointing you my company commander. We're short on field captains up here so you're Bloom's replacement. Sergeant Cody recommended you. Wild Bill and I go back a lot of years together."

"Thank you, sir."

"Sun Tzu was a Chinese warlord who lived six hundred years before Christ. Many of his military sayings are appropriate still today. I especially like this one. 'Regard your soldiers as your children, and they will follow you into the deepest valleys. Look upon them as your beloved sons, and they will stand by you even unto death.'

"Bear that in mind, Parker. It makes for dedicated soldiers. Good luck to you and Tuttle Company."

"Thank you, Colonel. I'll do my best for the men."

Chapter Fifteen

Rico

"It wasn't one of our people and it wasn't the Colombians. I would know. We got connections from here to Jacksonville. They're lying low because of your Brazilian bust. Meyer Lansky thinks its downtown."

"Downtown? What's downtown?"

"He has a source at the Justice Department. This person says he's heard rumors about a political involvement down here in Miami. All the source could give us was a name, 'The Peacock.' He didn't know any more about it, and was afraid to stick his nose in it."

"It still doesn't make sense. Why would anybody whack Jimmy?"

"Maybe he saw something he shouldn't have at the Three Feathers."

"Okay, but why would they kill him unless he knew something important? That newspaper reporter tied me and Cotton to Jimmy … Betty Lou, the hooker, might be a lead … our coke bust is another factor … that and the Brazilian kidnapping were both South American.

"What if some political ass-wipe brought in a ringer to protect his percentage?"

"That is definitely a possibility."

"An' me and Cotton are the monkey wrench in the money machine."

"Right … so now they're coming after you and John. No offense, but that's what I'd do. Eliminate the threat to the cash flow. It's Racketeering 101, McCoy."

John Franklin spoke. "How 'bout askin' your people to find out who wrote that note I got off Jimmy?"

"You got it on you?"

Cottonmouth pulled the paper out of his jacket pocket, handing the note to Rico.

"Not much to go on … lead pencil, printed letters, notebook paper. I'll give it to Luther. Maybe he'll see a pattern he recognizes."

"My guess is it's somebody new. It could be local, Spanish, or damn near anybody."

"We use Russians, Jews, Jamaicans, the Frogs, you name it. Money and drugs are pouring in from places I never heard of before. Miami is going to grow like it did during the Second World War. Twenty years from now you won't recognize the place."

Detective Franklin made an observation. "Why don't we buy some swampland up around Hollywood? It's nothin' but snakes and lizards now, but in twenty years it'll be worth a fortune. Miami's gonna boom just like Atlanta."

Rico glanced up at John Franklin with a respect he reserved only for a handful of men. His Jewish accountant had been urging him to purchase acreage in that same location. The dapper little man had already bought twenty-two acres himself, inexpensive marshland near the beach. How could such an ugly, unsophisticated, musclebound brute like Cotton know to do that? Rico made a decision.

"Bear with me a minute. I've been looking at a farm up off Ives

Dairy with eight hundred feet of oceanfront. It's $500,000 for a hundred and four acres. I figure for cash we might get it for $300,000, maybe $350,000. It belongs to a Japanese couple in Hawaii. You guys interested?"

"You mean like a partnership?"

"That's right. I could get killed any given day in my business. I want to leave something for my wife and daughters. You and Cotton are people I trust."

Cottonmouth spoke. "Real estate is uh sound investment. I got two hundred acres up in Georgia."

"I can see the headlines now," McCoy responded. "'Miami Detectives and Mob Boss Busted.' I never liked you, Rico, because of the rackets, but I'm beginning to change my tune. You and I are a lot alike. Cotton too. We make our living in a sewer. But we ain't half as bad as the shit we deal with."

"Your boy getting killed changed things."

"How's that?"

"I saw you for the first time as a father, not a lousy cop. That much we have in common."

"Yeah. I miss my Frankie."

Cottonmouth addressed them with his analysis of a partnership. "Rico needs us as much as we need him. Any double cross would mean the slammer."

"I'll tell you a secret, Basilio. People look at Cotton like a big ugly dummy, but he has brains I never had. He's saved my life twice since we been together."

"I always figured he was the smart one."

McCoy looked at Rico sideways then burst out laughing. Rico and Cotton just grinned.

"You talkin' three ways?"

"Yes, three ways. I got a hundred grand rat-holed, twenty-five or thirty more if I call in my markers."

"Me an' Cotton can get the rest. Give the Nips a call. If they're willing to deal we want to see it first."

"I'll get back to you as soon as I know something. I got a survey map. There's an old house down by the beach that looks like a southern plantation, tall columns, long winding staircase. It could be fixed up."

The wait lasted a little over seventy-two hours. Rico's offer of $300,000 was countered at $400,000. A compromise was reached for $365,000. The next day the three of them were walking the property, weaving through a tangle of underbrush, briars, ferns, and mangrove trees. Rico led them down to an antebellum mansion ninety yards from the beach. A bronze plaque on the front gate read "1905."

"A citrus farmer owned this land. He followed the railroad down here after the freeze of '94 that killed all the orange groves up north. Miami was the only place that survived the cold. After the Flagler Railroad was built in 1896, Miami went from wooden shacks to a boomtown overnight."

"Looks like that big house in *Gone With the Wind*."

"This acreage sits right in the path where Miami has to grow, plus we got eight hundred feet of beachfront. It won't take twenty years, McCoy. Developers will beat our doors off the hinges before you know it."

"Cotton, what's your take on this place?"

"Rico's right. Let's buy it."

A red fox watched from behind a buttonwood tree as the mobster and the two police detectives shook hands. Forty-five minutes later they were seated at a wooden picnic table in the upstairs barroom of Tobacco Road. Behind them lay the Miami River. Myron, the little Jewish accountant, had just arrived with his yellow notepad and a briefcase full of legal documents. Everyone else went downstairs when Rico asked for privacy.

"I took your advice, Myron. We're buying the citrus farm."

"That's wonderful, sir. It's a sound investment."

"That's what Cottonmouth said. That's him right there."

"Pleased to meet you, sir. Everyone knows Mister Franklin."

"This here is Detective McCoy."

"It's a pleasure, Detective McCoy. I'm sorry about your son."

The property was divided into equal shares with the right of survivorship going to the next of kin. John Franklin had no family so he named his Cajun princess as his legal heir. Any two partners constituted a majority with the right to sell, lease, or trade after a period of five years. Otherwise, all three partners could do as agreed upon at any given time. A title search was to be conducted.

A sales contract was drawn up and signed for $365,000. Legal papers were airmailed to the couple in Hawaii. Nine days later the money was transferred. The three partners had become owners of 104 acres on the Atlantic Ocean. Title was constructed in such a manner making it almost impossible to discover who actually owned the 104 acres. No one suspected at the time the significance of the citrus farm or the role it would play in the months ahead.

Chapter Sixteen

Lieutenant Overstreet

The Widow Maker

Four months had elapsed since Tuttle Company's encounter with the Vietcong on their first patrol below the Demilitarized Zone. The Miami Reservists, dubbed "Tuttle's Turkeys" by the Marines at Da Nang, had mastered their search and destroy operations, and the deciphering of French maps while patrolling the jungles around Hue, Quang Tri, and the provinces below the DMZ. Lieutenant Parker had matured as company commander. And always, several paces nearby, Master Sergeant William Cody watched over his lieutenants and enlisted personnel whom he referred to as "kinfolk."

Lieutenant Overstreet had become one of Tuttle Company's celebrities during a search and rescue operation near the Laotian border in the A Shau Valley. First Platoon had gotten pinned down when they ventured away from the safety of the jungle to investigate a downed B-52 bomber sitting in an open field. Six Air Force fliers were reported missing. What they encountered was a Vietcong machine gun nest overlooking the crash site.

They were exposed in open grassland with no place to evade the enemy gunner so they took refuge behind the huge bomber. Overstreet flanked the Vietcong, coming up behind them with Third Platoon. A firefight erupted. Lieutenant Overstreet crawled up and lobbed hand grenades inside the enemy bunker while Second and Third Platoon kept the VC busy with rifle fire. Six Vietcong were killed and one captured.

Today's mission was another sweep through the quadrant known as The Widow Maker. Tuttle Company remembered the place well. Last time they were there five of their company had reported in for fence patrol inside the Pearly Gates. Apprehension was in the air. Khe Sanh had been under attack for seven consecutive days.

The sky resembled dirty linen with a line of gray cumulous clouds hovering a hundred feet above the low-lying hills. It was raining, a fine mist but rain nonetheless. Tiny droplets of water coated their weapons and ponchos. The Huey helicopters made loud rotary sounds settling down in the landing zone. Leaves and twigs flew. The grass and bushes swayed back and forth from the prop wash of the chopper blades. Tuttle Company was on the ground. The date was January 29, 1968.

Parker, Wild Bill, and Lieutenant Overstreet stood shoulder to shoulder studying a map of the terrain up ahead.

"Right there looks like a good spot, about four kilometers. We could dig in and wait. If Charlie shows up we'll have the drop on the bastards."

"I like the elevation. That valley makes a good choke point."

"Move 'em out, Gunny."

Tuttle Company spent the rest of the morning slogging through grasslands, marsh, and heavy jungle. That afternoon they found the hill they were searching for which sat back against a higher elevation overlooking a narrow valley with a creek meandering down the middle.

Hill 409 was flat on top. The men dug foxholes around the perimeter, and settled down for chow. The rain had stopped.

Master Sergeant Cody was dreaming about the wind-up bird, a toy his father brought home from the Orient after serving his final tour in China with George C. Marshall. He was six then, and hadn't seen his father since he was four years old. The Chinese toy had a wind-up mechanism inside that made chirping sounds like a real bird. William loved his wind-up bird, and took it with him everywhere he went.

One day at school the class bully, Earl Honeycutt, grabbed the wind-up bird, threw it down on the hallway floor, and stomped it. Young William was expelled from school. Young Mister Honeycutt had to drop out of class for a week due to a variety of injuries. William's proud father took him and his mother to see Laurel and Hardy in *Big Business* that same afternoon.

Gunny was still dreaming when the sentry shook his arm. Wild Bill opened his eyes to see the concerned face of PFC Butler. Lieutenant Parker was kneeling beside them.

"Sir, we got movement in the valley."

"How many?"

"I can't tell, but we sure can hear 'em."

"Lead the way, son."

The moon appeared from behind the clouds. They saw them in the moonlight, a long column of enemy soldiers marching south along the creek bank. Tuttle Company was two hundred feet above the enemy column, looking down on them as they made their way beneath the Army's dug-in position.

Lieutenant Parker whispered to Wild Bill. "General Weyand was right. They're using Tet to infiltrate. That's why we're out here. The Marines are behind us. The Army is farther south."

PFC Butler posed a question. "Sir, what does Tet mean?"

"It's their lunar holiday, similar to our New Year's Eve. It's when the

Vietnamese people celebrate their birthdays all at the same time. That's just part of it. It's in a book I'll let you borrow."

Gunny spoke. "I better radio I Corps. I 'spect this is worse 'n it looks."

Lieutenant Parker told him, "Tell them the truce is broken."

Gunny radioed Da Nang, and had just returned to join Overstreet and Parker when the first artillery shell exploded on the side of the mountain above their heads.

"Commence Firing! Commence Firing!"

A second round detonated on the far slope of the plateau.

"Call the flyboys! We're in for it!"

Night resembled day from the muzzle flashes of hundreds of guns firing back and forth between the American troops and the North Vietnamese Army. Cursing, screaming, and the banging of grenades amidst the howl of automatic weapons filled the humid nocturne. Back up the valley a Soviet field gun was searching for the range on Tuttle Company. A shell exploded in the clearing atop Hill 409.

"Don't waste ammunition!"

"Squeeze 'em off!

"Keep them heads down!"

Wild Bill was walking behind his men barking orders, praising their *esprit de corps*, calling out for a medic when needed. The radio man, Billy Smith, parroted Gunny Cody stride for stride. Another 130 mm shell impacted on the mountain. Two riflemen went running past accompanied by Lieutenant Overstreet to fill a gap in the line. In the distance they heard the approach of a Cobra gunship. A shoulder-fired Strela-2 went streaking from the valley floor. The Cobra pilot veered violently, dodging the missile then swung around to attack.

"Gunny … help me …"

Collins lay on his back, the top of his head blown completely off revealing his bloody brains. The man beside him stared in horror at PFC Collins.

"Soldier! Get back to your position!"

William cradled the dying man in his arms, speaking softly to Albert in his last moments on earth. "I love you, Albert. Go to sleep now. You're going to be with the angels."

PFC Collins grasped Wild Bill's hand, stretched out his legs, and breathed his last breath. He was staring up into Gunny's eyes, a peaceful expression on his face. William lay the boy down gently, placed a poncho over the body and stood up, his legs soaked with blood.

"A brave soldier is dead! Kill those sons a bitches! Kill 'em all!"

The Tet Offensive was underway in more than a hundred towns and villages throughout South Vietnam. The Vietcong had thrown their entire force into the surprise attack. A lesser number of North Vietnamese Army personnel were engaged. The Offensive had been in the planning stages for more than a year. General Giap, Commander of Communist forces in the North, was against risking 85,000 men against the superior firepower of the Allies, but was overruled by the Politburo in Hanoi. The Grim Reaper watched and waited. The fate of the Vietnam War would be decided February 27, 1968, by Walter Cronkite, anchor for the *CBS Evening News*.

The battle raged back and forth through the night. Twenty percent of Tuttle Company had been wounded, eight men killed. Ammunition was critical. There wasn't enough. Medical supplies were down to a few boxes of morphine ampules and sterile bandages. Air support was stretched to the limit from the Hien Luong Bridge all the way south below Saigon. Drinking water was what they had left in their canteens.

A frightened PFC voiced his fears to Wild Bill. "We ain't gonna make it, are we, Gunny?"

"When we get back to camp I'm gonna wash your pie hole out with soap. Hell, yes, we'll make it if I have to carry you an' the whole damn company on my back!"

Gunny was dressing shrapnel wounds in the stomach of one of his corporals. The man lay on his back gazing up at Wild Bill. Corporal Lowery was groggy from loss of blood, and the effects of the morphine.

"I dreamed again."

"Tell me what you dreamed, son."

"I was with my girl at the high school dance. This song was playing … something about a dream and a candy-colored clown. Then it all changed … we were back at the drive-in restaurant. Sally wanted to go park someplace … I wanted to get some more vodka. Then it got all fuzzy … me an' Sally …"

Corporal Lowery passed out. Gunny stuck a field pack under his head, and moved on. Both medics were hurt so William Cody was assisting with the wounded. That helped the master sergeant keep abreast of the situation around Tuttle Company's perimeter.

The sky was changing color from deep purple to a pale yellow in the east. White fog shrouded the valley floor. The ground and the soldiers were wet from the falling dew. One sardonic combatant suggested the moon looked like the blade on Mister Bone's scythe.

"What do we have left?" Lieutenant Parker asked Gunny.

"One uh tha machine guns is busted. The rest got about two belts apiece. We got forty or fifty rounds per man. Two packs uh grenades. M-79s got seven or eight shells. An' two satchel charges. That's about it if you don't count piss an' vinegar!"

"About sixty minutes worth, give or take."

"Mostly take."

"Those satchel charges, can we stuff them with shell casings?"

"Good idea, lieutenant."

"What else can we do?"

"Semi-automatic only. I think we oughta move one M-60 to tha far end. Rifles can hold tha center."

"Sounds reasonable."

"Sir, may I say something personal?"

"You aren't going to get all weepy on me, are you?"

"Lieutenant Parker, it's been an honor. I've served with a lot uh lieutenants in my day. You're a natural born good 'un!"

"Thank you, William. Thank you for keeping their spirits up. You're a good 'un yourself."

"Yes, sir. I'll go see about that gun now."

"Billy, hand me that radio."

Parker shifted his weight to relieve the throbbing from the shrapnel splinters in his shoulder and left arm. He radioed the airbase at Da Nang for the second time that morning requesting resupply and withdrawal of his dead and wounded. The airbase was under attack. The insurgents had fought their way inside the forty-five-square-mile compound.

Lieutenant Overstreet came running over. "Any luck?"

"They said an hour. That means we better plan on two."

"Well, shit!"

"Make sure the men go easy on the ammunition."

"I've told 'em ten times. They know."

"Tell them they're an important part of all this. Tell them help is on the way."

"I will, John. Are you all right?"

"Steve, as bad as I feel this is the most alive I've ever felt."

"See to it you stay that way. I better get back to the men."

"Steve."

"What?"

"Take care of yourself."

Gunfire snapped their attention toward the perimeter of the hill. Several of the men were standing and firing their M-14s. An M-60 opened up. Automatic weapons down below reverberated back and forth between the hills. Wild Bill came running from the machine gun emplacement at the end of the plateau.

"Get Down! Get Down!"

A rocket propelled grenade detonated down the line. Heavy gunfire, yelling, a man began to pray. Another RPG exploded. Then another one. And another. Somebody was screaming. Two more M-60s added their staccato voices to the calamitous din. From the valley floor came the clamor of dozens of AK-47s. In the distance the Soviet field gun had fallen silent. The Cobra gunship had wiped out its Chinese crew.

"Get your asses in them holes! Don't give 'em a silhouette."

Sergeant Cody was everywhere, directing the fire, encouraging his men, telling them to shoot slow and deliberate.

"Don't waste ammunition!"

Lieutenant Overstreet was humping it back and forth with fresh magazines, bandages, and fragmentation grenades. A man went down in front of him. Steve pulled the soldier over beside Lieutenant Parker then ran back into the smoke and gunfire.

"Gunny! Lieutenant! They're coming up the hill!"

Cody grabbed a C-4 satchel charge and raced to the position where the soldier was sounding the alarm. He bobbed up for a quick look. Down the embankment about ten of them were bunched up in a gully parallel with the top of the hill.

Gunny chanced another look. About fifty feet he estimated. He lit the fuse and waited, counting off the seconds. The soldiers on both sides stared mesmerized at the high explosive. With three seconds to go Wild Bill swung the olive drab satchel high in the air. It struck the front of the gully, bouncing in. The ground rocked from the detonation.

An NVA boot with a foot inside struck the soldier standing beside Gunny on the shoulder. Tuttle Company let go a rebel yell. Out of the fog burst a screaming wave of NVA charging up the hillside. Overstreet and Gunny looked at one another.

"Select your Targettts! Squeeze 'em Offff! Don't Waste Ammunition!"

Wild Bill rushed back and knelt beside Lieutenant Parker. Wounded soldiers lay in bloody rows on either side of the two men, a smorgasbord of misery and suffering a long ways from home and mama's apple pie. Lieutenant Overstreet had carried several of the casualties on his shoulders from the breastworks of 409.

"It's time, sir. Better make that call."

"Broken Arrow! This is Tuttle Company! Broken Arrow!"

Lieutenant Parker relayed the time and position. The message went out to Hue, Quang Tri, Da Nang, Dong Ha, and Hoi An. Pilots in the area received the distress signal. Tuttle Company was being overrun.

Within minutes a pair of Skyraiders appeared. They came in low, one behind the other, strafing the hillside with their 20 mm cannons. It produced death and dying, but the NVA were battling their way inside the perimeter.

The fighting was savage and brutal. Men were hacked to pieces with machetes and entrenching tools.

From the southwest came another sound, a CH-47 Chinook helicopter carrying a 105 mm howitzer on cargo straps beneath the aircraft. Parker watched as the crew released the gun which went crashing

The Huey arrives.

down into the jungle. They were dumping boxes of artillery shells as they came in for a landing.

The instant the pilot sat down, the flight engineer jumped out. He observed the rows of injured men.

"We'll take the wounded. Leave your dead. More help is on the way. Leave the weapons here. We got battle damage. We'll leave our .30 caliber stuff with you guys."

Hand-to-hand fighting raged in the background while Gunny, Overstreet, and Smith helped the flight engineer and copilot load up the casualties. Bullets flew, some striking the helicopter. A sergeant staggered over with his left arm clutched in his right hand. It was severed at the elbow.

Lieutenant Parker was the last one onboard, making the total thirty-nine. Twelve boxes of belted M-60 ammunition sat on the ground as the aircraft lifted away. Thirteen dead men lay huddled together on a blood soaked earth beside the metal canisters.

Back at the perimeter, fifty-eight soldiers had beaten off the attack with bayonets, rifle butts, and their last rounds of ammunition. Another attack was forming up down in the valley. Gunny and the lieutenant hurried around the top of the hill distributing the precious boxes of ammunition. Several of the soldiers were wounded, but had chosen to remain with their buddies.

Steve, William Cody, and Billy Smith resembled doctors in a MASH unit. They had blood on their hands and sleeves, blood on their boots. Their fatigues were caked with blood.

"You two look like vampires." Lieutenant Overstreet snickered.

"I can't tell you how grateful I am we got John and the rest outta here."

"Same here, Steve. Them gooks woulda killed 'em for sure."

Billy voiced his opinion. "Those planes sure did help, sir. We were goners up until then."

"Skyraiders, Billy. We had 'em in tha Pacific, an' Korea."

A bugle sounded.

"Them bastards are at it again."

"Tuttle Compannny! ... Fix Bayonets!"

Steve sat down on an empty ammo canister, exhausted, blood leaking from two gunshot wounds.

"Lieutenant, if we make it through this horseshit I'm puttin' you in for a silver star."

"Gunny, I'd rather have us one of those mechanized flamethrowers."

"I'd give up my front seat in hell for a toaster my damn self."

More explosions and gunfire sounded!

The commotion rattled Private First Class Billy Smith. "Are we going to die, sir?"

Gunny pulled out a Baby Ruth and handed it to the boy. "Eat this! It'll make you bulletproof."

Fighting escalated across the front of the perimeter. Wild Bill hurried back to his men. The radio crackled. Billy, busily munching his Baby Ruth candy bar, handed the receiver to Lieutenant Overstreet,.

"Tuttle Company, are you still there?"

"We're here, what's left of us."

"This is Captain Camacho. I got three choppers I can bring in right now. The others went to the wrong LZ. They'll be here in a few minutes. Is it safe to land?"

"I'm Lieutenant Overstreet, sir. There's fighting, but you can land."

The Hueys swung around the side of the mountain, coming straight in on their skids in the center of the clearing. Gunny ran down the perimeter picking every other man. Thirty bone-weary soldiers hightailed it for the helicopters.

"Ten men to a chopper! You there! Pick up three of our dead and get onboard. Ten more! Step forward! Take three dead men with you. Last ten! Get your dead loaded, and get the hell outta here!"

The Cobra gunship had rearmed and returned, strafing the valley floor with rocket fire and a 7.62 mm minigun. The minigun made harsh buzzing sounds, firing twenty-two rounds a second.

The Hueys were almost out of sight when another call came in. "Tuttle Company. Come in, Tuttle Company."

"This is Lieutenant Overstreet."

"I'm the Sad Sack that got us lost. Can we still land?"

"Yes! Hurry, please. We got bookoo bad guys breathing down our necks."

Three choppers came down in single file settling along the base of the mountain. Wild Bill ran from man to man, bringing in the remainder of the company. Two machine gunners set up their weapons in front of the lead aircraft. Gunny deployed four riflemen in a semicircle around the gunners. The remaining soldiers loaded the rest of their dead in the aft helicopters, and lifted away.

"Okay, boys! Time to haul ass!"

An enemy machine gun opened fire at the end of the plateau. Dirt flew, tracers, a GI went down. Both M-60s cut loose. The door gunner joined chorus with the four riflemen on the ground. A swarm of enemy soldiers appeared at the crest of the hill.

"Get Onboard!"

Gunny grabbed an abandoned carbine and started blasting. The two machine gunners continued firing as they retreated through the door of the helicopter. The door gunner stopped momentarily, allowing the riflemen to climb inside.

Overstreet was helping the wounded GI toward the open door when a long burst from a Chinese machine gun cut them down. Gunny dropped his weapon, grabbed the two men by their shirt collars, dragging them toward the men reaching out to pull them inside. Rifle fire raked the side of the aircraft, striking Wild Bill in the back. Billy Smith and the door gunner hauled Gunny onboard, and the pilot soared out over the valley floor.

Master Sergeant Cody sat quietly in a pool of his own blood

with tears streaking his grimy cheeks. He was holding Lieutenant Overstreet's hand, softly reciting the 23rd Psalm, watching Steve's eyes turn the color of faded denim.

Chapter Seventeen

Sarah

What was it about growing old? Trudy wondered.

Father was fifty-one and still a handsome, athletic man. Mother was only forty-five and looked her age, even sixty. Alzheimer's was a terrible affliction. It took away one's dignity, and any chance for a normal life. Worst of all were those episodes when Mother came out of her fog, not knowing or remembering where she'd been. She always cried when she realized the extent of her illness. Father would hold her in his arms and sometimes cry himself. Then a day or so later she would drift away again.

Life was not fair, Trudy thought. For some it was, but not for the majority. She looked over at Dutch sleeping beside her on their shared blanket on top of the cabin. Dutch had turned off the engine so they could drift awhile and gaze at the stars. Sarah and Wayne were on the forward deck enjoying the night together.

Trudy viewed Dutch as one of a kind. An enigma in some ways, but totally suited for her. How ironic that they met under such unconventional circumstances. A stewardess and her smuggler! She almost laughed. Yet she wouldn't change a thing. He was her man now. And she was his lady.

She loved the way he held her when they made love, talking to her and kissing her. He was kind and gentle, afraid he might hurt her because he was so big down there. Sending her into orbit was a more descriptive term for their lovemaking. Golly! Just thinking about it made her weak and a little breathless.

Dutch stirred in his sleep. Trudy snuggled beside him and lay still. She enjoyed watching him sleep. He mumbled something, dreaming. She didn't wake him. She wanted to admire her champion in his most vulnerable state.

She laid her hand on his flat, muscular stomach. There was a scar there where the enemy soldier had cut Dutch with a knife. Thank goodness he survived. Trudy slid her arm across his stomach, gently holding him. It was all she could do to keep from placing her lips against his mouth.

What is the matter with me? Trudy smiled at her thoughts. *I've become a sex fiend. Five years is a long time to wait. That might have a little something to do with it. Oh, well, no big rush. We have the rest of our lives together.*

Dutch stirred and opened his eyes. "I must have dozed off."

"You did, but that's okay. I took advantage of you while you were sleeping."

"I knew better than to sleep on the job."

"Sleep any time you want, my darling. I'm not going anywhere without you."

"I like you saying that."

"Why do you like it?"

"Because I love you."

"Dutch, you're wonderful. You're like me. You aren't afraid to express your feelings. I love that about you."

"I dreamed about the children again."

"I'm sorry. I wish I could make it go away."

"Maybe when you and the girls start the hospital. That should help."

"Why do you say that?"

"I don't know. I enjoy thinking about it. Wayne and I will be helping poor kids."

"Maybe you'll get cured by Doctor Peters."

"Doctor, I need lots of medical attention."

"Take two kisses and call me in the morning."

"It only hurts when I laugh, Doc."

"Oh, my goodness. Your case is worse than I thought. You're going to need home care Mister Henry, with me looking after you."

"I can see us now. You'll be the blonde belle. I'll be in a wheelchair."

"A wheelchair?"

"Yes, because you take advantage when I'm sleeping."

"I can remedy that, sir. Proper exercise, lots of vitamins, avocados, and raw oysters."

"Be careful you don't kill the goose that laid the golden egg."

"That's funny. Why don't we call your penis 'Mister Gander'?"

"We'll name yours 'Miss Goosey,' I suppose."

"I like that. When we make love we'll just Goosey and Gander up a storm."

"You're absolutely an adorable mess."

"Look! A shooting star."

"There goes another one."

"Father believes they're lucky. He saw lots of them flying his night missions."

"I'm looking forward to meeting your father."

"Don't ask him about the war unless he brings it up."

"Why?"

"His group was assigned to bombing civilian targets in Germany. Places where factory workers lived. He still has bad memories about that."

"I'll be careful."

"He'll probably ask you about Vietnam."

"I won't mention the children."

"No, he would remember the civilians."

"Tell me about his hobbies. What does he like to do?"

"He works in his rose garden on Paces Ferry. He belongs to the country club there, pokers once a week with his buddies, enjoys playing golf. He has a collection of rare books. Some of them are quite valuable. He loves old movies. Father seldom goes out because he doesn't like crowds or small talk. He's a man's man."

"Being a chip off the old block, you're a woman's woman."

"Around you I blather on about sex and everything. You've corrupted me."

"I could tell this morning how much you enjoyed being corrupted."

Trudy laughed. "I love you, Mister Henry. I love you making love to me. I just love you to pieces."

He held her and kissed her, stroking Trudy's blonde hair. She clasped the back of his head with her palms, eyes open, smiling, savoring their tender kisses.

"I want us to travel and see the world. Then I want to have your children."

"You're the maestro, Miss Peach Blossom."

"I have a trust fund. Father's wealthy. After you and Wayne make your fortune I want you to quit this smuggling business. The thought of you getting hurt or maybe going to prison is too much for me."

"Boogie and I want to make a million apiece. That means two more of these trips. Will that suit you?"

"I suppose. Would you object to Sarah and I going with you on your next voyage?"

"I don't want you girls taking any chances."

"As long as it's nice like this I don't see how we'd be in any danger."

"I still think it's a bad idea. What if pirates tried to capture the boat?"

"You'd shoot them with those big guns downstairs."

"What about a typhoon?"

"I guess I'd wet my pants!"

Dutch laughed. "I guess I would too."

"Will you talk it over with Wayne, please, for me?"

"Sure. If he says okay we'll give it a try. It's getting light. Want to see if we can find some more whales?"

"Oh, yes. And when your watch is over we can go downstairs again." Trudy giggled.

Dutch ran the *Sea Queen* up to twenty-five knots and set the throttle. They were in no hurry to make port. A day's voyage lay ahead. The girls would disembark in Trujillo, then he and Boogie would begin their Gulf run back to Miami for their first big sale.

At 1024 hours Dutch noticed something in the water about a thousand yards to starboard. He swung the helm over for a closer look. At four hundred yards they could see it was a disabled craft, floating upside down in the ocean. Nearing the scene, Dutch slowed the torpedo boat to an idle. Floating in the water was the half-eaten corpse of a woman. A moment later they saw a man. He had a bullet hole in his forehead. Sharks had devoured most of him, leaving only the head and trunk area. There were two more bodies floating on the other side of the pleasure craft.

"Good God!

"Those poor souls!"

"Wayne, take the wheel. I'm going below."

Moments later Dutch came up the steps with a .50 caliber machine gun and a box of ammunition. Down he went for the second machine gun. Once both weapons were mounted on their pedestals and charged with a round in the chamber, Dutch turned and addressed the group. Sarah and Trudy had been talking back and forth the whole time with Wayne.

"This is what the captain warned us about. We can't do anything for them so let's leave them here. I'll call that number Tony gave us, and give them the coordinates. The military can sort this out. From now on we'll run with our guns loaded."

Sarah spoke. "Wouldn't something more powerful on the back of the boat be better?"

"A 20 millimeter has a range about like a .50 caliber, but it fires explosive shells. I like the way you think, Sarah."

"I'm way ahead of you, Dutch. Trudy and I want to go with you on your next trip. God gave me a gift. Sometimes I can sense things before they happen."

"Seeing this horror, you still want to come along?"

"Yes, I might be able to help you two avoid trouble before it starts."

"Hell, Sarah, what if you get killed?"

"What if you and Wayne get killed? Where does that leave me and Trudy? I can look after Trudy and myself. It's you and Wayne I'm worried about."

"This is crazy!"

"Would you rather she and I be left alone if you two knotheads get yourselves murdered in a gunfight?"

"No, but you're talking nonsense. This is serious business. You women ..."

"Stop it!" Trudy stepped between them. "I just found you, Dutch Henry. And I'm not about to lose you to a bunch of thieving criminals! We can get a bigger boat in Panama, and wrap up this business in one operation. I have a piece of real estate Grandfather left me we can use for collateral. Captain E'Manuel is willing to supply us with a cargo ship. Amanda told Sarah before we left. We were saving it for a surprise. We'll all make a fortune, or I could lose my two acres on Peachtree Road. I still have my trust fund so I'm set anyway."

Sarah smiled. "We could bring in a hundred tons, maybe more if Wayne can find the buyers."

Wayne was enthusiastic about a cargo vessel. "I know a couple of people with connections. I'll find out when we get home."

"Y'all beat anything I ever saw. I've fallen in with swashbucklers. With … with … three of the craziest people I ever met in my life … with … three of the finest, bravest, noblest … Oh, hell! Let's do it!"

Trudy hugged Dutch. "Honey, you aren't mad at me, are you?"

"I'm not mad, Trudy. I worry, though, about all of you."

"You say the sweetest things. Make that call and let's get away from this awful place."

Sarah motioned to Dutch. "There's something I want to do before we go."

Sarah said a prayer over the four unfortunates floating in the sea. The others bowed their heads in silence.

It was a Spartan farewell for the two young couples out from La Barra on their first sightseeing cruise. The pirates had raped the women, beating the men and forcing them to watch. Then shot all four of them for less than two hundred dollars in Cordoba currency, plus a few inexpensive watches and rings.

They sailed north. Dutch wanted them well away from the area in case the pirates were still around. They cruised at forty knots for two hours. Trudy fell asleep on a canvas recliner inside the cockpit. Sarah and Wayne were up forward discussing plans for their future.

Boogie turned and waved at Dutch to slow down. He and Sarah made their way back to the cockpit. Sarah was excited about something.

"Wayne and I have decided to get married before our trip to Panama. You two lovebirds care to join in the nuptials?"

Dutch grinned down at Trudy. "I think that's a marvelous idea."

Trudy smiled up at Dutch. "Yes! Let's do it in Atlanta. I want Father there, and Dutch's mother. We'll need a few days getting our ducks in a row. The Atlanta Marriott Downtown is a nice place to stay. Father attends Peachtree Christian Church just up the street. He can make the arrangements for us. We'll have a double wedding right there in the church."

Chapter Eighteen

Bait

"Cotton, this is Rico. Can you guys meet me someplace today?"

"Sure, why don't we grab a bite ta eat?"

"What're you in the mood for?"

"How 'bout Scottie's Drive In out on Collins Avenue?"

"Say one o'clock?"

"Okay. I'll round up McCoy and we'll meet cha there."

One o'clock rolled around with Rico pulling his Mercedes around back away from the crowd out front. Cottonmouth drove up a few minutes later with McCoy riding shotgun in an unmarked Ford Galaxie. Rico got out and climbed in the backseat. Cotton's .12 gauge Mister Whupass hung on plastic hangers on the rear of the front seat.

"Cotton, this shotgun suits you. You both scare the shit outta people."

"Bein' uh ugly sumbitch has its advantages."

"No offense, Cotton. I think you're quite the man."

"Let's order. I'm hungry," McCoy said.

They were almost finished with their barbecue sandwiches when Rico told them why he asked for the rendezvous. Rico didn't trust telephones because of FBI wiretaps.

"Meyer Lansky called this morning. One of his snitches thinks he knows who killed Jimmy. Two black guys at the Red Bird got drunk as skunks, laughing about how they beat a white man to death with a tire iron. He said one of them had a black eye and the other man had a busted mouth. Apparently they got more than they bargained for with Jimmy. They paid their tab with a hundred dollar bill. He followed them home and got the address. My boys checked it out."

McCoy took the piece of paper and read the names. "Looks like chicken tracks."

"They're Muslims, Malcolm X Muslims. They do hits for a thousand bucks a job."

"Got any idea who hired them?"

"I doubt if they know themselves. The way that usually works you get a phone call, you're given an assignment, then some foot soldier shows up with your money after you've capped some poor bastard."

"Any notion how to play this one?"

"I'm not sure. I know Muslims are bad news."

Cotton spoke up. "Why don't we bait 'em?"

"I don't follow you."

"Bait 'em with somethin' that makes 'em come outta their hole."

"What might that be?"

"Waste the two assholes!"

"Right on! Then maybe they'll come pay us a visit."

"Damn! You guys are crazy. I don't want my partners getting killed."

"Yeah, but if it works we'll get Mister Big. Jimmy was good people."

"I just had me uh brain wave," Cottonmouth said. "Leave 'em a note like they left on Jimmy."

"Let's lay off on that, Cotton. We don't want the newspapers involved in this."

"You're right, Willie. Rattle their cage an' keep the bastards pissed off."

"When you nuts retire, I want you as my bodyguards. Nobody would come within a block of you crazy bastards."

"Think your snitch can get us an itinerary, five or six days, maybe?"

"I'll slip Elmo a few twenties. Give me a week on this."

A call came in over the police radio. A theft had taken place at the Vizcaya Museum in South Miami. Rico said so long, and the two detectives drove away for another rendezvous with the usual misfits associated with Miami's Finest.

Chapter Nineteen

Poke 'n' Beans

The hour was half-past one on Saturday morning. Traffic had thinned to the occasional driver searching for another bottle of pop-skull or someplace to eat, affording the two detectives the cover they needed. The sweet aroma of cornbread and cabbage drifted through the neighborhood. A stark white moon hung high above Miami in a cloudless night sky.

Cottonmouth was sitting on the passenger side of the Ford Galaxie. They were in the parking lot of a dilapidated two-story clapboard building. It was the resident whorehouse, a block east of the Liberty Square ghetto known as "Poke 'n' Beans." Cottonmouth had Mister Whupass resting between his knees. Detective McCoy was driving, a Colt .45 in his lap. Elmo had done an excellent job of sleuthing the two killers.

"Here they come. Anybody lookin'?"

"Some drunk across the street just fell on his ass. You got a clear field, Cotton."

Cottonmouth waited until they were ten feet abreast of him in the trash-littered moonlight. They were dressed for the evening, the tall skinny one wearing a lavender zoot suit with a key chain down to his knees, while his friend sported a double-breasted green blazer accentuated by a brown derby hat.

"Hey, raghead!"

"Say what?"

"You brothers lose a tire tool?"

The two Negroes looked at one another. They were visibly angry at being called ragheads. The tall, skinny one slid a hand in his pants pocket.

"What chu want, white man?"

"I come to collect."

The Negro had a slight lisp from a missing front tooth. "We don't owe you shit, you dumb cracker."

"You owe me for Jimmy Four Eyes."

The tall man turned, pulling a pearl handle .32 from his pants pocket. Cottonmouth shoved Mister Whupass out the car window and fired.

BOOM!

The son of Islam did a half gainer from the impact of the lead shot before his head struck the pavement. The big man turned to run, but he was down to his last grains of sand in the hourglass of the living.

BOOM!

Big Man was blown sideways into eternity, his derby hat still on his head. Cotton stepped out of the unmarked squad car, walked over and shot Big Man in the ear. He returned to his first victim and blew his face all over the parking lot. Then he walked back to the squad car and got in.

"That'll screw up their heads. They'll think it was a Mob hit."

Detective McCoy drove slowly out of the parking lot. Their casual departure attracted no unwanted attention. The drunk lying in the grass across the street waved as they drove by. Ten minutes later they turned off 12th Avenue, east on 79th Street. The quest for those responsible for Jimmy Four Eyes and their own personal safety had begun.

Monday morning the headlines read, "Mob Hit in Liberty City, Two Gangsters Gunned Down."

Martin Luther King was assassinated April 4, 1968, turning Liberty City into a powder keg. The following weekend several of the city fathers visited Liberty Square in an attempt to quell the unrest. Negro citizens across the United States were angry and devastated over the murder of their beloved leader. Riots had broken out, costing the lives of dozens of citizens with hundreds more injured. Millions in property damage was reported across the nation.

Student war protesters trashed the Columbia campus in New York City, led by Mark Rudd, founder of Students for a Democratic Society. Labor unions and students aided by communist agitators in France forced a nationwide strike over wages. *The Heart Is a Lonely Hunter* was playing at the Miami theaters. It was a fitting backdrop for black men and women in America, many of whom believed they were disenfranchised from the American Dream.

"Have you seen those new miniskirts?" Rico asked.

"Yeah. Their ass is hanging out sayin', 'fuck me'!" McCoy responded.

"I ain't complanin'. I like purty girls."

"I do too, Cotton, but my wife hates it."

"How is your wife, Rico? Me and Cotton only met her that one time at the funeral."

"She's a sweet Italian girl. We been married since we were nineteen, great cook, great in the bedroom. Marie takes good care of me. My daughters are in high school now. Jemma is a freshman, and Crystal's a senior. I'm blessed in that respect."

In a rare moment of self-reflection, John Franklin mused about his own personal life. "My old lady is sick. She does dope."

"Maybe you should put her in one of those recovery places."

"I ought to. She might hurt herself one uh these nights."

"Cotton, I'm telling you as your partner and your friend. She's bad news. Get rid of that crazy woman before she burns the house down."

"Bill, when she's straight she's sweet as pie."

"Feeling sorry for 'er don't make it right."

"No woman ever liked me before."

Rico and McCoy stopped dead in their tracks. McCoy had never heard John utter a sad word about anything. He was always professional and hard as nails. Rico felt a wave of compassion enter the room. He tried to imagine himself in the big man's shoes."

"Is something wrong?" McCoy asked.

"Naaaw." Cottonmouth stared down at his hands. He appeared distracted, lost in another dimension.

McCoy asked again. "Is something wrong, John?"

"Well … I reckon they is."

"Tell us what's bugging you."

"Mattie has breast cancer."

"Shit! Why didn't you say something? I've been going on about what a bitch she is."

"She ain't your problem, Bill."

Rico addressed the two detectives. "We're all partners here, one way or another. Maybe we can help."

"She's worse lately. She ain't got uh lotta time left."

"At least we could make her comfortable."

"She likes bourbon whiskey, 714s, an' nose candy."

"I meant like a hospital."

"I won't put 'er there. She wants to die at home."

McCoy responded, "Daisy used to be a nurse. You care if she takes a look? It might help."

"I don't mind. Maybe get some uh that morphine stuff if she can. We got a prescription, but it's just pills. They ain't strong enough."

Rico spoke up. "I can get all the morphine you want."

"Get me four or five bottles an' a box uh needles. I'll give it to 'er myself."

The scene at the Franklin home reminded Rico of his mother's tales about Florence, Italy. There were crucifixes on the walls, a marble bust in the foyer of the Virgin Mary, and framed pictures of the crucifixion in the living room and over the dining room table. Rico had gone with Daisy and Bill McCoy to visit with Mattie. Daisy took one look at Mattie and asked the men to leave the room. A few minutes later, Daisy called them back in.

"I gave her a shot. She'll be better in a few minutes."

"How is she?"

"She should be in the hospital."

Cottonmouth sat down on the couch beside his Cajun princess.

"I never knew you had such nice friends, Johnny. Won't y'all come back an' visit us?"

McCoy was amazed at the change in Madeline. He'd seen her twice before, stoned out of her gourd. "Of course we will, young lady, whenever you want some company."

Mattie was a little groggy from the painkiller. "Johnny has spoken about you many times, Mister McCoy. He says you're friends."

"We've been friends quite a while, Mattie."

"I apologize for the house. I've been a little under the weather lately."

Rico made a suggestion. "Why don't I run out and get some food? It won't take but a few minutes."

Daisy McCoy spoke. "Good idea. I'll clean up a little while you're gone."

Bill tapped out his pipe in the ashtray on the coffee table and chimed in, "I'll help too, mama."

Cottonmouth was overjoyed at the results of the morphine. The liquid painkiller had brought back the woman he met five years ago in the Dade County Courthouse. Rico was back in thirty minutes with zuppa toscana soup, cioppino seafood stew, lasagna, peppered shrimp Alfredo, and five bottles of Italian red wine. It was a grand feast enjoyed by the three men, Madeline Xavier, and Darlene McCoy.

With the death of her son still fresh in her memory, Daisy had taken to the younger woman like the return of a prodigal daughter.

Chapter Twenty

Victoria Peters

Homecoming

Joyce Overstreet was sitting on her porch swing enjoying the quiet of the morning when a car pulled up to the curb in front of her house. She watched as two men dressed in military uniforms got out. One wore a captain's bars … Joyce bolted upright then jumped to her feet.

"Oh My God!" she screamed. "Oh, God! Nooooo!" She crumpled to the porch floor in tears, tearing at her blouse, beating her fists against the wooden decking.

The captain and the sergeant raced across the front lawn to stop Joyce from hurting herself. Captain Murphy held her in his arms while Sergeant Smith went inside for a glass of water. Joyce slapped the glass out of his hand, cursing the men.

Next door, Katherine heard the commotion. When she saw what was happening she telephoned for an ambulance. The paramedics were there in minutes. The scene was one they had witnessed several times that February. Another family member grief-stricken over the death a loved one, killed in Vietnam. Joyce was given a sedative. The Army men helped Katherine get Joyce next door to her house.

Captain Murphy gave Katherine a brief rundown on what happened. He told her that her husband had been wounded in the fighting, but that John Parker would recover. He was in a hospital in Da Nang. The captain promised Katherine he would telephone her as soon as he knew the details regarding Steve's body, and any additional information he received about Lieutenant Parker.

Katherine telephoned her pharmacy, explaining the situation. The pharmacist knew Katherine, telling her he would send something over right away. The pills arrived the same time as Shannon and Roger were pulling up the driveway. Roger broke down in tears. Katherine gave Roger one of the tablets.

Two days later Captain Murphy called, informing Katherine of the arrival of Steve's body at the Homestead Air Force Base the following Saturday. Thirteen additional bodies were coming home with Steve. John Parker was still in the hospital with a badly damaged arm.

Then the media got wind of all the casualties. It was in all the newspapers and on television. Families were devastated, grieving the deaths of their sons and loved ones. Citizens became angry. The Tet Offensive had turned the Vietnam War upside down. People blamed the president, the war protesters, the military, and General Westmoreland.

March 31, 1968: President Johnson stated he would not seek a second term as president of their United States.

"You know any uh them soldiers got killed?"
"Remember that kid at the funeral that Frankie had trouble with?"
"Sorta."
"He had his girlfriend with him, red hair, big knockers."
"Yeah, I remember her."
"Her old man, John Parker, got shot. I don't know anybody else."
"I remember now. How'd you know that?"

"The girl's name is Shannon Parker. I read it in the newspaper."

"Mattie read a lot 'fore she got sick."

"How is Mattie?"

"Kinda puny, but Rico's morphine helps 'er. I don't let 'er hurt no more."

"Ya know, Cotton. Rico's a standup guy. I always thought he was just another punk mobster, but I was wrong about him. He's a good man to have in your corner, especially with this Three Feathers murder."

"Heard anything yet?"

"Not yet. He's working on it. We'd get nailed by our guys."

"I'd grab Mattie an' skip town 'fore I'd go to jail."

"He did say there was a load of grass come up the Miami River last night."

"How'd he know?"

"He's got the unions in his pocket. One of them told him."

"Was it Colombians?"

"No, two white guys in a PT boat."

"Half the crowd in Miami is dealin' weed."

"Yeah, it's pretty funny. That dude with all the restaurants, and that other one with his hotels. They're about as straight as those Tin Pans over on Biscayne Boulevard."

John and Bill chuckled.

"Marijuana's okay. Nose candy an' that other shit I don't like."

"Rico doesn't like it either. But he takes his orders from that Sicilian zip."

"They's always some shit ass up top."

"Rico gave me the name on the boat. We should check it out."

"Okay. Mattie said six o'clock. She's fixin' crawdaddy salad. Good eatin'! Rico's wife is fixin' spaghetti."

"Daisy's bringing her tomato pudding dish. I'll get the wine if you'll rustle up some Jack Daniels.

"I owe Rico for gettin' me that morphine. Mattie done quit them other drugs."

"Good. I was wrong about Madeline. I like your lady friend."

Second Lieutenant Steven Overstreet was recommended for the Distinguished Service Cross by his division commander before his body departed Vietnam. A gravesite in the City of Miami Cemetery was donated in Steve's honor by the mayor and the city council. Various notables buried there included several American pioneers, Civil War veterans, Julia Tuttle, and William Burdine. Lieutenant Overstreet was laid to rest with full military honors wearing his Army dress uniform.

Homecoming was not what Katherine expected. Steve Overstreet was a war hero, dead and buried. Joyce and Roger were devastated. Shannon had absorbed the unhappiness within the two households, losing seven pounds in a month. Not the least of which, John had returned home a different person. Most nights he cried out in his sleep, struggling against his bed covers. Katherine prepared his favorite meals, engaged him in the bedroom, took him to church on Sundays, but still he could hear the gunfire, the explosions, and the terrible screaming.

John Parker remained quiet and withdrawn, sometimes sitting for hours on the front porch staring into space. He was nice to the children, made idle conversation with Katherine, but John was never completely there. Katherine sensed correctly that he was still in the jungles of Vietnam. That afternoon she purchased a bottle of Sapphire gin, sending Shannon next door to spend the night with Joyce and Roger. In the middle of their second cocktail, Katherine asked John a question.

"Do you feel guilty because you're still alive, and Steve is dead?"

John crushed out his cigarette, and took a sip of his drink. He appeared confused by the question.

Katherine moved closer on the couch, taking hold of his hand, and asked again, "Do you wish it were you instead of Steve?"

John looked at his wife, as though seeing her for the first time. "Yes, I do," he answered.

"Can you tell me why?"

John lit another cigarette, and stared away into the distance.

"I love you, sweetheart. Please tell me."

"I failed the men. I let Steve down. And I failed Gunny."

"Being alive doesn't make you a failure. Sergeant Cody told me so over the telephone. He said you would be okay after you learned to forgive yourself for being alive. He said you were brave, and he was proud of you. I'm proud of you too, John. We all are, Joyce and Roger."

For the first time, she had his full attention. "Gunny said that?"

"Yes, he did. He said you were a brave soldier. He said Steve was too. He said Steve saved a lot of lives. I asked Mister Cody to come visit us when he got back from overseas."

"Did he say he would?"

"He said yes, he would come. He asked me to wish you a quick recovery, and to remind you of the time the three of you got drunk in something called a slop chute. What's that?"

"A slop chute is a military bar where soldiers hang out and drink. We … Gunny said that?"

"Yes, honey. Gunny thinks the world of you. He told me he recommended you for another medal. I forget now what he called it."

"Gunny said that … about me and Steve … I wish Steve was …"

John began to cry. Softly at first then pained and mournful sobbing, tears filling his eyes and streaming down his cheeks. Katherine held his head against her breasts, rocking him gently, mascara streaking her own pale cheeks. They sat together like that for a long time. Finally she led him back to the bedroom, undressed John, and tucked him into bed. Katherine fixed herself another drink, returned to the bedroom, and took a seat beside a window. She sat there most of the night watching her man sleep. It was the first undisturbed sleep John had experienced since coming home with a crippled arm.

Saturday morning.

Katherine got up to see who was knocking on her front door. John was sitting on the couch reading *The Miami Herald*. "Ebb Tide" by the Platters was playing on the phonograph. Two men stood outside, a big man and another fellow about six feet tall. The shorter of the two was well tanned, almost bronze, with sun-bleached hair and eyebrows. The bronze one looked like … Katherine pulled the door open.

"Boogie Compton!"

"You must be the famous Katherine Parker, married to that no-good John Parker."

"Come in! Come in!"

John rose to his feet, a big grin on his face. "Wayne! Dutch! Am I glad to see you guys."

The men hesitated when they saw how much weight John had lost.

"Damn, man. We heard you'd been hurt."

"I'm okay. Tell us about your adventure. Meet any exotic dancing girls?"

"We met some girls, all right. We're getting married!"

"This calls for a celebration! Oh! Excuse me. Kat, this is Dutch Henry. Dutch, my lovely wife, Katherine."

Dutch took her hand and smiled. "You're everything John said you were. I'm proud to meet you."

Katherine smiled at John. "He does have big hands and big feet."

"Now cut that out."

They all laughed.

John made his way toward the kitchen. "I'll fix us some drinks. Then I want to hear all about this marriage business."

Fifty-five thousand dollars in hundred dollar bills lay piled on the coffee table in front of Katherine and John. Boogie had stacked them there from a leather briefcase he carried with him. He and Dutch chuckled at the reaction from the couple.

Katherine clasped her hands to her cheeks, her mouth wide open. "Oh, my goodness!" she exclaimed. "Look at that."

John just smiled, shaking his head in amazement. "Did you guys have any trouble?"

"We didn't, but we came across four dead bodies in the ocean. They'd been killed by pirates."

Katherine stared at Dutch. "That's awful! Did you see them?"

"No, they were gone. We radioed back to Panama. They took care of it."

John spoke, concerned for his two friends. "You never mentioned pirates."

"We didn't know. A captain in Panama told us."

"Do you plan on going back?"

"Sarah got us in with the military. They have a cargo ship they've offered to let us borrow. There's so much money involved we have to go back. We're talking millions here, John."

"Do you know how to operate one of those things?"

"A small one shouldn't be much trouble. We'll figure it out when we get there."

Wayne posed a question for Katherine and John. "We have more than enough money for expenses and whatnot, but I said I would cut you in as partners our next trip. Do you want to chance it again?"

Katherine looked at John and John nodded.

Katherine spoke. "Those pirates … what about them?"

Dutch responded. "We know they're out there. Nobody knows how many. My guess is four or five boats. The ship is armed. Captain E'Manuel confirmed that. We can radio Panama if we need help. There is some danger, but with their military protecting us I don't believe any half-baked pirates are a serious threat."

"Who's going with you?"

Boogie answered, "Trudy, Dutch, Sarah, and myself."

John spoke up. "I'd like some time for Kat and I to think it over. I haven't gone back to work yet. Can we let you know at the wedding?"

"Sure. We'll see you guys in Atlanta. Trudy's father is throwing a big party afterwards."

The double wedding at Peachtree Christian Church was a memorable affair. More than a hundred people were in attendance, including friends of Mister Peters, Dutch's mother, TWA pilots and stewardesses, and Kat and John, accompanied by Shannon, Roger, and Roger's mother, Joyce. The wedding march began and both couples proceeded down the aisle. Vows were exchanged. They kissed and embraced. Tears were shed by friends and newlyweds alike. All the pretty flowers amid the magnificent architecture gave rise to a sense of well-being and hope for a brighter tomorrow.

"Dutch, looks like I'll have to call you 'son' from now on."

"I'm proud to be a member of your family, Mister Peters."

"Sometime I'd like for us to sit down and you to tell me about Vietnam. That's a curious war we're fighting over there. Nothing like we fought in '43."

"Whenever you have the time, sir."

Trudy spoke softly. "Isn't he something, Father?"

"Yes Trudy, you've chosen wisely."

"I feel blessed by your wonderful daughter."

"She can be a handful at times, but I'm sure you'll manage well together."

Wayne's mother, Mildred Henry, joined the conversation. "Besides when I married your father and when you were born, this is the happiest day of my life. Thank you, Mister Peters. Thank you for this lovely reception."

"Please call me Winston. May I escort you to the bar for some refreshment, Mildred?"

"Why yes, Winston. I'd like that."

Wayne and Sarah were across the room sitting with John and Katherine at a table with Joyce Overstreet. Shannon and Roger were dancing to the music of the orchestra. So were Dutch and Trudy. The soft music reminded Joyce of Steve, filling her with feelings of melancholy, but she was thankful to be with her son and their friends away from Miami. Atlanta had a Southern charm about it that Joyce found comforting.

"I finally nailed you, Bilge Rat."

"You did, didn't you, Love Muffin. I'm a happy bilge rat."

John Parker was beginning to emerge from his shell. The church, the wedding, and Mister Peters' kind words had made him more aware of the importance of one's family. Steve was with God now. John was still a citizen of earth. He was coming to realize how much his family loved him, and how they worried about him. But always, Steve was there kneeling beside him at the base of the mountain.

Katherine noticed his faraway look and reached for his hand. "Honey, are you all right?"

"I was just thinking. I'm fine now. Joyce, are you feeling better today?"

"I'm glad I came. It's still difficult, but I believe Steve is out there someplace watching over me. That doesn't sound crazy, does it?"

Sarah got up, moved around the table, and sat down beside Joyce. Sarah took Joyce's hands in hers. The force was strong and gentle. The current flowed into Sarah.

"Joyce, you're one of the sanest people in this room ... you're a Mature Soul ... intuitive and wise ... you are evolving ... your search for spiritual purity is nearing the end of a long journey."

Joyce listened while Sarah concentrated, her eyes closed. Thirty seconds ticked by before Sarah said another word. Wayne and the others watched, fascinated.

"Steve's lineage dates back thousands of years … he's an Old Soul … Steve no longer requires the physical plane … Roger and Shannon will make you proud … I sense a bright future for two little grandchildren … love will find you again." Sarah opened her eyes as though waking from a dream.

Joyce had tears in her eyes. "Thank you, Sarah. You're a remarkable young lady."

"Oh, I'll do … right, Boogie?"

"The best soul in town, besides you, Joyce."

They all laughed.

Joyce experienced a sensation of emotional peace for the first time since the funeral.

A short while later John whispered in Wayne's ear, "We'd like to invest $20,000 if that's all right with you and Dutch."

"That's great, John. We'll be leaving for Panama right after the honeymoon."

Winston Peters' home on West Paces Ferry resembled the man himself: Victorian architecture, cathedral ceilings, rough-hewn beams, pegged flooring, leaded glass windows, arched doorways, and mahogany paneling, augmented by a stacked stone fireplace connecting the dining room with a stainless steel kitchen. The newlyweds, Mildred, Joyce and the kids, and John and Katherine Parker were there for Sunday dinner.

"'May you live in interesting times' is thought to be a Chinese curse attributed to Confucius. That's not the case. It was first spoken by Frederic Coudert in 1939 at the opening proceedings of the Academy of Political Science. He spoke about 'an interesting age.' Robert Kennedy used the phrase incorrectly with his Cape Town speech in 1966, referring to the Vietnam War.

"I propose a toast of good fortune for every person in this room. May you live in an interesting age."

"Well done, Father!"

"What a lovely thing to say. Thank you, Winston."

John rose from his chair at the table. "I wish to propose a toast in keeping with Winston's service to his country and Great Britain. May Dame Fortune ever smile on you, but never her daughter, Miss Fortune."

"Good one, John."

Joyce Overstreet, unaccustomed to speaking in front of a group, stood up. "I want to say something. I don't believe any of this is a coincidence. I believe we are here for some reason. I don't know what it is, but I'm thankful to be a part of it. Here's to all of you for being who you are. Thank you so much for inviting me and my son."

"Mom, that was cool."

Shannon lifted her glass of champagne. "To Roger Overstreet! May he hurry up and marry me!"

That brought the house down. Mister Parker laughed so hard he spilled his cocktail.

Roger scratched his head, rolling his eyes. Then he responded to Shannon's playful remark. "Men should never have given females the right to vote!"

More laughter …

Winston Parker addressed the gathering. "This is the first time there's been so much laughter in my home since my wife became ill. I wish she were here tonight, but Victoria's not well. Maybe next time she'll join us. Perhaps we are here for a reason, Joyce. I would like to believe that."

"It feels right," Sarah said. "Maybe we are destined to serve together for some common good."

Wayne turned to Sarah. "I like that, Sarah."

"I like you, Pumpkin."

It was a grand evening filled with laughter and good vibrations. And tasty food catered by Mary Mac's Tea Room over on Ponce de Leon. John thought again about Steve and Gunny the night they got drunk before the Tet Offensive. Joyce recalled making love to Steve the morning he left for Vietnam. Dutch envisioned the Vietnamese children playing beneath the bridge along the riverbank. Each in their own way was slowly coming to terms with their personal tragedies.

Chapter Twenty-One

The Contract

"I know it sounds nuts," Rico said, "but word on the street has it there's a contract out on two detectives. That has to be you two mugs. I don't know for what reason, but be careful out there. Vincent Alo heard it in the Greek's gambling house. They don't know who said it, where it came from, nothin'! I'm batting zero out here, but I've got my crew on the streets with their ears to the pavement. I should know in a day or two if it's for real or not."

Detective McCoy hung up the pay phone.

Detective Franklin asked his partner a question. "So … we gotta put them damn vests on again?"

"I guess we better. This heat is something else."

"Let's hit Tobacco Road an' get us uh cold one."

A blonde hooker wearing a pink bustier and pink miniskirt, black mesh hose with matching fuck-me pumps, and two female impersonators decked out in similar attire were sitting at the counter when McCoy and Cottonmouth walked in the back door.

Willie "Tomatoes" Tigerella was sitting in the far corner nursing a sloe gin fizz. Sitting with him was Lourdes, a midget prostitute who made her living servicing the downtown business crowd. In the other corner sat a criminal court judge, two well-connected drug dealers, and a half dozen drug enforcement officers. It was early. The street people, whores, gamblers, pimps, and the usual menagerie of rubbernecks hadn't arrived yet.

"I wonder why we keep coming here."

"Tha Road is uh distraction from our looney-tune jobs as flatfoots."

"Rico likes the place. He's not like us."

"Yes, he is, Bill. He deals with scumbags an' assholes same as we do. We're more alike than we are different. This place is our country club. Tha regulars are interestin' people."

"You shoulda been a damn shrink."

"Listenin' to people's shit all day would drive me crazy. I don't see how they do it."

"Maybe they're crazy to begin with. Like the rest of us."

A transvestite waiter brought their Pabst Blue Ribbons. He had a black eye and a split upper lip. Cotton gave him a five dollar bill and told him to keep the change.

"Why'd you give him three dollars and fifty cents?"

"Poor bastard needs a hand. Somebody done kicked 'is ass for 'im."

"How do you think we should handle this contract business?"

"It'd make more sense if we knew where it's comin' from."

"If Rico can't give us a name, we better think of something and pretty damn soon."

"They'll try an' lure us out someplace. That's the usual way."

"Which means … we'll be getting bogus calls at the station house."

"We can still make our rounds. Just don't drive up to the address no more."

"We better get some rifles. Mister Whupass ain't got much juice past a hundred feet."

"A 30.06 oughta do it."

"Finish your beer. Let's go check out that gun shop over on Miami Gardens."

A call came in three days later about a robbery in progress at the clubhouse in the Ollie Trout Trailer Park. Ollie Trout was a deluxe trailer park with individual tourist cabins where renters could park their automobiles right beside their cabins. It featured a pool, tables and umbrellas, a dance floor, plus an elaborate clubhouse with an outdoor bar, which made for tea dances and vacation entertainment. Ollie Trout was part of their beat.

Cottonmouth and McCoy parked down 107th Street, well away from the main entrance.

"Music's goin' full tilt. I don't hear nothin' funny."

"Grab the rifles. Let's go around back."

A few minutes later they came up behind the clubhouse. People were talking and dancing out front as if nothing was wrong. They waited in the shadows of a tall palm tree, watching and listening.

"Bill! Up there!"

A man had stood up on the roof of the clubhouse, peering out toward the entranceway. Then he crouched down out of sight.

"Looks like that contract's legit, all right."

"Let's take this bird alive. He got up there some way. You see a ladder?"

"Over there. He went up them steps."

Cotton and McCoy crept up the stairs with their rifles pointed toward the upper banister. A black man and a white man were crouched on the forward edge of a widow's walk. Both men appeared to be in their middle twenties. The white man wore a long ponytail. The black man had a shaved head.

"You boys lookin' for somethin'?"

The black man whirled, a machine pistol in his hands. Cotton and

McCoy both fired just as the Negro pulled the trigger. He was dead when he hit the wooden deck. McCoy's bulletproof vest saved him from four 9 mm slugs. A fifth 9 mm tore his britches, slicing a bloody groove along his inner thigh. The white man dropped his carbine, and raised his hands in the air.

"Don't shoot, mister. I give up."

"Who sent you?"

"Mister, I don't know. We got our instructions on the phone."

"I'll say this one more time, dirtbag. Who sent you?"

"I swear, Mister. I don't know. We got a package in the mail with pictures an' stuff."

"Cottonmouth … kill that son of a bitch!"

"Oh, God, sir … please … I don't know anything."

Cotton chambered another round, placing his rifle against the man's crotch. The man stared in horror at John's threatening persona, mesmerized by his scar and white birthmark.

"I think I'll blow 'is nuts off first."

The white man sagged to his knees beside his dead companion, leaned over, tenderly closing the black man's eyes with his fingertips, choking on his own misery and fear of dying.

"Please, don't … wait … I don't know … Oh, God … Please don't hurt me."

"A kneecap might be better. Then I'll do 'im."

"Bleed the bastard, Cotton."

Cottonmouth poked the man's knee with the blue muzzle of the Winchester … eggs and bacon splashed onto the walkway.

"Looks like Ponytail done lost his vittles."

"That nigger was the hitter. This fruitcake's his bitch. Cuff him!"

"Ya know somethin', Bill? There for a few minutes … I thought you was serious."

Chapter Twenty-Two

Front: Rico & Bootnose. Back: Eddie Nails & Fat Mike.

Broken Hearts

Rico was speaking. "I heard about Ollie Trout. That's a stupid place for an ambush."

"Makes sense when ya think about it. Who would expect a hit there?"

"You make a good point, Cotton. Listen, we got a problem."

"What's that?"

"The Feds are down here nosing around all over the place."

"You think they're after me an' Bill?"

"I don't think so. They're running around like squirrels so something's up. I don't know what it is. I haven't been able to get a handle on that contract, either."

"What about you an' the crew?"

"The Department of Justice is on Pennsylvania Avenue in Washington, DC. That's where Hoover runs his FBI from. That bastard bugs everything, including me. Well, we just pulled off the bug of the century. We got J Edgar's phone line tapped."

"No shit!"

"That's how we know he's not on our case. And we haven't heard a peep about you and Bill. A couple of times he's mentioned 'The Peacock.' That's the name we got from Lansky. Maybe this Peacock person is tied in with Jimmy's murder. Maybe he's the one after you fellas."

"Don't ring no bells. Keep lookin'. I'll go back in records at the station house."

"I asked one of my boys to pick up something special for you."

"Wha' cha got, Rico?"

"Phosphorus grenades."

"Honey, don't forget. We're having dinner tonight with John and Mattie. Pick up two bottles of that good wine Mattie and I like so much. Madeline's preparing a special dinner for us."

"Sure thing, Daisy. I'll be home around five-thirty."

Bill McCoy and John Franklin spent the afternoon going through the station house records. Bill took the Ts and John took the Ps. The records were old and dusty, packed in cardboard containers in a crowded storage room in back of the building.

"I ain't found nothin' but dead roaches in these damn boxes."

"That Peacock son of a bitch ain't in here."

"I'm gonna blow 'is ass clean to hell when we catch 'im!"

"Yeah, if he don't blow ours there first."

Madeline was pale and even more emaciated, but she was able to function around the house a few hours a day. Tonight she had prepared jambalaya for her guests, with dirty rice and cornbread dressing. John and Bill were having a Jack Daniels out in the living room before dinner. Mattie and Daisy were enjoying their chardonnay, planning a shopping trip downtown Saturday morning. Mattie needed a smaller dress size because of all the weight she'd lost. Bill had slipped off his shoes and was smoking his pipe when he remembered the police cruiser he left parked beside the curb.

"I better pull up the driveway or some kid might soap the windows again."

"You've got your shoes off, dear. I'll move the car." Daisy picked up the car keys and walked out the front door.

Moments later … *BOOOOM!*

Windows in the front of the house burst into the living room. The lights went out. Pieces of the patrol car slammed against the side of the building and on top of the roof.

Mattie, her face bleeding from flying glass, stared down in shock at William McCoy. Bill was bloody and incoherent, buried beneath an antique bookcase. Cottonmouth knew instantly what had happened. He dashed into the bedroom, then out the front door with his .12 gauge riot gun. The roof of the squad car was blown completely off, lodged in an oak tree. What was left of the automobile was in flames. Bits and pieces littered the roadway. Daisy was blasted through the roof, landing thirty feet from the vehicle. Broken and badly burned, Darlene McCoy was dead.

Cottonmouth used the telephone across the street to call Rico, then rushed back to attend to Mattie and William. Mattie was carried into a bedroom. A cold washcloth revived William. He struggled with John to go to his wife, cursing John, but Cotton held fast, refusing to let go.

"Don't see 'er like that, Bill. Please! Remember Daisy the way she was."

William broke down and cried. Cottonmouth held his partner in his arms.

A fire engine wailed in the distance, then an ambulance. A patrol car pulled up. All the neighbors were out in their yards or on the sidewalk. Several minutes later Rico pulled in.

Mattie wept brokenly, led by John to Rico's automobile. William had the vacant stare of a man struck a mortal blow. McCoy blamed himself for Daisy's death. Rico had tears in his eyes over the mangled body in the middle of the street.

Take 'em an' go, Rico. Get outta here."

"We'll be at my place, John. Come stay with me when you're done."

Twelve days later Madeline Xavier passed away in her sleep. Her physician told John she just gave up after Daisy died. The two detectives had lost their women to an unknown force which threatened to destroy both of them. The Miami Police Department had established no leads in the murder case. A meeting was held the following Monday morning at Tobacco Road. Rico brought his Mafia lieutenants with him. The doors were closed and locked.

"Boys, this is Cottonmouth, and Bill McCoy. Bill, Cotton, this is Eddie Nails, Bootnose, Fat Mike, and Harry the Hoop. Bootnose was a boxer back in the day. He knew Jimmy Four Eyes. He looks after our night trade for us. Eddie served two years in Korea with Uncle Sam. Eddie handles the unions, trucking, construction, and the docks. He got those pineapples for you. Fat Mike is a mathematical genius, perfect memory, butter and eggs, gambling, finances. Harry is our enforcer.

"McCoy and his partner are Miami Police Detectives. You know that. Treat them like men of honor. They're important to the organization. Some asshole is trying to kill them. Your job is to keep them alive. The only clue I have is a name Meyer Lansky gave me, 'The Peacock.' Find this Peacock, and it's worth ten grand to you."

Fat Mike asked the first question. "Why does this Peacock want these guys knocked off?"

"I don't know. The Colombians might be involved, but I can't make a connection there. I think the same person killed Four Eyes. There's an open contract out on Franklin and McCoy. We have to stop that and eliminate the source."

Eddie spoke up. "You think it's something to do with those FBI dicks? They were all over the waterfront and South Beach last weekend. I'll ask my dock bosses to nose around."

"It could be. I wondered about that."

Fat Mike spoke again. "Peacock must really be pissed to go after two coppers. That's plain crazy."

"They busted a big drug shipment a while back, killed five uh those Bogotá jerk-offs. I think it ties in, but the Colombians don't appear to be the ones behind the contract."

Bootnose offered his opinion. "Men spill their guts around pussy. I'll ask my girls to keep their ears open."

Harry pulled a .455 Webley from his shoulder holster, and placed it on the table. "Gun weighs uh ton. I'll get in touch wi' da beach owners. All dos guests comin' an' goin' might turn up dis Peacock. Rico, why don't you check wi' da gang a' da courthouse? Dos guys respect you."

"Good suggestion, Harry. I'll do that."

Curiosity got the best of Cottonmouth. He turned to the Italian killer at the end of the table. "Why do they call you 'Hoop'?"

"Gas starts buildin' inside a dead man, methane, CO2, hydrogen. Dem gases brings a corpse back to da surface. I put barrel hoops 'round a stiff. Chained together an' weighted proper, none uh my stiffs ever come up again."

Chapter Twenty-Three

Amanda Stone

Honeymoon

Sarah and Trudy were as happy as a pair of Louisiana mud ducks nesting on the bayou. Wayne and Dutch had married them, thereby making the stewardesses "honest women." At least that's what Boogie said before Sarah threw a biscuit at him over the breakfast table in the Dorchester of London. Sarah hit Trudy by mistake, but they had great fun together on their British honeymoon.

They visited the Tower of London where they saw the crown jewels, and the courtyard with its huge black crows where Anne Boleyn was beheaded. The Royal Palace, St Paul's Cathedral, Regency Park, plus a dozen other places in history.

A tour guide escorted them around Bath so Wayne could see where his father was born. His great-grandmother's grave was located in Bath Abbey Cemetery. His grandmother and grandfather were there. The great-grandfather was thought to have been lost at Waterloo fighting Napoleon. They visited the Roman baths, Stonehenge, and

King Arthur's legendary Badon Hill. Boogie Compton was proud of his English heritage. Sarah Compton was proud of her American husband.

The ninety-foot patrol boat, *Isabella*, met them twelve miles north of Old Bess in the Archipelago de Bocas del Toro. *Isabella's* captain escorted them through the strait of Boca del Drago which ran parallel with Colon Island. The strait was bound on either side by beautiful white beaches, lush with palm trees and tropical vegetation. The *Sea Queen* emerged in Almirante Bay, an inland sea of crystal blue waters with dozens of picturesque islands. Brown boobies enjoyed protected haven there on the Isla de Los Pajaros. Anchored before the port city of Boca del Toro, they saw the craft their hopes and dreams had rested upon ever since their decision to sail the vessel back to Florida.

"That's it?"

"We're going to sea in that … thing?"

Wayne and Dutch were angry, and not a little disappointed. It wasn't until they got within a few yards that they began to notice a difference. The cargo vessel was constructed to look old. Captain E'Manuel and Amanda Stone were waiting topside to greet them.

"Welcome aboard! How do you like my little ship?"

"You sure had us fooled. We thought it was an old rust bucket."

"Amanda informed me the four of you were married in Atlanta. Congratulations, my friends. Come! Amanda and I have a little surprise for you."

Amanda led the way. Sarah and Trudy were eager to know all about her relationship with the handsome and dashing captain. How was their courtship progressing? Had they discussed marriage? Was she going to remain with the airlines? Once they were seated Amanda tapped her wine glass for attention.

"Ladies and gentlemen, welcome aboard! For your dining pleasure today we have citrus salmon with watercress salad, broiled lobster tails, coleslaw with corn on the cob, and to wash it all down the delicious and ever-popular Lafite Rothschild. And for dessert we have something extra special … Tony and I are engaged to be married!"

Hoots and hollers! Tony slipped the ring from his pocket and placed it on Amanda's finger. Trudy and Sarah hugged Amanda. Wayne and Dutch were on their feet, shaking Tony's hand. Sarah filled their wineglasses, proposing a toast.

"To Amanda and Tony … long life and great happiness."

Amanda took a sip then raised her glass of champagne. "To us … the Six Musketeers."

They dined and drank, laughing and telling tales on one another. It was a memorable time for everyone. Amanda glowed with happiness. As the evening wore on Captain E'Manuel became more serious.

"This was a coal burner we converted into a diesel. *Gris Fantasmo* is a third the length of a Liberty Ship with a displacement of 4,154 tons. She has a 2,200 horsepower motor, dual rudders, a chromium drive shaft, and is fully operational from the bridge. She carries enough oil to go to Miami and back without refueling. Her best feature is speed. She can turn twenty-four knots. Cruising speed is fifteen knots. She has steel plating in her engine room, and a reinforced bow to deal with any pirates you might encounter."

Boogie was impressed. "Sounds like a destroyer without the guns."

"She has guns. Underneath those tarpaulins on both sides of the bridge you'll find twin .50 calibers. On her foredeck she has a 20 mm Oerlikon cannon. You also have a powerful two-way radio if you find yourselves in a situation. Those drooping antennas up top are just for show. Everything is held together with rivets and steel cables."

"Is it safe to leave the *Sea Queen* here?"

"My men will see to it no one disturbs your boat. Now if you will permit, Amanda and I would like to escort you into del Toro tonight after you've rested from your journey. There's a cantina there with an excellent floor show and dancing."

Sarah asked Tony where he got the name *Gray Ghost*.

"I read about your Civil War when I attended school in America. The South was the nation's breadbasket, yet they were taxed to excess. The North was more industrial, but paid less in taxes. In other words, those with the less influence in government were at the disadvantage. It is the same with every country.

"I especially enjoyed the exploits of your John Mosby, the *Gray Ghost* of the Confederacy. He rose from the ranks of private to that of a full army colonel, surviving the war and going on to serve with President Grant. May the *Gris Fantasmo* enjoy the same success as your elusive Colonel Mosby."

That night they remained onboard the *Gray Ghost* and all the next day. Captain E'Manuel and his soldiers acquainted the four adventurers with the bridge, navigational and radio equipment, the engine room and fuel bunkers, plus keeping the cargo hatches secure and hoisting and lowering the anchor. Sarah, Wayne, and Trudy were taught how to load and fire the machine guns. Dutch was familiar with the .50 caliber from his tour of duty in Vietnam. He devoted his attentions to the 20 millimeter Oerlikon. It was decided that Boogie would operate the ship if they encountered trouble.

Friday morning, the same gunboat escorted them back out Boca del Drago into the open sea. Five miles beyond the strait the four waved goodbye to the *Isabella*. Wayne set the throttle at fifteen knots, running parallel with the Panamanian coastline.

"Two hundred and nine tons! Do you have any idea how much money we're going to make?"

"Will it fill a breadbox?"

"About twelve million bucks! We'll have a million and a half apiece after Tony gets his share."

Sarah hugged Wayne. "I'm so happy you made me an honest woman."

Wayne laughed. "Where do you want to spend your second honeymoon?"

"Tahiti! New Zealand! China! All of them!"

"Sounds swell. Hey, Dutch, did you hear what those soldiers called our stuff?"

"You mean square groupers?"

"That's a funny name for a bale of grass."

"I'll remember that when I'm on the Rivera. Trudy and I been talking about spending some time in Australia, traveling the Far East, seeing Europe. You gonna keep the boat dock?"

"Yes. I can't leave Bubba-J. He's family now."

They journeyed on another six hours, Boogie always keeping them in sight of land. He was being careful until he mastered a feel for the ship. The 134-foot *Gray Ghost* was slower than the 78-foot *Sea Queen* but very steady, slicing through the waves with the nautical grace of a seafaring Madonna. A rain squall blew in from the ocean. The downpour lasted twenty minutes, lashing the decks of the *Ghost* and the glass windowpanes on her bridge. A rainbow appeared.

No one noticed a white speedboat following in their wake five miles behind the laden vessel.

Chapter Twenty-Four

A Viable Problem

It rained the day of Madeline Xavier's funeral at the parish of St. Rose of Lima. Mirror Lake across 105th Street reminded Cottonmouth of all the tears shed over Mattie and Daisy. Darlene McCoy had been laid to rest eleven days earlier.

Enrico Basilio's mobsters had become a permanent fixture in the lives of Bill McCoy and John Franklin. They were always watching from a doorway, an automobile, or behind a window curtain. Anyone suspicious was confronted and questioned. The Miami Police Department had no idea their celebrated detectives were being protected by the Florida Mob.

"You think we'll ever find who planted that damn bomb?"

"Rico said they got a few leads, but nothin' solid."

"They ain't got shit around here. We might as well be working for the Post Office."

"Let's get us a beer. They'll call on the radio if somethin' turns up."

"Is your shotgun in the car?"

"Yeah, I just got me another box uh shells."

They drove to Tobacco Road and parked in back.

A Ford pickup pulled in behind them on the south side beneath the trees. The driver watched as they entered the rear door. He walked across the gravel parking lot, taking a seat on one of the lawn chairs beside the barbecue cooker.

"Give us two Schlitz. Make sure they're ice cold."

The waitress was a tall, slender brunette with perky tits and a nice ass. She smiled for McCoy but he paid her no mind. Not an hour had gone by that he didn't think about Daisy lying dead on the pavement. Cotton could tell Bill was wound tighter than Dick's hatband. Then he thought about Mattie curled up in a fetal position the morning he found her. Maybe a few beers would do them some good.

"You gonna sell your place?"

"I been thinking about it."

"You can stay with me. Two of us together would make a harder target."

"I been thinkin' about that too."

"We could get us one a them yard alarms that warns you 'fore they get to the door."

"That's a good idea. We'd be waiting for the bastards."

Hot Pants brought their beers, slipping McCoy a note with her name and phone number.

"When Daisy was alive women never gave me a second look. Now they seem to know I'm not married anymore. Weird!"

"Women are strange creatures. I never did figure Mattie out, but she liked me in spite uh my looks."

"You have a good heart, Cotton. It's just hard to see behind that shotgun."

Cotton chuckled. "We done some damage out there. That's for sure."

"I still laugh when I think about you slamming that moron against the wall in the glove factory. You damn near killed him."

"Fuck him! He wouldn't give us a job."

McCoy laughed. It was the first time he actually laughed since the bombing. Cotton grinned at his own joke. The somber mood was beginning to lift.

"I wish Rico would find that sumbitch. I'd stick my shotgun up his ass an' blow 'is nuts in a tree."

"We live in strange times, Cotton. A redneck shot King. Some fucking A-rab killed Bobby. A crazy bitch shot Warhol. The Russians are in Czechoslovakia. And the Democrats in Chicago look like a three-ring circus from God knows where. The world is a fucking lunatic asylum!"

"You said it, Bill. An' Vietnam's goin' to hell like ever thing else. Our vests still in the trunk?"

"Yeah, we oughta get some new ones. Ours are falling apart."

"We got shot too many times!"

They laughed.

Hot Pants returned, flirting with Bill. Cottonmouth ordered two more beers. The place was empty except for a table of gay men gussied up in drag. One of them looked like Marilyn Monroe. A stranger appeared in the back doorway wearing a long white tunic. McCoy was reaching for his .45 when the stranger raised a Schmeisser submachine gun. Two shots rang out before McCoy cleared his holster. The stranger toppled to the floor, dead. They heard the truck start up in the parking lot, and drive out. Harry the Hoop had just saved their lives.

"That whack job Harry blew away was here on a work permit. We ran a check through Immigration. He's from Saudi Arabia," McCoy said."

"I know," Rico replied. Fat Mike has a wiretap in an Arab joint over on 135th Street. We couldn't understand a word until we got one of our students to listen in. You won't believe those nut jobs. Hoover's wiretap confirms everything the kid told us. Ever hear of Wahhabi?"

"Sounds like some kinda rabbit."

"It's a Muslim cult that believes anyone who isn't a Muslim has to become one or else."

"Or else what?"

"Or else they kill your ass!"

"What's that got to do with me and Cotton? We don't know any Muslims."

"Well, it's complicated. Seems those religious fruitcakes have a plan for us infidels. That's what they call Christians and Jews. They want to overthrow the United States."

"That's bullshit! How could one of those pissant countries overthrow anything?"

"Drugs and oil."

"I don't get what you're driving at."

"Watch for oil prices to start climbing. Oil could reach $100 a barrel in a few years. The real problem is narcotics. Look at our young people today. They walk around stoned, like zombies."

"I still don't understand why they're after me and Cotton."

"You've been busting drug shipments. These Wahhabis want those drugs to get through. Get people hooked. They even finance some of it. That big one you busted was one of theirs. That really pissed 'em off."

"You mean they're backing the Colombians?"

"Sometimes, it appears. The Colombian cartels just want our money. Saudi Arabia is spending a fortune over here building mosques to convert Americans to Islam. A lot of that is taking place in our own prison system."

"You mean the brothers?"

"Yes! Subvert the country from within. Then take over. Black Panthers, Malcolm X, Muslim Brotherhood, Islam this and Islam that. It sounds crazy as hell, but it's logical."

"Sounds like Uncle Sam's got his self a camel jockey problem."

"So do you and Cotton. It's called 'jihad.' That's the Arabic word for 'contract.'"

"Are they in Miami?"

"There's an old military building on Sharar Avenue. They bought the place and set up shop there. Get this. It has a brass peacock on the front door. That peacock was a mystical bird in ancient Persia."

"So that's our Peacock! How do you think we should go about this?"

"Eddie Nails is working on it. He's got some young Negro fellas on the payroll. They're scouting the neighborhood for us."

Ten a.m.

Rico telephoned the two detectives at headquarters. He had news, asking them to meet him at the Playboy Club on Biscayne Boulevard. He chose the Club because he was friends with the owner, and his cousin worked there. They were ushered into a small but elegant dining room. A pretty bunny brought their menus then left them alone. Eddie Nails rolled out a city map of Opa Locka.

"That's it, right there. This side here is a car lot, jalopies an' shit. That's a loan office over there, shysters an' more shit. Vacant lot behind the building, kids play back there. Good bakery across the street. I got me some fresh dinner rolls over there.

"They got this place fixed up like Fort Knox. Back door is bolted shut with 2 x 12s. Windows all got burglar bars. Twin doors out front are steel with those old-timey door handles that curve down. Flat roof and no crawl hole to climb out.

"There's eleven of 'em, twelve before Harry shot one. They're in by dark. They sleep there. They're antisocial as hell. Treat the blacks like shit. Pray all the time. Those bastards are bad news. My boys were afraid of them, an' they ain't afraid uh much uh nothin.'"

"Nails, that's excellent! Here, give this to the boys. Tell them thanks for me."

"Those kids idolize you, Rico. They'll probably take the money home and frame it."

"See to it they enroll in college next year. Too many black kids end up dead or in prison."

Cottonmouth posed a question. "Well, what do we do now? Shoot 'em, arrest 'em, what?"

"I read this in a comic book when I was a kid in Hell's Kitchen. Those door handles can be chained and locked. The porch is all wood, the building is wood, one way in and one way out. Burn it down with them in it!"

McCoy asked another question. "How would you do that?"

"Chain the front door, padlock it, lots of kerosene, and six men. One man does the door, then all of 'em douse the building with their five-gallon cans. Strike a few matches, climb back in the pimpmobile, and head for the barn. Flambé de Raghead."

"What about the fire department? It's not far from there."

"I'll turn in a false alarm at the Opa Locka Airport. Firemen will be driving around lost while our friends get nice and crispy."

McCoy spoke again. "That gets me and Cotton off the hook, payback for Mattie and Daisy. What about it, Rico?"

"How soon can you do it, Nails?"

"My boys can do it tonight."

"Don't leave anything behind, cans, matches, nothing that might be traced back to us."

The bunny was called back in and took their orders.

Three a.m..

Cottonmouth, Rico, and McCoy were sitting in Harry's truck one block down the street from the target. Six men ran away from the building, jumped in a van, and drove away. Flames licked the sides of the structure, growing higher and brighter by the second. They heard muffled yelling, banging on the front door. Soon the outside of the building was a roaring mass of burning timbers. There was screaming and gunfire. They were trying to shoot open the steel door. The flames were leaping as high as the trees.

KA-WHOOOOM!

The building exploded in an orange fireball, boiling up into the heavens. Structures on both sides of the blast caught fire. Building joists, studs, and flaming debris rained down in every direction. The steel doors with the brass peacock landed on the sidewalk in front of the bakery. Explosives stored inside the building had blown up from the heat.

"I've seen enough. Let's go."

Chapter Twenty-Five

Katherine and John

"Honey, which one do you think is best, Humphrey or Nixon?" Katherine asked.

"Probably neither one … Nixon, I guess."

"Why Nixon?"

"Well, Johnson screwed up the war, and he stuck us with more government, so I'm not so sure Humphrey wouldn't do the same thing."

"I like Humphrey. He seems like a nice man."

"Maybe so. They all seem nice until they get elected."

"I can't believe Jackie Kennedy married that Onassis. He's twenty-nine years older than she is."

"Maybe she has a taste for old Greek guys."

"You know something, John?"

"What's that, dear?

"You've got your sense of humor back."

"I do feel better. Gunny was right about getting used to being home."

"I wish he could come to the wedding."

"I do too. The kids would love Gunny."

"You never say much about him."

"Well, let's see now. He's older, going on fifty. Gunny fought in the Pacific during the Second World War. He was in Korea too. He calls that the 'Forgotten War.' He's about my height, maybe a hundred and seventy-five pounds. He looks a little like the Marlboro Man. Tough old fella. Divorced, gray hair, wife left him because he has a long blue tail."

"He does not!" Katherine laughed. "I like it when you get squirrelly."

John placed an arm around Katherine's shoulders. They were sitting on the sofa in the living room. "I won the blue ribbon when I married you."

Katherine kissed John on the cheek and laid her head on his shoulder.

"What brought that on?"

"I just feel fortunate I got you back from that awful place."

"I'm glad you got me back too."

They laughed, holding hands.

"Are you ready to eat?"

"Yes, I am."

"Okay, what would you like for dinner?"

"How 'bout spaghetti?"

"Want anything with it?

"Do we have any of those Grainger County tomatoes left?"

"I bought some more yesterday."

"I'd like some green onions with sliced tomatoes, and two pieces of pumpernickel."

"Some cake for dessert?"

"I want you for dessert."

"You are feeling better!"

"I don't say this often enough. I love you very much, Katherine."

She kissed John and hugged him. "Thank you, sweetheart."

"I wish we could find someone for Joyce."

"So do I, but she's not ready yet. She still talks about Steve."

"I never told you about Steve when I was hurt. He was all over the place, helping Gunny, running back and forth with ammunition and medical supplies, carrying the wounded over beside me at the base of the mountain. Steve and Gunny saved Tuttle Company."

"Don't upset yourself, dear."

"You're right. What about the honeymoon plans?"

"Joyce and I mentioned the cruise again. I think that's what they want to do."

"Imagine, our little girl going away on a honeymoon. It's hard to believe we've been married twenty years."

"You know what? Steve might be your guardian angel."

"How can that be?"

"Mister Cody said it. He told me you were both like guardian angels watching over your men. Maybe that's why Steve is always in your dreams."

"Gunny sure has a way with words. Say, he's not married!"

"You mean him and Joyce?"

"Yes! It wouldn't have to be obvious. We could have Joyce and the kids here when he comes to visit."

"That's a splendid idea. If they like each other, wouldn't that be something?"

"And they'd never know we did it."

"I never realized you could be so devious."

"Neither did I, but I hope it works!"

"Let's not get too hopeful, but it is a wonderful idea."

"Can we start that spaghetti now? I'm hungry."

Chapter Twenty-Six

Wedding Bells

Shannon and Roger were down on Pier 5 watching the boats come in. They went there often to visit their captain friend, Carlos Diego Antonio Garcia. Carlos was a former sea captain, a refugee from Castro's Cuba. He chartered his thirty-three foot Chris-Craft to vacationers who want to see the sights along the Florida beaches.

Moments earlier they had bumped into Shorty Dog on 4th Street. Roger recognized him as one of the football players who pushed him around in the filling station. Shannon recognized him too as the one who pulled her panties off while the others held her arms. Shorty came wandering along the sidewalk seemingly in a daze. Roger spoke to Shorty, asking if he was alright. When Shorty looked up and saw Sharon and Roger, he didn't act as if he knew them and kept on walking. He was disheveled and hadn't shaved for days.

Shannon stood staring at the retreating figure.

"He looks terrible. I believe he's on those drugs we heard about."

"I'm afraid you're right. Come on, Shan, I think I see the boat."

"Come aboard, my friends. I have Cuban tea for you today, very nice with lemon and honey."

"Where have you been? We haven't seen you for days."

"Oh, I have been away."

Shannon grew suspicious. So did Roger.

"You mean back to Cuba?"

Carlos chuckled in his light-hearted manner, pouring tea into three pewter mugs. "*Si*, a friend needed my boat."

"That's dangerous! What if you'd gotten caught?"

Carlos teased them. "Do you really want to hear my boring tale of adventure?"

"Oh, yes. Please."

"All right then, I will tell you. My cousin Immanuel was wanted by Raul Castro, Fidel's brother. It would have been very bad if the secret police caught him. Prison is not for that one. He is what you call the intellectual."

"Why were they after him?"

"His father was part of the 2506 Brigade. Those were the men who fought against Castro in 1961. His father was killed at La Batalla de Giron. Immanuel sabotaged one of their airplanes last December, and some of Castro's prison guards and secret police were killed. They would have tortured Immanuel for names then executed him."

"That's scary."

"There was no moon. He asked to meet with me at two in the morning."

"How did you find him?"

"Immanuel had with him the flashlight. He was waiting on the jetty at Isabela de Sagua.

"Weren't there patrol boats?"

"I heard only the one, miles away. Lady Luck was with us that night."

"Were you scared?"

Carlos chuckled again, a broad grin on his face. "I was how you Americans say, a little bit afraid."

"I don't blame you. I would be too."

"*Si*, he is the brave one. But he is safe now."

"Is he here in Miami?"

"He is safe. That is all I can tell to you. Now, tell me about yourselves. What have you been up to?"

"We're getting married!"

"*Mucho felicitaciones, mi amigos!*" Carlos rose from his seat, embracing his friends. "I am so happy for you. This is the time for you, no?"

Roger nodded. "Mother is better, and Shan's father is almost well. They asked if we were ready, and of course we said we were. They've been wonderful to us after what they've been through."

"I read about your Lieutenant Overstreet. Your father was very brave, Roger."

"I miss my dad a lot. I never knew that about him … until he was gone."

Carlos gazed into Roger's eyes, remembering his own sad adventure at the Bay of Pigs. "That is the way with so many. They never know themselves until destiny calls them. Then they become our heroes. Will you be married in Miami?"

"Yes, we want you to come if you aren't working."

"It will be my pleasure. Tell me where to go and what time to be there."

"It's at my house, 128 Judith Drive, Saturday morning at eleven o'clock."

"I will wear my white linen suit with the spectator shoes to celebrate your wedding."

Winston Peters had flown in from Atlanta. John Parker went through the ritual of walking Shannon down the aisle and giving her away. Joyce and Katherine sat beside Mister Peters during the nuptials. Carlos wore his white linen suit sitting next to Coach Caputo. The Sha Doobies were all present, and all the neighbors with the exception of one saleslady who was out of town. Little Willie John produced the ring, Roger slid it on Shannon's finger, and the preacher pronounced them man and wife.

"You may now kiss the bride."

They embraced and kissed, gazing into each other's eyes. A long coveted dream had finally come to pass. Then they turned and faced the gathering. They were surprised to see Detective McCoy standing at the back of the room.

McCoy made his way through the throng of smiling guests. "Garcia told me you two were getting married today. I dropped by to wish you good luck."

Shannon responded, smiling. "Thank you, Mister McCoy. My brand-new husband and I really appreciate that."

Roger laughed.

McCoy became businesslike. "May I see your father?"

"He's right over there." Shannon led the way holding Roger's hand. "Daddy, this is Detective McCoy. Mister McCoy, this is my father, John Parker, and our friend from Atlanta, Winston Peters."

Mister Parker was delighted. "Detective McCoy! I've read all about you in the newspapers."

"Thank you. May I see you two outside a minute?"

Winston Peters gazed into Bill McCoy's green eyes. What he saw there he didn't like.

"What's wrong, Detective?"

"Come outside, both of you. I don't want anybody to hear this."

Chapter Twenty-Seven

Sarah Ferguson

Dangerous Seas

Everyone was asleep except Dutch Henry. He was sitting in the pilothouse manning the *Gray Ghost* at a steady fifteen knots. Storm clouds had been gathering for hours so Dutch steered the ship toward deeper waters. He didn't want to run aground, blinded by a tropical deluge.

No stars were visible. Clouds continued building to the southeast, spiderwebbing the horizon with long fingers of lightning followed by rolling peals of thunder. Finally the rain came, lashing the window-panes with noisy gusts of wind and water. It was difficult to see beyond the bow of the ship. A flash of lightning revealed an angel standing in the doorway, a yellow raincoat about her head and shoulders.

"What are you doing up so late?"

"I love thunderstorms, ever since I was little. I came to share this one with you."

"Sit here in the pilot's chair. I'll stand behind you."

Trudy climbed onto the pilot's seat wearing her white silk pajamas, and Wing Dings footwear. Dutch slid his arms around her, holding her snugly beneath her proud breasts. He reached over turning off the cabin lights. The glow from the dials, the raging storm, and the mysterious sea surrounding the cargo ship was enchanting. He stood there holding Trudy, watching the ocean toss and roll with each flash of lightning.

"With you the dream never ends."

She smiled. "I know. It's the same for me. We're very lucky, you and I." Trudy turned and kissed him. "I can't get enough of you, Mister Henry. You've utterly turned my world around."

"I'm addicted to you, Miss Peters."

"And I with you, my love."

"Bloody Hell!"

"What is it, darling?"

Dutch leaned over the control panel staring into the night, waiting for the lightning. "There! See it?"

"Oh, damn! I'll get the others."

As soon as Trudy was out the door, Dutch radioed the number given him by Captain E'Manuel.

"Mayday! Mayday! This is the *Gray Ghost*! Mayday! This is the *Gray Ghost*! Three hundred miles north of Boca del Drago. Five miles off the coast. Three hundred miles north of Boca del Drago. Five miles off the coast. We are surrounded by pirates. Mayday! We are surrounded by pirates."

The radio crackled with static while Dutch waited anxiously. Thirty seconds ticked by. A minute passed.

"Mayday! Mayday! This is the *Gray Ghost*! This is the *Gray Ghost*!"

"I read you five by five, *Gray Ghost*. Sorry for my delay. I was scrambling the pilots. Are you under attack?"

"No! Not yet."

"How many craft are there?"

"I don't know. It's too dark, five or six, maybe more."

"Reverse course and steer for Panama. I have four fighter bombers warming up on the field. In exactly twenty minutes, switch on all your lights so the bombers can find you. Do not allow the pirates to board. I repeat. Do not allow the pirates to board. They will kill you, and steal your ship. Do you copy?"

"Steer for Panama ... lights on in twenty minutes ... waste the bastards."

"That is affirmative. Good luck to you, *Gray Ghost.*"

Sarah, Boogie, and Trudy burst into the cabin fully dressed.

"Did you reach Panama?"

"Four planes are warming up right now. We're to reverse course, and switch on our running lights in twenty minutes. That way they can find us. We have to fight. Our lives depend on it. Wayne, you take the wheel. Keep an eye out for the girls."

Boogie stood solemnly before them. "When I start my turn I'll go to full speed. Don't forget your helmets and flak jackets. Everything you need is in the lockers. And for God's sake stay behind your gun shields."

Dutch addressed the women. "Keep your heads down. Sight your targets between the gun barrels. Wait for the lightning. Remember, short bursts. Take one of the pistols from your locker for protection. Sing out if you need me. I'll be there as quick as I can."

They stood together in the dark as though to comfort one another. What seemed like twenty minutes lasted maybe twenty seconds. Nobody spoke. Eternity hung in the air. They embraced, kissed, and disappeared into the night. Wayne waited a full minute before he spun the helm hard to starboard, pushing the throttle all the way forward.

Trudy had just removed the tarpaulin from her twin mount .50 calibers, chambering a round into each machine gun when Boogie initiated his starboard turn. The *Gray Ghost* surged forward gathering speed. Two pirate craft in front of her opened fire, raking the pilothouse with automatic weapons. Glass and splinters of wood rained down on her and the guns.

Trudy marveled at her father's responsibilities facing the Focke-Wulfs and Messerschmitts flying his bomber missions over Nazi-occupied Europe. How frightening that must have been. This gun mount was her responsibility. The others depended on her. She must stay the course and complete her mission.

Dutch Henry was inside the 20 mm gun emplacement swiveling the long barrel around to bear on a dark shape seventy yards off his port bow. A bolt of lightning revealed a cabin cruiser with several men onboard, firing automatic rifles. They were shooting into the bridge, trying to kill the man steering the ship. They had no idea the *Gray Ghost* was armed. Dutch waited for the next flash of lightning.

Ghosts of the two husbands and their wives materialized before him. The dead Vietnamese children appeared, gazing up at Dutch with their curious brown eyes. Gunny and Moses Blue Pony stood at each shoulder lending him moral support. Silently, he promised his ghostly audience he would never allow the pirates to take Trudy or Sarah alive. He knew what they would do to them.

Sarah was questioning why the hell she hadn't sensed trouble. Was being in love clouding her ability to envision future events? No matter! She loved Wayne Compton. She loved Trudy. And she admired Dutch Henry. She would defend them with her life. Those assholes out there were trying to harm her friends. Sarah kicked the tarpaulin out from under her feet, sighted her weapons at the gun flashes nearest her, and squeezed the trigger.

Blossoms of flame shot from her gun barrels, tracers streaked into the night, geysers of water flew ten feet in the air, slamming into a boat fifty yards distant with six men onboard. Tracer rounds found the gasoline, and the fuel tank exploded.

Wayne had tied off the steering wheel and jammed the throttle wide open. Then he crawled underneath the control panel to escape the copper-jacketed storm flying through the pilothouse. Broken glass covered the floor. The radio was hit and knocked off its perch. Part of the wooden helm dangled from its steel surround. Papers, plastic charts, slivers of wood, and debris were everywhere. A quick glance at the speedometer revealed twenty-four knots. The *Gray Ghost* was performing as promised. Outside he could hear the chatter of the .50 caliber machine guns, and the *Pom Pom Pom* of the 20 millimeter deck cannon.

Lying on his stomach, Wayne pushed open the cabin door. The scene which greeted him was a surreal portrait of a madman's dream. An angry tempest howling above a windswept ocean, chain lightning spiderwebbing an ominous black sky, orange tracer rounds streaking back and forth between the *Ghost* and the pirate vessels.

The fleeing ship plowed on through the mountainous waves, her decks awash with seawater. A specter of evil had gained passage onboard, one of rape, torture, and murder. Sarah, the airline stewardess, the woman he loved, was firing point-blank into a host of boats shooting back at her. Bullets pranged off her gun shields. One craft in particular was too close for comfort, hosing the *Ghost* with automatic fire. Sarah swung her guns around, blasting pieces of the boat thirty feet in the air.

Spent cartridge casings rolled drunkenly about the pitching deck.

Wayne crawled on his hands and knees to the ammunition locker, dragging out two canisters. The drums were heavy.

Mascara streaming down her cheeks, hair flying in the wind, Sarah shouted above the Sirens' wail of the storm and the throbbing of the engine, "Hey, Bilge Rat, load these suckers for me!"

"Where's your helmet?"

"Some asshole shot it off my head!"

Wayne connected the new drums, slotting the belted ammunition into the breeches. He crawled back to the locker and got Sarah another helmet.

The outline of the moon appeared. The storm was beginning to pass.

"Put this on. I'm going to check on Trudy."

"Be careful, darling. I love you!"

"I love you too, Annie Oakley."

Wayne crawled back to the entrance, ducked across the pilot-house, and crawled out the opposite door. Trudy was struggling with one of the heavy drums, the right side of her flak jacket drenched with blood. Wayne crawled to the locker, bullets slamming into the wall, and pulled out a medical kit.

"Sit down! Let me bandage that arm."

Trudy slumped to the deck behind the machine guns, her back against the wall. "God, I'm glad you're here."

"Take it easy. I'll have you fixed up in a jiffy."

A bullet had sliced open the back of Trudy's forearm. Wayne bound it tightly with gauze, winding the arm with adhesive tape. Then he attached the drums of ammunition.

"Take a break, gunslinger."

"Thank you, honey. Is Sarah all right?"

"Sarah is her usual hell on wheels self. You stay put."

Wayne sighted the guns at a boat coming up alongside the *Ghost*. He squeezed the trigger. The twin .50s belched three-feet of flame, pouring a lethal stream of armor piercing steel into the pirate craft. They heard screams, and saw sparks flying. Pieces of the boat flew into the sea. The engine quit, and the craft drifted into the wake of the *Gray Ghost*.

Wayne didn't notice a grappling hook hanging from the railing. He heard a thud.

"Trudy, take over!"

He found her unconscious, a bloody gash in the side of her head.

They had shot her helmet off for the second time in ten minutes.

Dutch yelled up from the foredeck. "Sarah? Are you all right?"

Wayne called down from the bridge. "She's hurt, but she'll be okay. Trudy got shot in the arm. I took care of her. What about you?"

"I'm fine. Are you sure they're all right?"

"I'm positive, Dutch. Shoot those dirty bastards!"

A burst of machine gun fire from Trudy's quarter settled Dutch's apprehension.

"Same to you, Boogie! Let's roll!"

Wayne carefully bandaged Sarah's head, placing her behind the gun mount then positioned himself behind the twin machine guns. Two craft close together presented an ideal target beneath the silvery glow of the moon. Wayne engaged the trigger just as the 20 mm opened fire. Tracers split the night, geysers of water erupted around the two craft. The lead boat burst into flames. Wayne was adjusting his guns to fire at the second craft when he was knocked off his feet against the bulkhead.

Dutch could hear aircraft engines to the east. "Wayne! The lights! Turn on the lights!"

No response.

Fearing the worst, Dutch aimed his weapon in the direction of the bombers and fired off the remainder of his ammunition train. Tracers soared high into the heavens plummeting down a mile away into the sea. The pitch of the engines changed.

"Die, Yankee Dog!"

Dutch jerked around and ducked just as the man brought down a machete. It clanged against the steel breech of the Oerlikon. The intruder swung again, missing Dutch's throat by inches. Dutch slipped on a shell casing and fell over backward. The pirate swung wildly, cutting a gash in the fabric of Dutch's protective jacket. The man raised the machete with both hands, a malicious grin on his face. Dutch shot him under the chin with his .45 automatic.

With the approach of the aircraft, panic set in. The boats fled for shore. Dutch watched as the first fighter bomber flew in no more than a hundred feet above the waves. The pilot opened fire. It appeared as though Poseidon had released a sea monster from the deep. The pirate craft disintegrated into a thousand pieces. Dutch remembered Wayne, and went running for the stairs.

Wayne opened his eyes. "Where am I?"

Sarah got up from her chair and sat down on the side of the bed. Her head was wrapped in bandages. "You were shot. We're back at Boca del Toro."

"What's wrong with me?"

"They nearly shot your wing wang off."

"Bloody hell … does it … is it still there?"

"Three stitches. The anaconda is fine, baby, but the bullet broke your hip."

"Are you sure it's okay?"

"You'll have a scar, that's all. But you're going to be in bed awhile. You lost a great deal of blood, Wayne. Dutch stuffed your wound with gauze or I'd have lost you."

"What about you? How's your head? Where's Trudy?"

"I have a concussion. Seven stitches. Trudy has a fractured arm. Her doctor fixed it with a splint. Trudy got shot three times. That jacket she had on saved her life. She has these big purple places on her chest and stomach. We're lucky we got back alive."

"The last thing I remember I put a bandage on your head, then I started shooting those guns."

"Dutch found us. He said you were on top. Your blood was all over me so Dutch thought I was dead."

"Did Dutch get hurt?"

"Not a scratch. He's a brave man. Trudy and Dutch are well suited for one another."

"I damn near died when I found you lying there."

"Does it hurt much with me sitting on the bed?"

"No, I don't feel a thing."

"I want to snuggle up and take a nap. Do you mind?"

"No, honey, go on to sleep. I'm right behind you."

"You know something, Boogie?"

"What's that, Sarah?"

"You were wonderful out there."

"You and Trudy were the gunners. I was just the water boy."

"Hurry up and get well, Water Boy. Your wounded appendage needs some exercise."

Chapter Twenty-Eight

A Gathering of Eagles

"What I say here, stays here, off the record."

Cottonmouth had gotten out of the police cruiser and stood beside his partner. John Parker and Winston Peters both marveled at the size of the man. Cotton held out his size thirteen, and they shook hands.

"Your friends are mixed up in the smuggling business."

John Parker turned pale. He feared he and Katherine were in trouble. "Sm ... Smuggling?"

"Grass, weed, marijuana. Wayne Compton and Dutch Henry brought a load in two weeks ago in a PT boat. Now they've gone back to Panama for another load, a big one this time."

Mister Peters asked, "How do you know that?"

"Like I said, this is strictly off the record. A friend of ours is buying the shipment."

"Dutch Henry just married my daughter, and Wayne Compton married her best friend. Were you aware of that, Detective?"

"No, sir, we didn't know. But they might be in danger, all of them."

Winston Peters took a step nearer the two detectives. "Who're you talking about?"

"The same people trying to kill me and John."

McCoy told the story about the drug bust and how it ruffled the feathers of a group from Saudi Arabia living in Miami. He described the murder of Jimmy Four Eyes. He told of the attempts on his and John's lives, and how Daisy was accidentally killed. And about Mattie's passing. He explained the motives behind oil prices and drug addiction, and how that was supposed to cripple the United States. He revealed to John and Winston how he and Cotton exacted their revenge on the Wahhabis. And he explained about the wiretaps and the drug shipments. But he didn't mention Rico by name.

"Sounds like you're in the business yourself, McCoy."

Bill looked up at his partner, not sure how to respond. Cottonmouth nodded his head.

"We don't sell the stuff. But we have taken a shitload of money off the dirtbags. That's what started the drug war. We didn't know the Arabs were in on it until our friend tapped some phone lines to find out who was trying to nail us."

"You've certainly picked the cream of the crop to piss off," Winston continued. "From what I know about those drug cartels, they're a ruthless bunch of killers. As for those Arabs you mentioned, I was in Middle East once during the war. Muslims for the most part are nice people. The majority are poor, but some of those religious cults are absolutely nuts. They stone people to death, cut off heads, treat women like cows."

"Well, here's the rest of it. They have a contract out on me and John."

"Are you sure about that?"

"Our friend verified it on one of his wiretaps. A special team is being flown here from Saudi Arabia. He'll tip off the FBI, but I doubt that'll stop them. We came here to warn you about Compton and

Henry. Get them and the women someplace safe before the shit hits the fan. John and I can manage for ourselves."

Winston scratched his head. "You can't use your police force because that might land you in trouble. What does this friend of yours do for a living?"

John looked up again. Cottonmouth nodded.

"He's a captain with the Mafia."

John Parker shook his head in disbelief. "I don't believe this shit. Wayne and Dutch are in trouble. You're in trouble. Killers are on the way. And the Mob is involved. What else can go wrong?"

Winston had to laugh in spite of John's concern. "Isn't that enough for one day?"

"Hell, yes, but we've got to warn your daughter and the others. What about these detectives? Hells bells, what about them?"

Winston looked up at Cottonmouth. "You haven't said a word, John. Bill keeps looking to you for support."

"Bill lost his son an' Daisy. He ain't right yet."

"I'm sorry for both your losses. Tell you what, let's meet with that friend of yours and put a plan together. We did it in the military. Let's do one here in Miami."

"You mean you'll help me an' Bill?"

"I owe you that much for warning me about Trudy and my son-in-law. What about you, John? You want in on this?"

"Steve Overstreet was my next-door neighbor. He died saving a lot of GIs. He probably saved my life too. Ever since I came home I've felt like I had unfinished business. Count me in, fellas."

They met at the Leprechaun Bar on Bird Road. Detective McCoy made the introductions. Cottonmouth sat with his back against the wall, watching the front door.

"Mister Peters, Mister Parker, this is Enrico Basilio. Rico, this is Winston Peters and John Parker."

"I'm pleased to meet you, gentlemen. Please call me Rico."

They shook hands, and Mister Peters asked a question. "Bill informed us about this jihad business. Can you think of some way we might use it against them?"

"One of my men has a daughter majoring in philosophy. He asked her to type a report for us. I'd like to read it to you."

"Good idea, let's hear it."

"Arabia was a land of desert kingdoms. These were nomadic tribes that often fought amongst themselves as well as against their neighbors. Beginning in 1902 Abdul-Aziz bin Saud defeated one rival kingdom after another, founding the nation of Saudi Arabia in 1932. His chief supporters were the Ikhwan, a religious army of the Wahhabist-Bedouin tribes. Their goal was the unification and purification of Islam.

"The Prophet of Islam, Muhammad, was born in Mecca around 570 AD, and began preaching in Mecca in 610. He moved to Medina in 622 where he and his followers united the Arabian tribes into a single religious order under the banner of Islam. Muhammad died in 632. His successor was Abu Bakr, Muhammad's father-in-law, who became the leader of the Muslims as their first Caliph. He died in 634. Three more Caliphs followed after that. In a span of a hundred and thirty years the Muslim armies defeated the Byzantine armies, and destroyed the Persian Empire.

"The Qur'an, pronounced 'Koran,' is their Bible. It was written by the followers of Muhammad who revealed his visions to his scribes as he received them from Allah. The Koran is a book of laws, half prose and half poetry. Islam is more a religious ideology of conquest than a religion of peace. Islamic law is called Sharia. Sharia laws are enforced by the Mutaween, a private police force. They dictate moral and religious behavior.

"Wahhabis forbid all luxuries or any cultural imports from other societies. Basically, they hate everything modern, and dislike anyone who isn't one of them. The Koran states that infidels, any person not a Muslim, must be converted to the faith either by the word or by the sword. This may be accomplished, if taken literally, by any means necessary including treachery and war. The Wahhabis want to take the world and everyone in it back to the 7th Century.

"Saudi Arabia is the home of Islam, and thought to be where the first Arabs originated on the Arabian Peninsula. The United States has a large presence in Saudi Arabia constructing and modernized the county's infrastructure. King Faisal is viewed as a reforming and modernizing king, and is friendly to the United States. The Saudi people like him. But there is friction between the Wahhabis and the Saudi Kingdom.

"That's it in a nutshell. Those Wahhabis and their Muslim pals want to bankrupt America with oil prices, and wreck our society with drugs. McCoy and Cottonmouth got in the way which cost Daisy and, indirectly, Mattie their lives. So far we've killed a dozen of the bastards, but another group is on the way."

John Parker spoke. "I read something about Black Jack Pershing executing Muslim fanatics in the Philippines, and burying their bodies with dead pigs. That's supposed to have stopped a rebellion. Muslims view pigs as unclean beasts. Bury the body with a pig and his soul is unclean. The dirty soul can't get into Paradise."

Rico chuckled. "I guess we'll have to become sodbusters, raising pigs and chickens."

They all laughed.

Mister Peters confirmed the rumor. "I heard that same story when I was stationed in London. There may be something to it. Ask the college girl if she can come up with anything positive. If they're spooked by something that simple it could be their Achilles heel."

McCoy was skeptical. "How are we going to use pigs against a bunch of fanatics?"

"The citrus farm!"

They turned and stared at Cottonmouth. Rico smiled, amazed at his friend's insight into complex situations. The citrus farm would be the ideal place for an ambush.

John and Winston both were curious.

"What's the citrus farm?

They met again two days later at the Copacabana. Rico took his wife there often and knew the staff. The maître d' showed them to his finest table. Rico slipped the man a twenty dollar bill.

"Lucy found a number of references on General Pershing and the pig story. She wasn't able to confirm the story with eyewitness accounts or written testimony, but she did say it appears to be authentic. Lucy believes it's true."

"Do you really think this will work?" McCoy asked. "It sounds crazy as hell."

Mister Peters quoted an old military proverb. "If you find yourself in a fair fight, you didn't plan your mission properly."

"What if they find us first?"

"I know they're coming through Mexico. We have their embassies bugged, and I have my informers. We'll find them," Rico reassured McCoy.

Cottonmouth offered a suggestion. "Me an' Bill could bait 'em to the farm."

Rico responded. "What if we had a boatload of marijuana anchored at the farm? The Muslims might be tempted to steal the boat, and whack you guys all at the same time."

McCoy was confused. "What marijuana?"

"That boat Henry and Compton was supposed to bring here ran into trouble. It's back in Panama. We could use that as part of our trap."

Winston responded. "I called the airline for Trudy, but she hasn't returned my call. Are the boys all right?"

"Wayne Compton got shot in the ass. He'll be okay. Your son-in-law didn't get hurt. Here's the number in Panama. The girls are there with them. Use your hotel phone. I don't trust the ones here because of the FBI."

"Thank you, Rico. I really appreciate this. I don't like the idea of leaving Bill and John out there on a limb."

"They won't be on a limb," Rico said. "My crew and I will be with them."

Winston nodded his approval. "Do you have access to automatic weapons? "

"One of my men is friends with a weapons dealer."

"How 'bout Claymore mines?" John Parker asked Rico.

"How many would you suggest?"

"Six should do it, and a box of hand grenades."

"Sounds like you want in on this."

"We talked it over last night. Winston and I want to go with you."

"Gentlemen, I would be honored. My men would love meeting two war heroes."

Winston interrupted. "The real heroes are buried in Europe and Arlington Cemetery, and a thousand other places around the world. We did our job and came home. They weren't so lucky."

"I meant no disrespect, Winston."

"None taken, my friend, but don't introduce us as war heroes."

"Gotcha covered. Nails will get the hardware. Anything you want in particular?"

"With this bum arm I'd like a carbine," Parker requested. "They're light and easy to carry."

"Winston?"

"I'm familiar with the M-1 rifle. We qualified with those in basic training."

"McCoy?"

"I got my chopper."

"Cotton?"

"Ask Nails to get me uh machine gun an' eight or ten belts."

Rico reminded them again. "Remember now, we have to take one of them alive."

Recovery

Trudy was resting on a queen-size bed. She had two pillows propped up behind her back, and was talking with her husband. Trudy was recovering from the physical trauma of being struck by three high-velocity bullets in the sea battle. Her bulletproof jacket had saved her life. Her main injury was a bruised and very sore stomach.

"I spoke with Father. He was not happy."

"I guess he's pissed at me."

"He's mad at all of us. He said we have no business smuggling marijuana."

"Does he know you and Sarah were on the boat?"

"I couldn't lie, I told him."

"What did he say?"

"He said if he were here he'd give me a good spanking. Father was upset over Wayne too. I didn't tell him Sarah and I got shot. I'll explain that later."

"You father's right. I should have taken those pirates more seriously. The *Sea Queen* can outrun just about anything, but the *Ghost* is less than half her speed."

"It's not your fault, dear. We all wanted to go. None of us realized the danger."

"Captain E'Manuel warned us. I let my stupid ego get in the way."

"What could you have done any differently?"

"I'd ask Tony for an escort, and suggest you and Sarah meet us in Miami."

"We wouldn't leave you and Wayne alone."

"I know that, but I should have asked anyway."

"Father told me some of his friends in Miami are in trouble with a religious group of Muslims. He called them Wahhabis. Have you ever heard of that before?"

"No."

"They're from Saudi Arabia. He said they may be after the *Gray Ghost*, and we should get back to Miami as soon as possible. We can't leave Wayne here."

"Wayne should stay in bed 'til that hip gets well."

"What can we do then?"

"Let's talk it over with Sarah. How's your chest?"

"I'm better, but it still hurts. That bullet that hit me in the stomach was the worst."

"Thank God you weren't killed."

"You'd have a hard time explaining that one to Father."

Trudy and Dutch were in Boogie's hospital room visiting with him and Sarah. Wayne had a plaster cast around his hips, which covered his lower abdomen. He was not the exemplary patient.

"I hate this crap! Bedpans! It's humiliating!"

"Now, dear, remember where you are. Be a good boy and get well."

"Besides that, it itches."

"Here, use your coat hanger."

Sarah winked. Dutch and Trudy laughed.

Captain E'Manuel had seen to it that Wayne got one of the best hip surgeons in Panama. Doctor Torres put Wayne's hip back together with four stainless steel screws, and just under fifty stitches. If the bullet had been five-eighths of an inch lower and a smidgeon to the left, Wayne's conjugal duties as a new husband would have been a fading memory.

They were discussing their harrowing sea adventure and being rescued by a Catalina flying boat, when a knock came at the door.

"Tony! Come in!"

"*Buenos dias*, everybody. How's the patient today?"

Sarah answered for her husband. "The patient is coming along fine. All he does is bitch."

"That is a sign of progress, is it not?"

Sarah smiled. "He just likes the attention."

"Our pilots counted four disabled craft in the wake of the *Ghost*. You did very well. A fifth boat they weren't sure about, but there were bodies in the water. They accounted for four boats themselves. Several got away. The pirate threat appears to be over for a while."

Wayne asked a question. "Do you still want the *Ghost* to go to Florida?"

"I received a call this morning that concerns me. It was your father, Trudy. Have any of you ever heard the term, 'jihad'?"

Captain E'Manuel went on to explain what Winston Peters told him about the Wahhabi threat in Miami, how drugs played a role, concerns over Middle Eastern oil revenues, and about the Muslim jihad against the two detectives. He warned that they could all be in danger if the radicals discovered their whereabouts in Panama. Then he said something that surprised everyone.

Mister Peters wanted the *Gray Ghost* delivered to Miami.

Sarah foresaw a drama unfolding. "What does Mister Peters want with a boatload of square groupers?"

Tony answered. "I don't know, but I can tell you this. Trudy's father has friends in some very interesting places. We've started work to repair the damages. The *Gray Ghost* will be ready to sail in two days."

Dutch spoke up. "How do you plan on getting the ship to Miami?"

"I came here to offer you the job. Several of my men will accompany you."

"Will your government supply an escort?"

"That has been arranged."

Trudy said. "I should stay here. Sarah has a concussion, and Wayne needs more time to get his strength back. Then we can charter a plane and fly to Miami."

"I agree with my wife. Sarah has her hands full with the big baby."

Wayne joshed his friend. "You're just jealous 'cause I got two sweetie pies looking after me now. Seriously, Dutch, be careful out there, man."

Tony spoke. "You'll be well protected. I should have seen the danger before, but it never occurred to me the pirates would try and steal one of my ships."

Wayne mused over the situation. "I wonder what they're up to in Miami?"

Despite his bravado, Dutch felt a sense of unease. Sarah looked at him oddly as if she sensed it too. He felt responsible for nearly getting them killed. Was risking all their lives worth twelve million bucks? Hell, no! He felt ashamed at having gotten them involved in his marijuana dealings. Now Trudy's father was waiting for him in Miami. He wondered if he'd ruined the friendship with his father-in-law.

But he never would have met Trudy Peters if it hadn't been for Wayne and Sarah and the Panamanian connection. Tony and Amanda were wonderful people. So were Mister Peters, and Katherine and John Parker. Somehow he had become intertwined with all of them through a smuggling operation. He recalled Wayne asking if selling marijuana was an honorable thing to do.

Dutch kissed his wife goodbye, and followed Captain E'Manuel out the door. Ahead lay the journey home, and a date with an uncertain destiny.

Chapter Thirty

The Arab

A'zam Hussein Baz watched the runway slide by as the Air France 707 lifted into the skies over Paris. Below he could see the Eiffel Tower and the Arc de Triomphe, a beautiful city which had been spared the horrors of the Allied bombing campaign during the Second World War.

Degenerate French, he thought to himself. Filthy infidel swine! And those Americans! He remembered his cleric's teachings about the immoral race of capitalist infidel dogs, so many now trampling the sacred sands of his beloved Saudi Arabia. All must burn in the furnaces of hell. England! A gluttonous tribe of arrogant colonial savages! Spain! A stinking cesspool of Catholics!

Islam would retake the lands his forefathers had conquered thirteen centuries before. His hatred swelled and grew as he gripped the arms of his passenger seat, imagining himself the great Caliph of the Arabian Desert. If he were shot and killed he would be martyred.

Songs would be sung of his magnificent victories. Seventy-two virgins awaited him in Paradise.

A pretty stewardess passed A'zam's seat, walking up the aisle pushing a metal serving trolley. Her short skirt revealed a pair of shapely legs. He stared at her enticing bottom.

Disgusting! I must not view these unclean things. He turned away. She aroused him. He felt stricken, betrayed by his lustful thoughts. *It was forbidden!* He looked again, desiring her. He would mount her from behind across her service contraption, have his pleasure, then beat the woman for tempting him.

Passengers began ordering cocktails. The Atlantic flight would last several hours. *Spirits of alcohol were forbidden!* The woman beside him spilled a few drops on her skirt, pulling it up to sponge it off. *Bitch dog! Daughter of Satan!* She had short blonde hair with blue eye makeup, a painted red mouth, and protruding breasts. He coveted the blonde woman, desiring to rut with her like a canine in heat.

Allah, deliver me from these lustful distractions! Show me the beautiful images of Mecca and Medina. He envisioned himself as the reincarnation of Commander Tariq, sweeping the infidels from the Persian sands, reconquering Northern Africa and Spain. Then on to Great Britain! The Great Satan would be saved for last, the United States of America.

The airplane hit a pocket of rough air and several passengers spilled their drinks. Once again, the woman began sponging at her skirt. He saw her pale thighs almost to her panties.

"Pardon me, I'm so clumsy. My name is Betty, Betty Witt. What's your name?"

He felt suspended between the glowing coals of the Pit, and the eternal bliss of the Promised Land. *Imagine! An unescorted female speaking to him directly! Such transgressions were forbidden!* He struggled to compose himself and refrain from striking the woman in the face.

With Herculean effort, holding on to his armrests, he blurted out, "My name is A'zam Hussein Baz. I am a disciple of Muhammad."

"Who's Muhammad?" asked the retailing major from Texas University.

A'zam Baz felt as though he were going to swoon. His head swam, his eyes watered, his mouth opened and closed like a perch out of water. The nerve of this ignorant slut! May the wrath of Allah strike her blind! If he were home in his oasis village he would have her stoned to death, then left in the desert for the vultures.

"Mu-Muhammad is the father of Islam," he stammered.

"Oh, you mean that religious thing where the women wear those veils."

"That is correct."

"Seems pretty silly wearing those veils in all that heat. Why don't they take 'em off?"

A'zam didn't know whether to scream, pray, or burst into a fit. Take them off! Was there no end to this horrible creature's blasphemy? Doesn't she understand revealing a woman's face in public is a sin against the Qur'an, punishable by twenty lashes? Muhammad would be outraged! First he would give her to his men, then have her drawn and quartered, and her pieces thrown to the dune dogs.

"It is the Wahhabi way." He said evenly, his eyes never leaving her breasts.

Betty realized she was talking with a very strange and uptight individual. Betty had also picked up on his infatuation with her 36Ds. She noted his hands gripping the armrests, and his constant swallowing which made his Adam's apple bob up and down like a fishing cork. *Should a Texas girl have a little fun?* she asked herself. *Why the hell not!*

"Gosh, it's hot in here."

She unbuttoned the top two buttons on her blouse, revealing the swell of her voluptuous bosoms.

A'zam's mind flew straight into the side of an olive tree. Debauchery had him by the balls. He felt his loins succumbing to lust.

Betty wore a miniskirt. She spread her knees, fanning herself with a *Mademoiselle* magazine.

A'zam was experiencing difficulty keeping his breathing from running up and down the aisle of the 707 with its hair on fire.

Betty turned to ask him another question, pressing her left breast against his right arm.

"Allahu Akbar!" shouted A'zam. "Allahu Akbar!"

He bolted to the safety of the restroom to address his swollen appendage. The passengers looked at one another as if to question the man's sanity. Surely that one had eaten a bad fig.

Betty smiled. *Men are so silly*, she thought to herself. Little did she realize she was sitting beside an Arab killer on his way to a rendezvous in Mexico City with an elite squad of assassins. There they would be supplied weapons, and flown by private plane to a landing strip thirty miles south of Miami. She had no idea of the torture which would be inflicted upon her if A'zam ever got her alone. She had shamed him, and dishonored his god, Muhammad.

A'zam Hussein Baz spent the remainder of the flight huddled on a backseat in coach. He was convinced the stranger with the blonde hair and the breasts of a goddess was sent from the underworld to try and seduce him, thereby betraying his loyalty to al-Muwahhidun.

A'zam would soon be in the land of the hated Christians where his faith would again be put to the test.

Chapter Thirty-One

FBI Headquarters

"Sir, we got another message from San Antonio about those Muslims. They want to know if we should detain them or not."

"Same caller as last time?"

"Yes, sir. Miami."

"You know what that means, don't you?"

"No, sir."

"The Mob is nervous about the Colombian drug cartels. Apparently that Peacock outfit got involved. Eleven of the poor bastards got burned up last month."

"I don't understand, sir."

"Simple! The Italians want us to clean up the mess so they can carry on with business as usual."

"You mean they want us to protect them?"

"That's right. Then they'll make another fifty or a hundred million with their lousy gambling and prostitution and you name it with no more interference from the wetbacks or the sand niggers."

"And we end up with another dead agent, like Gary, Indiana."

"You're getting the picture loud and clear, Special Agent Carpenter."

"What should we do about it, sir?

"What would you recommend if you were the field commander?"

"Sir, I'm not sure I'd do anything. If they kill each other, it's no skin off our nose."

"Right, we stay out of it. You're going to make a fine agent, Special Agent Carpenter. Let the bastards kill themselves."

"I'll notify San Antonio right away, sir. I'll tell them, hands off!"

"Don't forget our luncheon today with that senior senator."

"Do you still want me to bring up Brazil, sir?"

"Yes, indeed! Pour it on thick like that syrupy dialogue he uses. Praise him as our great congressional philanthropist. Flatter his ego, express envy at his genius with those oil wells and mining interests in Brazil. Mention his ties with their military. And don't forget his villa overlooking the South Atlantic.

"I'll lay it on thick, sir. Then you give him the old skunk eye."

"Yes! I want that married prick to understand I know he's a political fuck with a mistress in Rio. He'll suck up like all the other congressional thieves and scumbags. This will assure us the votes we need in the Senate when the Bureau comes up for review. Then we can get on with the real business of exposing the communist bastards we got right here in Washington, DC."

Chapter Thirty-Two

Buttered Popcorn

"Honey, let's go see that new movie, *Charly*.

"What's it about, Shan?"

"It about a retarded man and a mouse named Algernon that have operations that make them smart. It's supposed to be really good."

"Sounds weird. What time does it start?"

"You have time for a shower. I'll fix my hair then we'll go."

An hour later Shannon and Roger paid their seventy-five cents at the Carib Theatre, walked inside the "Dream Palace," and took their seats. A newsreel highlighted the battles of Khe Sahn and Hue, Lyndon Johnson stating he would not seek reelection, and Richard Nixon talking about China. The newsreel ended with Hubert Humphrey speaking at a political rally in Wisconsin.

Cliff Robertson, "Charly," has the operation, and he and Claire Bloom, "Alice," fall in love. They plan on marriage and spending the rest of their lives together. Algernon dies. Charlie then realizes his increased intelligence is only temporary. Roger and Shannon both shed tears over the sad ending.

As they're leaving the theater Shannon asked her husband a question. "Have you noticed a change in my father lately?"

"Yes, he seems like his old self again."

"I don't mean that. There's something different."

"He saw a lot of people die in the war. That would make anybody different."

"That's not it. Something has changed. I noticed it last week."

"You're imaging things, honey. The movie upset you."

"I don't think so. He and Mister Peters have been going out a lot lately. And Mom said those two detectives came by the house last week while we were gone."

"Maybe you should talk to him if you feel that strongly about it."

Shannon slid over beside Roger as they drove out of the parking lot onto Lincoln Road. "You always make me feel better."

Roger placed an arm around her shoulders. "So that's why you married me, damage control!"

"I married you because you're so cute."

They chuckled merrily, heading north away from the theater on Washington Avenue.

Chapter Thirty-Three

Shorty Dog

The tears he shed resembled pearls of defeat from his collapsing world. They fell to the ground like dead leaves in a poisoned wood. There they sank into the coal-dust and cinder-encrusted earth like raindrops upon desert sands, forgotten by all but the man who put them there.

The pain was excruciating, like nothing experienced before. He felt as though Mister Bones was gouging him from the grave, taunting him with further pain and humiliation.

"Mother of God," he whispered. "Please make it stop!"

But God had long since departed his isle of misery, tending to other members of His dysfunctional flock. The world was a lunatic asylum, filled with vicious ten percenters, political lifers down at city hall, coke whores, dirty cops, and bat-fuck crazy. Only God held the key. Or maybe it was Beelzebub who managed the booby hatch. But there was no escape, no relief to be gained from good Samaritans, no more nights with the Salvation Army. Just the hot coals of a worldly hell he knew all too well from his addiction to the brown powder.

"Please," he begged. "I can't stand it no more."

He slid the glass bottle from his coat pocket and washed down another pill, another distress flare from his sinking Titanic. The warmth of the whiskey filled his belly and for a moment he felt almost normal. Then he cried again, lonely sobbing into the raggedy sleeve of the coat he wore.

"Why doesn't my daddy love me? Why won't he help me just a little bit?"

Shorty knew he had come to the final chapter in the pages of his novel. No love was his with the coming of dawn. No sweet doggie in the yard waiting to greet him. No white picket fence. No escape from his hateful addiction.

His codependency on the woman hurt worst of all. God, he missed her. He was nothing without the woman. A dried up husk of a man in a desolate world of lowlifes, misery, and brown powder. If only he could score a fix. She had the works, the needles, his reason for one more day on the Jurassic planet. Without the woman there was no more happiness, just lonely nights. No more pretty flowers, just confusion and tears.

His mother tried helping Shorty, but she threw in the towel after her marriage to the drunken longshoreman who didn't want Shorty hanging around anymore. The longshoreman beat Phyllis, and when the screaming stopped he beat Shorty, kicking him out of the house.

His father was a big shot in the mahogany-paneled star chamber of a downtown law firm. Why couldn't the old bastard take him in and give him a place to sleep? That wasn't too much to ask. It wasn't his fault Mama got knocked up by an ambulance-chasing son of a bitch. The lawyer turned his back on Shorty, refused even to see him the day he hitched a ride downtown to ask Mister Perry Mason to recognize him as his son.

In the distance a train whistle blew.

The man lay down in the weeds and curled up, cradling the whis-key bottle gently against his left arm. He was careful not to spill any. Another pill, maybe? No, whiskey first. Shoot, why not take them both? He took the plastic vial from his pants pocket and shook out another amphetamine. Then a Valium. If only his withdrawals would go away, he could rest then. He chased it down with a long pull of Old Gran-Dad, then curled up in the weeds and lay still.

Memories of the first time he met his father came drifting back through the emotional fog of childhood. The man had come to the house on Baker Street to visit his mom. Mother brought him out from the bedroom, and introduced him to the lawyer. Then they left him alone in the living room, and closed the bedroom door. He was almost two then. The man came to the house many times after that.

When he was four, the lawyer bought him a wagon. A yellow wagon. He didn't like yellow, and told the man he didn't like the color. The lawyer took it away. After that he never bought him anything. The lawyer didn't like the little boy. He just came to visit his mother.

The years passed them by, and he stopped coming to see his mother altogether. He remembered his mother crying. The boy asked her why she was crying. She told him the man she loved was going to marry someone else. The boy felt sorry for his mother. He cried too because he wanted a father and didn't have one. They cried together sitting side by side on a purple sofa in the living room.

Phyllis was insecure and brought men to the house. Strange men in the house made Shorty uncomfortable. He felt like his mother didn't love him enough to stay home with him on weekends, read stories to him, or take him to the park where he could play on the swings. Pretty soon he discovered beer and cigarettes. It wasn't long before he was drinking Boone's Farm and smoking marijuana.

He remembered the sound of the ambulance gurney bumping against the L-shaped turn in the hallway when they came to the house on Detroit Avenue where Alexandria lived with her mother. Mama was dying with a brain tumor. Alexandria wasn't breathing when they placed her on the gurney. He remembered they put a plastic thing over her face to make her breathe. Then they loaded him on another gurney, and drove them to the hospital.

The ambulance made a loud wailing sound like something lost from the herd, crying out for others of its own kind. When they reached the hospital they rushed them both into the emergency room. Alexandria was choking, trying to breathe. He drifted away then into another heroin dream.

When he woke up they had taken Alexandria away. He asked them where she was. The nurses avoided his eyes. He asked one of the doctors where they had taken her. The doctor just shook his head, and looked at Shorty like he was dirty with vomit or dog shit or something. Nothing was the same after Alexandria died. He drank more, shot up more. Nothing was ever the same after they buried his sweetheart.

The train whistle blew again. It was closer this time.

Shorty sat up in the weeds beside the railroad tracks listening to the approach of the diesel locomotive with its long caravan of boxcars. The metal wheels went *bump bump, bump bump* every time they passed over another thirty-nine foot section of steel track. Trains reminded Shorty of adventure and faraway places. He wished he could go there.

But there was no escape from the misery in his heart. Rejection by his father. A mother lost in her own mental neurosis. Drug addiction. His dead girlfriend. No money. No brown powder. No happy tomorrows. No more summers on the beach holding hands. He missed the woman terribly. He missed his mother. He missed not having a daddy.

Shorty was illegitimate. Nobody loved him. That's what he believed anyway, consumed with self-doubt and a terrible, empty loneliness. He couldn't function without Alexandria. Satan had nailed him to the gopherwood cross of clinical depression. It hurt! Why did Alexandria have to die? He needed Alex. He needed her now to give him the needle.

Was this God's punishment for blaspheming the church? He had sinned against God. Sinned against the woman he loved. Sinned against his own mother. Stolen money for alcohol and drugs. Lied to his friends. Lied to everybody he would pay them back. Pawned his soul into the fiery furnace so he could ride the lightning one more time.

Highs and lows, and a marble orchard in between.

Codependency consumed his mortal soul, filled his brain with maggots, black widow spiders, and diamondback rattlers. His drug habit had turned his stomach into a squirming mass of night crawlers, swamp leeches, fire ants, and poisonous cane toads. The two together rendered Shorty a quaking wreck of a human being with an inferiority complex which paralyzed him emotionally and a paranoia so intense he believed the FBI was coming to get him. They were out there to-night, someplace in the palm bushes and pine trees with their dogs and guns. They would hurt him if they caught him, put things on him. Maybe put things in him!

He could see the engine's big headlight coming down the tracks. The engineer blew his whistle. That was customary when approaching a road intersection. It was a clear evening with a thousand points of light in a black summer sky.

He remembered once as a child when his mother helped him catch lightning bugs. It was great fun. They put them in a Mason jar, after they punched holes in the lid with a kitchen knife so the insects could breathe. They caught dozens of the fireflies, and placed them in the glass container. The tiny insects lit up the living room. But the fireflies died. Mother said it was because of the soap residue left in the jar for doing the laundry.

The engineer blew his whistle again. The ground quaked a little. Shorty remembered the time they had a flat tire on the old bridge go-ing into Bal Harbour. They got out the spare tire and the car jack. That's when he noticed the bridge was swaying from the movement of the automobiles. It scared Shorty, and he began to cry. A trucker saw what was happening, and stopped to help his mother. After that his mother dated the trucker a while, but he was married so it didn't last long. Shorty liked the trucker. It made him sad when the truck driver went away.

Shorty didn't understand the term codependent, but without the woman he felt as empty as a number 10 Krystal bag. He wasn't tuned in much on drug addiction either, but he was a full-blown heroin junkie. Nor was he familiar with the psychology associated with paranoia. But the brown powder and pills and Old Grand-Dad and his own personal insecurity rendered him a codependent paranoid schizophrenic. He had found his bottom. Any lower and he would have to learn Chinese.

Being a drunk when he wasn't nodding out on heroin, or in mind-numbing reverse on Quaaludes, or blasted around the moon on west coast turnarounds rendered him incapable of rational thought. They were out to get him. He knew that, tasted it, breathed it, felt it like a poisonous snake wrapped around his thighs with his balls in its mouth.

Frankie McCoy's accident was a terrible shock. Months later Alex's overdose made his break from reality complete. Visions came and went inside his head. He lived in a dangerous underworld filled with drifting fog and shadows. Monsters dwelled there.

The ground shook as the train approached where the man sat in the weeds beside the rail road tracks. It was about two hundred yards up the line, coming full throttle. The engineer blew his whistle. The stars were beautiful. A full moon was shining down on Shorty Dog. One more pull on the bottle and he felt almost at peace. It lasted several seconds. Then the pain returned, and he cried again.

He stood up. The ground was moving beneath his feet. It felt like one of those crazy rides at the fair. But it wasn't so bad that he couldn't keep his balance. Even half drunk he could manage that. It was a little bit scary though, with the big engine swaying side to side thundering down the tracks. The engineer blew his whistle again which hurt his ears. The train made a loud rumbling noise as it approached the man standing at the edge of the ballast stones beside the steel rails.

Shorty took out his bottle, turned it up and drained it empty. The warmth in his belly felt good. The speed had kicked in, and he was flying high with those "*Ghost Riders in the Sky*." He loved that old country song by Vaughn Monroe. He used to listen to it when he was a boy on the Gallatin radio station up in Tennessee.

The man stepped out onto the tracks and turned to face the locomotive. Its bright light illuminated him as though he were staring into the cosmic eye of Almighty God. The whistle howled and screamed as the engineer yanked frantically on the lanyard. His life began to pass before his eyes, all the disappointment, all the hurt, all those things he had no control over. He was a bastard, a lost soul, and nobody loved him. But somehow he knew that he, too, was responsible. His decisions had been wrong decisions. No matter. He wasn't going to deal with that anymore.

"I'm sorry, God. I'm sorry I made such a mess of things. Please forgive me."

The engineer locked down on the brakes, but the train went sliding forward at 55 miles an hour. It would take nearly a mile to stop. The man stood between the tracks with his arms outstretched as though he were Christ on the cross. The locomotive was less than a hundred feet away.

"Lester! Get Up Here! I Need You!"

The fireman had never heard the engineer scream before. He burst from his place behind the levers and mechanisms for the big diesel engine. Lester tripped, falling against the engineer, spilling his coffee, grabbing the front of the engineer's coveralls.

"Oh My God!"

Shorty was thinking about the first time he and Alexandria made love. Neither one of them were hooked back in the day. It all started when they got involved with that Mexican drug lord who gave them money for helping distribute the marijuana, and later on the cocaine. He recalled how Alexandria loved snorting the white powder. Then they learned to cook the stuff in a silver spoon, and put it in their arms. Next came the brown heroin from South America which stole his Alexandria away from him.

Shorty could almost reach out and touch the glaring white light of his earthbound executioner, hear the desperate wailing of the locomotive warning him off the tracks, feel the quaking of the earth as tons of iron and steel bore down on him without pity.

It made no difference. He was happy in those final moments. He was going home to be with Alexandria. No more heartaches and tears. No more being lost and afraid. No more shakes and humiliation. He would fly up with the angels and touch the hand of God. They would be together through all eternity, happy, smiling, forever in love.

"I'm coming, Alex. I'm coming, sweetheart."

The grinding pain lasted only a second.

Chapter Thirty-Four

Winston's Remembrance

Rico had called a meeting with John Parker and Winston Peters, the two detectives, and two of his crew, Nails and Harry. The Muslims had arrived in Mexico. His attempts to involve the FBI had proven fruitless. Rico was concerned over the safety of Cottonmouth and McCoy.

"The ragheads landed in Mexico City this morning. My boys lost 'em in traffic. They were headed into town, but they could be on their way here for all I know. There must be forty or fifty landing strips around Mexico City. My bug in the Saudi Embassy went dead last night so Washington is out of the picture. We need to formulate a plan right now."

"What are the chances of finding them again if they're still in Mexico?" John Parker asked.

"Not good. We don't have the manpower over there we have here."

Nails offered his opinion. "I think we oughta concentrate on Miami. Arabs ain't that hard to spot."

The briefing triggered suppressed memories of briefings twenty-five years earlier. It was 1943 and Winston Peters was flying over Hellfire Corner above Dover. He and his squadron of B-17s were starting across the Channel when the P-38s and the P-47s came up to escort them. The German pilots were smart. They would wait over the Netherlands until the American fighters were running low on fuel.

His group was part of a British and American bombing raid. The Allies had been bombarding the target relentlessly for nearly a week. Two hours later he saw a red glow on the horizon in front of the Dixie Belle. As they approached at 18,000 feet a sight greeted them straight out of hell. Hamburg was in flames, smoke rising thousands of feet into a starry night sky. Everywhere there was fire and the drifting Christmas trees, flares sent up by the Germans to target the bombers. The boiling cauldron of flames illuminated the bellies of the aircraft giving them the appearance of flying crosses. Once again his mind filled with the rapid-fire detonation of the bombs, the chatter of the machine guns, a British Lancaster going down, and the monotonous drone of the Curtiss-Wright engines.

He would learn later that the temperature rose to fifteen hundred degrees while winds up to one hundred and fifty miles an hour tore through the city streets sucking oxygen into the conflagration. People were swept off their feet like pieces of paper and disappeared into the flames. The asphalt streets caught fire. Everything burned.

Colonel Pierre LaSalle was a prisoner of war in Hamburg. Captain Peters read his postwar account about the horrors inside the city, and the terrified residents trying to save themselves in the Elbe River. Forty-two thousand six hundred Germans were burned alive, suffocated, or blown to kingdom come. Another thirty-seven thousand were injured. His nightmares about the civilians in the firestorm never left him.

Captain Peters feathered a port engine spewing oil from flak damage just as his bombardier toggled their bombs. The ball gunner was stuck. His radioman was using a pry bar to get him out. Up ahead a

Halifax was being shot to pieces by a Focke-Wulf 190.

The bombers were buffeted around the sky by updrafts of heat from the firestorm. A tornado of flame rose thirteen hundred feet above the center of the stricken city.

"FWs at six o'clock!"

Loud bangs indicated 20 mm shell hits. The Dixie Belle shuddered then resumed normal flight.

"Winston, the tail gunner's hit."

"Get him out of there!"

"He's dead, Captain."

"Winston! Are you all right?" John asked.

Winston's face was contorted as though in pain. "Sorry … I … I was distracted."

John Parker had seen the thousand-yard stare before. He touched Captain Peters' shoulder with his damaged hand, one comrade of war to another. Rico hurried over and stood beside Winston. Cottonmouth, Nails, and Harry were up out of their chairs.

"I'm fine, let's get on with it."

"Are you sure? Is there anything I can get you?"

"If there was a problem I would tell you."

"Okay, then. Nails, what about our guns?"

"Me an' Harry got 'em stashed in the trailer park."

"You get mine?" Cotton asked.

"I got enough shit to start World War Three, including a brand-new .30 caliber Browning."

"What about grenades?" John asked.

"I got a boxful, an' those Claymore things you wanted."

Harry voiced a warning. "Cotton an' McCoy better lay low 'til we find doz fucks."

"I got the airport covered and the train station, but Nails is right," Rico agreed. "Our best bet is watching the city."

Winston asked Rico, "How many men can you muster?"

"I got the unions. Three hundred I know I can count on. My men number sixty-seven."

Winston smiled. "That should do it. We'll need a cover story for John and Cotton."

"We better watch our butts too," Harry cautioned. "Dem Colombos knows us. Dey got informers just like Rico. Doz bums is in on it!"

John wore a frown. "What about our wives and kids?"

Winston placed a hand on John's arm. "We should prepare the same way the Brits prepared for war. That means getting our families out of harm's way."

"Mister Peters is right," Cottonmouth told John. "This ain't no different from Japs or Germans landin' on South Beach. They're comin' to snuff our asses an' fuck with our country."

"This is some crazy shit!" Nails declared. "Arab fruitcakes comin' to fuck with Uncle Sam!"

John Parker suggested to Katherine that she and Joyce take a trip to the Virgin Islands while Winston was still visiting from Atlanta. John used the excuse that he didn't want his wife and Joyce bored with a lot of military jargon. The women were overjoyed at the prospect of a week of girl's fun in the sun at an international resort. It was Joyce's first respite since Steve's death.

Samantha and Roger were another matter. They were in school and couldn't just pack up and leave. So Rico assigned six of his best men to watch over them, night and day. The next afternoon Joyce and Katherine boarded a Delta jet bound for the islands. Roger and Samantha planned to fly down the following Friday afternoon and stay through Tuesday. It was the best John could muster on the spur of the moment. He felt conflicted for deceiving his family, but believed he was protecting them in doing so. If the Muslims or the South Americans knew about him and Winston it could prove disastrous not to get his family out of Miami.

Rico's wife was an old hand at laying low. She understood the nature of her husband's business affairs. Marie kept their two daughters inside the family compound with her and the bodyguards. Missus Basilio was told her husband was dealing with a confederation of international smugglers. Rico's home resembled a fortress in the fashionable seaside community of Golden Beach. If an emergency arose, John was to bring Roger and Samantha to the compound for safekeeping.

Chapter Thirty-Five

Night of the *Ghost*

With Boogie, Sarah, and Trudy safely hidden away in a small military hospital for politicians and officers, Dutch set sail for Miami with a complement of seven Panamanian soldiers to help operate the ship. A second 20 mm Oerlikon had been installed on the aft deck during repairs. That gave the *Ghost* two 20 mm cannons and four .50 caliber machine guns which was more than a match for any known pirate vessels in the region.

The ninety-foot gunboat *Isabella* sailed alongside the *Gray Ghost* a mile to starboard. She sported an assortment of weapons including her 88 mm deck cannon. The German eighty-eight was one of the most feared weapons of the Second World War. Its deadly accuracy was legendary.

John Paul Jones was acting first mate. His father was an American sea captain who married his Panamanian mother in 1942. Captain Richard Horatio Jones went down with his ship and all hands during the Battle of the Atlantic. A German wolf pack sank Captain Jones' and five other Liberty ships that fateful voyage. Salon never remarried, raising John Paul as her only child.

The tropical night had a sense of magic about it. Seas were running at six feet with phosphorous from the breaking waves blowing in the wind. The ocean was platinum from the glow of the lunar body overhead. Lightning forked the eastern horizon, but no storm clouds came their way. A fresh breeze blew from the south and the sky was black, studded with points of light from eons past.

A dark silhouette of the Costa Rican shoreline lay four miles to port. Shooting stars blazed their epitaphs across the silent heavens. It was midnight. The *Gray Ghost* was traveling north with the Equatorial Current. In the distance they could hear sperm whales singing to keep the pod together. Dutch and John Paul were in the pilothouse smoking Marlboros, and enjoying a fresh pot of Peruvian coffee.

"So you never knew your father?"

"*Si*, Poppa got killed five months before I was born. That is my one regret in life. I never met my poppa."

"Don't you have pictures your mother saved?"

"I have pictures. Mama dug them out before she died."

"What happened to your mother?"

"Mama had the cancer. It is the bad sickness, Captain Henry."

"I'm not a licensed sea captain. I was in the Army."

"You are the captain of this ship. Captain E'Manuel make you our captain. We obey you."

Dutch laughed. "I appreciate the promotion."

John Paul Jones liked Dutch Henry. The feeling was mutual.

"Captain E'Manuel say you brave man. You save this ship once before."

"I'll try and live up to Tony's confidence in me."

"Captain E'Manuel is good man. He is fair with his men. He treat us like brothers."

"We're all brothers when it comes to fighting. The only difference is skin color."

"I like the way you talk, *senor*. You smart man."

"Let's take a walk around the deck, make sure everything is shipshape."

"*Si* ... let me find my flashlight."

They took the steel stairs down to the main deck and began their inspection. The *Gray Ghost* was a deceptive vessel, painted light gray which gave her the ability to blend in with the ocean. Cargo ships did not have reinforced bows for ramming, were not capable of twenty-four knots, nor did they have 20 mm weaponry onboard. All that was in a class with lightly armed naval craft.

"Did you play sports in school?"

"I was good with the soccer, but I hurt my knee so I quit and finish the education. I was a good soccer player, but I like the Army better. It is the balanced and stable life. No surprises unless there's fighting."

"Do you have a girlfriend, John Paul?"

"Oh, si! She is a beauty. She takes good care of me."

"I have a woman too. Her name is Trudy."

"I bet she is smart like you, Captain Henry."

"Smarter! She was with me when ... "

A flash of light caught Dutch's eye. It was a mile or so beyond the *Isabella*. Then they heard the unmistakable whine of an incoming shell, followed by the rolling report of cannon fire.

A column of water exploded high above the masts between the two ships.

There was another flash.

"Get the men out of bed! Man the guns! Meet me on the bridge in ten minutes!"

A second column of water shot skyward beside the *Isabella*. Dutch took the steps three at a time, switched off the running lights, shoved the throttle forward, and turned on the radio.

"Come in, *Isabella*! Come in, *Isabella*!"

"I hear you, Captain Henry. It's the *Sea Witch*. She has never been this way before."

"What the hell is the *Sea Witch*?"

"Colombian gunboat! She has a five-inch main battery. You must run for it. She's after you!"

"No way! I'll follow you. You're outgunned."

"God bless you, sir. We are crossing the T now!"

The eighty-eight belched flame followed by an explosion amidships on the *Sea Witch*. The *Sea Witch* fired again. A blast ripped a hole in the stern of the *Isabella*. The *Gray Ghost* was out of range, but John Paul had both 20 mms firing high in hopes of scoring a few hits. The added firepower might distract the *Witch's* gunners.

It took Dutch three agonizing minutes to complete the starboard turn and fall in behind the *Isabella*. He was in range! An incoming 127 mm shell blasted a gaping hole in the starboard side of the *Ghost*. Diesel fuel began pouring into the sea. Her twin .50 calibers opened fire. Tracers filled the night between the three combatants.

Dutch knew the *Witch* would target the pilothouse so he was hunched down peering out the windows when a five-inch shell hit the funnel and blew the roof off. Dutch was knocked to the floor. There were sharp burning sensations in his back and legs. He got back up. The *Isabella* was listing to starboard but still manning her eighty-eight, her 40 mm Bofors firing nonstop.

The eighty-eight belched flame again, striking the *Sea Witch* at her waterline. She was taking on seawater the same as the *Isabella*. Another hit from the five-inch battery and the *Isabella* began to settle. *Isabella* fired her last salvo. It clipped a wave and burst in midair.

A loud explosion aft wiped out the 20 mm Oerlikon and its two-man crew. Dutch looked out to see them sprawled on the deck beside their mangled weapon.

John Paul burst through the port door, his left hand wrapped in bandages. "I apologize for my tardiness. I had the little accident."

"You're right on time, John Paul. Does our forward battery have ammunition?"

"Si! They have plenty. The second gun she is no more."

"I know."

Another explosion rocked the *Gray Ghost*. When Dutch and John Paul regained their balance the forward gun crew was gone, blown overboard.

Another blast hit them.

The *Gray Ghost* shuddered. Fumes in the aft fuel locker had ignited setting the fuel oil ablaze. Her .50 caliber guns were silent now. John Paul and Dutch Henry stood looking at one another in that age-old ceremony between men who know everything is on the line, and one mistake means the end.

"John Paul, I want you to go down and see if the forward gun still works."

"I will do it, my brother. God be with you."

"God protect you, my friend."

As his companion departed the cabin Dutch recalled Boogie's remark about one's honor being in question in the drug smuggling business. Grass was no big deal, but Dutch knew that sometimes it led to other things such as heroin or cocaine. Trudy and Sarah had told him stories about people getting hooked on drugs after smoking marijuana just once. Some of those people were dead now. Dutch felt the harsh grip of responsibility, a deep sense of melancholy, and the unbearable sadness of being alone.

All this killing and murder over a lousy load of cannabis!

Dutch swung the wheel over savagely, turning the bow of the ship ninety degrees, locking the throttle forward against the control panel.

Pom! Pom! Pom! Pom!

John Paul was still alive!

A terrific blast blew away part of the floor beneath his feet. His legs went numb. His ears rang from concussion. Blood stained his khaki trousers turning them black. The *Witch* loomed ever larger as the *Ghost* bore down on her amidships. She couldn't escape. There was too much water in her belly.

A five-inch shell struck the foredeck of the *Ghost*, glancing into the sea. The blast surrounded the ship with a white, ghostlike mist. And for a few seconds she resembled her namesake.

Higher and higher her bow rose against the silhouette of the *Witch*.

Two hundred yards to go!

Machine gun bullets peppered *Ghost's* superstructure, glass flew, slivers of wood fell.

Pom! Pom! Pom! Pom!

"Go, John Paul! Go, you magnificent son of a bitch!"

One hundred yards!

The *Ghost* was turning 300 rpms, churning up a violent sea in her wake. Dutch heard yelling and gunfire.

The *Witch* fired again. A 127 mm projectile whistled through the wrecked pilothouse into the night, past Dutch's ear.

Fifty yards!

Flames billowed from *Ghost's* ruptured fuel locker. Dutch could feel the heat.

Pom! Pom! Pom! Pom!

He wondered what it felt like to die.

The crash of metal against metal made a shrill, screaming sound. Rending and grinding, banging and scraping, the agonized cry of a ship being struck a mortal blow. The *Gray Ghost* had cut the *Sea Witch* nearly in half.

Dutch Henry reversed his propeller, full throttle; more grinding and rending of tortured steel. Slowly, the *Ghost* began to pull free.

Backing away fifty yards, Dutch placed the telegraph in Stop, and went looking for John Paul. He found him facedown in a pool of blood, unconscious beside the Oerlikon.

He knew he should flood the fuel locker and put out the fire. Save the *Gray Ghost*. Save the valuable cargo.

Trudy and Sarah appeared in his thoughts. He thought about Wayne and stuffing his leg with surgical gauze to stop the bleeding. He remembered believing Sarah was dead. That was gut-wrenching. And the woman he loved, shot three times. It was a miracle the four of them were still alive.

He recalled the two couples they found in the ocean, half devoured by the sharks. The first sea battle came to mind, and all those men who died fighting for a better way of life.

Across the moonlit waters the *Sea Witch* was sinking beneath the waves. Some of them had survived. He could distinguish their heads bobbing in the ocean. The survivors from the *Isabella* were rowing a lifeboat over to rescue them.

His thoughts returned to his loved ones, Trudy and Sarah, Wayne and Bubba-J. He thought again about his father-in-law. Mister Peters was not a fan of drug smuggling. He was probably ashamed of his son-in-law. Winston Peters, war hero. Dutch Henry, drug smuggler. His mother would be heartbroken when she found out.

Dutch looked down at the brave man unconscious at his feet. Then the children appeared. They came and stood around him, the little Vietnamese boys and girls with their trusting brown eyes and friendly, smiling faces. The brown-skinned youngsters brought tears to his eyes, and for several moments Dutch wept for the lost children. He wept for the dead soldiers. And he wept for himself.

Dutch got hold of John Paul beneath his arms and pulled him around to the port side of the ship which still had a lifeboat intact. He loaded John Paul in the boat then swung it out over the railing ready to be launched.

Then he returned to the pilothouse and radioed an SOS.

Finding the seacocks in the forward hold wasn't easy with bilge water up to his knees from the collision. He opened just one, and the sea came rushing in. Dutch could barely see with his flashlight batteries going dead, but he knew the kids were down there with him. Their presence gave him comfort.

He wished he could hug them, but that was not possible.

Chapter Thirty-Six

It Begins

Cottonmouth was sitting at the bar waiting for Mama to bring the cheeseburgers. Mama didn't serve meals to her customers, but she did favors for the two detectives. McCoy had gone down the street with Harry to buy a tin of Price Albert pipe tobacco. She had just set the cheeseburgers down on the counter when gunfire erupted outside.

"Mama! Shotgun!"

Mama Maybell tossed Cottonmouth her sawed-off .12 gauge double barrel which she kept under the counter ever since Jimmy Four Eyes got himself murdered in the alley.

He ran out the rear exit, going around the side of the building, up the alleyway toward the front of the Three Feathers. Forty yards to his right he saw McCoy lying on the sidewalk. Harry was kneeling beside him. They were behind a steel mailbox and a rickety newspaper dispenser. Across the street sat a white van with an AK-47 poked out the back window.

Harry bobbed up and fired a round. McCoy let go with his .45 automatic. Ricochets, sparks, and newspapers flew in the air. They were trapped in a vulnerable position. The van began backing up.

A pair of telephone poles blocked the driver's view of the alleyway. Cotton eased along the side of the building up to the corner, slid the shotgun between the brick wall and the two poles, and fired both barrels at once. Windows in the van shattered. A man screamed. The van roared away.

"You idjits tryin' to get yourselves killed?"

Harry was disgusted with himself. "Doz fucks caught me off guard, Cotton. I was eyeballin' dis girl's ass an' wham! Dey like ta got us."

McCoy was incredulous he was still alive. "Harry knocked me down or I'd be dead as a doornail!"

"Saudis or Colombians?"

"Colombos!"

"How do you know that?"

"Dey wadn't no goats in da car wid 'um."

"Seriously, damn it!"

"They cursed at us in Spanish."

"Come on you two comedians. Our burgers is gettin' cold."

Back inside the tavern the patrons gathered around the trio asking one question after another. Finally Mama told them all to go sit down, and leave her guests alone so they could eat. To settle their curiosity she ordered a round of drinks on the house. That had the desired effect. Inner-city gunfights were not uncommon over turf wars or racial tensions.

"Did you get a look at 'em?"

"Just a voice."

"I don't like this. We got two groups gunnin' for us now."

"Get da coppers involved. Dey don't know nuttin' 'bout you guys an' shit."

McCoy liked the idea. "That would keep the greasers busy while we hunt the ragheads."

Cotton agreed. "I think you're right, Harry. Tell Rico we'll call 'em in, okay?"

"Okay, Cotton. Dez burgers is good!"

Departing the Three Feathers they elected to check out the neighborhood. Thirty minutes later they hadn't spotted anything suspicious. Harry suggested a cold beer. When they pulled in the rear parking lot at Tobacco Road they saw a white van parked beneath the shade trees, facing SW 7th Avenue. McCoy slowly drove by. Windows on the driver's side had been blown out by buckshot. Cottonmouth got out and walked around to the other side of the vehicle with his .45 in his hand. There was a dead man lying on the back floor. Part of his face decorated the interior of the van.

Further inspection revealed a blood trail leading from the driver's side of the van to an empty parking space. They had stashed a second car in the parking lot. One man dead and one injured, maybe more. McCoy made the call to headquarters to start the ball rolling. With the police involved the Colombians would have their hands full. That would give the detectives and Rico the freedom they needed to locate the Wahhabis.

Chapter Thirty-Seven

Men of Honor

Rico Basilio and Winston Peters were waiting at John Parker's home on Judith Drive. John had just left on a run to the liquor store to purchase a quart of Wild Turkey. Nails and Harry were due in fifteen minutes. So were Cottonmouth and McCoy.

Minutes later John pulled back in the driveway with Nails and Harry right behind him.

The two Mafioso carried two duffle bags inside and lay them down in the middle of the living room floor. McCoy and Franklin drove up, exited the police vehicle and walked inside. John set about mixing cocktails for his guests.

When everyone had their drinks John proposed a toast. "To the success of our mission."

Winston Peters followed suit with a second toast. "To absent friends."

Rico removed his jacket and took the floor. He was wearing a shoulder holster with a Walther PPK.

"Men, you all know about the fracas down at the Three Feathers last Wednesday afternoon. Detective McCoy has called in the police which was an excellent idea. It gets the Colombians off our backs so we can concentrate on the Arabs. They're here. I got the tip last night. I don't know how many or where they are, but we'll find them. I have nearly four hundred men out looking right now.

"The *Gray Ghost* hit a snag. She was sunk in a sea battle with a Colombian gunboat. Panama also lost a gunboat in the action. A number of men were killed. Dutch Henry survived with … "

Winston Peters lurched to his feet, visibly shaken. "My daughter? Was Trudy onboard?"

"No, Winston! The girls are safe and sound in Panama City."

"Thank God!" Winston sank back in his chair. "Is Dutch badly hurt?"

"I have a story to tell you, Mister Peters. It seems Dutch Henry has become a celebrity. He's the toast of Panama City. They're taking care of him in a military hospital. Wayne Compton and the women are there with him."

"What are you talking about?"

"He rammed a Colombian gunboat called the *Sea Witch* with the *Gray Ghost*, and sank the ship. He's credited with saving the lives of thirteen men, five of them Colombian sailors who were taken prisoner. That son-in-law of yours is something else, Winston. He sank a gunboat with a cargo ship. That takes some pretty big cojones!"

"Well, I'll be jiggered!" Winston Peters stood up and addressed the gathering. "I'm going to tell you something I don't want repeated outside this room. With all this drug business back and forth, which I do not approve of, I was beginning to think Trudy had made a mistake. I should have known better. My daughter is a brilliant woman. It sounds like she caught herself the brass ring when she married Dutch Henry."

John responded to his friend. "I believe she did, Winston. Dutch and Wayne are patriotic individuals. A little wild at times, but so were we at their age."

"I'd like ta meet doz guys," Harry chimed in.

"I'll see to it, Harry," Winston responded. "We'll have ourselves a real do when this is over."

Rico turned to Nails. "Show 'em what you got."

Nails pulled out a .30 caliber Browning machine gun and laid it across Cottonmouth's knees. "I got the tripod and some boxes of ammo out in the trunk. I can get more anytime you want it."

Cottonmouth picked up the heavy weapon with one hand, smiling like a kid with a new toy. He ran his fingertips over the sleek metal receiver and the long gun barrel with sincere appreciation. "Thanks, Nails. I sure do like it."

"Any time, Cotton. You ain't like no cop I ever met before."

Nails rummaged around and pulled out an M-1 assault rifle, an M-1 carbine, and a .45 caliber Tommy gun. Then he opened the other duffel bag and dug out two Browning Automatic Rifles.

"I got these for Harry an' me. The rifle is for Mister Peters an' this carbine's for Mister Parker. Rico gets the chopper. I gotta trunk fulla ammunition. Them bombs is still at the trailer park. I got some other stuff too."

Nails pulled out an M-79 grenade launcher. "The gun dude said this thing has a range of four hundred meters. You could blow them A-rabs away in the next county. He gimme thirty shells."

John Parker was impressed. "That is one serious piece of equipment. We had those in Vietnam."

William McCoy stood up and addressed the group. "Bill and I want to thank each one of you for helping us. Before Rico and you guys got involved we knew our days were numbered. My Daisy got killed. Then Mattie passed away. The way things turned out we're doing something good for our country. Me and Cotton are blue collars, but we're damn proud to be a part of this outfit."

Winston turned in his chair and faced McCoy. "Every man in this room comes from humble beginnings, John. You and Cotton are valuable assets. We're damn proud to have you. And yes, it has come down to us fighting for our country. Maybe that's what Joyce Overstreet meant when she said our friendship wasn't a coincidence."

Nails responded. "Maybe this ain't no coincidence, but I'd like to think if I get whacked I died for a good reason. This country's been good to me. I got no complaints. The funny part is nobody will ever know but us."

Rico smiled with pride when Cottonmouth added his analogy. "We're Americans. It's what we do. Ain't nobody else got the balls."

Chapter Thirty-Eight

The Citrus Farm

The Republican National Convention was held at the Miami Beach Convention Center August 5 through August 8, 1968. Richard Milhouse Nixon, Vice President for Dwight David Eisenhower, was nominated on the first ballot. Nixon chose as his running mate Spiro T Agnew, Governor of Maryland. "Let's win this one for Ike!" was one of Nixon's campaign slogans.

Three months earlier US troops had been dispatched to Venezuela to protect Mister and Missus Nixon from communist-inspired violence as they toured Latin America on a goodwill tour. Similar protests occurred in Peru. French Algiers was awash in civil unrest. Iraq and parts of the Middle East were in chaos. Cuban rebels kidnapped forty people, mostly American sailors and Marines near Guantanamo Bay. Sputnik had just rattled the doors of the military world. Mao's Cultural Revolution was in full swing. And Leonid Brezhnev had consolidated his power as Premier over the Soviet Union.

Hundreds of thousands of Chinese citizens were being starved and murdered by Mao's Red Guards. Soviet dissidents simply disappeared when taken into custody by the KGB. North Korea, Romania, and Haiti were dictatorships of pure evil. Africans were slaughtered in wholesale numbers. Others were taken prisoner and sold as slaves on the black market. The planet was a three-ring circus of conquest, war, famine, and death. Good people, the majority, didn't want to get involved. Meanwhile, women's liberation groups targeted the Miss America Beauty Pageant in Atlantic City.

"Cut across 5th then turn up Alton Road. Once you get past Sunset Lake the traffic should thin out. These convention people are worse than sea gulls. They're into everything."

Nails nodded. "You said a mouthful, boss. Bootnose got so many Republicans callin' for hookers he can't keep up with 'em. Said he borrowed some Puerto Rican girls from Black Willie last night."

Harry responded. "I like dat Willie. He treats doz broads nice."

"Willie is a savvy businessman. Treat the hookers like ladies and they'll be loyal to you. Bootnose is a good example. Remember when that politician from New York broke Ruby's arm?"

"Yeah, boss. Boot took Ruby to da hospital den caught da guy. Poor Yankee bastard."

"That's the point, Harry. The girls respect Bootnose because they know he'll protect them from the bullos and the cortigianos. Johns treat our girls right or get their teeth kicked in. They still with us?"

"Two cars back, boss. I'm watchin' in the rearview mirror."

They were on their way to the citrus farm. The two detectives, with John and Winston in the backseat, were following in a blue Pontiac. Twenty minutes later they drove down a sandy driveway to the old plantation manor beside the ocean.

The red fox came out to observe from her vantage point behind a blackberry bush near her burrow beneath a eucalyptus tree. The curious little fox remembered the man creatures from weeks earlier."

"Some place, huh?"

Winston loved the farm. "Damn, Rico. This is great.

"This is McCoy's, Franklin's, and my retirement plan. Land will be worth a fortune someday."

"Yes, it will. This is a very impressive investment. Say, if another piece like this turns up let me know about it. I have some money in London drawing three percent interest. That barely keeps up with inflation."

John Parker voiced an interest. "Same here, Rico. Katherine and I have a few dollars in the bank."

Rico responded,"I'll ask an agent I know. See what she can come up with."

"Where should we dig?"

"One of the boundary lines down by the water might be good."

"We could leave it open and let the animals do the job."

"I'm concerned about bones when we sell the property."

Cottonmouth spoke up. "Let 'em think this is it. I'll take tha bodies out in tha swamp for the gators."

Rico nodded. "I never thought of that."

Harry agreed with Cotton. "It's da smart move, boss. No evidence ta cause trouble."

Nails disagreed. "The swamp's okay, but me an' Harry takin' 'em out a few miles is better."

Rico turned to John and Winston. "What do you think?"

"Do the ocean! Sharks will eat the evidence," John answered.

"I agree with John. A hunter might find something out in the boondocks."

Cottonmouth nodded. "I'll help you guys when it's done. It's gonna be a stinkin' ass mess, though!"

Chapter Thirty-Nine

Joyce Overstreet

Joyce and Katherine

The Five Star Hotel sat atop a rocky bluff on a peninsula between Charlotte Amalie Harbor and the Caribbean Sea. On the backside of the island was the Atlantic Ocean. A Mafia family owned the hotel. Katherine and Joyce had no idea Enrico Basilio had arranged their reservations which cost John Parker nothing.

Saint Thomas is one of approximately fifty islands and serves as the capital for the Virgin Islands. The islands are the remnants of volcanic activity dating back many centuries. Christopher Columbus discovered the region in 1493 on his second voyage from Spain.

Shannon and Roger had arrived the night before. "Mom, I just love this place. I wish Daddy was here."

"I do too, dear, but he's involved with Mister Peters so we have to let them do their thing."

"Do you think being a veteran is like being in a fraternity?"

"Something like that. Soldiers experience horrible things in wartime. It bonds them together as men. It's a little like us ladies having babies. That's our spiritual connection as mothers."

Joyce smiled. "You'll be joining the club soon enough, Sam."

"Roger and I want two little ones, a boy and a girl."

Katherine teased Joyce. "You've been quiet as a church mouse ever since we sat down to breakfast."

"This place is so elegant I keep losing my place. And weren't those blueberries delicious? What do y'all want to do today?

Roger was enthusiastic about Buck Island. "We could go snorkeling."

Katherine replied, "I'd like to sit by the pool and get some sun. How 'bout you, Joyce?"

"And a pitcher of rum punch!"

"You and Shannon run along. We'll be here by the pool working on our Saint Thomas rum diet."

"Don't get knee-walking, you two."

"Now there's an idea. Take care of Shannon, you."

"Don't worry, Mom. I will."

Two hours later the women were ensconced on their wicker lounges by a kidney-shaped pool imbibing their second pitcher of rum punch. Joyce was in a reflective, melancholy mood. Katherine was nearing her tiddly zone.

"I been thinking."

"What about, dear?"

"I don't understand it."

"Then it's probably a crock."

"I keep wondering about God."

"What has God done to piss you off?"

"I don't understand why they're so many shitty people in the world."

"Shitty people are like lawyers, there's one on every corner."

"None of it makes sense to me."

"The Bible says it's man's will."

"Man's will doesn't give babies cancer. Or make pets die. Maybe the people who wrote the damn thing were passing the buck."

"Tell that to Harry Truman."

"Korea was a fine example. Communist soldiers killing people like rats."

"I don't try to understand. It's too complicated."

"You think I'll go to hell for doubting God?"

"We'll go together. I'll keep you company." Joyce laughed.

"I don't have those answers, Joyce. Nobody does. It's a matter of faith."

"I have faith, but since Steve died I've misplaced mine somewhere."

"I know, honey."

"That's what I don't understand. Good people die, and bad people go on living."

"I don't know. Ever since John came home he's been different, detached, off in his own world someplace. When Mister Peters came to town, he changed. John's his old self again."

"I know how hard you tried to fit me in when John came back, and Steve didn't."

"I was worried about you, and about John."

"I talk to Steve at night, when I'm in bed and the lights are out. Sometimes it feels like he's there."

"He probably is, sweetie."

"I close my eyes and imagine him lying in bed beside me. It's very comforting."

"Does he say anything?"

"I think he does, sometimes. I think he'll be there for me as long as I need him."

"Don't let go Joyce, not until you're good and ready."

"I'm glad you understand."

"Growing up in an orphanage you learn things early."

"What things?"

"Well, you learn about loneliness, making your own way, and people you can trust."

"I trust you."

"I trust you too, baby."

"I love you Kat, you dear wonderful thing."

"Wanna screw?"

Joyce cackled. "Yes! But you aren't built right."

Katherine grinned. "I'm glad we're friends. You're a sweet person, Joyce."

"We've come a long ways together."

"Miles to go before we sleep."

"I read that poem in high school. I never did understand it."

"Me neither. It's probably about cabbages and kings, and who cares?"

"Let me fresh up your drink, honey pot."

"Don't mind if you do, Miss Joyce."

"I've been wondering lately about John and Mister Peters. Seems like they're up to something."

"Samantha said the same thing last week."

"You think we're imagining things?"

"I'm not sure, but I think we should check into it."

"I believe so, Kat. I don't want us losing one of them like we did my Steve."

Roger and Samantha were just returning from their snorkeling adventure when a stranger walked up and handed Katherine a note. The man was tall and handsome with the bluest eyes she had ever seen. He wore a tailored summer suit and a white silk shirt open at the collar. The man smiled politely, telling her the message was to be read in his presence.

Katherine opened her envelope.

"Dear Mrs. Parker

Please come to the front desk immediately. Bring Mrs. Overstreet, Roger, and Samantha with you.

Drago Eldorado

Hotel Manager"

Trudy's Injuries

"Does it hurt?"

"How'd you like to have shrapnel dug out of your rear end?"

"How much was there?"

"Legs and all, seventeen pieces."

"At least they didn't shoot it off."

"You're a sex fiend!"

"You know I love to tease you."

"Seriously, for a few minutes out there I thought I wasn't going to make it."

"It's terrible about those six men. They only found two of them."

"Is John Paul all right?"

"Yes! He's better."

"He really was brave facing down that big gun. John Paul was out there on the forward deck firing his 20 mm point-blank into the *Sea Witch*. Last time they fired it shot right past me or I'd be with Davey Jones for sure. Then we hit 'em amidships."

"It's in all the papers. You and John Paul are big heroes."

"We did our bit. The real heroes are those dead soldiers. I hope the newspapers mentioned them."

"All their names are in the papers, and I quote, 'killed in heroic action against sea bandits.'"

"Anything out of Colombia?"

"Not one word. It seems the Colombians don't want the world to know about their defeat in a sea battle."

"I'm sorry about the ship. I guess you'll lose your inheritance in Atlanta."

"No, dear. I had Tony take out a policy with Lloyds of London before you left. It cost a pretty penny, but nothing like losing our property on Peachtree Road."

"Man, you're smart. I sure got a good one when I married you."

"Oh, I took pity on you. You needed a keeper."

"Have you heard from your father?"

"He called this morning, said for us to stay put until you and Wayne are well enough to travel."

"Does he know about the *Gray Ghost*?"

"He went on and on about it. You're a terrific individual in the eyes of my father, Mister Hero Man."

"I'm glad. I want your father to like me."

"He does. They all do, sweetheart."

"How's Wayne?"

"Cranky as ever, but he'll be able to use a wheelchair soon."

"When can I get up?"

"The doctor said two days. You have to heal some before you can be up and around."

"Does your stomach still bother you?"

"No, just a big purple bruise."

"I like purple bruises."

"I might show it to you when you're better."

"You know what I was thinking just before I rammed the Witch?"

"What, dear?"

"I was thinking I might never see you again."

Trudy bent over the bed and kissed her husband's forehead. A tear fell on his cheek.

"Don't cry, baby."

"I'm so proud of you. I would have died if you'd been killed out there."

"I have something to tell you, Trudy."

"What?"

"I don't want to do this smuggling thing anymore."

Trudy sat down on the bed beside her husband. "That makes me very happy. I don't want you risking your life ever again. We'll have a great life together just the way we are."

"You're the boss, Miss Magnolia."

"Now I have something to tell you, Mister Henry."

"What?"

"Sarah and Wayne feel the same way you do. Wayne has his marina, and I have my trust fund. We don't need anything else to make us happy."

"How 'bout a couple a kids?"

"Oh, honey! You just blow me away sometimes."

"A Little Dutch and a Little Trudy. They'll have the best Granddaddy in all Atlanta."

"I look forward to being a mother. We'll travel some then you can make me pregnant."

"I'll make that a special project for Mister Gander to come a-courtin' Miss Goosey."

"Gosh, just thinking about it … well, golly."

"That works both ways, sugar plum. Think we can make do here on the hospital bed?"

"No siree!" Trudy hopped off the bed. "You have to get better before Miss Goosey welcomes Mister Gander for a social call."

"Well, okay. Do me a favor, please."

"Sure, baby."

"I'd like a vanilla milkshake."

"I'll go downstairs and ask them to make you one."

"Get yourself a shake while you're at it."

"Yes, something sweet would be nice. I'll get one for John Paul too."

When Trudy returned from the kitchen with three vanilla milkshakes on a plastic tray she found an attractive young woman sitting on a chair beside John Paul's bed. He was propped up, asleep, with his right arm in a sling. His left hand was heavily bandaged.

The lady rose from her chair when Trudy entered the room. "My name is Pilar. Are you Missus Henry?"

"Yes, I'm Dutch's wife."

"John Paul told me about your husband. He saved my Johnny's life."

"Would you like a milkshake?"

"I would love one, thank you. I will tell John Paul you were here. His doctor gave him a sedative to make him sleep."

"How is he today?"

"He will be all right. He was shot, and his hand is broken."

"Is there anything Dutch and I can do?"

"Please come visit my John Paul."

"I'll come back tomorrow. My husband bragged about John Paul. He's a very brave man. "

"I will tell my Johnny. He'll be so happy to see you and your husband."

Back in the room Trudy handed Dutch his milkshake. Trudy seated herself beside the bed to enjoy her treat. There was blood on the sheets. Trudy pulled the blanket down, rolled Dutch over, and reattached a bandage to his hip.

"You're going to have to be still or you'll make them come loose."

"Yaz'um, Nurse Ratched."

"Mister McMurphy, would you prefer your lobotomy in the morning or the afternoon?"

"I take it all back!"

"Wise choice, smarty pants. John Paul has a pretty girlfriend. Her name is Pilar, long black hair, green eyes. A perfect size two."

"I'd like to see them."

"Maybe Sunday, if the doctor says you can get up."

Sarah entered the room. She was carrying a bouquet of orchids and a box of chocolates. "I picked the posies. Tony sent the candy"

"Put 'em in there."

"Trudy, find us something. I'm not going to use his water pitcher."

Trudy left the room and was back in a minute with a vase from the nurse's desk.

"How's Boogie?"

"He's coming along. He'll be up in a wheelchair tomorrow morning."

"That's good news."

"He wants to talk to you about expanding the marina. I don't want him getting his hopes up so I thought I'd run it by you first. Would you be interested in a partnership?"

"I think that's pretty cool."

Trudy voiced a concern. "We're going on vacation when we leave here."

"What about when you come back?"

"Well, it's not that far from Atlanta. I guess we could summer in Florida and winter in Georgia."

"The marina is a very profitable business, but Bubba-J is getting old and Wayne needs help. That hip is going to slow him down. And we have a hospital to build, remember? We need you both."

"Gosh, boat people and airline passengers. We'll have our hands full."

"Say yes, Trudy."

"For the beautiful and ever-engaging Sarah Compton … Yes, Trudy!"

Dutch responded. "Hey, don't I get a say around here?"

Trudy pointed a finger at Dutch. "You hush up or I won't show you my spots."

"Yaz-um, Nurse Ratched."

Sarah laughed. "I love you guys. I'll tell Wayne."

Dutch spoke to his wife. "Come over here and kiss the new boat dock owner."

"Yes, Mister Henry."

Chapter Forty-One

The Mansion

The men had returned to the citrus farm with their weapons and explosives to set up what John Parker termed a "kill zone." That involved the best locations for weapons placement, and the removal of vegetation and trees that might hinder target selection. The detectives were called away at the last minute for a homicide over in Hialeah. Winston and John were present, Nails, Harry, and Rico, plus ten of Rico's crew. Nails was busy placing Claymore mines every thirty feet parallel with the driveway. Winston and Rico were upstairs in the mansion determining the best fields of fire from the second-story windows. Harry was down on the beach helping the men bag sand.

"Dez mothers is heavy!" Harry was bathed in sweat as were the crew.

Winston laughed. "Damn, Harry, you guys look like field hands."

"Dis is worse'n hoopin' stiffs!" Harry placed his sandbag at the base of an upstairs window. "Youse guys stack 'em to da windowsills. Ain't no slugs gettin' thru dat."

A procession of sandbags proceeded up the winding staircase until the bedrooms resembled bunkers. Bruno brought a chainsaw he used to clear scrub trees blocking the view. The trees were cut up and dragged back in the underbrush. A rented backhoe sat in the driveway, its front bucket stacked high with sandbags.

"Put da rest uh dem bags in front uh Nails an' Mister Parker. Vico, give us sum uh dat music you like."

Vico Esposito switched on his portable Heartbeat radio. Big Mama Thornton was wailing "Ball and Chain."

Harry smiled, mopping his brow. "I love dat kinda music, Hank Williams, Ralph Stanley, John Lee Hooker. Reminds me uh bein' a kid again. Dem was good ole days."

Vico responded to Harry. "I like that T-Bone Walker an' Bessie Smith, Louie Armstrong. You ever hear Johnny Lee sing 'Cherokee Fiddle'?"

"Now you're talkin'! How 'bout Webb Pierce an' 'There Stands the Glass' or Ferlin Huskey an' 'Gone'?"

"Oh, man! An' Kitty Wells singin' 'Honky-Tonk Angel'?"

John Parker was showing Nails how to arm a Claymore mine.

"Your blasting cap goes down in either one of these holes. Then reel out your wire behind it. This is your M57 firing device. When Mister Raghead gets within fifty or sixty feet, push the lever. Bang! He's hamburger delight."

"You say its fulla BBs in there?"

"Seven hundred little steel balls, blows their ass away like a big shotgun."

Winston Peters asked Rico a question. "How far do you think it is from here to that big tree over there?"

"I'd say seventy-five or eighty yards."

"I'll set my sights up one click. That should do it. Where'd you get the old hammer shotgun?"

"It belonged to my grandfather. Anzolo fought with the Italian Resistance. The SS murdered him."

"I flew over Italy a few times, but I never landed there."

"The war devastated my country, but things are better now. A lot of the men were killed. Some of the widows have trouble making ends meet. I send money to my cousin Vinnie in Salerno. He makes sure they have food and clothes on their backs."

"You're a good man, Rico. I never thought I'd say that about a Mafioso."

"Thanks, Winston. That means a lot coming from you … even if you aren't a Catholic."

They laughed.

Harry appeared in the doorway. "Boss, I found uh spot."

Rico and Winston followed Harry out of the house and down an animal path to a cluster of tall mangrove and palm trees. Behind the trees was a bowl-shaped depression covered over with bushes and grapevines.

"You can't see it from the driveway or the house. This is good, Harry."

They retraced their steps up the driveway to the backhoe.

"I'll make it about five feet, boss."

Rico's car phone started ringing in the Mercedes. "Rico here."

"Boss, remember you told me to follow Cotton an' McCoy?"

"Yes?"

"I followed 'em over to that murder place. They was three cop cars an' this ambulance was there."

"Go on."

"When our guys left, guess who pulled out behind 'em?"

"Arabs?"

"Two of 'em in a Hertz Chevy. I'm behind 'em right now."

"Listen, Freddie, stick with 'em but don't let them see you. We need to know where they're staying. Call Blackie for backup. Switch off when he finds you."

"Got it, boss. I'm callin' Blackie soon as I hang up."

"Listen up, men. Gather round over here."

Everyone stopped what they were doing and assembled in front of Rico.

"Freddie has spotted two of our Muslims. We'll be pulling out of here in a few minutes so finish up what you're doing. Harry, you stay and dig the hole. Nails, you stay with Harry. Take turns sleeping tonight. We don't want kids coming in here to park and getting hurt."

Harry climbed up on the machine. "I got cold beer in da cooler, sandwiches, an' sleepin' bags. We'll be snug as bugs in a rug, boss."

"Did you remember your mosquito repellant?"

"Shit!"

"I thought so. Here! I brought an extra bottle."

"Thanks, boss."

The red fox watched as the automobiles pulled out and drove away. A yellow machine, a pickup truck, and two of the man creatures remained behind. The little fox wondered what those creatures were doing in her backyard digging in the sand. It troubled her. She didn't like the man creatures. She fretted she might have to move away and find herself another place to raise her kits.

Chapter Forty-Two

The Castaways

They were at the Castaways on Collins Avenue. The motel complex sat on a small jetty of land surrounded by the Atlantic Ocean. The restaurant was a square-shaped building with glass walls and an A-frame roof on each of its four corners. The Teamsters Union owned the motel. Jimmy Hoffa stayed there when he was in town.

Rico was presiding. "You won't believe where the bastards are staying."

"I'll bet someplace creepy."

"No! They're up the road at the Sahara Motel."

John Parker laughed. "That's funny, camels out front and a camel-shaped pool."

Winston Peters made jest. "It's perfectly logical, keeps them from getting homesick."

"Blackie stayed in his car last night and counted heads." Rico continued. "I had a police sergeant go in this morning and check the register. Ten Saudis! They don't know we're on to them or they wouldn't use their country of origin. That gives us the advantage."

"Yeah, but they probably know what Cotton and McCoy look like."

"That plays into our hands too. Cotton said he and Bill will try and lure them to the farm. If we can get them out there their goose is cooked!"

"What if they don't fall for it?"

"We'll manage that situation when we come to it. Keep your weapons handy until this thing blows over. Nails, if you're going to use that grenade gizmo keep a box of shells with you. All of you need enough ammunition for a sustained fight. And keep your eyes and ears open. We don't want them getting the drop on us."

Harry spoke up. "How we gonna do dat lure thing, boss?"

Cottonmouth leaned forward with a Schlitz in his hand. "Me an' Bill go in tha Sahara, see. Pretend we're lookin' for a drug dealer or somethin'. When they spot us we'll bait 'em to tha farm. Then we call Rico on 'is car phone. Gives you mugs time to get out there an' get set up."

Rico responded. "You two be careful. I don't want my partners getting a premature set of wings."

The meeting adjourned and everyone left except Nails, Harry, and Rico. There was serious business to discuss which did not pertain to the situation at hand.

Rico asked, "Did you find out anything?"

"I talked to Bootnose. He thinks it's true," Nails answered

"Fat Mike said da same thing," Harry confirmed.

Rico was troubled. "Can you two handle it by yourselves?"

"You tell us when, boss!"

"We can't chance it right now. The timing is all wrong."

"He goes to that gambling joint ever Wednesday night. Two torpedoes is always with 'im. Me an' Harry got it figured. They's a stand uh trees beside the parking lot. He goes late so it's dark, see. Me an' Harry can wait in the trees."

"I wish we didn't have this to deal with."

"He's a stupid ratfink, boss. All he does is snort coke and lay broads. He wants you whacked 'cause you run the show now. His pride is makin' 'im nuts."

"If da bastard had any pride we wouldn't be in dis fix. He's a lousy stinkin' bum!"

"We've got to wait. Cotton and McCoy come first. I gave my word."

"Okay, boss. I'll have da boys keep der ears open. But if youse gets knocked off I'll kill 'im myself!

Nails agreed with Harry. "Me an' Hoop will snuff them macaroni snappin' *faccia di stronzos!*"

"Our Italian blood runs deep. Your loyalty is a thing of honor. You will be my underbosses when we take control of the organization. If I get bumped off do your thing then take over. Fat Mike knows all the lawyers and politicians. Trust Cottonmouth and McCoy. They're my partners. See to it that Marie and my daughters are cared for. Now let's go."

New Orleans

Katherine sat staring out the window at the patchwork of farms, houses, and villages five miles below. The sky was pale blue like the eyes of a newborn, with wisps of cirrus clouds passing beneath the belly of the aircraft. She thought again about the warning Mister Eldorado had given her and Joyce, an odd statement about Americans being in danger of kidnapping. He'd whisked them off to the airport, and away they flew.

She'd tried calling John the day they left, but got no answer. She made a mental note to purchase one of those answering machines when they got home. Samantha and Roger had missed most of their Virgin Islands vacation, but it didn't seem to bother them. Those two lovebirds were happy no matter where they were.

Joyce was different.

When the hotel manager told them about the kidnapping Joyce turned and whispered, "This is screwy."

Since they were the only ones to leave the hotel, Katherine suspected Joyce was right. Other guests were Americans, but they remained behind.

"Something is going on, Kat. I can feel it."

"I think so, Joyce. Our leaving makes no sense. I'm worried about John and Winston."

"What do you suppose it could be?"

"I have no idea. That's what bothers me. John has never kept a secret from me before."

"Why in the world would they book us to New Orleans, then back to Miami?"

"Mister Eldorado said it was the only flight out this morning. This whole thing is crazy."

Katherine sat thinking. "Unless … somebody really is after us."

"Don't say that. You're scaring me."

"It's the only thing that makes sense. A flight to New Orleans would throw off anyone expecting a flight from Saint Thomas. Didn't Mister Eldorado say someone would meet us at the airport?"

"Yes, he did! I'd forgotten about that."

"Then I suggest we do like he said."

"Oh, Katherine, I'm afraid for us and the children."

"Pray, Joyce. Pray for John and Winston."

They landed at Moisant Field and disembarked into the New Orleans International Airport. A tall man wearing sunglasses, a New Orleans Saints pullover, and blue jeans, and a slender brunette in a jogging outfit with her hair done up in a ponytail greeted them. Each produced credentials identifying themselves with the Central Intelligence Agency. The four travelers were led to a private room away from the main floor of the terminal.

"I know this is hard for you to understand, but you must do as we ask for the sake of John Parker and Mister Peters. Success with what they're doing would be in jeopardy if you returned to Miami. You yourselves might be in danger."

Katherine was frustrated and angry. So were Joyce and the kids.

"This is crazy as hell. What are they doing that got you people involved?"

Ruth Townsend, the CIA agent responded, "We can't reveal that. It's classified. But I can tell you your husband and Mister Peters are working with some very professional people. They're in good hands."

Katherine went off on the woman. "Good hands, my ass! It sounds like they could get themselves killed with all this secrecy bullshit."

George Brown tried to reassure her. "Your husband is a patriot. What they're doing is for the country."

"Fuck the country! I want my husband back! He's been shot already. I don't want him getting hurt or maybe killed."

"But Missus Parker ..."

"If it's so goddamned important, you go do it!"

George Brown changed tactics. "I served in Vietnam just like John Parker and Steve Overstreet. My best friend died over there. The Vietcong caught Richard and tortured him before they hung him in tree. I was wounded in the Ia Drang Valley."

George's reference to Vietnam calmed Katherine and Joyce somewhat.

"John got hurt during Tet. Joyce's husband was with him. Steve got killed helping his men."

"I know. We were briefed with their military records before we came to meet you."

"Can't you tell us anything more?" Joyce asked.

Samantha was on the verge of crying. "I don't want my daddy getting hurt again."

Ruth spoke. "Part of this has to do with smuggling. Drugs are flooding into the United States from all over the world. It's become an epidemic. We do what we can to stop it but thousands of people are smuggling, and thousands more are taking bribes to let the contraband in. We need all the help we can get. Please try and understand."

"I understand if John gets killed my daughter won't have a father. And I won't have a husband."

"I sympathize with you, Mrs. Parker. But it goes beyond drugs. It's about national security."

"I don't believe it!"

"They're dealing with people from another part of the world. That's all I can tell you."

"I still don't understand why John and Winston got mixed up in this."

"Katherine, they chose to be involved because they love their country. All of you must accept that and wait this thing out. It should be over in two or three days."

"I don't like it one bit. What if Mister Parker gets killed?"

"It's like my gunny sergeant used to tell us in Vietnam, Roger. 'Do your job, trust in the Lord, and you'll be home before you know it.'"

"But, sir, this isn't Vietnam."

"I know, son. I sympathize with each one of you. Ruth and I thought this was crazy when we heard about it, but it's extremely important. Mister Parker is doing something that's good for our country. I understand that's difficult to accept, but give him the credit he deserves. He and Mister Peters are brave men. So are the others involved in this."

"Can't you tell us who they are?"

"No, Samantha, I can't. It's classified. Our government doesn't want this getting out."

"Mom, I'm so scared I'm sick to my stomach."

Katherine was accepting the fact that there was nothing she or Joyce could do to stop whatever John and Winston had gotten themselves into. It reminded her of the time John and Steve boarded the military flight for Vietnam. Joyce was physically ill that afternoon. Now it was her turn.

The suite accommodations were nice. They were near the airport in case they received a call saying they could go home. Each in their own way worried about the future, and what it might hold if John or Winston were killed. It was a terrible night in the lives of four innocent people. Ruth supplied them with a vial of tablets to calm them and help them sleep.

Samantha and Roger had taken a pill each and fallen into a restless slumber. Katherine swallowed two tablets, but her anxiety kept her awake. Joyce took none. She knew Katherine needed her.

"Kat, honey, lie back and close your eyes. I'll get a warm washcloth."

Joyce returned from the bathroom, placing the cloth over Katherine's eyes and forehead.

"Joyce, I never knew how bad it was what you went through over Steve. I'm sorry. I wish I had known then what I know now."

"You did a wonderful job looking after me. I have no complaints."

"I'm afraid for him, Joyce. I'm afraid for them both."

"They're grown men with military training. If anybody can make it they will."

"Would you bring me another washcloth, please? My head is splitting."

"Of course, honey."

Joyce returned and placed another warm cloth on Kat's forehead. "Feel better?"

"Yes, thank you. You're my best friend, Joyce."

"I love you too, baby. Try and get some sleep. I'll sit here by the bed."

Katherine was emotionally and physically exhausted. Finally, she drifted away to that distant realm where dreams are born. She found herself behind the lunch counter at Woolworth's Department Store.

The young man sitting down the counter was John Parker. He'd ordered a chicken salad sandwich and a Dr Pepper. John was supposed to ask her out on a date to the beach. They were going on a picnic to-gether, but John never even looked her way.

Hey, John, I'm over here. But Katherine couldn't move or make a sound.

John! John! Take me to the beach.

But John couldn't see her. She was invisible. John paid his $1.05, left a fifteen cent tip on the counter, and got up to leave.

John, she cried. *Please don't leave. John, come back.* But John turned and walked out the door.

She was inside the church wearing her wedding gown. It was a pretty little dress she'd picked out herself. Katherine felt very glamor-ous. She'd gone to the hairstylist to have her hair done, her nails too, but something was wrong. The pastor kept looking at her as if to ask a question. Where's John Parker? Katherine looked around. There was no one in the church but her and the preacher. "Where's John?" she asked with tears in her eyes. But John Parker wasn't coming. There was no John Parker. They never met at the lunch counter.

The hospital scene was one of joy and confusion. Katherine was scared silly. She looked forward to the baby, but this was going to hurt! Her doctor informed her it was a little girl. She and John had decided to name the baby Samantha. Her feet were up in the stirrups, and the doctor was down there ready to assist the little newcomer. But some-thing was missing. Where the heck are the nurses? She felt her tummy. Her stomach was flat. She wasn't pregnant! "Where's my baby?" she wailed. There was no little Samantha. She and her husband had never gone to the beach that special evening when John got her pregnant. Katherine reached for the doctor's hand, but the doctor wasn't there.

The dream shifted to her backyard on Judith Drive. John Parker and Winston Peters were both gazing at something in the backyard next door. They were crouched down behind the lawn furniture with guns in their hands. The birdbath was between them and the big azalea bush. From the corner of her eye Katherine saw movement. A man with a large pistol was creeping up behind Winston and her husband. He raised his weapon pointing it at the back of John's head. The man began to squeeze the trigger.

"NOOO! Stop It! Stop It!" Katherine was tearing at her bedsheets, screaming.

Joyce, half asleep, bolted upright "Katherine! Stop That!"

Samantha and Roger jumped out of bed, running into the room.

Joyce held Kat's face between her hands. "You were dreaming, baby. It's all right. You were dreaming."

Chapter Forty-Four

Farewell to Some

Rico was sitting behind the wheel of his armored Lincoln Continental in the driveway at the citrus farm. His bodyguard, Adolfo D'Angelo, was riding shotgun beside him. The man was tall and angular with jet-black hair and black eyes like his Gypsy father. Adolfo had one of the BARs between his knees. A bandoleer of magazines lay on the front seat between them. John and Winston sat in the backseat, John with his .30 caliber carbine, and Winston with the M-1 assault rifle.

Tension was in the air. Cottonmouth had called that morning saying it looked like the ruse was working. The Hertz Chevy and a Hertz Ford were trailing the two detectives from the Sahara Motel. Cottonmouth had set the plan in motion by insulting one of the Arabs while he and McCoy pretended to be searching for a drug dealer. The Muslim didn't take kindly to being called the sexual suitor of his own mother.

Nails and Harry were a few yards down the driveway in Harry's pickup truck. Nails had possession of the second Browning Automatic Rifle. Harry carried the M-79 grenade launcher.

Six additional men sat in an armor-plated Cadillac beside the pickup truck. Everyone was waiting for a call from Cottonmouth to confirm when he and McCoy would be arriving. It was a hot day. No one wanted to park the automobiles behind the house, and leave the comfort of their air conditioning until they were certain the Muslims were on the way.

Cottonmouth had instructed them to sit tight. He and McCoy were playing it cool, taking their time leading the Wahhabis to the citrus farm. He said it might take thirty or forty minutes.

Ten minutes ticked by … fifteen … twenty minutes. Rico was reaching for the car phone when it rang.

"This is Rico."

"We're in trouble!"

"Where are you? Adolfo! Get the others ready!"

"West Dixie Highway a quarter mile north uh 207th Street. We're in a sharecropper shack."

"Right or left? I'm coming from the farm."

"Right! McCoy drove through tha front wall. He's hurt!"

"Hang on, John! We'll be there in five minutes!"

Adolfo jumped back in the front seat. "Ready, boss."

Rico floored the Lincoln, fishtailing out the driveway onto SE 7th Street heading west. He saw Harry in his rearview mirror come out of the driveway sideways, burning rubber, with the big Cadillac right behind him. Rico slowed the Lincoln down to forty, bouncing across the sandy median onto the southbound lane. The truck and Cadillac spun across the median, slinging a cloud of yellow dust in the air.

Rico pushed the accelerator to the floor. The fuel-injected engine gave vent to a guttural squall like a wounded animal. In seconds they were traveling 100 miles an hour.

William McCoy knelt on a plank floor in front of a shattered window with a three-legged oak table and a raggedy-ass mattress stuffed with goose feathers and old newspapers between him and the wall. The two-bedroom structure was 1930s, dilapidated, and falling to ruin. He'd sprained his wrist maneuvering off the highway, and dodging trees coming up the front yard. A bullet had creased his skull. His shirt and jacket were crusted with blood. Crashing through the front wall of the house had saved their lives.

Cottonmouth had pulled an ancient wood stove out from the kitchen to the second window beside McCoy. The squad car sitting in the living room served as a protective barrier behind the two detectives. Cotton piled the living room furniture against the front wall creating a jerry-rigged bunker on that side of the room. An oak tree growing out of the floor and through the ceiling between them and the kitchen shielded them from the rear of the building. Outside ten Jihadists were advancing on the rickety structure.

"How's your head?"

"I think they knocked some sense into it."

"What about?"

"We need a life!"

Automatic gunfire showered glass and pieces of wood down on both men. McCoy bobbed up and fired a burst from his Tommy gun. More gunfire poured into the building, causing the window frame to fall out on top of McCoy's head. Cottonmouth was trying to sight the .30 caliber through a hole in the wall above the baseboard.

"Pop 'em again so I can see where they are."

McCoy held the submachine gun above the windowsill and squeezed the trigger. Return fire appeared from both sides of a slatboard shed. Cottonmouth cut loose. The hammering machine gun blew boards and greenery in the air. The tool shed groaned, leaned sideways, and fell over in a pile.

Thump!

A rocket-propelled grenade burst through the wall bouncing on the far side of the cruiser and exploded.

"I smell gas."

"Whatever that was punched a hole in the tank."

Thump!

A second rocket grenade burst through the side wall, exploding with a loud bang.

Wooomp!

The gasoline fumes ignited. Flames quickly engulfed the left side of the living room.

"Can you make it?"

"I sure as hell ain't stayin' in here!"

Crawling over the glass-littered floor toward the kitchen they heard a noise on the back porch. Cottonmouth tattooed the rear wall with his machine gun, blowing the kitchen door off its hinges. A man screamed.

"Let's go!"

The cruiser's gas tank exploded just as they ran for daylight. Concussion knocked them sprawling through the backdoor into the yard.

"Bill, up there!"

They ran hunched over for a stack of cinderblocks in the tree line. Bullets plowed the earth around both men. Cottonmouth fell. Bill grabbed John by the hand hauling him back up. Behind the block pile each man paused to catch his breath.

Cottonmouth was in pain. "They got me in the ass again."

"Is it bad?"

"Naw, it just hurts like uh bitch."

"Gimme your gun."

Bill rested the barrel on top of the concrete blocks and blazed away. Cartridge casings bounced about in the dry leaves. The Wahhabis scattered, scrambling for cover.

"Looky here."

"What?"

"Little kitty cats."

"Holy cow! They're babies."

Cottonmouth stuffed the kittens two each in the front pockets of his bulletproof jacket."

Out front they heard the welcome squalling of automobile tires. Rico had arrived.

Gunfire, explosions, gunfire, and more explosions followed ... the Wahhabis were giving back as good as they got.

"Fuck This Shit!"

McCoy stood up, blasting the Arab positions with the remainder of the .30 caliber ammunition belt. The smoking machine gun wrought havoc amongst the Muslim intruders.

"That'll settle their hash ... Awww Jesus!"

The machine gun slid from his hands. He crumpled in the dry leaves, blood spurting from a wound in his throat.

"BILLY!"

His life ebbing away, McCoy grasped his partner's hand, looking up into Cotton's eyes. "So long, Johnny ... take care ... uh those little kitties ..."

William McCoy died in the arms of John Franklin as the firefight reached a thundering crescendo. Waves of gunfire, bursting M-79 rounds, and exploding hand grenades overpowered the Muslims. Two were taken prisoner. The rest lay dead among the sunflowers in the noonday sun.

When John reached the shoulder of the highway where Rico's men were holding the two Wahhabis at gunpoint, the Muslim with a bleeding facial wound spat on John Franklin.

"Fuck you, you infidel freak!"

Cottonmouth whirled, snatched the fanatic off his feet, slamming him down violently against the hood of the armored Cadillac.

He grasped the man's ankles, smashing him into a mailbox, snapping it off at its rusted metal base. The body lay crumpled on the sandy right of way, ribs protruding through a bloody shirt, its spinal column shattered.

John seized the second jihadist by the throat.

Rico yelled, "Stop It! Goddamn You, Cotton, Stop! We Need That One!"

John Franklin hurled the terrified Muslim into a drainage ditch.

"Where's McCoy?"

"Billy's dead."

"I'm sorry, Cotton. We didn't know."

John and Winston approached Detective Franklin cautiously. "Come over here and sit down. You need medical attention."

John noticed Cotton's pockets moving. "What's that?"

Cottonmouth pulled out one of the kittens, a black-and-tan one. The little thing began to purr and lick the blood off his sticky fingers. That's when John Franklin cried.

Chapter Forty-Five

End of the Line

Rubberneckers began lining the highway. Sirens wailed in the distance. A fire engine and several police cruisers were on the way. Harry
and the crew loaded up the bodies in the back of his pickup truck then
Harry took off for the farm. Two of Rico's men were dead. Those they
placed in the trunk of the Cadillac. Adolfo, Nails, and Cottonmouth
were taken downtown to see the Jewish physician who attended Rico's
crew. McCoy went with them. Cottonmouth refused to abandon Bill
McCoy's body to the care of anyone but himself.

A'zam Baz lay back against the front seat of the Lincoln Continental,
his hands bound behind his back. Rico was driving. John and Winston
rode in the backseat. All their weapons were in the trunk. Harry had
taken the Wahhabi guns with him. The scene was well policed except
for the hundreds of spent cartridge casings, the charred Miami Police
cruiser, and the burned-out building.

A'zam spoke. "You may kill me, but others will take my place.

Stupid Americans have no idea what Wahhabi has in store for these United States. You will be conquered. It may take a hundred years, but Allah will win."

Winston asked a question. "What makes you think we won't use the atomic bomb?"

"You will never use your atomic bombs. Your politicians are cowardly and stupid. They will do nothing to turn world opinion against them. They are corrupt and degenerate with the sex and the alcohol. Islam will destroy America!"

Rico took a turn. "Is it true your believers don't drink alcohol or smoke cigarettes?"

"That is very true. Unlike the West we are clean and pure."

Rico continued. "I heard Muslims like hamburgers, cold beer, and barbecue pork."

"No! We do not eat such garbage, especially pork. Pigs are filthy animals."

"Hear that, gentlemen? Pigs are filthy animals."

Rico turned down the driveway into the citrus farm. Harry and Bootnose were waiting at the bottom of the hill. Bootnose had brought an ice cream truck. The truck sat beside the yellow backhoe. John opened the car door allowing A'zam to step out.

"I suppose now you will kill me. That is not important. I will be martyred by my people. Seventy-two virgins await me in Paradise."

Winston posed another question. "What if you don't make it to Paradise?

For the first time A'zam appeared uncertain, not so sure of himself anymore.

Rico spoke. "Show 'im, boys."

Harry grabbed the man by his arms, steering him past the machine to an open pit behind the high stand of trees. At the bottom of the ditch lay the nine corpses of the elite assassin squad. Bootnose stopped at the ice cream wagon, bringing a pair of five-gallon buckets over to the edge of the ditch. He removed the lids, dumping the contents of one bucket down over the bodies. Then he went back to the truck and returned with two pigs' heads. He tossed those in.

A'zam began to scream. It was all Harry could do to hold him. Bootnose came over to help.

Rico gave the order. "Put him in!"

Bootnose and Harry shoved A'zam into the pit. Then Bootnose emptied the second bucket of guts all over the protesting Muslim.

Harry taunted him. "Youse ain't goin' to Paradise, ya miserable fuck. Youse is goin' to hell! No virgins, pally. It's seventy-two Virginians with pitchforks an' butcher knives!"

The once proud A'zam Hussein Baz became a screaming, sobbing hysteric. Covered with pig blood and pig entrails hanging around his neck, he stumbled from one end of the grave to the other with his wrists behind his back, beseeching Allah to save him. Eternal damnation had him by the gonads. Finally the terrified man fell to his knees, sobbing uncontrollably.

"That's enough. Get him out of there."

Harry and Bootnose jumped in the hole and untied his hands. They had to lift A'zam out of the ditch. He had collapsed into a state of shock.

"Take him down to the beach and clean him up. I got a shirt and jeans in the trunk."

John spoke. "That's the damnest thing I ever saw. A grown man going batshit over a bucket of guts. I feel sorry for the little bastard."

Winston spoke. "It's a sad thing seeing a man broken. I feel the same way you do, John. That young individual is the victim of a religious order being bastardized by a group of fanatics. The Nazis brainwashed Germany the same way. The Vatican had a similar problem eight hundred years ago."

Rico opined. "You know what? If it ever comes down to a war

between us and them, we know how to kick their asses now without destroying half the planet."

Winston agreed. "He's right about our politicians. Most of them are cowards, and they have been compromised by all the money and power. It would be up to ordinary citizens like us working in league with the Armed Forces to save our country."

John suggested they go to the beach.

"I'll get the clothes. Let's go down and help the crew."

"Good idea. We have to get Jihad Johnny ready for travel."

Next day A'zam Baz was placed on an airliner bound for Saudi Arabia. He had been instructed in no uncertain terms what would happen to any Muslim returning to Florida with the intention of harming Cottonmouth, any of his friends, or the United States. They would be shot and buried with pig entails so they could never enter the Kingdom of Allah. A'zam thanked Rico for sparing his life. He departed Miami grieving his dead comrades whom he believed were doomed to walking the corridors of hell for all eternity. Harry and Bootnose had already removed the bodies from the citrus farm, and dumped them far out in the Atlantic Ocean.

Chapter Forty-Six

Cottonmouth

John Franklin was downtown in his Chief's office at the Miami Police headquarters.

"I'm sorry about McCoy. He was a fine detective. You two made the department proud. But that has to end today, now. I think you understand why, John. With all your good qualifications, you've become a liability to the department. Too many people know about your connections with the Mob, and they have their suspicions about those drug cartels. If you weren't such a public figure, the brass would probably bring you up on charges.

"That badge you carry in your pocket sets you apart from the criminal elements we deal with every day in this fucked-up metropolis. You've become associated with those elements, so I'm forced to ask you to resign. I hope you can appreciate my position in this situation. Personally, I think you're a great detective, but it's my sworn duty to protect the reputation of this department."

"Ain't no hard feelins, Captain. I been thinkin' 'bout quittin' anyway."

"What about funeral arrangements? We could give William a good sendoff."

"No thanks, Chief. Rico took care uh that."

"Have you heard what happened last night?"

"No! Is Rico okay?"

"The Sicilian is dead. Rico is the big boss now."

"You got Rico all wrong, Chief. He's a crook all right, but he's uh honest American crook."

"Cotton, sometimes I can't tell if you're brilliant or just plain nuts."

"Chief, sometimes I ain't so sure my damn self."

They both laughed.

Cottonmouth laid his badge and his .45 automatic down on the desktop.

They shook hands.

"Take care of yourself, Johnny. Come see me once in a while."

"I will, sir. Take care uh tha city for me."

After the door closed and his footsteps receded down the hallway, Ruth Townsend and George Brown emerged from the back room.

The Chief was concerned over the man he had just forced to resign. "You think he'll hook up with Rico?"

The CIA man responded. "I hope so. What a team those two would make."

"What do you mean by that?"

"Chief, those two guys are what Uncle Sam needs in the coming war."

"You mean another Vietnam?"

Ruth Townsend answered the white-haired police chief. "Washington has pissed Vietnam out the window. We'll survive that. Next time around all the chips may be on the table. We'll need men like John and Rico to help defeat the Fifth Column we have right here in our own backyard."

Chapter Forty-Seven

Daisy

The Reunion

"I don't understand her."

"He's a good man, Kat."

"But look at him. He's ugly!

"Beauty is in the eyes of the beholder, dear."

"Oh, bullshit! He looks like something out of a Dracula movie."

"Katherine, he's one of the bravest men I ever met."

"You don't understand, John. He's friends with that mobster."

"Honey, that's what I'm trying to tell you. That's where Winston and I were last week."

"You were with that mob guy in that gunfight?"

"Yes!"

Katherine grasped the armrest of the sofa and sat down, her complexion fading from tan to a whiter shade of pale. John went to the kitchen to fetch his wife a soda. A knock came at the front door. John opened the door holding a bottle of Grapette in his hand.

Cottonmouth was standing there in a newly tailored blue suit, a red-rose necktie, and a brown pair of Bally Continentals. Joyce was beside him, all smiles in a flowery City Triangles outfit with a strand of white pearls around her pretty neck. Winston Peters stood behind them in his pinstriped Ralph Lauren holding two bottles of Polish champagne.

Cottonmouth spoke. "Hi, Mister Parker!"

"Come in, everyone. I've been expecting you."

Joyce entered, walked across the room, and sat down beside Katherine. Cotton ducked his head to pass under the doorframe, followed by Mister Peters.

Winston performed the introduction. "Katherine, this is my good friend, John Franklin. John, this is Katherine Parker."

Katherine swallowed hard, extending her right hand which disappeared in a massive paw with broken knuckles and white scars on the backside. She looked up at the white birthmark and the jagged knife scar down the front of his face. Katherine was surprised by the eyes. They sparkled.

Before Katherine could mount a conversation another car pulled in the driveway. It was Rico and his wife, Marie.

Winston made the introductions.

By now Katherine had arrived at the "Oh Wow" stage. She liked Marie whom she found adorable. Rico was quite charming, but she'd read so many stories about him in the newspaper. John Franklin was nice too, but big enough to pick up the coffee table and beat them all to death with it. They frightened her.

John laid a hand on Katherine's shoulder. "Honey, these are my friends. I want them to be your friends too."

Winston handed Kat her second glass of champagne. The bubbles tickled her nose. Winston spoke glowingly of the Mafia boss and the former Miami detective. Joyce reassured Kat, holding Katherine's hand and smiling. John beamed like a proud father. The people in her living room reminded Kat of Rick's Café Américain in *Casablanca*. It intrigued Katherine. There sat the evening news, and her husband was a part of it.

"Excuse me a minute. I want to call the children."

Fifteen minutes later Samantha and Roger pulled up the driveway. When they walked in they were both astonished by what they encountered in Katherine's living room. Winston introduced them while John brought in additional chairs.

Curiosity finally had its way. Katherine asked Joyce the pivotal question. "How did y'all meet?"

"John came to my door by mistake. He was looking for John and Winston. The poor thing looked awful so I asked him to sit down on the swing while I made ice tea. We talked awhile. He told me about Mattie and Daisy, and about William getting killed. Then he took me out to the car and showed me his four little kittens. He named them Daisy, Frankie, Mattie, and McCoy. I knew right then I liked this man."

"Golly, Joyce. I'm … I'm happy for you."

"May we borrow a pillow, please? John is recovering from a gunshot wound."

Roger retrieved a pillow from the bedroom and handed it to Cottonmouth. "Do you remember me?

"Sure do! You was at Frankie's funeral. Your lady friend was there too."

"We got married."

"I know. Me an' Bill was outside talkin' to your daddy an' Mister Peters."

"Is that when the trouble started?"

"Naw, it started before that."

Rico addressed Katherine. "I want to apologize, Katherine. I'm the one who ordered Drago to send you and your family to New Orleans. Some very bad people had discovered you were in the islands. John and Winston asked me to get you out of there. I'm sorry I frightened everyone, but it was necessary."

"Who are they?"

"It's a long story, Missus Parker. We've been asked to keep it under our hats. I can tell you the Central Intelligence Agency got involved after Winston telephoned Washington. You met two of them."

"The papers said it was those awful drug people from South America."

"That was part of it. Your husband and Winston saved one of my men after he'd been shot."

"Oh, My God!"

"It's all over now. No more *High Noon* drama."

"John, if you do something like that again I swear I'll have a heart attack and come back and haunt you!"

Everybody laughed.

"Honestly, I'm proud of you both. I just don't want any more surprises."

"I promise, Kat. From now on I'm yours to boss around the hacienda."

Winston opined. "Word of honor, Katherine. I won't get John involved in any more shenanigans."

Samantha went up to her father and hugged him. "I love you, Daddy. Mister Peters, you're the greatest."

Marie spoke to Katherine. "We'd like you and your husband to join us tonight. We have box seats at the opera."

"Golly, I'm not dressed to go anywhere nice."

"You have time to dress. We could have dinner before the show."

"I've never seen an opera before."

"The Met is performing *Turandot*. One of the neighbors said their "Nessun Dorma" is wonderful."

John spoke. "Put on that little black dress you like so much."

"Everyone, I'll be ready in a jiffy. John, your blue suit would look nice with my dress."

Chapter Forty-Eight

Eddie Nails

Winston Peters, Rico, Harry, and John Parker quietly opened the door to Eddie's hospital room. They didn't want to wake him if he was sleeping. A cute little redhead was bending over her patient checking his temperature. Eddie had his hand up her skirt.

"Eddie, me darlin', you cut that out right now. I'm not that kinda lassie."

"Let me pet your sweet bottom, Vicky."

"Stars an' garters, Eddie, if I let ya handle me bottom ya'll get all lovin' like an' hurt yer naughty self."

Harry imitated the pretty nurse. "Oh, Eddie, me darlin', if I let ya squeeze me buns will ya buy me uh diamond ring?"

The Scottish RN fled the room, her face the crimson shade of a ripe strawberry. Winston and John couldn't stop laughing. Rico just shook his head, rolling his eyes.

Rico addressed his friends. "See what I have to deal with … sex maniacs!"

"Reminds me of London during the Blitz," Winston responded.

Nails was grinning ear to ear. "Veronica digs me."

"Dat babe was a looker!" Harry observed.

"She's hot for me, boss," Nails declared. "I promised I'd take 'er to Italy, buy 'er some new threads, the whole enchilada. I think I'll marry tha broad."

"You have good taste, Nails," Rico said. "Good luck with the little redhead. How're you feeling today?"

"If it wasn't for them guys standin' beside ya, I'd be pushin' up daisies. Mister Parker and Mister Peters saved my bacon. I'm sorry we lost Marko an' Luther. McCoy too, he was a good egg."

"I took care of the funerals, gave the widows their allowances. I buried McCoy next to Daisy, Frankie, and Mattie. That's what Cotton wanted."

"You're aces, boss."

"Have they told you when you can go home?" Rico asked.

"The sawbones said I should be outta here by tha middle uh next week. Vicky said she would come over an' cook for me. I can be back on the job in two weeks, ten days maybe."

"There's no hurry. Some of the boys were asking about you."

"Ask Bootnose to swing by, boss. Vicky's got a girlfriend. I met 'er … pretty lady!"

"Do you remember getting shot?" John asked.

"I remember some of it. Them ragheads had my ass over a barrel 'til you and Mister Peters started blastin'. I passed out when ya come an' nabbed me."

"It was touch and go there for a few minutes. You went down, out in the open, bullets flying all over the place. Then McCoy cut loose with that .30 caliber. We got the man behind the privy then ran to get you."

Winston added, "Crucial events sometimes appear in slow

motion. That's what I recall when we ran out. I can't explain it. I just knew the three of us were going to make it."

"Dats when Luther got kilt. Den Marko bought da farm," Harry said.

"McCoy saved the day," Rico said. "It was an even fight until he opened up. Those Wahhabis were tough hombres."

Nails posed a question. "I wonder what happened to the one Bootnose poured crap on?"

"I felt sorry for the little bastard, but he was kind of funny thrashing around in that hole," John replied. "I never felt that way in Vietnam. Steve and Gunny and I tried to kill as many as we could."

"Dats where ya got da bum arm?" Harry asked.

"Shell burst. It killed the man standing behind me."

"Dat musta been uh bitch!"

"Vietnam is the bitch. Politicians are losing the war."

Rico looked puzzled. "Cottonmouth said something odd the other day. He said there would be another war, here in the States. I should have asked what he meant, but I didn't."

"John Franklin is an amazing individual," Winston said. "He's exceptionally well read, plus the man has street smarts. That's more than you can say for the crowd in Washington."

Nails made a face. "I never liked politicians. They're like mouthpieces, liars an' bull-shitters."

A knock came at the door. It was the little redheaded nurse with Nails' lunch. She smiled politely, not letting on how much they'd embarrassed her that morning.

"Eddie, me dear, it's time to get some food in ya."

Rico said, "Veronica, you have a good man there. Take good care of Eddie."

"I will, sir. Are you Mister Basilio?"

"Yes, I am. This is Harry Vento, Winston Peters, and John Parker.

We'll leave now so you can get your work done. Please call me if Eddie needs anything." Rico handed Veronica one of his personal cards.

"I will, Mister Basilio. It was nice meeting you gentlemen."

Driving back in Rico's Mercedes, John addressed the men in the automobile. "I think I know what Cotton meant about another war. France had a Vichy government after the Nazis took over. The United States had a Nazi Party plus an active Communist Party up until Pearl Harbor. Now we have war protesters marching in the streets. Eisenhower sent three hundred military advisers to South Vietnam after the French pulled out. He believed in the domino theory, that communism would spread like a plague if left unchecked.

"Roosevelt screwed up by not helping Ho Chi Minh when he asked the president to declare Vietnam a sovereign nation. That might have gotten the French off the backs of the Vietnamese people. France was an ally against Germany, so Truman refused to do anything after FDR died. Ho then turned to Moscow for help.

"Right or wrong, we're over there fighting the communists from Hanoi, Moscow, and Peking. We're winning our battles, and losing the war. The Tet Offensive was the turning point. That was a disaster for North Vietnam, but American television played it up like a big defeat for the Allies. Makes you think, doesn't it?"

"Makes me think we've got enemies, right here in our American press." Rico said.

John agreed. "Indeed we do. Our press is lousy with socialists and communists. The term Left is a pig with lipstick. Its Bolshevism all dressed up in pretty words. A lot of governments hate our guts. It doesn't matter why, they just do. We have the same problem right here at home. Some people don't like us being a superpower. Others object to capitalism. Religion offends the atheists, and so on and so forth. So they call themselves 'Liberals.'"

"I never heard dat before," Harry said.

"Cottonmouth warned of a coming war," John said. "If the Right wins, we'll carry on much as we do now. If the Left takes control, we'll descend into a dictatorship similar to Cuba or one of the Soviet Bloc countries. Revolution will follow sometime after that."

Rico changed the subject. "Let's have dinner tonight at the Copa. I'll call Joyce and Cotton."

"Me too, boss?"

"Yes, Harry. You and Nails are going to manage the Family when I'm out of town."

Dutch and Winston

Two months had elapsed since the shootout on the Dixie Highway. Dutch and Trudy were booked on the Queen Mary to begin their world tour in five more days. They were staying at her father's home in Buckhead in North Atlanta. Dwayne and Sarah were back in Daytona looking after the boat marina with Bubba-J. Dwayne walked with a limp now, using a hickory cane. John Franklin had recently purchased Joyce Overstreet a one-and-a-half-carat white diamond engagement ring.

Trudy was immersed in conversation with her husband. "I talked with Amanda this morning. They're planning their wedding for next June. They want us to come and bring Father and everyone. Do you think we should invite John Franklin and that Rico person?"

"Of course we should."

"Okay, just so you don't go getting tempted by all that easy money again."

"Don't worry, Miss Peach Blossom. I've learned my lesson. We're lucky one of us didn't get killed."

"You can say that again. I still can't believe I shot those big guns."

"You were magnificent, the Pirate Queen of the Caribbean!"

"I didn't feel too queenie when they shot me in the stomach."

"You scared the daylights out of me. Sarah did too! It was like a dream, wasn't it?"

"A bad dream, but wasn't it exciting? I'm glad we did it."

"Winston wasn't too happy."

"I never did confess about getting shot between my boobs or on my tummy."

"Are you still going shopping?"

"Yes, I need another bra and a new pair of shoes for the trip."

"You've got a closetful now."

"A girl can never have too many shoes."

"I like you better not wearing a bra."

"I can't go on the boat like that. I'd look like a hippie."

"Don't wear one when nobody's around."

"Maybe I'll not wear one in bed tonight."

"Right on, Miss Goosey!"

Trudy left, and Dutch went in the library where Winston kept his collection of books. He was scanning the titles when he came across a skinny little novel, *The Moon Is Down* by John Steinbeck. Dutch opened the cover and there was the great man's scrawl, an original probably worth hundreds of dollars. He sat down in one of the easy chairs and began to read. The Nazi occupation reminded him of Indochina. Sleep took Dutch in a matter of minutes. He dreamed about the children.

The dream was disjointed and troubling. He was down in the hold of the *Gray Ghost*. The children were down there with him, but they weren't dead anymore. All seven of the Vietnamese youngsters were gathered around their American friend. He'd opened a seacock, and the ship was starting to sink. Then the flashlight went out. It was pitch-black in the hold. Dutch couldn't find the stairwell leading topside. The children clung to him, frightened, beginning to cry. Seawater continued to rush in. The steel I-beams began to pop and groan. The ship was going down.

Dutch was mumbling, trying to say something, when he felt a pressure on his shoulder. He jerked awake.

Winston Peters was standing over him with a glass in his hand. "You were talking in your sleep, son. Care for a mint julep?

"Why … uh … yes. I was having a dream. "

"Trudy mentioned your dreams. I know a good therapist I can send you to when you get back from your trip. He's one of the best in Atlanta."

"Thanks. I might try that."

Winston mixed another mint julep, handing it to his son-in-law with a cloth napkin. "Trudy told me you dream about dead children."

"Yes, sir, little Vietnamese boys and girls."

"Care to share it with me?"

"I guess so. It's always the same, three little boys and three little girls. The Vietcong hacked off their arms because we gave them vaccinations."

"I have dreams like that. We bombed civilian targets over Germany."

"Did your dreams ever go away?"

"I still dream about the civilians in the fire. Therapy helps."

"I'll go see him when I get back."

"How's your drink?"

"Excellent! There's something I want to tell you, Mister Peters."

"You're my son-in-law, Dutch. Call me Winston."

"I sank the *Gray Ghost*."

"You sank that ship?"

"We had enough marijuana onboard to keep Georgia stoned for a year."

"Trudy said it was worth twelve million dollars."

"I sank the *Ghost* knowing Trudy might lose her property on Peachtree Road."

"You didn't know about Lloyd's of London?"

"No, sir, I didn't."

"Why did you do such a thing?"

"A lot of men died fighting over that cargo. That was part of it. I know what drugs do to people. I've been fooling myself for years about marijuana."

"It does lead to other substances, so I've been told."

"I did it partly because of you, sir."

"What does marijuana have to do with me, Dutch?"

"It made me ashamed. I didn't want the reputation of being a drug smuggler."

"So you sank twelve million dollars, plus Trudy's inheritance if the ship hadn't been insured?"

"I'm not sure I could have saved the *Ghost*. She was on fire and shot all to blazes. Her bow was damaged and she was taking on water. Everyone was dead except me and John Paul. I might have been able to flood the fuel locker and put out the fire, but I didn't try. I didn't want the responsibility of anyone else dying because of me."

"That is one incredible story, my boy."

"John Paul was out cold and I was bleeding like a stuck pig, but I'd do it again if faced with the same situation. Drugs are part of what's wrong with America, that and our dumb-ass politicians."

"Does Trudy know?"

"You're the only one I've ever told."

"Dutch Henry, I'm damned proud of you. What you've accomplished is an amazing feat of courage. You've sacrificed a great deal of money over your convictions. That takes real guts!"

"Thank you, Winston. Your friendship means more to me than that money."

"Trudy got a good man when she married you. You made your old father-in-law very proud when Rico told me about those sea battles. Thank God all of you survived."

"Did Trudy tell you about getting shot?"

"She explained about her arm, and about Sarah getting hurt."

"Trudy and Sarah manned the machine guns. Wayne piloted the ship. I was on a 20 millimeter. Trudy got shot in the stomach and the chest. Her bulletproof jacket saved her life. Wayne was nearly killed, and Sarah got her helmet shot off her head twice. The second time knocked her unconscious. I never got a scratch."

"Good Lord! This calls for a second round."

Mister Peters mixed the mint juleps and they resumed their conversation.

"I hope I haven't betrayed your daughter's confidence, Winston."

"No, Dutch, I suspected there was more to it, but I didn't press the issue."

"Trudy and Sarah are two of the bravest people I ever met. Did she tell you they built a hospital in Panama?"

"Yes! I was very pleased when she told me about that."

"They have plans to build another one. Sarah is friends with the Panamanian military. Her stewardess friend Amanda is marrying one of their officers next spring."

"I've been saving this as a surprise. I'm going to help them with their next project."

The front door closed and Trudy entered the room, her arms full of packages. "Well, what mischief have you two managed to stir up?"

Winston smiled back at his daughter. "I didn't know I had two gunslingers in the family."

"You told, didn't you?"

"I blabbed, Miss Peach Blossom."

"Daddy, I didn't tell you because I didn't want you to be disappointed in me."

"Disappointed? I'm so proud of you both I could puff up like a danged hop toad!"

"Am I missing something here?"

"Tell her, son."

Dutch hesitated, not sure how Trudy might react. He didn't want his wife to think him a fool.

Winston prompted Dutch again. "Go on. Tell her what you did."

"I sank the *Gray Ghost*."

"You did what?"

"I went down in the hold and opened a seacock."

"But why? You were so keen on making a million dollars."

"I found something out there I lost a long time ago. I got it back with John Paul and those brave soldiers."

"What was that?"

"My honor as a man."

Trudy dropped her packages in the middle of the floor, plopped her bottom down on Dutch's lap and kissed him. Winston Peters sat nearby on his tan leather sofa with a big smile on his face, proud as a gray-haired possum up a persimmon tree.

"A girl couldn't ask for a better father or a better husband. I just love y'all to pieces.

Mister Peters got up to mix his smiling daughter a mint julep.

US Senator Henry Clay of Kentucky first introduced the drink to Washington, DC at the Round Robin Bar in the Willard Hotel during his tenure in the nation's capital. Henry Clay was the eighth, tenth, and thirteenth Speaker of the House of Representatives. The mint julep has been a staple of Southern culture and hospitality for over two hundred years.

John Franklin married Joyce Overstreet in the same church where funeral services were conducted for Madeline Xavier.

Trudy decided she wanted to become pregnant in Sydney, Australia. Dutch Henry happily obliged his blushing bride. The blessed event took place on the veranda of their hotel suite overlooking the Tasman Sea during an electrical storm. The following morning Trudy sensed a change had taken place in her body.

From there they traveled on to New Zealand, Japan, China, Israel, and Russia. They returned home from Rome when her swollen belly began causing Trudy back pains. She gave birth to twins, a five-pound baby girl and her four-pound seven-ounce baby sister. Trudy named her daughters Zephyr and Zelda.

Cottonmouth had predicted a Florida boom. It came in the form of escalating real estate values, tourism, a wave of new Floridians, and high-rise condominium buildings sprouting up like mushrooms. Few realized a large part of the Miami skyline was financed and constructed with illegal drug capital.

Chapter Fifty

Doctor Bach

Katherine and John Parker had just left for Saint Thomas on their second honeymoon. The kids were on their own now. The neighborhood had finally adjusted to Cottonmouth living in their midst with his new bride next door to the Parkers. At first the neighborhood children all ran away in fright from John Franklin. Time passed and they began coming up to the big man to touch his hand, and ask him questions.

Nails, Harry, and Rico were in the lounge at the Blue Mist Motel on Collins Avenue relaxing and having a few beers.

"Where'd you get the fancy clothes?"

"Margot bought dez duds. You like 'em?"

"Bell bottoms look good, Harry. I like the jacket too."

"Who's this Margot?" Rico asked.

"Nails' girlfriend fixed Bootnose up wid Mazie. Den Mazie innerduce me an' Margot."

"Margot's your girlfriend?"

"Yeah, boss. Margot's a doctor."

"You're moving up in the world?"

Nails explained. "He sure is, boss. Margot was a sawbones in Vietnam. She's been with Mercy Hospital five years now."

"Harry, that's wonderful. It's about time." Rico smiled.

"She knows about our business." Nails added.

"You told her?"

Harry answered. "No, boss, da whole hospital knows. You got respect der."

"Just be careful what you say around the ladies."

"Margot's a smart kiddo. She's cool too, carries uh snub-nose inner purse."

"Why does she carry a gun?"

"Da war made 'er dat way."

Rico sighed. "I'll have to meet these ladies and see what you rascals have gotten yourselves into."

"You'll like 'em, boss," Nails replied. "Veronica an' Mazie is RNs. All of 'em was in Vietnam together."

"Let's take them out to dinner one night soon."

Harry had been watching what was going on behind Nails' and Rico's backs. The place was empty except for them, and three young ladies sitting around a table across the room. One of the girls was crying. Harry got up and went over to see what was wrong. Rico and Nails watched as Harry introduced himself, and sat down at the table. A few minutes later he came back and took his seat.

"What was that all about?"

"Somebody broke in der room an' stole der money."

"Did they report it?"

"Yeah, cops ain't gonna do nuthin.'"

"It's not big enough to fool with."

"I give um some dough."

"That was very kind of you, Harry."

"Dey said I look like Barry Gibb. Dat was worth uh hundred bucks."

"Having Margot around has brought out your positive side."

"Thanks, boss. I like dem Bee Gees."

"Me too, boss," Nails added. "I never was nuts about them Beatles."

"The Bee Gees will be here in concert in a few weeks. I'll pick up some tickets for you and your lady friends."

"Dat would be swell, boss."

Rico paid the bill and they started for the front door. Sunlight caught the metallic glint of gunmetal. Nails knocked Rico under a table. Harry dropped to one knee and opened fire. Glass and wood splinters exploded around Harry from a shotgun blast.

Blam! Blam! Blam! Blam!

Rico and Nails were down on their knees tending to Harry. He had taken buckshot in the face and his left shoulder. The girls ran over to help. So did the bartender. The dying shooter lost his shotgun out the window as a black sedan sped out the driveway.

"Get Me An Ambulance!"

"Boss … dey fucked up … my new threads."

Rico had tears in his eyes. "You wonderful idiot! Don't you die on me!"

Harry grinned up at Rico, and passed out. The girls were sobbing. The bartender ran for towels, stuffing them inside Harry's sports jacket to slow the blood. Nails inserted a stack of linen tablecloths beneath his head. In the distance they could hear the ambulance coming. Rico picked up Harry's bloody revolver and stuck it in his belt.

"Harry? Can you hear me?"

Harry opened one eye. Margot was leaning over him on the operating table. He was at Mercy Hospital. Mazie and two additional RNs stood ready to assist. They had clothed Harry in a hospital gown. Rico and Nails were outside in the hallway. Bootnose was on the way with five of the crew.

"Margot?"

"We're going to put you to sleep. I have to get the pellets out."

"Am I gonna croak?"

"No, darling, I won't allow that to happen. Breathe deeply now, we're putting you under."

"Margot … I gotta tell ya somethin' …" Harry drifted away to dreamland.

Three and a half hours later the operation was over. Doctor Margot Bach was out in the waiting room explaining the procedure to Enrico Basilio.

"Double-ought buckshot has the same diameter as a .32 caliber bullet. Two pellets were lodged in the bursa. We found another pellet in the supraspinatus tendon. His clavicle was fractured. The deltoid muscle required sutures. His rotary cuff is going to be stiff, and may require a second surgery.

"There was a pellet lodged in the rear socket of his left eye. Doctor Greene got that out with a probe. The optic nerve was badly bruised, but did not rupture. His eyesight should return to normal after the swelling goes down. He'll have headaches and double vision for a few weeks. The left cheekbone was shattered. If those two pellets had been a few inches higher … well, Harry was lucky today."

"That's the second time Harry saved my life."

"I wonder if you know what a good man you have there, Basilio?"

"Margot … may I call you Margot?"

"You may."

"I've become quite aware of that lately. Please call me Rico."

"I care about Harry. He's more than just a stooge, Basilio. He's a man of honor."

"I know, Margot. I apologize if I've offended you."

"I am offended. I don't want Harry getting killed protecting your gangster ass."

Nails and Bootnose stood there with their mouths hanging open. The only person who had ever talked that way to Rico was Detective McCoy. They were more astonished by what came next.

"I deserve that, and you're right. Harry deserves better. How long will his recovery take?"

"Three weeks until he can use that arm again."

"Why don't the two of you take a vacation? All-expenses paid. A colleague of mine has a hotel in Saint Thomas. It's a beautiful place."

Margot eyed Rico coldly. "Are you trying to buy my friendship?"

"No, Margot. I want to give something back to the man who saved my life. You're his woman. I want you to go with Harry and nurse him back to health. Make him happy. He's never had a real girlfriend before."

Margot's stern face broke into a smile. "You're not such a bad son of a bitch after all. I think I'll take you up on that."

"Then you'll go with him?"

"I'll have to request a leave of absence."

"Leave that to me. I'll handle it."

"Are you married?"

"Yes, I am. Her name is Marie. We have two lovely daughters."

"I'd like to meet her someday. I bet she's nice."

"She's a wonderful lady. You'll like Marie. There are others I want you to meet too."

"I'd like that, Rico. I'd like that a lot."

Chapter Fifty-One

Langley Headquarters

Fat Mike had done his homework. Even so, his connections with lawyers, judges, the police establishment, and the Miami underworld had revealed nothing. It was baffling. No one knew where the hit came from. Then an unexpected source called Fat Mike on his private line.

"Who is this? How'd you get this number?"

"I know everything about you Michael, your wife and kids, the name of your dog. Now shut up and listen."

"You're lying!"

"Dog's name is 'Poochie.' Your son is 'Daniel.'"

The line went silent on Fat Mike's end.

"You still with me?"

"I'm listening."

"You'll find what you're looking for on the Dixie Highway ten miles south of 344th Street in Florida City. There's a green mailbox on the left side of the highway with no numbers. You'll see a hangar and a landing strip out in a big open field. There's a compound there with four frame houses beside a grass runway. That is the same Colombian dirtbag that brought in those Arab dirtbags from Mexico City. Tell Harry everyone wishes him a fast recovery."

The line went dead. Rico's consigliere was still busy scribbling notes.

Ruth Townsend leaned back at her desk in Langley, Virginia, with a smile on her face. She always got a kick out of pulling the rug out from under smug members of the opposite sex. Fat Mike, for all his connections, was no match for the Central Intelligence Agency.

George Brown, her partner, stood gazing out the office window at the Potomac River. "I wish I had known Wild Bill Donovan."

"What would you have said to him?"

"I don't know. It would have been an honor just shaking his hand."

"We'd have made a great team back in the day with Wild Bill and the OSS."

"Did you know he won the Medal of Honor in World War One?"

"I read the man's bio. What do you propose we do about our situation?"

"There's nothing we can do but wait."

"That's all we ever do is wait, watch, and shuffle papers."

"It comes with the territory. We'll make our move when the time is right."

"I'm glad you're my partner, George. I'd probably shoot some Ivy League pussy."

"Have faith, Ruthie. We're still the good guys."

Chapter Fifty-Two

The Airfield

Charles and Blackie reconnoitered the compound with a pair of infra-red field binoculars. They did it from a hilltop a mile and a half from the airfield. Two sentries were always on duty after sundown. Cars and trucks came and went, but the best they could determine was a dozen people lived there full time. A pair of C-47 cargo planes flew in, unloaded, and flew out once a week. The pilots and copilots usually spent the night.

Rico called Cottonmouth for some advice. John Franklin was schooled in explosives. That accomplished, Rico contacted the Miami Airport asking when the next moonless night would be.

Adolfo D'Angelo was an expert marksman. He lay in the grass by the fencerow waiting for the two sentries to get farther apart. That way the one still standing wouldn't realize his partner was dead. The other members of the raiding party waited patiently on either side of Adolfo, making no sounds. He needed all of his concentration for the M14 infrared sniper rifle. As forecast, there was no moon.

His first shot made a funny *pomp* with the silencer attachment. One down and one to go. At four hundred yards his second shot missed. Instead of running for cover the man looked around to see what made the strange *zap* when the first bullet flew past his ear. He never knew what killed him.

"Okay, let's go!"

Seven men went scrambling down the embankment beside the highway and across an open field toward the four frame houses. The grassy field resembled a fairyland with hundreds of glowworms illuminating the ground cover. It was a dark night laced with mystery and intrigue, but there were stars overhead. Fireflies blinked their silent messages, reminding Charlie of his childhood which seemed a thousand years ago. In the distance a train whistle made its mournful presence known. Halfway to their objective they halted to allow the men carrying the boxes time to rest. Minutes later they reached the first structure.

Adolfo took charge. "Remember now, set your box right in the middle of each house. Blackie, you take yours inside the hangar. Frado will string the cord. Don't make no noise. We don't want them assholes wakin' up."

A fifty-pound case of dynamite was placed against the side of each building with a detonation cord running from box to box, and farther on inside the hangar for the airplanes. Blackie was assigned the task of lighting the fuse to a blasting cap attached to his end of the cord. The hangar was empty. He waited for his six companions to make it back to the highway then he struck a match. Blackie had allowed himself three minutes of fuse.

A noise on the back porch of the third house caught Blackie's attention. There was a man standing there smoking a cigarette. One minute ticked by. The man casually smoked his Chesterfield. Two minutes. Blackie lay in hiding outside the hangar anxious to make his get-away.

The fuse was down to a few inches when the smoker flipped his butt out in the yard and went back in the house. Blackie ran for it. He'd covered a few feet when the world behind him detonated.

The hangar lifted off its foundation. All four houses exploded into thousands of timbers, chunks of drywall, and flying shingles. A shock wave carried Blackie up off his feet, slamming him down against the ground. He lay there stunned, watching the flaming chaos that once housed human beings. He tried to get up but something was wrong with his foot.

A fuel dump for the C-47s went up in a boiling cloud of fire, setting the surrounding trees ablaze. From the highway they could see Blackie sitting in the field beside the burning buildings. Minutes later Adolfo and the others came running to the rescue.

"His ankle's busted … Frado, Charlie, get the bus!"

Headlights came bouncing down the gravel driveway. Blackie was quickly loaded on the backseat, given a bottle of grappa, and covered with a blanket. Charlie backed the vehicle up then swung around and roared back out the gravel drive. The fields were burning. Miles away people began reporting an unknown explosion. By the time the authorities arrived, the Red Cross bus was passing back through Florida City.

Margot was discussing Blackie's broken ankle with Rico. "Third time's a charm. That's three in a row you've brought in here."

"I like Mercy Hospital. I was here myself a few years ago."

"I know your Doctor Gavri. He's a good physician."

"I like you better. You're not afraid to tell me when I'm out of line."

"What you need is a good kick in the shins once in a while."

"Why do you say that?"

"You get a little full of yourself being the big *ong chu*."

"What's that mean?"

"It's Vietnamese for 'man boss.'"

"I have a friend who got hurt over there. His buddy was killed."

"I treated hundreds of boys like that. After a while you can't remember their faces anymore."

"Is that where you met Mazie and Veronica?"

"Actually, we met here at the Fontainebleau. I was in the lounge getting pleasantly drunk, and they had just graduated from nursing. We got pretty out of hand that night."

"So you decided to go where you could do the most good?"

"Something like that."

"I met your Veronica. She seems like a nice girl."

"Ronnie was seeing a captain with the Special Forces. They were real tight. He went out on a mission one night and came back in a body bag. After that she stopped dating until she met Nails."

"I think they're in love."

"I hope so."

"What about you, Margot?"

"I didn't date in country. Too much drama and death everywhere you looked."

"What attracted you to Harry?"

"Harry makes me laugh. I feel safe when I'm with Harry."

"You don't seem like the kind of woman who would be afraid of anything."

"For two years the Vietcong had a bounty on our heads. We went out with the helicopters to pick up the wounded. That was against the rules, but our commander allowed it. We saved several boys doing that. A couple of times the VC almost got us."

"I understand. My enemies have tried to get me."

"Blackie said dynamite blew up right behind him. What in the world were you doing?"

"That was payback for Harry and Cottonmouth's partner, Detective McCoy."

"Who's Cottonmouth?"

"Somebody you'll meet soon. He's a big fellow, smart as a whip."

"Sounds like he should be working for you."

"John was a Miami police detective. He's retired now, just got married."

"I'm into characters. I'd like to meet your Mister Cottonmouth."

"You'll meet John Parker and Winston Peters too. Winston flew bombers in World War Two. John is the soldier that got shot up in Vietnam. Those two certainly qualify as characters."

"Harry and I are leaving on our vacation Friday. When we get back why don't we all get together?

"I'll arrange for a table at the Copa. We'll all get pleasantly drunk."

"You're all right, Rico. Don't go and get yourself killed while we're gone."

"I'll try not to. I think the threats are over for a while."

"Thank you for the trip. Harry's all excited about going."

"I'm glad. You two have a nice time."

"Blackie has to stay off that foot for five weeks. He can use his crutches."

"I'll see to it, Doctor Bach."

Chapter Fifty-Three

Noah's Ark

June 1981

The CIA agents had arranged a secret meeting at Winston Peters' home in Buckhead, Georgia. Three additional intelligence agencies were present: Marine Corps Brigadier General Robert Kurtz with Military Intelligence, Bonn, Germany; Lydia Sams with MI-6, London, England; and Uriah Frank with the Israeli Mossad, Tel Aviv, Israel. Also present were John Franklin, Enrico Basilio, and Army Major General Jack Marshal with the Joint Chiefs of Staff, Washington, DC.

They were seated in Winston's library enjoying sweet tea and apple pan dowdy. Winston had just shown them his rose garden. The Paces Ferry acreage was purchased in 1924 by his father, Jacques Parker. Mister Parker made his first million in Coca-Cola stock in 1928. With that fortune he invested in banking and industrial bonds. Then 1929 brought financial chaos. The Dust Bowl of the 1930s only contributed to his and the nation's woes, portrayed in John Steinbeck's *The Grapes of Wrath.*

Ruth Townsend was briefing them. "It's a shadow government inside our Federal Government, taking over the country."

General Marshall voiced a doubt. "We've heard scuttlebutt to that effect before, but nothing concrete has surfaced. Are you sure about that?"

Ruth Townsend continued. "There's a political conspiracy inside the Washington beltway. We're staking our careers on it."

"We'll be staking more than our careers if what you say is true. That's high treason, with the possibility of military intervention."

"We have a Fifth Column, General, a socialist cadre of malcontents no less a threat to these United States than Red China or the Soviet Union."

"Tell us what you have, Ruth."

"As you're all aware, Vietnam was a political chess game. Lyndon Johnson never committed our Armed Forces to full-scale war. Nor did he use sound military judgment. Johnson was a political dealmaker, not a military man. He believed Ho Chi Minh would cut a deal someday, and everybody would go home happy.

General Marshal interrupted. "A number of my colleagues and I argued against Johnson's handling of the war. We were told to butt out and mind our own business."

Ruth continued. "LBJ started this lash-up. His Great Society opened the floodgates for every pothead liberal in the country. The State Department is a prime example. Education is another one, also Energy, Agriculture, and Labor. Once they get a foothold and advance through the promotional ranks, they bring in more of their own kind. George and I have watched socialism spreading in Washington ever since Senator Church and Congress cut off aid to South Vietnam.

"Jimmy Carter was the icing on the cake. Carter is Manchurian down to the soles of his little red-and-yellow bunny slippers. He got on famously with Castro, supported the communist Sandinistas in Nicaragua, and gave away control of the Panama Canal. Carter brown-nosed every communist thug on the planet: Ethiopia, Syria, Haiti, North Korea, and that Romanian tyrant, Ceausescu. But his most outrageous blunder, besides wrecking the US economy, was Iran.

"General Kurtz, share with the group what your people dug up."

"The Marines hated that pious, Bible-thumping prick!

"Iran was the US-trained linchpin for our defense policy in the Middle East. The Shah was a dictator any way you cut it, but he was considered modern by Middle Eastern standards. That's why the mullahs hated him. Carter didn't approve of this arrangement, pretending White House support while secretly undermining the Shah at every turn. He pressured Pahlavi into releasing political prisoners. Carter even ordered our CIA to stop paying bribes to the mullahs to hold down their religious rhetoric against the Shah. Then Mister Self-Righteous insisted Pahlavi initiate democratic reforms or he would withhold our military support. The Shah was seriously ill so he finally gave in to Carter's demands. That led to his overthrow in 1979. He came to the US for cancer treatment, and died in Egypt in 1980.

"Carter's actions ushered in the Ayatollah Khomeini. Khomeini is a throwback to the 7th Century. His bloodthirsty henchmen executed twenty -thousand Iranians right off the bat. Khomeini brought back Sharia law, forcing the women to wear those awful burkas. Millions fled the country. The bastard spawns terrorism against anyone who doesn't kiss his crazy Muslim ass. And because the Shah was treated in the United States the Ayatollah ordered his followers to seize the US Embassy. They held our people hostage four hundred and forty-four days. President Reagan put a stop to that nonsense.

"Meanwhile Moscow saw Carter as all hat and no cattle so they marched into Afghanistan hoping to use that as a springboard for taking over Iran, then Pakistan. Saddam Hussein, who's as ruthless a killer as Khomeini, sensed a power vacuum in his own backyard so he attacked Iran. Thousands are dying in two desert wars because of that numbnuts peanut farmer."

George Brown, Ruth's partner, spoke up. "Most people don't know the real Jimmy Carter. He lost Nicaragua in a similar fashion. Uriah, tell us what you know about President Carter and the Somoza regime."

"My Uncle Benjamin was the only family member that survived Dachau. He found me in a jabneel in Poland. I was only four then. Uncle Bennie took me to the land called Palestine. What we found there was fighting between the Arabs and the Jews. The Arabs had sworn to drive the Jews into the sea. I remember all the singing and dancing the day we heard a Nicaraguan ship had made port in Tel Aviv. President Somoza was a great help in our struggle to become a Jewish nation.

"He was assassinated in 1956.

"Luis, his eldest son, ruled Nicaragua from 1956 until his death in 1976. That's when Tachito took over. Luis ruled more humanly than his father, but Tachito Somoza was like the old man. In 1979 his National Guard was fighting for their lives against the Sandinistas. Tachito requested help from Israel. Carter forced Begin to recall a ship bound for Nicaragua with arms and ammunition. I felt bad when Begin gave in to Carter, but the prime minister's first responsibility was to Israel.

"Carter threatened to cut off military aid to Israel if Begin allowed the ship to go on. The regime collapsed, and Tachito was overthrown. Carter denied him asylum in the US. The Sandinistas killed him a year later in Paraguay.

"The Somozas were a corrupt and unpopular dictatorship, but the Cuban- and Soviet-backed Sandinistas are even worse. Whether by ignorance or design President Carter blew off Nicaragua and Iran for regimes that hate the United States."

George said, "What we have on Capitol Hill is a systematic dismantling of our Federal Government as it was known during the forties and fifties. Patriotism is frowned upon. Socialism is rampant all over Washington, and God is practically a dirty word in certain circles.

What's happening is criminal. Carter is part of it. So are many of the bureaucrats.

"Labor unions have become political pawns for the Democratic Party. All they care about is money and influence. Look at the anti-American rhetoric all over the front pages of *The New York Times*, and the *Washington Post*. They crucify President Reagan every day. William Buckley refers to the *Post* as 'Pravda on the Potomac.' *The Times* is little more than a cheerleading squad for Big Brother. They never endorse a conservative candidate or less government. Hollywood is the same way. Back in the day they made patriotic films and family pictures. Now it's sex, violence, and putting down Christianity.

"The ACLU is a national disgrace. So is the EPA, SEIU, even our own Central Intelligence Agency. Many of our own people don't want to see the problem. They like their nice, cushy jobs and those cocktail parties over in Georgetown. Don't rock the boat. Go along to get along."

"You think this has to do with the UN?" Winston asked.

"It has everything to do with the UN!" Lydia Sams declared. "Those cheeky bastards have coveted one world government ever since Ike Eisenhower. Roosevelt gave them a taste of socialism with his New Deal. That started the ball rolling. The United Nations is a hotbed of tin-pot dictators and wanking Soviet sods who want to see the West brought to heel. They want our money! And they want a world dictatorship with them running the bloody show. The UN stopped solving problems ages ago. They've become a dodgy mob of nepotism and self-serving greed. If your politicians had any balls they'd kick them out of the country."

"Congress lost their balls in Korea and Vietnam," Rico said. "My question is what are we going to do about this? It sounds like the Kremlin has moved from Moscow to Capitol Hill."

"Global control is their lord and master, Uriah Frank said. "A fellow by the name of Saul Alinsky wrote a book, *Rules for Radicals*. Lenin and Mao believed in armed revolution. Alinsky died in 1972, but he was much more humane. He penned a master plan for infiltrating and taking over the Federal Government without firing a shot. He coined the term 'community organizer.' That's how Alinsky spread his message. You have state representatives in your own Congress promoting his communist ideology.

"Another gentleman we're keeping tabs on is George Soros. He's an atheist Jew, the same as Alinsky. Soros is Hungarian-American. He's a financial wizard who supports communism and one world government. His influence is a growing threat on two continents."

Cottonmouth asked, "Is that why you asked me an' Rico?"

"Yes, John," General Kurtz replied. "We may need your help. Ruth and George think the world of you and Rico. You're smart, you're patriotic, and you've experienced some of what we may be forced to deal with in the future. I thought that pig business was brilliant."

"That was Johnny Parker's idea."

"Do you know anything about the Bilderbergs?"

"Can't say as I do, sir."

"They're a secret society of the world's richest and most powerful men and women: bankers, business leaders, kings and queens, politicians. They control the World Bank, the Federal Reserve, the European Union, you name it. They meet once a year to discuss ideas, and make plans for what direction they want the world to go in. Their goal is the same as Soros and Alinsky, government control. They would govern as puppet masters behind the stage at the United Nations.

"There's only one thing that stands between them and their utopian objective."

Cottonmouth answered. "That would be our United States."

"Give the man a cigar! As long as the United States survives in her present form there can be no one-world government. America has to be brought down to a socialist order with no greater influence than France or Germany. Then the UN and their political cronies will take control. Our job in the West will be to fund the United Nations with our tax revenue. Our Armed Forces would be reduced in size, and used to maintain order around the globe. Step out of line and the World Court will sentence you to Leavenworth or something worse, like Natzweiler."

"Well, I'll be dogged!" General Marshall declared. "Staff and National Security have been discussing the Bilderbergs. They're worried about the labor strikes in Poland and a possible reprisal by the Russian military.

"It pains me to say this, but we have a similar situation at the Pentagon. Men and women in uniform openly supporting appeasement with dictators like Deng Xiaoping and Kim Il-sung. It's a sorry state of affairs. Those people would be dishonorably discharged or court-marshaled during our war years with Japan and Germany.

"It appears military liberals are no different from civilian liberals. They argue constantly for compromise. Give it to them, they spread their crazy bullshit, and you end up with a roomful of Bolsheviks."

Ruth Townsend spoke up. "We suspect an attempt will be made to take over the Democratic Party. It's unclear how that might come about, but George and I have been following this thing ever since South Vietnam began falling apart in 1974. Everything we've turned up points in that direction. The Republicans won't fall for such malarkey even though half of them are as thick as two short planks. It has to be the Democrats. They'd vote for Mussolini if it kept them in office."

"I have something to say," Winston Peters said. "Back in '64 three of us pilots were flying food and medical supplies into what became known as Bangladesh. That particular mission we had a layover of thirty-six hours before flying back to Bangkok. One of the soldiers gave me an English copy of the Communist Manifesto. I was struck by how it laid out ways to overthrow a country. Two in particular I found chilling. Take away religion, and make the workingman dependent upon the state. That's exactly what's happening in America.

"First they banned God from the classroom. Then they started

Welfare. Welfare is a trap. It gets people hooked. Congress is destroying the traditional values of millions of black families, making them
dependent on government handouts. It also assures those same con-
gressmen of the black vote.

"Now they're doing it to the whole country. They shoved abortion
down our throats. Then pornography was legalized. Homosexuality is
next. Joseph Goebbels and the liberal politicians in Washington have a
great deal in common."

"I have nothing against gay people, but the way it's played up in
the press we're the bad guys," Uriah Frank stated. "I never harmed a
homosexual in my life, but every time there's an incident the media
points the finger at us. The same thing happens with white-on-black
crime. We're all a bunch of racists. But let a black man kill a white
person, and you might see it in the newspaper once or twice. Then
it's gone. Liberals control the press, they control education, and they
control television."

Lydia Sams said, "Ain't that the full monty! If the editor twits and
their handwringing nudniks would get out of the way the world would
be a much nicer place to live."

 "We're accused of the same thing with Jews," Rico observed. "Me,
I like the Jewish people. But they usually vote for some lamebrain politician. Why is that, Uriah?"

"Best I can tell, our ancestors brought it over from the old country,
Germany, France, Russia. They lived under socialism so long they can't
seem to get it out of their system. It's like a mental disorder with them."

"What we've discussed here today has treason written all over it,"
George Brown said. "What do you suggest we do to stop it?"

Cottonmouth spoke up. "Each one of us has uh specialty.
Concentrate on that. Find recruits. Build us uh network."

Rico smiled with respect and admiration at the broad-shouldered
figure sitting beside him. The big man had a mind like a computer.
No wonder he and McCoy worked so well together. He missed Billy

McCoy. But he was thankful he had such a wise friend he knew he could rely on.

Lydia Sams agreed. "John hit the nail on the head. I have an aunt who's friends with Maggie Thatcher. I'll ask her to arrange a confab with the PM. Maggie's a loyal Brit, and she's certainly one of us."

"We have meetings two and three times a week at the Pentagon, usually a lot of hot air about nothing," General Marshall said. "This has been the most compelling discussion I've heard since Ronald Reagan got shot. I can think of an admiral and a couple of generals we can rely on."

"A conspiracy seems obvious," General Kurtz added. "You see it all around you: welfare, congressional turncoats, debt, and those left-wing news people who scheme and lie about everything. Nikita Khrushchev told the Western ambassadors in a speech at the Polish Embassy in Moscow in 1956, 'We will bury you.' People thought he was referring to the atomic bomb. What he actually meant and said in a later speech, 'The proletariat is the undertaker of Capitalism.' Our own people are doing a great job of digging our graves."

Ruth Townsend responded. "We've identified the problem. You know about Harry Hopkins and President Roosevelt, Julius and Ethel Rosenberg, and the Red Scare during the McCarthy era. It turns out Senator McCarthy was right. There were Red spies embedded in the US Government.

"That was bad enough. Now we have members of Congress plotting to turn our United States into a socialist *piñata* with Washington bureaucrats swinging the sticks. Two CIA teams working with George and me have put together dossiers on suspicious politicians in Vermont, New York, Massachusetts, Illinois, and California. We have additional information on people at the State Department, the Department of Education, and the Department of Defense.

"Foreign countries involved include Cuba, China, Russia, Iran, Syria, and North Korea. Sharing information and working together, we'll get to the bottom of who they're collaborating with here in the US.

"Two important people we have in our corner are Congressman Charlie Wilson with the House, and Gustav Avrakotos with our Central Intelligence Agency. Those two characters are patriotic individuals.

"I'll leave you with this in closing. We have a dedicated friend in the White House."

George Brown continued. "I suggest we meet again in six weeks at a different location. We don't want to attract attention. In the meantime Ruth and I will keep you posted on any new developments that crop up. Keep a secure telephone handy. Our call sign will be 'Noah's Ark.'

"Destroying people in Washington is political gamesmanship. That's not our purpose. Political turncoats are the game we're after. Ruth and I will use our office as much as we can without tipping off the Agency. All of you must use caution with your own investigations.

"Once we have a Judas in our sights we can leak the information to the people we trust in the news service, the military, or up on Capitol Hill. If that doesn't remedy the problem, we'll move on to Plan B … John and Rico.

Ruth added, "Have a safe trip, everybody. God bless you. And good hunting."

The meeting adjourned.

Everyone except Winston headed off for the Atlanta Airport to catch their respective flights home. Winston Peters sat alone in his library cogitating over the enormity of what had been discussed. He was sad over the passing of William Saroyan. Winston had several of his books. *My Name Is Aram* was his favorite. They had been friends since 1952.

Winston was tempted to bring Dutch into the fold, but had promised himself he would protect the boy for his daughter's sake. He didn't want Trudy becoming a widow. Then he remembered his friend in Congress whom he'd served with in the 8th Army Air Force in London.

Rico and Cottonmouth were seated together in first class onboard a Delta jet bound for Miami. Rico was enjoying a gin martini. Cotton had asked the stewardess to bring him three one-and-a-half-ounce bottles of Tennessee sour mash whiskey. He mixed the whiskey with Royal Crown Cola in a Dixie cup.

"If I drank all that I'd fall out in the aisle."

Cotton laughed. "You don't weight two hundred an' forty pounds."

"What did you think about the people we met today?"

"Ruth an' George we know. They're good people. I wouldn't want them dogging my trail. That Army guy is a thinkin' man. He'll be cautious with anybody he brings in. I like that Marine general. He's a tough ole codger. The Israeli is another thinker. Mossad is one uh the best in tha world. Lydia, the Brit, reminds me uh 007. She's sharp, good lookin', an' one hard-nosed customer. I like 'em!"

"That's what I wanted to hear. You're a better judge of people than I am. My favorite of course is Winston. He's a little older, but that man has moxie and a good head on his shoulders."

"Rico, we're gettin' into somethin' big, bigger 'n' anything I ever tackled before."

"I know, John. Later on things might get rough, but it's something we have to do. America is a lot more important than you or me. I feel honored that Ruth and George included us in this."

"Damn right! I been thinkin' tha same thing."

Rico fell silent thinking about his crew and the people he knew in Miami. Something at the back of his mind kept nagging at him, but he couldn't put his finger on it. Then it popped in his head clear as a bell. Doctor Bach! She was perfect. Rico smiled, knowing he had just made his first selection for Ruth and George, and the approaching struggle to rescue the Republic from the clutches of Karl Marx.

Contact the Author

To Contact the Author, visit his website at:
McAnallyFlatsPress.com

Or write to him via the publisher at:

Larry Henry
c/o McAnally Flats Press
4809 Riversedge Road
Louisville, TN 37777